Belong to Me

"Shayla Black is known for her hot writing, and this doesn't disappoint . . . Not to be missed." —*Night Owl Reviews*

"Blisteringly hot and equally emotional, *Belong to Me* is outstanding! . . . Packed with intrigue and scorching sex; Shayla Black should be on every erotica fan's must-have list!" —*Reader to Reader*

"Sultry, sensuous, and solidly the single most favorite book I have read the entire summer!" —*Romance Junkies*

"Ms. Black totally hit this one out of the park . . . Word of warning—the scenes are so intense you just may have to sit inside a walk-in freezer while reading them. Holy Hotness! This one is a winner." —*The Romance Reviews*

Surrender to Me

"Full of steam, erotic love, and nonstop, page-turning action, this was one of those books you read in one sitting." —*Night Owl Reviews*

"Delicious and entertaining, the scenes are unforgettable, and the characters are to die for. Fabulous read!" —*Fresh Fiction*

continued . . .

Delicious

"Shayla Black creates emotional, searingly sexy stories that always leave me wanting more."   —Maya Banks, *New York Times* bestselling author

"Too *Delicious* to put down . . . a book to be savored over and over."
                                                          —*Romance Junkies*

"Make sure you have something to cool yourself down with, for this one is a scorcher."   —*The Romance Readers Connection*

"The characters, the drama, the suspense, the eroticism, and most importantly the heart-stopping romance all combine to make *Delicious* a perfect read . . . sizzling hot and one for the keeper shelf."
                                                          —*The Romance Studio*

"Another winner from Black . . . will thrill erotica and mystery fans alike."
                                                          —*RT Book Reviews*

"Erotic, emotional . . . suspenseful."   —*Joyfully Reviewed*

"An absolute winner."   —*Fallen Angel Reviews*

Decadent

"Wickedly seductive from start to finish."
                                  —Jaci Burton, *New York Times* bestselling author

"A lusty page-turner from the get-go, *Decadent* lives up to its title, grabbing readers from the very first chapter and not letting go until the very end with a shuddering climax worthy of any keeper shelf."
                                                          —*TwoLips Reviews*

Wicked Ties

"A wicked, sensual thrill from first page to last. I loved it!"

—Lora Leigh, #1 *New York Times* bestselling author

"Not a book to be missed . . . Just be sure that you have something cold to drink while reading it and hopefully someone there afterwards to ease away the ache."

—*A Romance Review*

"Absolutely took my breath away . . . *Wicked Ties* wound itself around me and refused to let go. Full of passion and erotic love scenes."

—*Romance Junkies*

Strip Search
(writing as Shelley Bradley)

"Packs a hell of a wallop . . . an exciting, steamy, and magnificent story . . . If I had to rate this book out of ten, it would certainly get a fifteen! Twists, turns, titillating and explosive sexual chemistry, and memorable characters—readers can't ask for more. *Strip Search* is highly recommended!"

—*The Road to Romance*

"An exciting contemporary romance with suspenseful undertones . . . the love scenes are particularly steamy. This book would be perfect for readers who enjoy their romance with a hint of suspense."

—*Curled Up with a Good Book*

"Blew me away . . . a great read."

—*Fallen Angel Reviews*

"The twists and turns in *Strip Search* make for an intriguing climax . . . Bradley is a master of tying love and mystery together. I highly recommend this book."

—*MyShelf.com*

continued . . .

Bound and Determined
(writing as Shelley Bradley)

Mine to Hold

SHAYLA BLACK

HEAT
NEW YORK

THE BERKLEY PUBLISHING GROUP
Published by the Penguin Group
Penguin Group (USA) Inc.
375 Hudson Street, New York, New York 10014, USA

Penguin Group (Canada), 90 Eglinton Avenue East, Suite 700, Toronto, Ontario M4P 2Y3, Canada
(a division of Pearson Penguin Canada Inc.) • Penguin Books Ltd., 80 Strand, London WC2R 0RL,
England • Penguin Group Ireland, 25 St. Stephen's Green, Dublin 2, Ireland (a division of Penguin
Books Ltd.) • Penguin Group (Australia), 250 Camberwell Road, Camberwell, Victoria 3124, Australia
(a division of Pearson Australia Group Pty. Ltd.) • Penguin Books India Pvt. Ltd., 11 Community
Centre, Panchsheel Park, New Delhi—110 017, India • Penguin Group (NZ), 67 Apollo Drive,
Rosedale, Auckland 0632, New Zealand (a division of Pearson New Zealand Ltd.) • Penguin Books
(South Africa) (Pty.) Ltd., 24 Sturdee Avenue, Rosebank, Johannesburg 2196, South Africa

Penguin Books Ltd., Registered Offices: 80 Strand, London WC2R 0RL, England

This book is an original publication of The Berkley Publishing Group.

PUBLISHING HISTORY
Heat trade paperback edition / June 2012

Library of Congress Cataloging-in-Publication Data

Black, Shayla.
Mine to hold / Shayla Black. — Heat trade paperback ed.
p.   cm.
ISBN 978-0-425-24551-4
1. Life-change events—Fiction.   2. Triangles (Interpersonal relations)—Fiction.   3. Stalking—Fiction.
4. Family secrets—Fiction.   I. Title.
PS3602.L325245M56   2012
813'.6—dc23
2011051845

PRINTED IN THE UNITED STATES OF AMERICA

10 9 8 7 6 5 4 3 2 1

Acknowledgments

For fans of the Wicked Lovers series. Your dedication has been an inspiration to me. I can't thank you enough for your kind words and support. Thanks to Chloe Vale for helping me keep my head screwed on straight during this process, and to Angel Payne for her unending enthusiasm for these characters and this story. Special appreciation goes out to Christie Von Ditter for her help and honesty, for doing so much to organize and manage my administrative life so I can focus on writing books I love. Also a big shout-out to Rhyannon Byrd. You never fail to make me smile. And lastly, to the Wicked Lovers role-players on Facebook. It's like a whole new playground, and I love the way you've adopted the characters near and dear to my heart and taken them into your own.

Chapter One

"TYLER, are you aware that all the girls at Sexy Sirens have nick-named you Cockzilla?"

He laughed. That rich, deep sound Delaney Catalano hadn't heard for two long years sang in the humid May air, making her heart clench. After all the trials and miles—and lately, the bullets—she never believed she'd hear Tyler Murphy's familiar voice again. Certainly, she'd never imagined hearing it in BFE, Louisiana, as she hid in the shadows of his back patio like some sad stalker. She wasn't at all surprised that a group of girls had given him a moniker about his sexual prowess. Women had always crawled all over him, and perpetually single Tyler liked it that way.

Once upon a time, his antics had made her laugh—until De-laney had experienced him for herself. To this day, she remembered exactly how good he'd been. She pushed the thought aside.

Peeking around the corner, she saw Tyler's broad shoulders and upper back encased in a charcoal gray T-shirt. His blond hair had been cut brutally short, exposing the strong column of his sun-kissed neck. He lounged in a chair, his forearms looking bronzed, heavily veined, and vital under the patio lights. Around a table, he was surrounded by a virtual harem: two redheads, a platinum blonde, a Latina brunette, and an auburn-haired model type—each totally gorgeous.

Some things never change. Not that it should matter to her. He'd been her friend first and foremost. And he'd never been hers to lose.

"And that's a bad nickname why?" Tyler returned to the stunning blonde beside him, lifting his bottle of beer to his mouth and taking a long swallow.

As the other women laughed, Delaney glanced over her shoulder, hoping like hell that she hadn't been followed. She breathed a sigh of relief when it appeared that she was alone. How nice would it be if her most pressing problem were others' opinions? How nice would it be if someone didn't want her dead?

"Ladies . . ." the blonde's voice warned. "This is not funny. Remember the plan?"

"Alyssa is right," said the brunette with sinful curves. "We're worried about you."

"That's very sweet, Kata, but acting like you care isn't going to persuade me to watch another crappy Twilight movie with you."

"You liked it," Kata accused.

Tyler snorted. "You wish."

He probably had liked it more than he wanted to admit. Tyler liked high-testosterone thrillers, but he'd admitted under the influence of Señor Cuervo that he kinda liked chick flicks, too. Once upon a time, he'd been Delaney's buddy of choice to curl up on the couch with and rent movies, she remembered with a wistful smile. Then reality crashed back in.

"Focus." Alyssa snapped. "This is an intervention. The girls and I all agree that you need help."

"C'mon. I'm not a drug addict or an alcoholic. I'm no danger to myself or others."

"Wrong. You're dangerous to womankind," the auburn-haired

beauty cut in. "Can you make it a whole day without getting in some stripper's thong? Our guess is no."

Delaney grimaced. Yep, same old Tyler. He'd always liked women easy and flashy. One reason—among many—she'd never taken his flirting seriously. Then again, it wasn't his flirting that had been her downfall.

"Ouch, Kimber. You wound me." Tyler slapped a hand dramatically over his chest.

"Cut the crap," she demanded. "You *can't* make it a whole day, can you?"

"Sure, I could. But why torture myself? I have to do something to stave off the loneliness."

"I don't need any more catfights onstage about who's getting Cockzilla tonight," Alyssa chimed in again.

"No catfights at a strip club? You're kidding me? Your patrons *loved* the action. Better than Jell-O wrestling. Got a rise out of me."

The women in Tyler's life were staging an intervention, and he wasn't taking it seriously. Delaney wasn't really surprised. He would always be Mr. Good-Time. What did surprise her, however, was that none of the women seemed to be fighting over him. Yet, anyway.

"Wait. Are you here to tell me that you're suddenly available and want me all to yourself?" he challenged the gorgeous blonde. "You know I'm all over that."

"We *all* know." Another woman scoffed and waved her hand. "I haven't known you that long, but seriously, a stiff wind could get a rise out of you."

The lovely redhead with the sultry brown eyes wore a wedding ring. Then again, bands of gold had never stopped Tyler before. She ought to know.

"You noticed, Tara? I'm touched."

"Don't give me that," Tara scolded. "Alyssa is being really serious. We all are."

"Really? It's not a joke?" With a sigh, Tyler turned back to the blonde. "Okay. What's up, boss lady?"

"I can't have girls fighting and quitting because you're too busy playing musical beds," Alyssa said. "Someone is going to lose every time, and it's creating a fucking mess that I don't have time to clean up. I hired Jessi to replace Krystal, who left because she didn't like being last on your booty-call list. Tyler, Jessi has been with me for three days. *Three!* I found out this afternoon that you've already tapped that, more than once."

He fidgeted in his seat. "After her first shift, she asked for an escort to her car. The parking lot was dark and empty. I helped her out."

"By nailing her in the backseat?"

"There's more room in a Civic than you'd think."

"Tyler, I know you like to keep things light, but please be serious for a minute." Alyssa's voice rang with frustration. "Jessi came crying to me when she found you and Skylar in the dressing room last night after closing. Do I need to enact a strict no-anal-sex policy at the club?"

"I didn't mean to hurt Jessi's feelings. I thought she knew the score. I'll talk to her." He frowned. "I'm confused about one thing. I've bounced there for almost two years. What I do with the girls has never bothered you before. What is this really about?"

There was a long pause, and Delaney watched a few of the women lift glasses of wine and sip nervously.

The other redhead, the one with the baby bump, clutched a water bottle and shifted in the seat. "We think it's time you settled down."

"Morgan . . ." he warned. "Don't try spreading your matrimonial joy on me. Just because you're all blissful with your monogamy doesn't mean I'm in any hurry to get there."

So the redhead's baby bump wasn't his doing? *Never mind. It's irrelevant. Focus.*

"You're going to have to grow up," Morgan pointed out.

Alyssa wagged a finger in his face. "Skylar just turned twenty-two. You're, what, a decade older?"

Actually, Tyler was thirty-four. Delaney remembered his thirtieth birthday party, during happier times, back when she and Eric—

She shut down that thought and listened to the conversation.

"I didn't know she was that young. Sorry." Tyler shrugged. "We weren't exactly exchanging vital statistics."

"No," Alyssa jumped in. "Just bodily fluids."

"Hey, I always wear a condom."

Tara grimaced as several others groaned. "Eww. I don't want details."

"I'm just saying . . . Let's not get technical," he defended. "So I'm older than she is. I'm not the first guy to date a younger woman."

"Fucking in the back of the club isn't dating." Kimber sighed.

"Clean up your man-whore act." Alyssa looked dead serious. "Or in ten years, you're going to be a walking stereotype, a middle-aged Lothario hitting on young chicks with your snazzy sports car."

"I don't have a sports car, and even if I did, with a name like Cockzilla, everyone would know that I'm not overcompensating for anything I might be lacking."

Alyssa smacked her hand on the table. "Damn it, are you listening to us at all?"

Tyler sighed. "Yes. Joking aside, I will curb some of my . . . activity at the club. I appreciate your concern. But seriously, I'm not looking for any kind of happily ever after."

"Too bad," Kata cut in. "We're going to find you one."

He stiffened. "Oh, I get it. You have someone in mind."

"Well, I thought it would be nice if you'd talk to my cousin, London," Alyssa suggested as if walking on eggshells. "She just moved here. She's very sweet and could use a friend."

"Hell no."

Kata stood, putting her hands on her very curvaceous hips. "Are you refusing because she's not a size two?"

Tyler shook his head. "I've got nothing against girls with a little extra cushion. But that one has purity written all over her. No fucking way. Alyssa, you don't like the way I treat your dancers, but you want to unleash me on your little virgin relative?"

"So what if she's a virgin?" Alyssa argued. "You have a really kind, loyal side that would be good for her."

The gorgeous blonde had gotten that part right. He'd once proven that he'd do *anything* for a friend.

"He does," Kata agreed. "I might not be here if that weren't true."

"If you can just keep your pants zipped long enough, she'll see it. And you'll get to know her, too, and—"

"Nope." Tyler finished the last of his beer and slammed the bottle on the table. "I'm done here. If you ladies want to stay and finish your wine, you're more than welcome, but there's no way you're pairing me up with anyone."

"Where are you going?" Tara, closest to the sliding glass doors, moved her chair to block his path.

He scooted her out of the way with a nudge of his powerful thigh. "Anywhere else. Bye."

When he disappeared inside the house, Delaney panicked. It had taken her forever to track him down. She was at the end of her cash reserves and the end of her rope. Time had run out. No way could she wait until he felt like coming home again to confront him. There was too much at stake.

Dragging everything she loved and owned behind her, Delaney

clung to the shadows, watching for anything suspicious, and ran for his front door.

* * *

THE doorbell rang before Tyler could escape the house. Damn it, if this was another meddling female trying to tell him how to run his life, he was going to shove a bottle of wine in her hands and send her out back with the rest of them. He had better things to do, like slap some sense into his buddies. What the hell had possessed all of them to marry such interfering women?

Clenching the knob with almost as much gusto as he gnashed his teeth, Tyler yanked the door open with a curse on the tip of his tongue. It died abruptly.

Oh. My. God.

He drank in the sight of the familiar, petite brunette. He knew those wary blue eyes, framed by thick, dark lashes, and that sweet oval face. Her stubborn chin. That wide bow of a mouth. His heart pounded. He found himself unable to take a breath. "Delaney?"

The sight of her hit him like a fucking two-by-four in the solar plexus. Was it even possible that she stood at his door? Or was he hallucinating after two silent years of wondering what the fuck had happened?

"Hi, Tyler."

She shifted nervously, looking too damn tired and rumpled. Her dark hair hung in an unraveling braid. She wore no makeup, a faded T-shirt, and had dark circles under her eyes. By her side sat a black duffel bag on wheels. Something else squatted near her, around the corner. He couldn't see more than a blue, waist-high plastic handle stretching vertically for about two feet.

What the hell? She refused to have anything to do with him for two years, then came to his door unannounced, bringing every-thing she owned?

"You're a tough man to track down," she murmured, then glanced over her shoulder at the empty street bathed in twilight. "Your alias threw me."

Scowling, he crossed his arms over his chest. Yeah, he should invite her in, but last time he checked, she'd thrown him out of her life.

Of course, she wouldn't show up now with luggage unless she was desperate . . .

"I was under the impression you'd rather I get and stay lost," he drawled.

She shook her head, her dark braid swaying in the valley between her soft breasts, the ones with the pretty berry red nipples he'd never forgotten, no matter how many fake tits he'd fondled in the last two years. Tyler ignored the stirring of his cock and swallowed back the memory.

"I'm sorry for the way things ended." She bit her lip. "I know this is awkward—"

"As hell. Yeah. Where's Eric?" He glanced down at her left hand, clutching the rolling duffel bag. Her ring finger was bare.

"We're divorced."

Fuck. And there came the two-by-four to his gut again. Tyler didn't ask why; he knew the answer.

"I'm sorry as hell, Del."

And he was. But there was a selfish side of him having a full-on, get-down party at the news that Del was single again.

Self-consciously, she rubbed her thumb under her naked ring finger. "Thanks. It was final sixteen months ago. I haven't seen much of him since." She pursed her lips together, glanced behind her at the quiet street again. "We don't talk a lot."

Son of a bitch, he'd bet the split was ugly. And why did she keep glancing behind her?

"Delaney . . ." Tyler didn't know what the hell to say. It wasn't *all* his fault. But a good deal of the blame rested on his shoulders. The need to know why she was here now also kept circling his brain.

"It's okay. I know you have company and that this is uncomfortable. I know I handled everything between us badly in the past. I'm sorry. I regret it like hell."

Delaney's blue eyes filled up with tears. As she fought them back, Tyler resisted the urge to comfort her as he had when they'd been friends . . . then more.

"Can I come in? There's something we really need to talk about—and we shouldn't do it on your porch."

Everything inside Tyler seized up. The last time they'd talked, she'd asked him to leave, then cut him out of her life. Whatever was on her mind, it would be heavy. She hadn't come all the way to Lafayette from Los Angeles to shoot the shit.

Despite everything, how the hell could he say no? He'd ruined her life, and deep down, he'd been pretty damn sure that would be the outcome the second the deed was done. He owed her. Besides, he'd never been in love . . . but he'd come perilously close with Delaney. ·

"Sure." He swallowed, grabbed her duffel, and stepped back. "Come in. How did you know I had company?"

Delaney glanced at the object with the tall plastic handle beside her, the rest hidden by the exterior wall of the porch. She looked distinctly uncomfortable. "I rang the doorbell a bit ago, and no one answered. So I popped around to the side of the house and . . . saw that you weren't alone."

"They're my buddies' wives." He'd meant the words as an explanation, a defense. Then he winced. God, Delaney probably already imagined—with good reason—that he was fucking each and every one of them.

"It's none of my business." She glanced at the hidden object beside her again, then the empty street behind her. "I came because I need your help. Really badly and right now."

"You look tired, Del. And too thin. Come in and tell me what you need."

She drew in a deep breath, then bent to the hidden item just beside her. A trunk? A dolly? Did she mean to move in?

A moment later, she straightened up, clutching a child. A little boy. He was deadweight in her arms, half asleep, his face against her shoulder, thick blond hair askew. Tyler's heart skidded to a stop.

The kid's meaty hands and feet peeked out beyond the arms and legs of his Spider-Man pajamas that were just a bit too small. He hooked one arm around Delaney's neck, then began rubbing an eye with his little fist. Then the kid turned. That little face possessed the Murphy nose. His own green eyes, uncertain and watchful, stared back at him.

Tyler's entire body went cold. His jaw dropped as his mind came to a screeching halt. *Oh God. Oh fucking God . . .*

"Tyler, meet your son, Seth."

His son. Tyler had known this kid was his at a glance. A thousand emotions pelted him at once. Shock blazed through his system first. Wonder crashed in next.

He had a son. He and Delaney had created life together that beautiful May night when he'd finally stopped seeing her as a friend and had little choice but to touch her as a woman.

But she'd never bothered to tell him. Had she even tried to find him or just decided that he was irrelevant and had the child on her own?

Fury swept over him, relentless. One scathing accusation after another perched on the edge of his tongue. Gritting his teeth, he pushed it down for the boy's sake.

"Hi, Seth," he spoke in soft tones, then speared Delaney with a glare that dared her to defy him. "I want to hold him now."

Suddenly, Tyler ached to. This was his son. *His* . . . with her.

Regret made Delaney's mouth tremble as she nodded. She kissed the little boy's head, then whispered, "It's okay, little man."

Seth frowned and watched him suspiciously, but went into his arms without a fight. Then Tyler was holding his son for the first time, wrapping him as tightly in his arms as he dared.

He tried to swallow, but his throat felt too tight. His jaw ached. His heart beat fast, like a fucking racehorse at the Kentucky Derby. Something warm flooded his chest. Tyler had never fallen instantly in love with anything or anyone, but Seth seized his heart in a single moment. He kissed the little boy's forehead, and the feeling swelled tenfold.

"Why am I just now finding out about him?" Tyler tried to keep his voice calm and even. But his eyes accused her. What he really wanted to know was how the fuck she could have robbed him of the first fifteen months of his own son's life.

She glanced at the street behind her again apprehensively and shimmied out of the porch's light. "You have every right to be angry. Things were complicated, and you became impossible to find once you moved out of state. And I know those seem like poor excuses. At the end of the day, I didn't know what to tell you or if you'd even care. You can take it out of my hide later. I'm sure I deserve it. But right now, I need your help. I need you to protect Seth." She swallowed, her red-rimmed eyes looking stark and afraid. "Someone is trying to kill me."

* * *

TYLER'S face changed immediately, closing up, tensing. Cop mode; she recognized it. He might not be an LAPD Vice detective anymore, but some instincts never changed.

He dragged her into the house, then rolled her duffel and their son's stroller into the little foyer. Shoulders taut, he slammed the door, then locked it behind him.

When he turned to her again, his green eyes were laser sharp and focused. "Tell me everything."

Delaney licked her lips, her legs about to wobble out from under her. She was starving and exhausted. All of her cash had gone toward feeding Seth and buying gas. She hadn't dared to use her credit cards.

Her thoughts were racing, and her son stirred restlessly. He'd been cooped up for days. Now that he was awake, he would want to roam around. As a mother who knew the bastard after her didn't care if Seth was collateral damage, she was terrified to let the little boy out of her sight.

Sensing her problem, Tyler gently rocked him. "Hey, it's okay."

Seth frowned. Delaney handed the little boy the last of his apple juice from his sippy cup and a few animal crackers in the colorful but dented box.

Once he settled down, she risked a glance at Tyler. The man was waiting for an explanation—and not patiently. Where to begin?

"You remember Martin Carlson?"

"One of L.A.'s upcoming assistant district attorneys, right?"

"Yeah."

"Slimy bastard."

"That one, yes." She sighed. "You know how Eric always teased me about reporting on fluff pieces, like society baby showers and dog shows, when I first started writing for the *Times*?"

He shrugged. "Of course."

"So I pushed and pushed my editor, Preston, for meatier stories. On New Year's Eve, he assigned me to cover a party that Martin Carlson and his wife were giving. During the party, I sneaked away to call the babysitter and check on Seth. I overheard Carlson on the phone, talking. He threatened that he'd better see the money show up in his Cayman account or the police would be banging on the door the next day. Then I heard Carlson specifically call Double T by name and tell the guy not to fuck him over or he was going to find his ass in prison and his operation shut down."

Thunder rolled across Tyler's face. "The gangster Double T of the 18th Street gang?"

"Precisely," Delaney said grimly. "Everyone who knows anything about the drug scene near the Pico-Union district knows that he rules his turf with an iron fist. Carlson didn't see me, thank God. It was a short conversation, two minutes max. But after that, I started digging. I wanted to write a story that would blow Preston away."

"Oh, fuck. Double T isn't the person to get all tenacious and crusading about."

"Preston said the same thing. He wanted me to call the feds."

"Clearly, you didn't listen." And Tyler looked more than pissed about that fact. "So Double T is trying to kill you because you know some of his crap?"

"I think it's Carlson, actually. I got my hands on a copy of one of the evidence logs down at your old precinct, Rampart. I'm pretty sure it was tampered with. A whole bunch of guns and bags of white powder, supposedly with Double T's prints, suddenly turned up missing. I took a picture of the original log. Carlson and some beat cop went in the evidence room. But when I looked again, it only listed the beat cop's name. I hunted that rookie down and found out he'd supposedly died during a drive-by."

The frown that crossed Tyler's face wasn't comforting. "Gangsters don't usually shoot cops without provocation. It brings too much shit raining down on their head, which is bad for business."

"Exactly. No one else died in the incident, either. One shooter, one bullet, which seemed even more fishy. So I kept investigating. I found one of Double T's lieutenants, Lobato Loco, who wanted to make a power play, so he was willing to talk off the record. He didn't like his boss giving the ADA a cut of the money and figured that he could eliminate the problem and Double T at once by snitching anonymously to a reporter. He said he'd sign an affidavit to that effect.

"Armed with information, I went to Carlson's office and asked him about his dealings with Double T on the record. Of course he denied everything, but after that, shit started happening fast. I went to the police, but none of Eric's buddies wanted to lift a finger to help the bitch who'd cheated on him, least of all that creep, Becker the Pecker. So I had to fend for myself, especially since I didn't have any tangible proof of Carlson's guilt."

"Motherfucker," Tyler muttered. "Did you tell Eric this? You might be divorced, but he wouldn't want you dead."

"I left messages. He didn't call back." She pressed her lips together, watching as Tyler got angry all over again.

In some ways, Tyler had always been more protective than Eric. Her ex-husband had always said that she was strong and capable. He'd never seen her as needing a champion. Tyler had his affable moments, but underneath, he was pure caveman. He'd threatened to bust up just about any asshole at Rampart who'd dared to ogle her or acted a bit too friendly.

"Wait!" She pushed a hand against Tyler's chest when he looked ready to charge forward and find someone to beat the crap out of.

But her fingers encountered hard muscle, bulges, sinew—all male. Delaney gulped and withdrew her hand from the burning heat of Tyler's skin. Too often, she'd mentally replayed their night together and remembered the utter masculine perfection of his body. The way his lips had lingered on her neck, his rough fingertips had scraped every inch of her flesh, his sex-roughened growl had talked her through each one of the five orgasms he'd given her in that sublime hour.

Those thoughts wouldn't help her now. Lives were on the line.

"What the fuck am I supposed to wait for? I'm going to tear Eric a new one. And Carlson was always a fucking prick, more concerned with his own ambition than justice. If he's threatening you, I'm going to put a stop to it."

"You can't." She shook her head. His urge to help her was sweet . . . but misguided. "I started this. I have to finish it. Lobato Loco will only talk to me. No one else knows the facts like I do. Or has cultivated the contacts. But I can't keep Seth in the middle of this danger. After the bomb destroyed my Toyota—I'm so glad I hadn't strapped Seth in his car seat before I started the car with my key fob—I realized that—"

"The prick bombed your car?" Now Tyler sounded beyond furious. He'd gone deadly, with his jaw clenched damn tight. Delaney wasn't sure she'd ever seen him so enraged. "They meant to kill both you and our son?"

"Me more than Seth. Focus. All the admittedly circumstantial evidence I'd collected against Carlson was in that car, and now it's gone. He means business. So I need you to protect Seth. It kills me to ask this of you." She pressed her lips together, her eyes watering as she stroked her son's arm, then gripped his little hand. "So please, don't make this harder. I don't want to leave him, but I'd rather he be alive with you than dead with me. No one knows you're his father, and no one will think to look for him here. I have to go back to California and fix this mess. While I do, please keep our son safe."

Chapter Two

CLENCHING his jaw, Tyler stared at Delaney. Clearly, the woman had lost her mind if she thought for an instant that he was going to stay behind and babysit while she threw herself headlong into danger. The bad shit was his department; she'd never faced it, and he'd be damned if he let her do it alone.

But he also knew Delaney. If he argued, she'd only dig in her heels. Tyler weighed his words carefully. "I'll be very glad for any time you give me to get to know Seth."

She released the pent-up breath she'd been holding and closed her eyes. "Thank you."

"But before I agree to anything, we're going to do a little bargaining, angel."

He intentionally sent her his most dazzling smile, the one that had been melting hearts and panties since he was thirteen.

Delaney knew him too well. Her eyes narrowed. "What do you want? Spit it out."

If anything, his smile widened. "Who says I'm going to ask for much?"

She snorted. "Oh my God . . . Do you forget how many times I've seen that expression? You're going to ask for the moon, then act like it's nothing. Then you'll ask for the stars, and smooth talk me until I either (a) think it was my idea or (b) thank you for the suggestion— or both. Not this time, buster. I'm not listening. This is one request I know you won't refuse me. Regardless of what happened between us in the past, I know you don't want to see your son die."

"Absolutely true. But I'm also not willing to let you walk out the door again without some assurances that, from here on out, I have some parental rights." Which was true, but not his primary concern at the moment.

Surprised crossed her face. "You want visitation?"

At the very least, but they'd do details later. "Something like that. But I also want you to think about what you're doing. What happens to Seth's emotional stability if his mama leaves him with a stranger, then comes back in a pine box?"

She closed her eyes. "I'll have to figure out how to not die, I guess. I'd walk away from this, if I could. But Carlson is going to come after me no matter what. He's not going to leave a loose end like me hanging."

No, he wouldn't.

"I can't take Seth with me. Carlson won't care if he becomes collateral damage. My baby is too young . . ." She sobbed, sniffed, then tried to find her fortitude to press on. "I'm his mother, and I'm choosing life and safety for him."

Over her own. *Damn.* Tyler respected the hell out of her for this, but he also wanted to throttle her. He stroked his chin absently, hashing out a plan. It wasn't perfect and it forced him to prioritize objectives, but he could roll with it. If he achieved his primary goal—keeping Delaney safe and eliminating Carlson—then the rest of his wants might take care of themselves.

"Del, you need someone to watch your back while you clear up this mess."

"I need someone to watch Seth's back more."

For some reason, he found it incredibly sexy that Delaney was such a devoted mother. He wasn't equating her mothering skills with his desire to fuck her . . . Rather, it was seeing her fierce side, her determination, that started his blood pumping south of his belt buckle again.

"Understood. We'll work it out." He'd have to move carefully or his plan would backfire. "You look exhausted. Sit down. When did you last eat? Sleep?"

"It's not relevant." Delaney shook her head, sinking into the recliner beside her. "Are you going to help me or not?"

"We'll get there. Before now, how hard did you try to find me?"

She heaved an exhausted sigh. "We're going to play this game, huh? Okay, if you want me to be honest, not very hard." She pressed the heel of her hand to her forehead. "As soon as Eric found out I was pregnant, we separated for good. I was dealing with a lot—a new place to live, morning sickness, being served divorce papers . . . you being gone."

"You told me to leave." And goddamn it, if she hadn't meant that, he was going to string himself up for listening.

"I did. Eric couldn't handle what happened between us. I thought giving us all some time and space would help."

Her request had damn near destroyed Tyler, but he had lived with it because he'd thought it would help Del and Eric. He'd thought he was giving her what she needed. But clearly not.

Still, in the long run, Del was better off without her ex-husband.

Delaney's breath trembled. "Then Eric told me that you'd moved out of state and left for good."

Tyler froze. "Did he lead you to believe that I didn't want to come back? That I wasn't dying to call you twenty times a day and find out if you were okay? Because that's complete bullshit."

Those blue eyes of hers turned up to him, wide, teary. "He didn't say anything, and I didn't know what to think. Your reputation with women . . ."

The same one Alyssa and the other girls had been nagging him about fifteen minutes ago, before Delaney had knocked his world upside down—for the second time in his life. Ironic that his long string of conquests had come back to haunt him with a vengeance. His own Karma boomeranging him in the ass. And every friend he'd made in Lafayette would know it in the next few minutes.

"Is that really why you didn't try harder to reach me? I would have helped. I would have done whatever the hell you wanted."

Yes, he'd been best buddies with Eric since shortly after becoming his partner in Vice. But in some ways, he'd been closer to Delaney, connected more with her sense of humor, her intelligence. Something about her . . . He hadn't really tuned into what that was until he'd been balls deep inside her and falling for her fast. Until it was too late.

She shook her head. "I needed a father for Seth, and we both know you're short on commitment. At first, I was angry that you'd left without another word. I was tired and pissed and hormonal. I told myself it would serve you right to not know about your child." Tyler opened his mouth to object, and Delaney waved him off. "It lasted ten minutes. Then I felt . . . abandoned. I figured you'd gone on a case. But then your PI business closed and you didn't come back. I knew you must be using an assumed name, and it would take me time to find you. Eric certainly wasn't going to help me."

Mentally, Tyler added that to the list of Eric's infractions and planned to gleefully beat the shit out of him for being a raving douche.

"And I guess . . . there was a part of me that wanted this child to be *mine*. Everyone else in my life had left me—my parents died, Eric divorced me, you walked away—but this baby . . . I could raise him with love and get back unconditional love in return. I didn't mean to be selfish. I think"—she blew out a noisy breath—"I was just hurting. I know it was lousy. I'm sorry."

Fuck, she'd always had a way of diffusing his anger, and today was no different. In her place, he'd have been so angry, he'd have done serious damage.

She sobbed once, then clapped a hand over her mouth, trying to hold it in. Tyler crouched down next to her, settled a quizzical Seth into her lap, then wrapped his arm around her. She clutched her son, then stiffened, retreating into the back of the chair—away from him. Tyler sighed, all kinds of pissed off at the disappointment gnawing in his gut, then gave Del some space.

"You need to eat, angel. And rest." He stared down at his son, now patting his mother's hand as if he understood that she needed consoling. "How about you, Seth? Want a peanut butter sandwich?"

Delaney's head whipped up. "He's allergic to peanut butter. I'll make a list of his allergies and write out his routine."

Great. That would come in handy—for someone else.

"What can he eat?"

She wiped away her tears impatiently, then sent a wobbly smile to Seth. "We like eggs, don't we? We eat lots of eggs."

"Egg!" Seth gave her a snaggletooth smile.

Tyler grinned. Well, hot damn. Eggs had always been one of his favorite foods, too.

"Eggs it is."

"Thanks." As if she realized that she'd smiled at him, too, Delaney blinked and looked away. "Can I use your bathroom? I need to change Seth."

Tyler pointed down the hall, and she grabbed a diaper bag from the stroller. "Take your time. Scrambled with cheese?"

"You remember how I like eggs?" She bit her lip, as if trying to conceal the fact that it pleased her.

Fuck that. He was going to find out exactly how she felt. The whole shitty house of cards may have toppled once, but he'd be damned if he wasn't going to find a way to rebuild it at least enough to be on good terms with his son's mother.

But he was beginning to suspect that wouldn't be enough for him. Despite looking ragged and tired, Delaney was still one of the sexiest women to him. So sharp in some ways, innocent in others. Determined, brave . . . stubborn. Yeah, he was going to have to get past the walls she'd erected if he wanted to play a role in her life beyond Seth's father.

"Of course, I remember."

"But you don't like cheese in eggs." She frowned.

Ah, and she remembered, too. He shrugged. "I can adjust."

After a cock of her head, like she was trying to figure out exactly what he meant, she lifted Seth and carted him down the hall. The second the door shut and locked, Tyler sent out a quick text, then darted toward the patio. All the instigators of his "intervention" still sat there, drinking and clearly trying to decide how best to direct his life. He was about to give them one great big heaping dose of help.

Sticking his head out the back door, he glanced at the ladies. "Come inside. Have I got a surprise for you . . ."

* * *

DELANEY thanked God for the long countertop in the bathroom and laid Seth out. No doubt, he had to be wet by now.

"Da da da," her son babbled.

Yeah, that's your daddy. Tyler had seen it immediately. It *was* obvious and probably better than having to prove Seth's parentage to him. But it hadn't escaped Del that Tyler hadn't yet committed to staying here and protecting Seth. And if she knew that man, he had something up his sleeve. Whatever ran around in Tyler's half-crazy head, she couldn't let him derail her. He had all kinds of incentive to keep Seth safe that no one else would. She was sticking to her guns. If she didn't make it out of this alive . . . at least she knew Seth would be safe. And loved. Tyler, for all his seemingly carefree ways, had tremendous capacity for caring.

After a quick tug of Seth's clothes, the wet diaper came off. A fresh one replaced it, then Del righted his shorts. She looked longingly at the shower. How she'd love to bathe with Seth, hold his little body close to her and revel in the skin-to-skin contact. She'd only stopped breast-feeding a few months ago, and she missed having him that close. Showers were like gold to her now.

But this wasn't the time.

Quickly, she set Seth on his feet, used the toilet, then washed her hands. "Ready?"

In response, Seth blew air out of his lax lips, making noises like a car engine. She smiled softly, sniffing back fresh tears. He was little boy, through and through. She'd miss him desperately while she tried to nail Carlson to a wall and did everything in her power to make it back to her son alive.

Suddenly, a knock interrupted her thoughts. "You okay in there?"

"Be right out, Tyler."

Gathering her things and taping up Seth's wet diaper, she drew in a deep breath and stepped out of the bathroom, down the hall, and into the kitchen—with the five other women from the patio. She stopped short.

They didn't make any bones about staring at her with rampant curiosity.

Then the gorgeous platinum blonde stared at Seth and gasped. "Oh my God, Tyler. He looks just like you. Is he . . ."

"Yep. Mine." Tyler's expression was unreadable, but Del sensed a smile somewhere in there. Her mind racing, she tossed away Seth's diaper. What the hell was this about?

"You're just now telling us about him?" the pregnant redhead challenged.

The athletic, auburn-haired beauty tapped her foot. "Of course. He gets in the middle of all our shit, but notice that he doesn't fess up about his own."

The curvy Latina frowned. "True, but I don't think that's the issue this time. See how he looks at the boy, with curiosity and wonder. How long have you known?"

"Ten minutes."

The women collectively gasped.

Del held Seth tighter. "Look, I didn't know exactly how to find Tyler. And . . . what's going on here?"

"Ladies, this an old . . . friend, Delaney Catalano. And my son, Seth."

"Nice to meet you. He's precious," the other redhead, this one with the dancing dark eyes, said. "Tyler made him eggs. Can I feed him?"

Snapping around, Delaney spied a plate on the counter. Sure enough, steaming eggs and toast sat beside the stove. Seth saw, too—and lunged.

The platinum knockout caught him before he squirmed head-first out of Del's grasp. She scooped him right up against her chest and took him over to the eggs, calling over her shoulder, "I'm Alyssa, Tyler's boss. I've got a little girl just about the same age as your boy. I probably won't have more children, so I'd love the opportunity to spoil your son. Come on, Tara. Grab a spoon." She tickled Seth's cheek. "You hungry?"

"Wait!" Del reached for Seth. "I'll do that. He's—"

"No need," Tara chimed back, then giggled. "Gosh, Tyler. He looks so much like you. Except I actually like him."

"Funny." Tyler rolled his eyes. "You've met Alyssa and Tara over there." He pointed at the two women fussing over Seth—who looked to be eating it up, along with the eggs. "This is Kata, Kimber, and Morgan."

After nodding a greeting, Kata, the Latina brunette, took out her phone and started texting. Kimber, the auburn beauty next to her, got the same idea and whipped out her cell, too.

"Hold up there, girls. C'mon . . . Don't do this."

They both looked up with big Cheshire cat grins. Kimber tapped out a few more keys, then hit send. "That should have Deke here in . . ." She glanced at her watch. "About five minutes. Less, if there's no traffic."

"Oh, good. He'll tell Jack for me." Morgan, the pregnant red-head, smiled. "I need to recharge my phone."

"I'm sure Deke will be happy to tell Jack," Tyler drawled. "Isn't that great?"

He said it sarcastically but looked relatively pleased. Del didn't know who Deke or Jack were, but she got the quick idea that, despite his protests, Tyler had orchestrated this scene for some reason.

"What's going on?" she demanded. "Who are these men you're talking about?"

"Just my friends, who will hopefully come collect their wives so that we can talk privately."

"My husband isn't coming for me until the navy gives him leave again in a few months. I can stay." Kata grinned.

"I'm in the same boat," Tara added, nodding.

"But Hunter and Logan did give you a place to stay until they returned home. Do you need help remembering where it is?"

Though the women looked completely different, they wore identical pouts. "We're trying to be helpful."

"You're trying to cause trouble." Tyler turned to Del. "They're married to the Edgington brothers. Navy SEALs . . . who will spank both your asses red when I tell them what pains in *my* ass you've been."

"That's it. I'm bringing over *New Moon* and *Eclipse*," Kata insisted. "I'm tying you to a chair and forcing you to watch them. Hunter has taught me some interesting knots."

What kind of people were they, openly discussing spanking and bondage? She sent Tyler a questioning glance. He just smiled in a way that didn't give her any comfort.

A moment later, a booming growl sounded from the front part of the house. "What the hell is going on?"

A big hulk of a blond man bounded into the kitchen, holding a little boy just a bit older than Seth very comfortably in one beefy arm. Lord, at nearly thirty pounds, lugging her baby around took a lot of her strength. Yet this man didn't seem to require any effort to cradle his son, a veritable mini-me of the man himself.

"Check this out, Deke." Kimber sent a meaningful glance at Seth, still being fed and cooed by Alyssa and Tara.

The big, blond man's gaze followed Kimber's, then his jaw dropped. "Holy shit! Um . . . shoot."

Tyler crossed his arms over his chest, looking more pleased by the second. What was up with that?

"He looks just like you, man." Deke motioned to Seth.

"The way our son looks like you?" Kimber rushed over to pick up the boy in Deke's arms. "Hi, Caleb. Miss Mommy? I missed you."

The little boy just smiled at the gorgeous woman, then giggled when she lifted his little race-car T-shirt and kissed his belly.

"Well, isn't this an interesting turn of events?" came a voice from the doorway.

Del whipped around to face another man who'd sauntered into the room and propped himself against the wall. Dark hair, equally dark eyes, a serious sense of leashed power. He wasn't someone to fuck with. She got that instantly.

"Isn't it, Jack?" Tyler agreed.

"Can't wait to hear these details."

She didn't know who all these nosy strangers in Tyler's business were, but she didn't like the feeling that he suddenly had a whole team of people on his side—a virtual family at his back—while she had no one. As usual.

Since the whole room seemed focused on Jack, as if waiting for a cue, she decided to nip this in the bud now.

"I'm Delaney Catalano." She approached Jack with hand outstretched. "The boy is *my* son, Seth. It's great to meet you. I really have to talk to Tyler privately. Not to be rude, but would you mind leaving and taking everyone with you?"

Jack took her hand and shook it. "Nice to meet you, too. Tyler, you good here?"

Tyler sent her an unreadable gaze. "Maybe you could hang here for just a minute."

"No sweat." Jack approached the pregnant redhead, dropped a kiss on her forehead as he stroked her little baby bump. "How are my two favorite people today?"

Their mutual love and devotion was so painfully obvious, even ten feet away. Envy lashed through Del, and she looked away. So many times as her body had been expanding and changing during her pregnancy, she'd wished for Tyler's comfort. Some sense of his approval or caring. Instead, she'd been lugging boxes, wading into depressing divorce decrees . . . It had all turned out for the best, but welcoming a new life into hers should have been a happy time. Without Tyler, it had been bittersweet.

"Is someone going to tell me what the hell is going on?" Deke demanded. "Y'all texted me for a reason."

Every eye in the room turned to her. Every face held an expectant expression. Delaney sighed. They weren't going to leave, and this was some kind of gang-up-on-the-stranger thing. *Fine.*

"I have a dirtbag in L.A. trying to kill me. Really, the fewer people who know this the better, but since you're all standing here, waiting for me to spill my junk, there it is."

Jack raised a brow, then glanced at Tyler. "Did you bring us here so she could hire us?"

Del frowned. "For what?"

"Jack and Deke are in the personal protection business, angel. And they're the best."

With a shrug, Jack drawled, "You're no slouch, either. The job offer is still open."

Deke shook his head. "He's been too busy enjoying the . . . benefits of working for Alyssa too much for that. The scenery at a strip club is way better."

Figures. Del shook her head. She already knew Tyler had a long string of strippers on his beck-and-booty-call list. It didn't bother her, really. Well, not much. Besides, now that she had stretch marks and her clothes often smelled like baby vomit, there was no way she could compete, even if she wanted to.

Tyler shrugged. "I might finally take you up on that offer, Jack." The entire room froze. Apparently, this was big news. Whatever. She had herself and Seth to think about.

"Yeah?" Jack nodded. "When?"

"Now is good."

Del approached Jack. "Look, if you're in the personal protection business and done with your HR functions for the day, I might be interested in hiring you. I can't get my hands on my money until the guy trying to kill me is behind bars, but—"

"Stop." Jack's voice snapped with command. Then, with a deep breath, he eased his shoulders back, expanded his chest. He seemed to grow six inches in two seconds. His demeanor completely changed. Any hint of affable was gone.

Automatically, Del obeyed, closing her mouth. Then she frowned.

"That's not fair, my love," Morgan murmured. "Using that voice on her . . . It's mine."

"And you'll stay out of this, or you'll hear lots of that voice later. If not, as soon as this pregnancy is over, I have a new single tail with your name on it."

Morgan shivered and gave him a secretive smile.

Del didn't know exactly what a single tail was, but she was getting an idea. And Morgan seemed completely happy. Who the hell were Tyler's friends these days?

"Look, Mister . . ." What the hell was his last name?

"Cole," he supplied.

"With all due respect, I don't have time to stop. This man almost killed me and my son three days ago. I'm leaving him here with Tyler for safekeeping. I'd prefer to come home to Seth in one piece, and I could use your help doing it."

Jack glanced at Deke. They both turned to Tyler, who said nothing, but she sensed lots of silent communication.

"Look, I get that you've got your man code or whatever, but I'd like to be a client. If you can't take the job, please refer me to someone who can." She heaved a frustrated sigh. "I don't mean to be bitchy, but it's been a terrible few days."

"Clients by referral only. There's no one I can credibly recommend to you in Los Angeles. With my wife pregnant, I'm not leaving town. Deke has his hands full with his family and existing caseload. However, our newest associate would be happy to help." Jack gestured to Tyler.

Damn it! That was Tyler's game, setting himself up to be her safety net.

Del shook her head. "He's staying here with Seth."

"You know, your son looks like he's in really good hands." Jack nodded toward Alyssa and Tara fussing over Seth. Kimber had joined in, while Kata dug through the diaper bag and picked out some of his toys, to his squealing delight.

"I'm not leaving him with strangers." Even the thought made Del's heart stop.

"No one will ever suspect that the boy staying with Jack or Deke is Seth," Tyler pointed out. "My friends would protect him with their lives, and you know I don't say that lightly."

He didn't, but that hardly meant that she was leaving her little man with people she'd met ten minutes ago, especially when one was talking openly about whipping his wife. But Tyler could be stubborn as the day was long. The best way to deal with him wasn't to go through him, but around.

"I'll think about it."

Tyler grabbed her shoulders. "Will you? Really?"

His touch was a shock. The feel of his fingers wrapped around her arms buzzed across her skin, singed through her body—made her remember that night she needed to forget. She shrugged out of his grip. "I said I would. Leave it."

He looked unsettled that she wouldn't allow his touch. No, pissed off. God, she didn't have the time or patience for this game that being near him played with her head. That part of her life was done, gone. She had to focus on taking down Carlson and keeping Seth alive. She and Tyler would work out his parental rights afterward.

"Did someone say there's a hungry woman here who needs to be fed?" Yet another voice rang out from the direction of the front door. It slammed a moment later.

Alyssa made a beeline for the arched opening to the kitchen and met a gorgeous man with hair like midnight silk hanging around his shoulders. "Hi, honey."

"Sugar . . ." He pressed a quick, demanding kiss on her mouth, hugging a beautiful blonde baby girl against his side, her wide blue eyes and curly, pale hair a soft riot framing a pouty little bow of a mouth.

Holding out her arms to the baby, Alyssa pulled the girl against her chest. "How's my little Chloe? You have a good day with Daddy?"

Then the man raised his face and glanced across the room at her. Oh, wow. Was that really . . . "Luc Traverson?"

When she choked out the question, everyone laughed.

He rolled gorgeous dark eyes, then regarded her with a blinding smile. "Yes, ma'am. I got a text that you're hungry?"

So he'd come over here to cook food? For her? Del turned to Tyler. "He's married to your boss?"

"Ex-boss, thank you very much," Jack clarified.

Tyler nodded. "Ex-boss, yes."

"And who sent him here?" Del asked. Was this real?

"Jack might have mentioned it when he called earlier, since I ignored the text from Tyler." Luc slung an arm around the svelte, sexy Alyssa.

"So you just . . . came over to cook for me?" That astounded Del. A world-class chef with a growing TV and cookbook empire dropping everything to cook for a stranger?

"And to see for myself the woman who gave birth to Tyler's son." Luc glanced at Seth. "Yep, dead ringer. But he's cuter than you, Tyler. Since you're not working for Alyssa anymore and clearly have your hands full, does this mean that you'll finally stop hitting on my wife?"

Del's gaze zipped across the room to Alyssa. Instant jealousy bubbled in her gut. She tamped it down. Tyler wasn't hers, never had been, and this gorgeous blonde was absolutely his type. Tight dress, fuck-me mouth, stunningly gorgeous. Del felt ridiculously inadequate—as if she needed any help in that department. Right now, she felt every minute of the two years since she'd last had sex. Somehow, being mommy had allowed her to push aside that sexual part of herself. At the moment, she felt as sexless as cardboard.

Alyssa slapped Luc's arm. "Would you stop causing trouble and cook?"

He shrugged and turned to the refrigerator. "Anything you don't like, Delaney? That's your name, right?"

"Y-yes. You don't have to do this. I'm honored, really. But I'll be fine."

"You last ate when?" Tyler cut in right beside her.

When had he inched that close?

"I'm said I'm fine."

"That wasn't the question, angel." Tyler's voice was soft but firm. She knew when he put his unyielding hat on, and this was one of those times. A meal wasn't worth an argument, especially when she needed it.

"Yesterday at lunch. I split a sandwich with Seth."

Everyone stared at her like she'd grown two heads. Suddenly, Kata rushed to pull out a chair from the table in the eat-in kitchen. Tyler shoved her into it. Alyssa pressed a water bottle into her hands, along with a hunk of cheese.

Del stopped arguing and ate it gratefully. If she was going to fight off Carlson, she'd need her strength.

"I don't like bell peppers," she told Luc. "I'm allergic to shellfish."

"She also hates mustard and pickles," Tyler added, staring straight at her. "Coffee with creamer only. Lightly toast everything. She has a real thing for strawberries."

His knowledge of her was intimate, and his direct green gaze challenged her to remember exactly how well he knew her. It was just food, but somehow Delaney felt as if he'd opened her up again. She dropped her gaze to the slate tile beneath her feet, feeling her face heat up.

Suddenly, the chair to her left scraped against the flooring, and she looked up to find Jack plopping down beside her. "Go with Tyler. We'll watch Seth. Between Deke, Luc, and I, he'll be completely safe. We'll also do whatever investigating we can from here to support you. Tara over there is a whiz of an analyst. Come back to your son in one piece."

When Jack said it, the suggestion sounded reasonable . . . right up to the part where she had to leave her little boy with people she didn't really know. They seemed nice enough—but *seemed* wasn't good enough for her. Only Tyler had a really vested interest in Seth's future and continued well-being.

Before she could answer, Luc set an omelet in front of her, filled with chunks of ham, spinach, mushrooms, onions, and tomatoes. He'd drizzled a light cheese sauce that smelled over-the-top heavenly. A piece of wheat bread, lightly toasted, and a handful of fresh strawberries sat to the side, along with a cup of creamed coffee. She now had a meal made by *the* Luc Traverson. Surreal . . .

Del inhaled deeply and almost fainted in bliss as she dug in. "Thank you so much."

He looked at her with a kind smile that only made him more gorgeous. Alyssa was one lucky woman. "You're welcome. It would have been better, but . . ." He turned to Tyler. "Go to the grocery store and stock up. You eat like a five-year-old."

"Hey, I had fresh fruits and vegetables. Sorry I don't keep foie gras and caviar for you, Your Highness."

Okay, so no love lost there. Yet . . . when Tyler needed help, Luc had come. They all had. Again, she was amazed by the incredible sense of family he had among all these people. Yes, they'd rushed over to gawk at her and Seth, but they'd stayed to help. God, she wished she had even half the support system he did, and she realized how much she'd closed herself off from everyone after Tyler had gone, after her divorce. Del shook her head as she moaned around another bite. She'd rectify these deficits in her life after this crap with Carlson was over.

Seth toddled over to her and plopped at her feet with one of his toys. Little Caleb followed, then Chloe wanted down to join in the fun. Del gnawed on her lower lip, then took her last bite of food. Seth missed his preschool, his friends. He was cranky without his routine, his naps, his fun time. Guilt pounded her. For the millionth time, she wished she could make all this go away for him. For them.

And none of these thoughts did her a damn bit of good.

After wiping her mouth with her napkin, she set it down. "I'm stuffed. Thank you, Mr. Traverson."

"Luc," he corrected. Then the chef looked at his wife. "Ready to head home?"

Alyssa nodded, and within moments, they were gone. Tara and Kata left directly behind them with a friendly wave and air kisses for Seth, followed by Deke and Kimber. Jack and Morgan loitered for a moment.

"Deke and I will be around later to discuss our plan of action. We're going to help you. And you need to trust that Tyler is going to do everything to fix your problem. Listen to him; he knows what he's doing."

That sounded an awful lot like an order. Given his profession, it wasn't a stretch to guess that he'd either been military or law enforcement in the past. But she didn't work for him, and she wasn't about to just fall in line with his plans. She had the solution worked out in her head—one that didn't risk both of Seth's parents and leave him with strangers.

"Thank you for your opinion, but this is my son and my life. I have to think about it."

"We understand." Morgan patted Tyler's arm. "You've got a tough cookie there. Good luck."

With that, the couple departed, leaving her alone with Tyler, who sent her an unfathomable stare. His cop stare. God, she hated it when she couldn't read him.

Seth's childish noises faded to the background. The air turned thick. Crap, why was her heart beating faster?

Tyler leaned over her, bracing his hands on the back of her chair and crowding his way into her personal space. His ridged abdomen, apparent through his tight T-shirt, was right in her line of vision. She didn't dare drop her gaze lower to see if she had any effect on him. She wanted to . . . Instead, she tipped her head back to glare up at him.

"So, angel . . . let's talk about how this is going to go."

Chapter Three

DEL swallowed at Tyler's nearness. God, for years she'd basically crawled on his lap and never thought of him as more than a pal. One night had completely rewired her body and left her painfully attuned to him. Shoving the thought aside, she planted her palms against the corrugated expanse of his stomach and pushed him away.

"No, here's how it's going to go, Tyler. Seth and I are going to take a shower. Then you can read to him, if you like. After that, he and I are going to sleep. If you don't have a spare bed, I'll go find a motel and see you tomorrow, but—"

"I have a spare bed. You're not going anywhere."

Because it suited Del's plans, she didn't argue. "Fine. Thank you. As long as you understand . . . you keep your distance, and I'll keep mine."

Tyler clenched his jaw. "Damn it, Del. I didn't hurt you the night that we . . . made love."

Physically, no. It would almost be easier if he had. Instead, he'd given her one amazing climax after another, tripping her over the edge of pleasure in ways she'd never even conceived of. Certainly in ways that Eric had never managed.

But she wanted to throw his words back in his face and point out that he had other ways to hurt people besides physically. The seeming ease with which he'd left her without a backward glance had been damn painful, especially after she'd realized how badly she needed Tyler. It hurt more now to realize that, since they'd parted, he'd been getting busy with his usual bevy of strippers and easy lays. Not that she was surprised, but . . . had he thought about her at all?

She shoved the question aside. It wasn't his fault that she cared about him more, that not having even a small part of his heart crushed her. In truth, when Tyler had left, he'd only done what she'd asked.

"I won't hurt you now," he added into the silence.

Because I won't let you. "I'll come find you when Seth is ready for his story."

Tyler hesitated, his green eyes probing. For what? A chink in her armor? Any hint that she wanted him? A sign that she hated him? Maybe she was reading too much into it. At the end of the day, she'd been another piece of ass to him—one careless enough to get pregnant. He was more concerned about Seth, as he should be. She needed to forget whatever emotions might have been between them and move on.

Finally, he nodded. "Towels are under the bathroom sink. Shampoo and soap are in the shower. Take your time."

With that, he was gone, grabbing for the phone at his belt before he'd even left the room. Probably going to confer with Jack or Deke again.

Del sighed. It didn't matter if he was mad. Seth mattered. No guilt, move on. She'd functioned like that since her divorce—or tried. It was a good motto now, too.

She picked Seth up. He fussed at being separated from his toys, so she also selected a little plastic football he could play with in the shower, which calmed him down.

Minutes later, she stood under the hot spray, letting Seth play at her feet while she washed herself and her hair. She'd even found a fresh razor in the top drawer and availed herself of it. After a final rinse, she almost felt human. Then she quickly scrubbed Seth, working around his little football until he was clean.

As soon as she pulled back the shower curtain and emerged, she noticed that her duffel was missing. The last of her toiletries and clothing. Tyler, that rat, had sneaked in here while she'd bathed and taken her stuff?

Wrapping a towel around herself and setting Seth on another, she stormed out the door. "Tyler, goddamn it!"

Moments later, she heard the hum of the washing machine, saw him prowling through the bag and setting aside a diaper and pajamas for Seth.

He spun and eyed her with a stare that heated so quickly, she clutched the towel even tighter to her chest and took a step back.

Why the hell was he looking at *her* like that?

Water dripped from the ends of her hair, over her shoulders, down her arms. The air-conditioning kicked on. Her nipples beaded under the thin towel. And those green eyes of his zeroed in, staring unabashedly.

Delaney sucked in a breath. A quick glance down proved his erection packed the front of his jeans. She remembered every inch of the reason he'd stretched her almost painfully when he'd entered her and left her deliciously sore the next day.

"No. Do *not* go there."

"Where?" He tried to look innocent.

Tyler innocent? She stifled a snort. When he'd been four. Maybe.

"Stop with the . . . sexy glances. Why did you take my bag?"

Tyler suppressed a smile and held out Seth's things. "Just trying to help. I took the clothes in the baggie that I presumed were dirty and started washing them. You don't have a gun in your luggage."

"I wanted to get Seth out of the way before I brought out the firepower."

"What if you were followed? What if someone had attacked you?"

She'd thought of it, but still didn't feel as proficient with a pistol as she'd like, certainly not good enough to carry it around and make it actually threatening. "I rarely got out of the rental car, but I was afraid if I had a gun 'handy,' that it would be too easy for someone to turn it against me. You know that's what happens statistically."

Tyler ambled closer and rubbed the back of his neck. "Yeah. I'm going to adjust your comfort level with firearms first chance we get, angel. You don't get to say no."

For a moment, Del wanted to balk. She didn't like guns. In that moment, she didn't like Tyler, either. But he was right. It was for her own good—and Seth's. She nodded.

"Good." He lifted some of the damp ends of her hair between his fingers and rubbed, his gaze delving deep into her.

For a second, Del couldn't breathe, and she fell back in time, Memorial Day weekend two years ago. The hint of summer, the smell of beer, the laughter . . . then the feel of Tyler's hands peeling off her clothing, his cock burying deep inside her as Eric's eyes darkened with arousal.

"Angel," Tyler murmured, his thumb brushing softly across her cheek. "I'm glad you came to me. I wish you'd come sooner."

Her belly knotted, and her breathing turned shallow. Unless she wanted to fall into his arms and repeat her mistake all over again, she needed to pull away.

She stepped back, forcing nonchalance. "We've both moved on."

Anger tightened Tyler's face. "I'm not letting Seth out of my life again."

Her first instinct was to argue. Where the hell had he been for the last two years? But that was unfair; she'd sent him away. And she had to put Seth first. "He'd benefit from a father figure. We can work together on visitation. I don't need child support."

Tyler grabbed her arm and dragged her closer. "Stubborn woman. Don't doubt that we're going to work this out. Every last detail."

He meant that, and his adamancy surprised her. "Never took you for the fatherly type."

"One look at his face changed everything for me, Del."

She couldn't argue that. The entire stretch of her pregnancy, she'd felt disassociated from the fact that a child was growing inside her and focused on how this would further affect her job, her body, her life. The moment she set eyes on Seth's face, he'd become the most important priority, hands down. As far as she'd been concerned, everything else would work itself out.

"Fair enough."

"When the timing is better, I want to hear about every moment I missed."

A part of her tried to hate him for wanting to be so involved, as if he'd implied that she wasn't a good enough parent all by herself. Another part of her was so damn touched that he cared about their child. She swallowed back tears. It had been a long time since she hadn't felt alone. Allowing herself to feel at all close to Tyler was dangerous for her on so many levels . . . She stepped back.

"Of course."

Suddenly, Seth, wailing his displeasure, toddled around the corner, dragging his bath towel. Del ran for him, trying to juggle her own towel and get a free hand to pick up her son. Tyler beat her to it, scooping him up against his broad chest and dusting a kiss on his ruddy cheek.

"Let's get dressed for bed, Spidey."

Seth patted Tyler's face and smiled.

Del couldn't help it; her heart melted. They looked so very much alike. Seeing the affection beginning to bring them together choked her up. She turned away.

"We got this," Tyler insisted. "Go get yourself ready for bed. And take this with you."

Reaching into his back pocket, he withdrew a big gray T-shirt that said LOUISIANA CAJUN COUNTRY, with a cartoon of a bearded man riding an alligator next to a tiny rowboat, holding a shotgun.

It was one of the ugliest things she'd ever seen. "To sleep in?

"Sure." He slanted her a considering glance. "Unless you still sleep naked."

"My sleeping attire is irrelevant. Thank you." She plucked the shirt from his grasp, then turned away without another word.

Back in the bathroom, she shut and locked the door, blinking furiously and trying to bring her breathing back under control. But Tyler's scent, all woodsy and male with something so vital, lingered on the shirt. He was like smelling pure testosterone. And she had no choice but to wear the damn thing. With her bag elsewhere, it was this or the towel.

With a dusting of hand lotion and finger combing her hair, she whipped the shirt over her head—and went weak-kneed. God, his smell enveloped her, was all over her—right under her nose, against her breasts, skimming down her abdomen to her thighs, brushing her pussy as she straightened and opened the bathroom door again. With every step, she felt that shirt against her skin, like he surrounded her.

No way could she sleep in this without going insane. Tyler had been potent the night he'd gotten deep inside her, and she'd reveled in his heady, masculine scent.

It was twenty times worse now because she knew exactly what she was missing.

Shoving the thought aside, she pushed out of the bathroom, made her way to the kitchen—and stopped short.

Tyler sat on a barstool with a beer in one hand, the other wrapped around Seth, now dressed in a fresh diaper and clean pajamas. He'd perched his son on his lap and was reading one of Seth's favorites books about animals at a barnyard dance. Her baby boy was all smiles and turned to look up at Tyler with wonder, as if he recognized someone important and special.

Tears hit her eyes like a pickax. Damn, what was wrong with her tonight? She'd known that coming here and facing her past would be emotional. She'd had no idea what sort of reaction to expect from Tyler—but this was almost as sweet as her wildest dreams. On top of all the danger, adrenaline, and sleeplessness, Del felt her emotions crashing off a cliff.

Without missing a beat, Tyler finished the book and closed it, then handed Seth to her and hopped off the barstool.

"Give Mommy a hug," he told the boy.

Seth threw his chubby little arms tightly around her neck and squeezed. Del came apart, clutching her little boy tightly against her as she tried to hold the sobs in.

Her little boy pressed a sloppy little kiss near her mouth before Tyler gently pulled Seth away and wrapped an arm around her waist, bringing her tight against his chest. He felt so solid and alive. His heart beat loud and strong under her ear. More of his forestlike scent surrounded her, and Del realized this was the first time she hadn't been terrified since . . . that night.

"Let it out, angel. I'm here."

She sobbed against him once, twice. God, how easy would it be to lean on him. And how unfair.

Stepping back with a shake of her head, she swiped away the scalding tears. "No. My problems. My cross to bear. I'd just be grateful if you'd take care of Seth for me. I'd die if anything happened to him."

"He's going to be fine. So are you. Deep breath."

She drew in a shuddering breath, then let it out, already feeling better. But she'd be lying if she said she didn't miss Tyler's warm embrace.

"Okay, it's all ready," a booming voice called from the archway behind her.

Del gasped and spun around, pulling her T-shirt down. She was acutely aware of the fact that, since Tyler had swiped her bag, she'd had no panties and wasn't wearing any now. The shirt covered her ass and then some, but . . .

Deke strolled in, looking like he was suppressing a grin. "Did I interrupt something?"

"Don't sound so hopeful, pervert." Tyler crossed the kitchen to the refrigerator and threw Deke a beer. "Any trouble?"

"Nope. Slick as butter."

"Thanks, man."

"No problem."

What the hell were they talking about?

"Can you give us a second?" Tyler asked his buddy.

"Sure." Deke twisted the top off his beer with a beefy fist, then tossed the cap in the garbage. "I'll plop in front of the TV. There's a basketball game with my name on it."

"Thanks."

With that, Deke whipped past them and into the family room. Tyler held Seth in the cradle of one arm, biceps bulging. Del tried not to notice as she swept past him and grabbed her duffel bag off the counter with one hand, holding her T-shirt down with the other.

Tyler suppressed a smile. "Come with me."

With a sigh, Del followed. A part of her wanted nothing more than to get away from him. But she'd be gone soon enough. If he wanted to talk to her, she owed him that.

Pulling her comb out of the bag, she dragged it through her hair quickly, then stashed it as she followed him out of the room and down the hall. When they arrived at his guest room, she saw a playpen set up in the corner with a colorful blanket and one of Seth's toys.

The sight stunned her. "You did this?"

"I called Deke. He brought it over and set it up since Caleb isn't using it now. Kimber and Alyssa both sent over some foods their kids like, along with extra diapers. Kata and Tara are promising to go on a shopping spree tomorrow for Seth, so if he needs more clothes or toys, just make a list."

"I don't have any more money with me."

Tyler's jaw tightened. "Would you stop trying to do every god-damn thing on your own? He's my son, too."

She'd offended him, damn it. Del sighed and sat on the edge of the bed. "Sorry. Habit. What did you want to talk to me about?"

"You're not going off alone. There's no way I'm going to let you throw yourself into danger that's over your head."

"But—"

"No. You're what, five feet five, maybe? And a hundred twenty pounds, dripping wet? But you're going to single-handedly fight off a ruthlessly ambitious ADA trying to have you killed and the gang-land assassin trained to do it? Are you listening to yourself?"

"I'm not going to fight them with my bare hands. I'm just going to dig up evidence and write a solid story that will expose Carlson for the creep he is. I need to do it fast. Word on the street is that he's going to run for district attorney. If he does and wins, it's not like he's going to indict himself. We've already established that I might be the only person standing in his way. He isn't going to let this go."

Tyler kissed Seth's head, then held the boy out for her to do the same. Del scooped him up and inhaled his familiar soapy, boyish smell, wondering if this would be the last time she held him. Her heart tripped, stopped—then started breaking at the thought.

Before she could change her mind, she maneuvered to the far side of the playpen and set Seth inside. Already, he rubbed his eyes. When he saw one of his favorite plush toys, shaped like a tow truck with a smiley face, he grabbed it, tucked it against his body, and closed his eyes with a sigh.

"We can't talk in here without keeping him awake," she whispered.

With a glance at Seth, Tyler nodded and held out his hand to her. Del glanced at her duffel. She *really* should wear underwear to any conversation she was going to have with Tyler. Then again, if he truly wanted her out of them, she'd already be naked and flat on her back in the middle of his bed. He was that good.

But now, he was merely speaking to her as a concerned friend, the mother of his son. That look he'd given her earlier . . . well, she'd cut him off. Since then, he'd respected her boundary. Mostly.

Silently, he led her down the hall, around the corner, and into his bedroom. He shut the door, and she stiffened.

"If Seth starts crying, I can't hear him."

"Then make this fast and agree that you can't fight this battle alone. I won't let you do it, Delaney."

"Don't make this harder than it already is. It's not like I'm looking forward to leaving Seth, much less with a father he barely knows. But he and I have no future if I don't go."

Tyler advanced on her, growling with anger. "You may well wind up dead if you try to play the hero all by yourself. Like I asked before, what the fuck do you know about taking down a corrupt public official and evading a street killer?"

Delaney swallowed. God, he was big. She'd forgotten just how tall and solid and male he was. "I'm not going to run into the city with flashing lights and announce my presence with a bullhorn or try to single-handedly round up the bad guys with guns blazing. I just need to collect a little more proof, and as long as they don't know I'm back in town, it shouldn't be too dangerous. In the last week, I've learned how to lay low, disguise myself. Maybe I'll hire a PI in L.A. to help me. I'll think of something. I'm not stupid."

Tyler stalked even closer. "Being too brave for the situation is. Goddamn it, I'm angry with you right now."

"Because I'm leaving you with a kid you don't know and aren't prepared for? Forgive me, but I don't have more appealing options. Even if he's your son, do you think it was easy to come here and ask for your help?"

As soon as she said the words, she knew she was being unfair. Nothing he'd said or done since she'd arrived indicated he was less than thrilled with having Seth here. But the alternative, admitting that Tyler's anger was wrapped up in concern for her, was too sweet to bear. A tiny part of her would love to lean on him and let him fix all her problems. She couldn't do that to him.

"*What?* I'm happy Seth is here."

"I know. I'm sorry. I'm just . . . so tired. I haven't slept in days." And she was making a bad situation worse. That had to stop. No one liked a bitch.

"Damn straight. I wish to fuck you'd come here about . . . oh, twenty-three months ago. What I'm saying is that, even if you think you're just fact-finding, it's potentially dangerous. You're not equipped for the kind of threat you're going to be facing. You need to let Deke and Kimber or Luc and Alyssa keep Seth while I go with you to fight these fuckers."

It was so tempting to give in and have his strong, comforting presence beside her. But she couldn't accomplish her task if she was worried about Seth. Tyler might be a playboy, but he was also a protector. No way would he let anything happen to their son, and that would give her the reassurance and strength to do what she must.

"Please, let me go. I know best, really. If you'll just . . . do this for me—"

"You mean leave you now when you need me most, just like I did after I touched every inch of your body and got deeper inside you than any man ever has? Leave again, simply because you asked me to? Because you think you know best?"

Tyler advanced even closer, and suddenly, his bedroom door was at her back. He planted both of his large hands on either side of her head and leaned in. Her heart picked up speed viciously. That woodsy, testosterone-oozing scent swamped Delaney, and her legs trembled beneath her. She flattened herself against the door . . . but Tyler kept coming closer, leaning in, his green gaze darkening, drilling into her.

"How well do you think me listening to you worked out last time?" he challenged.

Terribly. Eric had eventually screamed that Tyler slinking off only made him wonder how long they'd been fucking each other. Her protestations otherwise had fallen on completely deaf ears. The positive pregnancy test had been the death knell of their marriage. By then, Tyler had been long gone, and she'd missed him so much. But . . .

Delaney closed her eyes. "This is different."

"Yeah. It's worse. Seth could lose you for the rest of his little life. *I* could lose you forever instead of for two years. Not happening, angel. Last time I saw you, I listened to you about everything. This time? It's my way."

Tyler cradled her face in his big hands. His stare zeroed in on her mouth. He pressed the length of his body against hers. The thin T-shirt she wore did nothing to protect her from the blistering heat of his body. He notched his heavy, steely erection against her mound. Delaney's heart stuttered.

And then his lips hovered right above hers, his head cocking to the side as his gaze ensnared her. He lowered his mouth so, so close. She curled her fingers into fists at her sides so that she didn't wrap her arms around him, her legs around him, and beg for everything he could give her—safety, comfort . . . feverish desire, shattering pleasure.

He exhaled against her mouth, parted his lips. God, she couldn't breathe. Already, she wanted him desperately. Her heart pounded. Her pussy ached. If he kissed her, it would only make everything ten times more difficult.

"Don't," she whispered.

He hesitated, dropped his head near her ear. "*My* way, Del."

Then Tyler nipped at her lobe with his teeth. A shiver wound through her, all the way to her toes.

She didn't get in another breath before Tyler's lips took hers, at first hungry but searching, as if testing his reception. The past, his long list of conquests, the pain between them—all instantly obliterated in the comfort of his solid embrace. His aching familiarity. His seductive kiss. There was no way she could stop the welcome bubbling inside her. Her lips turned pliant, yearning.

An instant later, Tyler groaned, bulldozing his way into her mouth. His heat crashed over her, inside her, surging low in her belly—then spearing deep between her thighs. The warmth of his breath as he seized her mouth and shoved her lips farther apart with his own burned her up. His arms twisted around her body, jacking her tight against the inferno of his taut muscles and steely cock.

She gasped into his mouth. He went deeper, even as his palm

worked under her shirt, branding the suddenly feverish skin of her back, holding her against him without a breath of air between them.

Without conscious thought, she whimpered, her body melting into his, hands fisting his T-shirt, then clutching his shoulders to drag him closer. She opened wider for the hot thrust of his kiss. Needed it. Tyler gave it to her, then grabbed her thigh in one hand, slung it over his hip, and pressed harder against the needy flesh throbbing between her legs. She moaned.

Then Del caught herself.

No, no, no . . . Please let the response shimmering inside her be like a mirage on a hot highway, glimmering with promise. Not real.

Because if it was, she was in a whole world of trouble.

But it felt all too genuine, too intense. It had been so long since she'd experienced the tug and pull of attraction, that agonizing want making her sink against a man's body.

Now wasn't the time to be distracted. Her life—and her son's— were on the line.

Delaney tore her lips from his and turned her head away. She'd love to push him aside and tell him that he didn't affect her in the least. But her trembling and panting were dead giveaways, along with her heart galloping madly in her chest. Tyler wasn't stupid or blind. His stare was all over her, weighty and scorching, cataloging her reactions. Her breath hitched at the thought. Her only consolation was that he was breathing hard, too.

Don't let him kiss me again. If he laid his lips on her now, she'd be toast.

Gently, he tucked a finger under her chin and forced her to look at him. "Del?"

What the hell did he want her to say? Was he looking for permission to continue?

She shook her head. "Don't do that again."

A muscle in his jaw ticced. "Why did you come to me? Honestly."

"I had nowhere else to turn. Please don't make me regret it. Just . . . watch Seth for me. I'll be back as soon as I can."

With that, she twisted out from beneath the solid warmth of his body and turned, yanking frantically at the doorknob. Damn it, she had to get free before she did something with Tyler that she'd regret.

With a low curse, he stepped back and let her go. Then she was in the hall, running toward the guest room as if she was on fire.

Because she was, and Tyler had done that to her with a single kiss. Del had no illusions; he'd let her leave his bedroom because he'd chosen to. If he ever decided to put his hands on her again, chances were he wouldn't release her until they were both utterly sated—because she feared that she wouldn't be able to find the willpower to say no.

* * *

WHAT the hell was going through his head? Tyler winced. He knew the answer to that question, and it wasn't G-rated. Damn it, Delaney flipped his switch in a way it hadn't been turned on in forever. Why was it that one reluctant kiss from her had been better than any blow job he'd gotten from Alyssa's girls? It was more than the addicting flavor of her kiss, more than the feel of her pussy against his denim-covered cock, getting hotter with each second.

As he watched Del's sweet little ass sway down the hall while she sprinted back to safety, he started asking himself some hard questions. Why had he kissed a woman who'd said "no"? For the same reason her quick little breaths and hungry eyes got to him. He wanted her—bad. Beyond sense. Beyond scruples. After he'd gotten over the initial shock of seeing her at his door and knowing that he'd fathered a son on her, desire had settled in, vicious and unrelenting.

Why?

He didn't want to delve too hard for the answer.

His dick couldn't seem to think past the fact that he'd pinned her against his bedroom door and felt every inch of her soft body against him, her shy little tongue touching his before retreating, her pert nipples hardening against his chest. And Jesus, those little gasps and whimpers? He groaned and swiped a hand across his face.

If this had been strictly about desire, he'd be okay. He'd rip his jeans off, take himself in hand, and settle matters quick. He'd done it many times in his life. But right now, his own hand wasn't going to do a damn thing to cool the throbbing settling deep in his cock. It wanted to fuck. Hard. Now. Until he was exhausted. And no one except Delaney would do.

Wasn't that a bitch?

With a sigh, Tyler sat on the edge of his bed. It wasn't wanting her that agitated him. Desire was easy. What he felt for her was far more complex.

Drawing in a shuddering breath, Tyler adjusted his hard dick in his jeans, willing his erection to subside. The last thing he wanted was a verbal ribbing from Deke.

Finally under some control, he stalked back to the den, TV blaring a Dallas Mavericks game. Feeling itchy, edgy, he plopped down on the dark leather sofa next to Deke.

"I saw Delaney race back to her room like her ass was on fire. I take it you kindled that?"

Was this his way of meddling? "Shut the fuck up."

Deke barked out a superior laugh. "You got it bad, you poor bastard. And she's trying hard to hate your guts right now."

Tell me something I don't know. Tyler gave his buddy the finger.

It only made Deke laugh again. Then he slowly sobered and glanced at his cell phone. "I need to keep Kimber in the loop. How long do you think it's going to take Delaney to run?"

"A couple of hours. She's going to wait until she thinks I'm good and asleep before she makes a move."

"Likely so."

"I should pretend to hit the sack."

"Sounds like a plan. I'll crash on the couch. She'll have no idea I'm here. But . . . can we wait just a few minutes? This game is getting good."

"Yeah?" Tyler tried to get interested. Instead, he stared sightlessly at the TV, everything swimming before his eyes as he remembered another hot May evening . . .

Chapter Four

Los Angeles—two years earlier

"WHY'D you knock? It'll take me two weeks to answer the door. I unlocked it a few minutes ago. Just come in."

At the sound of his friend's voice, Tyler entered the house with his key. Eric sat in his wheelchair as he had every day for the last three months, since the fucking suspect Tyler had been chasing sneaked up on Eric and capped a cheap shot in his back, grazing his spine and paralyzing him from the waist down. The doctors hoped the injury was temporary. But maybe not. The good news was, for the first time in forever, Eric looked clean, healthy, freshly shaved. Almost happy, given the grin stretching across his face.

"I'm here with beer, as promised." Tyler held up a twelve-pack.

Eric rubbed his hands together, his dark brows rising. "That's a nice appetizer, but tell me you brought something harder."

"Oh, did I neglect to mention the Jack?" Tyler grinned, then pulled a half gallon of whiskey from behind his back.

"That's what I'm talking about!" Eric wheeled himself into the living room, then motioned Tyler to follow. "Ice that shit down and let's get started."

"Where's Del?" He looked around the little character Craftsman house she and Eric had bought last year, shortly after their first anniversary.

"On her way. I can't believe you both took the whole weekend off." Eric stuck out his hand. "Thanks, man. For everything. For saving my life after the shooting, for being there during the surgery, for taking care of the yard since I can't."

Tyler shook his hand. "Hey, you'd do the same for me. We've walked through fire together. I'd do it again."

Eric nodded, his dark hair groomed for once. It was even short again, like he'd had a trim. Tyler hoped to God that meant that he was finally ready to stop being angry with the world and get on with his life. Even if he couldn't return to Vice, even if he never walked again, Del needed him to start recovering mentally and be the guy he'd been before the shooting. Caring for a man so lost in self-pity and depression weighed on her. She'd been so busy meeting Eric's needs that she hadn't seen to any of her own. She'd lost sleep, lost weight. Tyler tried to shoulder as much as he could for her, but the stubborn woman kept insisting that she was fine.

They'd all been looking forward to this long Memorial Day weekend. Tyler handed Eric a beer, hoping this would be Eric's turning point. Then he grabbed a cold one himself.

"I hate that you quit the force." Eric sounded genuinely regretful. "I feel responsible."

Tyler didn't regret it. "It wasn't the same without you. That new partner they tried to give me was all kinds of gaping asshole. The PI gig is a nice change, being your own boss, making your own hours. Some days with the force, I just felt helpless. Too much case load, bureaucracy, and red tape. So many douche bags on the street, willing to roll over an innocent for fun and cash. So little justice for victims."

"I know you hated that part of the job. I guess I kind of accepted that it came with the territory. I'm not sure that always made me the best cop." Eric shrugged. "But that's irrelevant now. I'm not going anywhere anymore."

At Eric's uncomfortable laugh, Tyler tried not to wince. Maybe Eric wasn't moving on, after all. The guy needed to be more positive about his future. The doctor had given him a 50 percent chance of rehabbing back to normal. His loss of functionality might only be the result of swelling where the bullet embedded near his spine, near thoracolumbar vertebrae eleven and twelve. At worst, the nerve damage was minimal. In that case, he'd probably never do anything more than work a desk again, but he might walk. In the back of his mind, Tyler wondered why Eric wasn't happier to be alive and have a wife who still loved him.

A thousand times, Tyler had wondered why he hadn't been the one to take the bullet. No one in his family gave a shit about him. Sometimes, he felt guilty for still walking, for being whole, while Eric was stuck in a wheelchair. If only they'd waited for backup . . .

"You will. You're recovering." Tyler tried to sound positive, then took another sip of his beer. He had to keep Eric thinking happy thoughts, looking forward to the future. "And when you're up again, maybe you should tell Captain Rogers to fuck himself and come work for me. I follow a lot of cheating spouses and shit, but I also help people. Just this week, I think I found a guy's long-lost, run-away sister. He hasn't seen her in almost fifteen years. It's a good feeling to put families back together. Tell me you don't want to be a part of that and keep more of the pay."

"Chasing cheating spouses sounds crappy."

Yeah, and seeing all the infidelity had put Tyler off of marriage. Not that he'd been a deep believer in the institution before. God knows, his parents had sucked at it before his father split. Eric hadn't been perfect, either.

Tyler took another sip of beer. "But I don't have Rogers yelling at me, and it pays the bills."

"I guess the cheating cases are cheap entertainment, too. Like free porn, eh, man?"

Before he could reply, the back door opened. "If you two are swapping porn collections, I'm going shopping."

Del breezed in, wearing a beige pencil skirt that hugged the slender curve of her hips, a silk blouse in a shade of blue that reminded him of a male peacock's feathers, and shiny black high heels. The latter she stripped off the second she cleared the kitchen. Then she spotted them sucking down brews and doubled back to the kitchen, pulling the pins out of her glossy, mahogany hair as she went.

When she emerged again, she clutched a beer and handed it to him with a pleading look. After Tyler twisted off the cap for her, she downed a long sip with a groan. "God, that tastes like Friday. Thanks." Then she turned her smile on Eric. "Hi, handsome."

"Hi, gorgeous." Eric turned on his megawatt smile, flashing white teeth against that dark Italian skin of his. That smile had persuaded more than one girl to part with her panties in the five years they'd been partners. If Eric had been fully functional, Del would likely have gotten some action tonight.

But neither of them had been remotely sexual since the shooting. Tyler knew it bugged the shit out of Eric. The guy flat loved fucking, the raunchier, the better. He'd drunkenly confessed once that Del wasn't that into sex. Glancing her way, Tyler thought that was a shame. She definitely had all the right curves in all the right places. A damn pretty girl. But more, she gave off this vibe . . . subtle, but undeniably sensual. Teasing. Then again, part of her appeal for Tyler was that she was off limits. Sure, he'd been attracted to Del when he'd first met her, but she was Eric's. Tyler refused to break the buddy code for a woman, no matter how appealing.

For the last two years, he'd put all sexual thoughts of her aside—well, as many as he could—and regarded her as a good friend he drank beer and watched TV with . . . who also happened to have a great rack. Since then, they'd established a great platonic connection. He'd never been friends with a female and was surprised that he actually enjoyed spending time with her, even without the sex.

Delaney turned to him, eyes narrowed. "You started drinking without me. How many beers do I have to drink to catch up?"

She would absolutely keep up with the boys if he challenged her. She had determination and grit. He liked that about her. It had seen her through the darkest days of Eric's recovery.

"Not telling. You'd better change clothes and get started if you have any prayer of lapping us in the alcohol department."

With a little mock pout, she stuck out her tongue and flounced away. Tyler laughed and swatted her ass. "Move faster."

When she rubbed her offended cheek, Eric laughed deep and loud. It was great to hear the sound. Even Del glanced over her shoulder with a grateful smile.

Relief flowed through him, almost peaceful, at seeing the couple on a more even keel. These were the people he knew—happy, teasing—not the gloom-and-doom grouch bringing down the end-of-her-rope worrywart.

This weekend was going to be good, for all of them. For Eric's sake, he'd glossed over the fact that PI work could be boring. Finding a missing woman in Lafayette, Louisiana, had been the only interesting case he'd taken since starting his business a few months back. He'd have to go out there next week and sew the case up. Maybe a change of scenery would be good. Lately, he'd felt really . . . unsettled, unsatisfied. No clue why. Lingering concern for Eric?

Moments later, Del emerged holding her beer, wearing a pair of denim short-shorts with rhinestones and white stitching across her sweet little tush, along with a deep red V-neck tank that flowed around her slender figure. He'd always liked that shirt on her. Good color, and it showed off her breasts. Eric smiled, and Tyler bet she'd worn the shirt so her husband could appreciate her, even if he couldn't do anything about it. Tyler tried to shove aside the fact that he appreciated the hell out of it, too.

"So?" she asked, tossing back a healthy swig of beer. "Pizza? Should we call now? I didn't get to eat lunch today."

And her bottle of beer was nearly empty.

"Lunch flew the coop on me, too," Tyler complained. "Damn executive fucking his secretary over lunch at the little love nest he keeps for her. Why don't these dumb asses ever close the drapes before they drop trou and go at it?"

They all laughed. As he described the couple's sexual gymnastics, they finished their first beers and started the second. It wasn't long before they popped open a third.

"Hey, Tyler." Del sent him a saucy stare. "You still dating that skank at the strip club on Wilshire?"

He tensed, looked at Eric—who glanced away. Shit. He needed to change the subject fast. Now wasn't the time for this cat to come out of the bag. "Destiny and I didn't 'date.' We just fucked."

Del rolled her lively blue eyes. "Duh! I was being polite, you horndog."

"Okay. Then, no." He grinned. "When the 'dates' got boring, I moved on." And that was enough on that. He turned to Eric. "So, what did the physical therapist say this morning?"

As they discussed Eric's recovery, they opened their fourth beer each and had a contest to see who could suck it down the fastest. After Tyler's easy victory, his memories of that night started getting hazy.

With the beer gone, they broke out the whiskey. But soon that bottle was gone, and the sun had barely set. Then they broke into Del's stockpile of wine while they raided the pantry and munched on some chips and salsa. But they never managed to order that pizza.

Critical mistake. The worst move? Allowing the alcohol and his dick to form the committee that made his decisions. Yeah, epic fail there. After that, everything went to shit.

Suddenly, Deke bounced beside him on the sofa. Tyler blinked, returning to the present as the last four seconds of the basketball game ticked down.

Just before the buzzer, one player made a killer three-point shot, and Deke rose to his feet with a fist pump. "Yeah, the Mavs won!"

"Nice." He dropped his voice to a whisper. "I should 'go to bed' now."

Deke's demeanor changed instantly, becoming all business. "I'll, um . . . let myself out the door."

"Want a pillow or blanket?" Tyler whispered.

"Nah. I'll be fine for a few hours."

Plenty of time for Del to flee. She couldn't wait to leave him and throw herself into danger. *Damn it.*

"Good night. Thanks for the playpen, man," he called out for Del's benefit.

The front door opened, closed. Ten silent seconds later, Deke returned to the family room and settled on the sofa. With a nod in his buddy's direction, Tyler headed to his bedroom, stripped down, and slipped between the sheets.

As he lay in the dark, he tucked his hands behind his head. The day washed over him. He had a son. Ten fingers, ten toes. So perfect. So life altering. A precious baby boy who'd need a father to teach him to play catch, learn right from wrong, help him become a good man—something his own father hadn't stuck around long enough to do. Tyler's eagerness to embrace fatherhood surprised him; he'd never thought much about kids . . . but he already loved that little boy, would lay down his life to keep Seth safe.

But thinking of the child led Tyler too easily back to the night he'd been conceived.

His mind drifting back to that unseasonably hot evening in Los Angeles two years ago, he recalled the instant the mood in the room had changed from drunk and jovial . . . to sexually supercharged.

"You're lucky, dude," Eric intoned. "I miss fucking. Nothing like sinking balls deep into a tight, wet cunt. I'd kill to have that again."

"Hey!" Del slapped him on the shoulder.

"With you, of course, babe," he hastily added. "Hell, I'd even settle for watching."

Suddenly, Eric raised a brow at Del, then slid a stare back at him, a slow smile spreading across his dark face.

Tyler feared he knew what the next words out of his friend's mouth would be. "No."

But as the thought of taking Del to bed entered Tyler's head, lightning streaked through him, shocking, unrelenting. Fuck if his cock didn't get hard at the mere thought—and not just slightly. In seconds, he'd gone from zero to dick of steel pressing insistently and painfully against his zipper.

"C'mon," Eric cajoled, his words not as sharp as his stare. "For me. I'm dyin' here. Help a guy out. I need to remember what it's like to really fuck a woman. I need something to look forward to."

On the chair across from him, Del leaned forward, bracing her forearms on her knees. Tyler could see straight down her tank top, to the barely there white lace bra. The overhead lights clearly illuminated her fair, slightly peachy-toned cleavage and the rosy brown of her nipples through the lace.

He hadn't thought it was possible, but he got harder. Tyler's gaze crawled up to Del's face, to her rosy, bee-stung lips, to her sultry, slightly unfocused blue eyes with their thickly fringed lashes. She blinked, met his stare, her own questioning.

How would her kiss taste? Would she orgasm with her eyes closed and a moan? Or with her gaze wide and surprised, screaming for the man who'd delivered it? He'd wondered more than once over the years. And as the questions rolled through his mind again, Tyler swallowed down a hot ball of lust. It settled south, making the throbbing of his cock like an insistent, nagging ache. Del was his best friend's wife, and with every one of these thoughts, he sank deeper into a thick cesspool of guilt. But now that Eric had planted the possibility of being Del's lover in his head, Tyler wondered how the fuck he was going to keep his hands off her?

He just would. Eric was like a brother . . . who'd had enough booze to be a few sandwiches shy of a picnic. Sober, he'd know this was a really fucking bad idea.

"Are you asking Tyler to sleep with me?" Del's voice slurred just a hint. She looked adorably confused. "You want me to have sex with your best friend?"

This was his cue to get up and leave, even though his dick really wanted to stay and party.

Before he could find his feet, Eric hammered his point home. "I'm asking him to be our middleman, Del. But it will be like you're with me, like it's my cock sinking into you, like me making you come."

She nodded, then frowned. "But won't that be . . . cheating? Won't you be hurt?"

"No, babe. You're not sneaking behind my back. I'll be right here, and I'll feel like you're with me." He grabbed her hands, then sent Tyler a pleading glance. "I might not ever be with her again. You're the only way I have to experience that. The only one I trust."

Tyler sucked in a shuddering breath. "Dude, she doesn't sound okay with it, and I won't do this against her will."

Del laid trembling fingers on his forearm. He could still see down her shirt, and he was so damn hot for her that he had to restrain himself from kicking aside his chair, pinning her to the sofa, then getting deep in her pussy and fucking her breathless.

"I—I'm willing," she whispered to him, then turned to Eric. "I—I mean, if this is really what you want."

"Yeah. Oh babe." Eric trailed his fingers down her cheek, dark eyes bright with gratitude. "Sex will give me something to look forward to while I rehab, something I can focus on and work toward when the therapy gets hard. Whaddya say, Ty?"

Scrubbing a hand across his face, Tyler paused. The fraction of his brain that wasn't alcohol soaked was sober enough to wonder what would happen if he crossed the friend line with Del. Sex was usually casual as hell to him . . . but she wasn't a meaningless fuck. A woman that smart, compassionate, and together deserved more than to be banged in a drunken orgy of whiskey and hormones because her husband wanted to watch.

But Eric, for all his faults, hadn't deserved to be shot near the spine and paralyzed, either. Still . . . Tyler wondered, if he agreed to Eric's request, how would his pal truly feel tomorrow about the fact that his best friend had fucked his wife?

"I've never asked you for anything this important," Eric pleaded. "I've been thinking about this for a few weeks now. I *need* this, Ty."

Damn it. Eric had been thinking about this sober? The guy had never pleaded for anything, not even his life when the asshole who'd shot him stood over him with a gun and threatened to do it again. Tyler wanted to do what was best for everyone . . . but his thoughts were complicated by the undeniable fact that he wanted to grab Del, strip her, lay her flat, and get his cock inside her ASAP.

Still, he hesitated. "I don't know, man . . ."

Eric's face closed up. "I'm asking too much, aren't I? Sorry. 'S okay. I'll ask Jim Becker. He'll do it."

Yeah, because Becker the Pecker would fuck anything that moved. And he stared at Del like a piece of meat every time she walked in the precinct. Eric knew that. Tyler's chest tightened at the thought of Del in the creep's clutches.

"Fuck no! Becker wouldn't be good to Del. He won't care about her experience or treat her like she's special."

"Maybe . . . maybe not." Eric shrugged. "I have to hope for the best. You're my first choice, but if you're not able . . ."

Tyler shook his head. *Not able?* He snorted. Right now, he felt like he could fuck Del ten times without pausing. "Dude, are you really sure this is what you want? And you, angel?"

"I want whatever is going to bring Eric and me closer together," Del whispered, eyes tearing up. "The last three months have been . . ."

Awful. He knew. She had to have felt like she'd awakened to a never-ending nightmare. Nothing in her life was the same anymore, least of all her husband.

"Yeah." Eric nodded emphatically. "I don't mean the idea to sound kinky. I just need to feel like a man again. I need something good."

How about an ice cream cone?

Once upon a time, Eric would have been too self-assured to make this request, no matter how drunk. Tonight showed just how desperate he'd become. How the hell was he supposed to turn down this plea?

Tyler palmed the back of his neck, then decided to shoot straight. "Dude, you know me. You know my reputation."

"Yeah. You love 'em and leave 'em. I don't think for one second that you'd try to stake any claim on my wife."

Eric had him there. He wasn't the forever type. His mother had been saying it since he was a kid. Hell, he, Eric, and Del had even joked that he usually didn't stay more than five minutes post-orgasm. But he respected Del too much to fuck and run. Where did that leave him?

"If I do this, you need to understand that I'm gonna be thorough and make sure she enjoys every minute, because your wife is hot. I'll definitely enjoy it, too.

"I know." Eric nodded. "I want her to enjoy it. She probably needs the release. I don't even think she's spent any time with her battery-operated boyfriends lately."

"Eric!" She batted his shoulder playfully.

The thought of Del masturbating just got Tyler hotter. Fuck, he wanted her bad.

"Will you do it?" That pleading note was back in his buddy's voice.

Did he really have a choice?

Taking a deep breath and hoping they didn't all regret this, Tyler nodded. "I'd do anything for you, man. You know it."

He also hoped to God that after he thoroughly enjoyed fucking his best friend's wife, he could live with the guilt.

Eric beamed, then shook his hand. "Thanks, man."

"Um, any boundaries?"

"Nah. I trust you to do what's right."

A bad choice on Eric's part. Tyler feared he'd be unable to stop himself from unleashing a whole bunch of naughty fantasies on Del and pushing every one of her limits.

Eric grabbed her and pulled her in for a quick kiss before snagging the wine bottle and taking another long swig. Then he turned to Tyler. "You gonna kiss her?"

Fuck, he wanted to. At the suggestion, need surged through his body, settling into his inflamed cock. How would she feel against him? Around him? Curiosity was eating him alive.

She climbed off Eric's lap, then drew in a deep breath that lifted her pretty, pert breasts. Her nipples were already hard, but she stared up at him through her dark lashes, her blue gaze surprisingly shy. She bit her lip.

"Del?" Tyler held out his hand to her. His own shook.

After a moment's hesitation, she nodded, then curled her fingers around his.

Desire jolted its way up his arm, short-circuiting his brain. More blood rushed south. Tyler swallowed. *Go slow. If you don't calm the fuck down, you're going to inhale her. Scare her. Hurt her.*

Apparently, Del mistook his pause for reluctance. She stepped against him, grabbed his face with both hands, and jammed her mouth against his in a desperate kiss.

That was all it took to unleash his hormones off the chain. His conscience quickly followed.

He fisted both hands into her long hair and yanked her head back, arching her body against his. With his lips, he shoved her own apart. He didn't just kiss her; he violated her mouth, plunging inside, dying to taste her completely. Possess her.

She moaned, rubbing that lithe little body of hers against him, accepting everything he gave her. Her flavor detonated like a bomb in his system, setting fire to his skin, dropping hot lava into his veins. As she wrapped her arms around his neck, desire settled with relentless insistence in his iron shaft, his heavy balls.

"That's it." Eric hissed the words. "God, that's hot."

Tyler jumped back as if he'd been scalded. He breathed like he'd run a fucking marathon, his lungs pumping hard and fast. A gorgeous flush stained Del's cheeks. Her mouth, always full, now looked downright red and swollen. She swiped the tip of her tongue across her bottom lip inquisitively, as if trying to taste his kiss all over again. The sight grabbed him by the cock and yanked hard.

"Don't stop now, babe." Eric wheeled close enough to caress her waist, her breast, then tugged at her shirt. "Take this off. And your bra. Remind me what gorgeous tits you have. Show Tyler."

She gave Eric a shaky nod but turned to him for confirmation. Insecurity crawled across her face. She bit her lip again, turning an even rosier red. Did she think for a second that he didn't want her? Probably. Whatever attraction he'd felt for her had been one-sided, and he'd done his best to bury it. After all, the concept of sex between them had never been even a whisper until five minutes ago.

With Eric watching, Tyler stepped into Del's personal space and cupped her breast through the red silk. He dragged his thumb across her nipple. It drew up tight and needy at his touch. She whimpered. Del was welcoming him? Oh hell, that turned him on. She probably did it for Eric's sake, but Tyler pushed that fact aside. Tonight, she'd let him fuck her. Suddenly, he couldn't think of anyone he wanted more.

He snagged her gaze, held it as he thumbed her nipple again. "Take it off, Del. Show me your breasts."

Her breath caught. She licked dry lips, sending another spark of desire through Tyler. Then she crossed her arms at her waist, grabbed the hem of the tank, and whipped it over her head.

Tyler blinked, stared. Del was . . . utopia. She'd been a contemporary dancer for years, and it showed in the firm lines of her delicate shoulders and arms. Her stomach was flat, the long, lean line of her abdominals visible under flawless skin. Her low-rise shorts clung to slender hips. But her gorgeous breasts had him stuttering. All natural, a perfect mouthful, they were beyond arousing. He wondered how he'd ever look at her again and not see her this way, tentative but flushed, her breathing almost as hard as her nipples, so pretty through the white lace.

Tyler swallowed. "The bra, Del. Off. Now."

Aw, hell. He couldn't even form complete sentences. But she understood exactly what he meant. Holding his gaze, she reached behind her back and released the hooks. A second later, the underwire contraption with the wispy lace slithered to the floor.

Fuck. Me. He almost swallowed his tongue. The palest skin of her body surrounded the most succulent pinkish brown nipples he'd ever seen. Wide, hard, drawn up so tightly, as if begging for a warm mouth to cradle them. Tyler was more than happy to oblige.

"Pretty, isn't she?" Eric said proudly.

The stuff of wet dreams. "Yeah."

"Come here, babe." Eric crooked a finger at her. "I want to touch you."

She complied, and Tyler had to bite back a protest. But Del wasn't his, so he stood silently and watched as his buddy placed a soft kiss on her lips, then ran his knuckles across one of her nipples. "Don't forget to look at me. I want to see your eyes. I want you to think of me."

Hell no. That was Tyler's first instinct. He kept the words in. He was doing a favor for a buddy, not greedily fucking the guy's wife for his own pleasure. His head—both of them actually—needed to get on board with the plan.

Del gave Eric a tremulous smile full of devotion. Tyler wanted one of those with an ache that didn't make sense. He'd never have it from her. The thought was a stab in the chest.

But he'd have her body tonight, and he planned to devour every inch he could.

Tyler grabbed Del's arm and pulled, yanking her into his embrace. With an insistent grip, he clutched her nape, pulled her flush against him, and devoured her mouth again. Those sweet berry lips, her shy tongue stroking and retreating, her little catches of breath as he grabbed her firm little ass and hoisted her against him, notching her pussy right against his cock.

"Fuck, that's hot," Eric murmured.

He liked what he saw? There was *way* more coming. Tyler vowed that he wasn't letting go of Del until she was completely sated. If he had his way, she'd stay under him until she was wrung out, sore, and smiling from ear to ear.

He tore at the fastenings of her shorts, undoing them and shoving down the denim, along with her little lace thong, in one swipe of his big hands. Once they reached her knees, he stomped them down with his foot, his mouth fastened to hers hungrily as he savored her taste.

Del didn't hesitate or back away. She clutched his shoulders, rubbing herself against his body. The second her shorts hit the ground, she shoved his T-shirt up his torso and over his head.

"Tyler . . ." She skimmed her palms over his chest, dragging her fingertips across his sensitive nipples. "Are you sure? I mean, if you don't want . . ."

Her? At this point, only an army could drag him away from Del. Maybe. If they were really insistent.

"I'm good. Are *you* sure?" he croaked out.

Nodding, she explored his skin again so lightly that goose bumps rose all over his chest. He sucked in a deep breath at the feel of Del's hands on him. God, that was spec-fucking-tacular. They'd barely started, and already Tyler wanted to beg for more.

He couldn't wait to get his cock deep inside her sweet pussy. And it would be sweet, he could already tell, as he swiped his fingers across her smooth flesh there. Eric had told him once that she waxed down south, and Tyler appreciated a bare cunt. Correction: bare, wet cunt. Hers was perfect. Fuck, he could get lost there.

He tripped a finger across her clit. *Hmm, already getting hard.* But her appeal went beyond the way she looked or felt. Del had held his hand in the emergency room once after he'd tangoed with a perp's knife and needed twenty-three stitches near his kidney and hip. She'd shown him how to cook more than frozen meals. Last year, after her parents' deaths, she'd clung to him during the funeral as Eric and the other pallbearers carried the caskets to the graves.

Tyler loved her openness. Del was totally, completely real. No plastic smiles, no silicone, no artificial bullshit designed to impress. Every emotion, every expression she laid bare. No hiding, no fronting. Just beautiful honesty. That took guts he didn't always have. And he admired her for it.

"That feel good?" He rubbed her clit again.

She gasped, and her head fell back as she melted under his touch. "Yes . . ."

"You'll have to get her off manually, and it'll take time," Eric coached. "And she doesn't usually come during sex."

Yeah? Tyler stared down into Del's face. She flushed, averting her gaze. Eric had embarrassed her. Did she think for a second that not climaxing was *her* fault? Tyler loved the guy like a brother, but if he wasn't manning up to Del's lack of orgasm during sex . . . well, Tyler would be more than happy to show Eric that he was wrong.

In fact, impatience clawed at Tyler. Everything about her body said that she was hungry. For him or just for sex? Whatever. He'd gladly feed her need.

He trailed openmouthed kisses along the hot satin skin of her neck as he shoved a finger inside her cunt. Instantly, her flesh clamped down on him as if trying to suck him deeper.

"Damn, you're tight." He leaned in, nipped at her ear, and whispered, "How long has it been for you, angel?"

Del grabbed his shoulders, eyes wide as he stroked her, mouth gaping. "S-six months."

What the fuck? Tyler tried to wipe the shock off his face. He'd give Eric a pass for the last three months. But before that? He'd been too busy fucking Destiny and had neglected Del completely.

Tyler stroked her again, deeper, slower. Eric thought *he* needed this? He'd bet Del needed it more. Who'd been holding her and reassuring her lately? Telling her that she was beautiful, desirable, worthwhile? Tyler vowed to fix that tonight.

She gave him a shaky nod, mewling and gyrating on his fingers. A pretty flush crawled up her chest, to her face. Her breathing shallowed as he rubbed at her clit. Then he pressed on that sensitive spot inside her.

Del dug her nails into his shoulders. "Oh my . . . Yes!"

Amazingly, she already felt moments from climaxing. Over the years, Tyler had seen a lot of women in the throes; he knew the signs. *Not responsive?* Eric had to be a flaming idiot in bed because Del was about to combust. Damn, he couldn't wait to see how she reacted when he had every inch of his cock buried inside her.

"You going to come for me?" Tyler whispered.

She swiveled her hips again, panting against his neck. When he bent and laved each of her nipples with his tongue, then drew one deep into his mouth, Del sucked in a deep breath. Her pussy squeezed like a vise on his fingers, then began to pulsate. She screamed as she came.

Tyler's entire body hummed at the sound.

He thumbed her little knot of a clit through a long, wrenching climax. Shit, her pelvic muscles were strong, and he couldn't wait to feel them clenching around his dick. He'd kiss her, trap her screams in his mouth as he rode her from one orgasm to the next.

"Babe, that orgasm was intense," Eric said. "Wow, you *did* need it. How do you feel?"

She whimpered. "I still ache."

Eric stroked her thigh. "We'll fix you."

The second her pulsing muscles let up, impatience clawed Tyler. He grabbed the snap of his jeans and wrenched it open, shoving his zipper down. Since he usually went commando, nothing else stood in their way.

His cock sprang free, and he palmed it, stroking slowly as she caught her breath and backed up, watching him with wide eyes.

"Holy shit." The whisper slipped out of her mouth, as her gaze fused itself to his cock. She blinked, and then blinked again. "Seriously?"

Tyler shrugged. He'd been told before that he was big, but he'd never had problems fitting. "We'll go slow." *Though it will kill me.* "I won't hurt you."

That seemed to dissipate her fear. "I know."

Eric wheeled over to the sofa and used his arms to lift and throw himself onto the cushions, then leaned against the arm. "I need to see more. God, I remember how much I'm missing. I want this back. I'm going to work to get this back."

Del smiled at Eric, then turned to him. As she did, her expression turned saucy. "You're not shy, right?"

Tyler snorted, his blood on fire. "Whatever you've got, angel, dish it out. I can take it."

She liked the challenge—her smile said so. Then she dusted kisses across his jaw, her fingers skimming, teasing down his torso, to his thighs. She gripped his cock in her hand, stroking with authority and a clever grip.

He groaned long and loud at the pleasure screeching through his body.

She giggled. "I'll bet you thought us old married broads were dull."

He'd never thought that about Del. He'd certainly never think that about her in the future. She knew way too well how to run her thumb over the sensitive head, then gently scratch on the nerve-laden indentation just beneath. Tyler sucked in a breath.

Then she started shimmying down his body until she sank to her knees.

"Del. Jesus, don't— Oh, fuck me, that's good."

Her mouth closed around his cock like hot velvet, all soft and wet and welcoming. Tyler gripped his fists in her long hair and eased deeper into her mouth. It was like quicksand, sucking him under until he felt as if he was drowning. Tingles hammered through his cock, down his thighs, and when she swirled her tongue around the head of his dick, then tried to take him to the back of her throat, he groaned.

"That's so hot," Eric murmured. "You know how, babe. Give it to him. Yeah . . . Fondle his balls."

Shit, it was like Eric could read his mind. Instantly, Del complied, her fingers cupping, stroking, sliding. Those tingles swirled, concentrated. He looked down at her lush little mouth, lips parted so wide, trying to accommodate him in that hot silk haven. She'd never take all of him, but when her lips slipped down another inch of his cock, Tyler thought he was going to lose his mind.

A blow job was a blow job, but this . . . Damn, how was he going to keep it together and not come down her throat in the next thirty seconds? Knowing it was Del's hot little mouth all over him was killing him. He wanted to take her in every way possible. In that moment, he couldn't deny a primitive urge to stake a claim.

Using his grip on her hair, he eased back. "Lick the head."

She did, just like she'd eat a fucking ice cream cone, laving as if he was a delicious treat she'd craved. And she looked up at him through those lashes, dark blue eyes soft and sultry. Aroused.

"Now lick your lips," Eric told her.

Tyler watched her sweet pink tongue cover her top lip in a slow sweep before darting inside again. Then it emerged again, the tip tracing the sexy little line in the middle of her bottom lip as it turned glossy and slick. Her chest rose and fell more rapidly with each moment. And still she never looked away.

"Good, babe. Now let him fuck your mouth. Do it slowly."

Crap, Eric was trying to kill him, and Tyler would object if it didn't feel so fucking good.

Del thrust out her tongue again, this time cradling the underside of his cock, then slowly luring it back, drawing him back into her mouth.

He tightened his fists and threw his head back. "Del. Goddamn it . . ."

Then she made it twenty times worse, taking his cock even deeper in her pretty mouth and humming around it. She swallowed, and the head bumped the tight, working muscles of her throat. Pleasure spiked through his system. The tingles were becoming a storm, centered at the base of his spine. His balls felt heavy, loaded.

Grimacing, he yanked on her hair and dislodged himself from the sweet grip of her lips. He glanced down, seeing her blink in confusion, in arousal. Her wet lips, her dilated eyes . . .

"I have to fuck you now." Tyler heard the desperation in his own voice and winced.

She gasped, then a kittenish smile curled the corners of her mouth. Tyler wished he could put that sexy, mischievous look on her face every fucking day.

"Yeah," Eric interjected. "Do it, dude. Bend her over the sofa right next to me. I want to kiss her and play with her."

While Tyler fucked her. He gritted his teeth. This so wasn't what he wanted with Del. He'd like a cozy bed at her back and hours on end to explore her. He wanted to suck her nipples raw, taste that pretty bare cunt, get drunk on her flavor. But the driving urge to get deep inside her and pound away until she screamed his name was shutting down his good sense.

Reaching down to his discarded jeans, he pulled a condom

from the pocket. Palming it, he helped Del stand, brought her against him, then brushed his thumb across her lip. No matter how badly his cock ached for her, he forced himself to ask, "You're sure?"

She gave him a shaky nod, then whispered, "Please."

The little word damn near undid him. He thumbed her hard nipple, caressed the long, lean line of her belly, then slid his fingers back over her pussy. Fuck, she was even wetter than she'd been just after her orgasm. Given how hard he planned to fuck her, she was going to need it.

"Face me," Eric demanded.

Tyler didn't want that. He'd give anything to stare into Del's eyes, watch them widen, watch her lips part, as he sank every hungry inch of his cock into her. He held in a curse. This wasn't his show.

Before he let her go, he cupped her cheek and settled his mouth over hers. He ached to be inside her utterly, devour her whole. Instead, he curbed himself, reassuring her with a deep, slow stoke of his tongue against hers, showing her silently exactly how gently but thoroughly he planned to fuck her. When he finally lifted his head and stared into her eyes, she gripped his shoulders and stared breathlessly.

She understood him completely.

"Face Eric, angel."

Del sent him a last glance, begging for reassurance. Whatever she saw on his face settled her. She nodded and turned.

As he donned the condom, Tyler couldn't deny that the view from the back was every bit as luscious as the front. That firm, round ass . . . The long line of her spine bisecting the flawless, peachy-hued skin of her slender back . . . The exaggerated nip of her waist, and the graceful slopes of her shoulders . . . The long, silken strands of her hair brushing her back, then the curve of her ass as she tossed her head impatiently.

When was the last time he'd wanted a woman this much?

Never. And he wanted her so much because no one was like Del.

Tyler palmed her hips, gently guiding her to bend over the arm of the black leather sofa, bringing her face inches from Eric's.

"You look hot, babe." He brushed a kiss over her mouth, reached out to toy with her nipples.

Fuck. Suddenly, Tyler didn't like watching Eric touching Del. Over the years, he'd seen his buddy kiss her many times. He'd heard a story or two about the escapades of their honeymoon. But tonight, in this moment, Tyler wanted Del to belong to *him*.

He intended to claim every inch of territory he could. He'd feel like shit about it tomorrow, but right now . . .

Fitting his hips to her ass, he slid his cock between her cheeks and laid his chest over her back. Del gasped. Yeah, the heat was intense. Tyler closed his eyes and let sensations wash over him. He should probably feel guilty for wanting her so much, but he refused to acknowledge it tonight. Del needed him—with any luck, half as much as he wanted her. The breast Eric didn't fondle, Tyler cupped, toying with the engorged tip, rolling it between his fingers until she gasped.

"I'm going to fuck you, angel," he whispered for her ears alone. "We'll work and wriggle. You'll gasp and tighten. But you're going to take every inch of me. And you're going to come for me. Understand?"

"Yes," she breathed.

"I want to hear everything you're feeling. Every second, every stroke. I have to know this is what you need and that I'm not hurting you. Stop talking, and I stop fucking. Are we clear?"

"Please." She wriggled back against him, her voice breathy.

Perfect.

Taking himself in hand, Tyler fitted the head of his cock to her tiny, slick opening and began pushing his way inside slowly.

Oh hell. What a constricting little vise of pleasure. Hot and tight. Sinful and so fucking necessary to his next breath. All attached to the woman making his blood sing like no one ever had.

As he shoved in the next inch, then another, she tensed, gasped. He gripped her hips tighter, forcing himself to pause.

"Does it hurt?" It had been a long time for her.

"Yes," she panted. "Give me more."

Who the hell was he to turn that down? And how the fuck would he ever get his sanity back afterward?

Chapter Five

DELANEY stared at the ceiling of Tyler's guest room. Weariness pulled at her. The bed was insanely comfortable, and Seth's deep breathing coming from the playpen relaxed her. She didn't lie to herself; being this close to Tyler made her feel safe. How easy it would be to snuggle down, close her eyes, and drift off. Here, she could almost forget that a bomb meant to kill her had exploded not quite four days ago.

But she couldn't think of her comfort now. Seth's safety was more important. Though Tyler hadn't known the boy more than a handful of hours, she had no doubt he would move heaven and earth to keep his son from danger. That had to console her. She would return to Los Angeles, investigate very quietly, write a kick-ass article, and lay low until it released. Once she'd nailed the bastard, she could come collect Seth . . . and say good-bye to Tyler.

He had a full life here in Lafayette, and she was both envious of and happy for him. But Tyler had always made friends easily. Once he cared about a person, he was as loyal as the day was long. He'd give a friend the shirt off his back.

Or his friend's wife the release she'd desperately needed.

Del tried to keep thoughts of *that* night at bay. But like a song she couldn't banish from her head, they came back. The heat, the alcohol, Eric's pleading request. And the pleasure. Dear God, she'd never felt anything like the ecstasy Tyler had given her that night, hadn't even known it existed. She remembered the moment he'd pressed inside her, slowly possessing her until all thought had fallen away, leaving only him and the searing need.

Those memories tumbled through her exhausted brain. No matter how tired she was now or how drunk she'd been then, everything about that night was crystal clear. Tyler bending her over the arm of the sofa. Eric brushing a kiss over her mouth, before glancing around her to watch Tyler press his thick cock into her pussy slowly, without mercy.

Though she had whimpered, she'd loved it.

This was really happening, Del remembered thinking two years ago. She was going to have sex with Tyler Murphy.

As he'd penetrated her that sultry night, she'd tried to swallow against lust, but it was useless. His huge hands engulfed her hips, and need flared through her, hot and unrelenting. He pushed deeper into her, stretching her, then withdrew again, only to inch in once more, so grindingly slow. The raw ache he spurred nearly drove her insane.

"Tyler, please . . ."

It wasn't the first time that night she'd begged. And it definitely hadn't been the last.

Del knew she should put a stop to this before the situation careened any further out of control. She'd stood in front of her family and friends—including Tyler as best man—only two years ago. That day, she'd promised to love and honor and be faithful to Eric for the rest of her life. Then, everything had seemed so natural and easy.

The days had become weeks, then months. Her husband's job consumed him, and it wasn't easy to know that he saw drug dealers and prostitutes all day. She'd talked to other cops' wives and knew that, behind the badge, they were still men who could be swayed to ignore crime for money or sexual favors. Not that she believed Eric would take either, but . . . the last few months before his shooting, they'd been more like friends than spouses, doing crosswords, watching movies, eating together. Their lack of connection was probably her fault. She'd been stressed, worrying that because she covered fluff pieces in a nothing section of a financially shaky paper, she'd lose her job. Whatever the reason, sex between them had stopped.

She'd begun to wonder if someone else was picking up her slack.

Then Eric had been shot, and everything else ceased to matter. Then, there'd been nothing but endless days in the hospital, pain, and sleeplessness, along with the grim fear that he might not live, and if he did, would he ever walk again? Del knew she'd take care of him, regardless. After all, in sickness and in health. But as time had crawled by, he'd grown more surly. Angry at her, at the world. Affection had ground to a complete halt in favor of snide disdain and petulance. Never had she imagined this side of Eric. He'd become a completely different man. And she'd despaired that she'd ever reach him again.

Would letting Tyler fuck her in Eric's place finally change something?

She remembered Eric brushing his lips over her jaw, down her neck. She'd closed her eyes and kissed his cheek in return, searching desperately for that connection she'd once felt with him, praying to find it. Praying that she was doing the right thing to save them.

Even if she wasn't, Del didn't think she could stop. Her body was burning up. It wasn't just the pleasure that had her crying out. She *needed* to be held, loved. Reassured of human comfort. Tyler clutched her tightly, suffusing her with a searing heat that made her ache down to her toes.

Since the second Eric had been wounded, Tyler had been by her side. He'd helped with the insurance and departmental paperwork. He'd taken care of her lawn and household repairs. He'd picked up the pieces when she'd been too distraught to carry on . . . or when she'd cried. If she called, he was never too tired or too busy. In some ways, he'd been more devoted than Eric ever had been. While she knew that love for his friend—not her—made him so loyal, she had to believe that he felt something for her.

God, she wanted to be wanted, to feel alive. Wanted to share something vital. And she craved all that with Tyler. Guilt was eating her alive. Her feelings made her a terrible wife. A terrible person. But . . . human. In this one moment, she wanted to be selfish— before she resumed caring for a man she wasn't entirely sure loved her anymore.

"Tell me what you want, angel," Tyler whispered.

She wriggled back on his cock, but he held her steady with those strong hands, controlling her until she answered.

"I ache." She sobbed.

"I know. I'm going to fix it." But he didn't move.

"C'mon, man. Fuck her!" Eric urged.

Yes, please.

Tyler's finger dug deeper into her hips. He spread his legs a bit more, stabilizing himself, before he pushed another scant inch of his cock inside her. She clawed at the sofa and looked at Eric in helpless surprise as pleasure tore through her.

"She's tight, man," Tyler growled. "So fucking tight. I won't hurt her."

"Don't worry. She wants it," Eric argued, taking another long sip of wine from the bottle. "She's goddamn begging for it. Shove it in her cunt and make her take it."

Her husband seized her lips, took her mouth with his own, stabbing his tongue inside ravenously. Then Tyler eased in another inch between her folds.

Dear God. She couldn't breathe. Tyler fired up nerve endings she'd never felt before. He surrounded her, warm skin sizzling her back, hot breath in her ear, fingers dropped to her thighs, clutching them possessively. He was on her—in her. Overwhelming her. Del tore her lips from Eric's with a gasp.

"Am I hurting you?" Tyler growled, sounding at the end of his restraint.

"Yes. No." She tossed back her head and groaned. "I don't know if I can take more, but I want it."

"See," Eric said. "She wants it."

"Damn it," Tyler cursed. "The goal is pleasure. Not porn," he tossed at Eric. "Not pain. You have to relax for me, angel."

He withdrew a fraction, scraping along her nerve endings. Then his fingers drifted over her clit again as he dragged his cock through the shallow channel of her vulva, coating himself in her juices, back and forth, bumping the little bundle of nerves he circled.

Unbelievably, need spiked again. She rarely orgasmed twice, so the desire balling in her belly, tight and urgent, pressing down on her made her thrash and mewl. "Tyler . . ."

"I know. I feel it, too." He fitted the head of his dick at her opening and began pushing in again. "Just let me in and let go."

She couldn't hold in a gasp as he parted her wet flesh with the blunt tip of his cock and forged deep, spreading her so damn wide. As he opened her, her flesh stung, burned, trying to take every bit of him she could. The thick, hot feel of him stole her breath. And still he kept thrusting forward, stretching and working with absolute focus.

"You look fucking hot," Eric murmured, fondling her nipples before twisting them.

Behind her, Tyler groaned. "Fuck, she just clamped down on me."

"Sweet." Eric manipulated her nipples again. They felt tight and raw and burning. Her body hummed, tensed, waiting for something more.

"Back the fuck off for a minute," Tyler snarled. "Let me finish getting inside her."

He hadn't yet? Already, she felt deliciously split in two.

Del breathed out. It had been so long since she'd felt her blood roaring, her pussy aching—and it had never been like this. She'd been so focused on Eric and his needs that she hadn't even used her vibrator once in the last three months. So she was totally unprepared for Tyler.

But beyond the pain, he was making her feel like a woman again. She couldn't disappoint him. This was supposed to be for Eric, but somehow, it had ceased being exclusively about his sexual needs.

She should probably be angry that Eric wanted her to sleep with another man. But right now, she was damn glad. And she owed Tyler. He'd stepped across his personal boundaries to give her immense pleasure and made her feel treasured. No way would she repay him by failing to give him her all.

Drawing in a deep breath, Del forced herself to relax her pelvic muscles and open in welcome. She wriggled back against him, sucking in a shocked breath as he sank deeper than before, deeper than she'd ever had a man. God, she'd never felt anything so consuming. With his tight grip and controlled breaths, she sensed Tyler's restraint, his concern for her—and the desire burning inside of him. It spilled on to her, urging her to tilt her hips to take even more of him.

On a long groan, he eased the last of his cock inside her, settling so deep, she gasped and clawed at Eric's forearms, eyes wide.

"I'm in." Tyler's voice sounded like gravel. He panted.

"You should see her face, man." Eric grinned.

"Look at me," Tyler demanded.

Del paused, trying to school her features, but there was no way to hide the confusing, sublime pleasure-pain drugging her system. So she looked over her shoulder at him, letting him see how much he affected her.

"Good girl," he praised, his green eyes burning.

Brutal lust stamped across his face, and her body liquefied as she met his stare. She'd known Tyler wanted her enough physically. He was hard, after all. But the sheer force of it stunned and excited Del. Desire, dark and compelling, gripped her. Blood ran thick and hot in her veins. It looked like she wasn't the only one afflicted.

"Jesus." He withdrew slowly, letting her feel every inch.

Then he shoved his way back in, and she gasped. And nearly came undone.

"Babe?" Eric called.

She turned to look at her husband again, his brown eyes desperate as he grabbed her hand, brushed his palm across her cheek. Del closed her eyes and sank into the sensation of feeling utterly adored by them both for a perfect moment.

"She's ready now." Tyler circled his arm around her waist and pressed kisses across her shoulder.

Eric nodded. "Give it to her."

"Remember, talk to me, angel. I can't see you, so I need to hear you."

"O-okay," she managed to get out. What she really wanted to do was scream at him to hurry up and fuck her.

"How do you feel now, Del? What do you want?" Tyler smoothed a hand across her ass.

"Please." Her voice trembled. "I need . . ."

God, did she. Having Tyler at her back, deep inside her, as he exercised his iron control blistered her with something so beyond desire, she had no name for it. She only knew if he didn't take away this fiery ache that gaped inside her soon, she'd implode.

"What, angel?" He wrapped his arm around her and fitted his

fingers over her clit, swirling slow circles around the screaming little bud. "You need to come?"

It sounded selfish to admit, and guilt slid through her for demanding more of Tyler. But the ache assailed her, pressing down until she could no longer hold it in.

"Yes." She couldn't catch her breath. "Yes!"

"Del?" Eric asked, frowning. "Again?"

Explaining herself wasn't at the top of her agenda now, especially when Tyler took her confession as a sign to get busy and began shuttling in and out of her in a measured, maddening pace.

She climbed toward the pinnacle, sobbing. Every one of Tyler's strokes generated friction that robbed her of words and coherent thought. His rough fingers twirled over the sensitive bud of her clit, driving her even higher.

"Let me have it, Del," he demanded gruffly. "Come for me, angel."

Pleasure spiraled, centering deep in her womb, before it sucked her deep. Blood roared in her head until she could only hear her beating heart. Then Tyler's relentless thrusts pushed her over the edge, breaking her open, and hurtling her into a thick pool of pleasure.

"Yes!"

He moaned. "Damn, you feel good on me. That's it. Yeah . . ."

"Fuck." Eric jammed his mouth over hers. "You look hot, Del. Whatever he's doing is working for you because you've never gotten off like that."

Del whimpered. "It's been so long . . ."

Any moment now, Tyler would pump into her hard, fast, coming in a shout and a rush. She wasn't ready to let him go yet, but she'd already been too selfish. This night was about Eric's wants.

"That was so fucking pretty, Del," Tyler breathed into her ear. "Do it again for me."

Come? If he'd asked her an hour ago, she would have sworn it wasn't possible. But with the thick slide of his cock inside her and every one of her senses attuned to him, he was making her a believer.

Eric cradled her breasts in his hands again, thumbing her swollen nipples and sending a jolt straight to her pussy. "Good luck, man. Two is really her limit."

Tyler just grunted. "Fuck that. Faster or slower, Del?"

Normally, she laid back and waited for Eric to finish. But Tyler wasn't going to take that. He was going to make her participate in her own undoing. And she loved the idea.

How would Eric feel about it?

"Faster," she gasped. Tyler would want it that way. It would send him racing to climax.

"Liar." He whacked a playful slap across her ass and slowed his pace.

The increased friction lit her pussy aflame again almost immediately. She sucked in a huge breath and clawed the arm of the sofa. Nothing had prepared her for this kind of thrill.

"Move with me," Tyler demanded.

Del rocked back into him as he established a rhythm, deep, steady, and overwhelming. And he held a possessive arm around her as he crashed into her again and again, the flat of his palm sliding over her mound as the pressure rose. The need swelled. Then the explosion became inevitable.

With a scream, she careened over the edge a third time. The orgasm was low and long and deep. Pulsing, throbbing, taking all her energy and will.

Afterward, exhaustion swamped her. Her body went limp. Her eyes almost refused to open . . . but Tyler still kept slowly thrusting his way into her.

"Fuck, that's amazing, Del," Tyler praised.

"It is, babe. It really has been too long for you." A line worried itself between Eric's brows as he frowned.

Was he concerned that she'd been so deprived or that she melted in another man's arms?

A moment later, it didn't matter as Tyler hit a spot so deep inside her that it sent her racing headlong for climax again. Her tissues swelled. Each thrust burned low, sensations gathering so deep, all so new. Her entire body tensed, thighs trembling as she hung between insanity and thrill.

Tyler groaned long and loud. "Jesus. I'm pressing against her cervix. I feel her against the head of my dick. So damn snug. She's killing me."

Del cried out at the cacophony of sensations hurtling her deeper into pleasure.

He eased back immediately. "Am I hurting you?"

"No!" she panted. "Don't stop."

She didn't even take a breath before he shoved his cock into her so hard, he knocked the sofa a few inches across the hardwood floor—and her senses all to hell. She took a soaring cliff dive off the edge and flew into a consuming, throbbing bliss. Her shout of satisfaction roared in her ears as her swollen walls pressed down on Tyler relentlessly. Surely, he'd follow her into orgasm.

He didn't.

Del realized that a few shocked seconds later when he started pumping hard and steady into her again. The room spun. Her vision swam. And still, Tyler continued fucking her.

Eric grabbed her arm. "Del . . . oh my God."

"You okay?" Tyler demanded.

Better than okay. Del nodded, happy and sated.

"A nod doesn't do it. Talk to me."

His voice kept getting deeper and deeper. That shouldn't turn her on. She should be incapable of being aroused at this point.

As he surged into her again, he brushed every stimulated inch of flesh all the way up her pussy. Del knew for certain that she was still fully capable of being aroused.

"Tyler!" she tensed.

"Yeah, angel." She heard the strain in his voice. "Tell me you can take more."

The idea was crazy, beyond insane . . . "I can."

"Good. I want to see you come again. Your skin flushes, your body shudders. It's so fucking hot."

"Dude, I don't think so . . ." Eric looked skeptical—and perplexed.

She'd have to say something to explain her shamelessness—no idea what—but that was later. Right now, Tyler strummed his fingers over the bundle of nerves between her legs and drove her up, up, up as he pressed his cock deep once more, making her nerve endings beg.

"She can," Tyler assured. "She's clamping down on me. Her clit is hard. I can get another orgasm out of her."

"I'm fine," she forced herself to say. This wasn't supposed to be about her pleasure, and suddenly, she wondered if Eric was ready for the experience to be over. "Don't worry about me, Tyler. Do what you need to do."

"And leave you hanging? Fuck no. What I need is to see you come again. Will you do that for me?"

Eric's dark gaze snagged hers, probing, raw. His expression tightened—and that kicked her in the gut. What did she say with her lover demanding more and her troubled husband looking on? She blinked, her mind raced. The silent moments stood thick.

Tyler ceased all movement. "I told you earlier, Del, you stop talking, I stop fucking."

Anguished pleasure ratcheted up inside her, damn near stopping her breath, her heartbeat. She gripped leather from the sofa cushion in her hand and cried out.

"That's not an answer," Tyler growled.

"Give him a goddamn answer," Eric snarled, grabbing her chin. "Can you come again?"

Lie? Don't lie? Del suspected that each man wanted a different answer. How could she betray Eric? But how could she fail Tyler after all he'd done?

Her husband stared with burning eyes, waiting.

"You're thinking too hard. Your body wants it bad, angel." Tyler pressed his cock deeper in her pussy. "Tell me the truth."

She bit her lip to keep her keening cry in, but she failed. "Please."

Before she finished speaking, Tyler thrust into her again—and lit her up like a city skyline. Eric clenched his fists, his mouth pressing into an angry line. She could feel the fury radiating off of him now.

Tyler paid him no mind and murmured in her ear, "You ever been taken anally?"

Del had pondered it. Some of her friends admitted to loving it. Eric had mentioned it a lot early in their marriage, but she'd always shied away.

Tyler pushed her hair off her damp neck, letting his lips linger just below her ear. "Yes or no, angel."

"I—I . . ."

He withdrew from her pussy and plunged two fingers inside her. Purpose driving him, Tyler rubbed a spot against her front wall, just behind her clit that had her eyes bulging and her breath stuttering.

"No wonder you're burning me up. You have one hot, tight cunt, angel. I could stay here all night."

"She's exhausted." Eric's voice was low and tight.

Del frowned. Did his objection really have anything to do with her well-being?

Tyler blew Eric off. "Not entirely. I can make her come."

Could he ever . . .

The thought had barely crossed her mind when he pulled his fingers free. Immediately, he eased those two digits into her untried backside—at the same time he shoved his cock deep in her clutching, swollen pussy again.

Nerve endings roared, swirled, gathered, tensed. She held her breath, the world stopping completely, except for her roaring heart. Tyler pulled back, then slammed home again, his fingers in her backside creating sensations she'd never imagined and couldn't repress. She went off like a fireworks display, all explosions and bright colors behind her eyes. Her body jerked, shuddered. She'd never felt anything so intense.

"You'd like having your ass fucked," Tyler murmured silkily in her ear before she'd even caught her breath. "I'd love to give it to you so sweet and slow that you'd cry."

Del believed he could do that. And, God help her, she wanted it.

"You're not going anywhere near my wife's ass." Eric's eyes had darkened from annoyance to condemnation. "Are you done yet?"

"Don't be a prick," Tyler groused. "With as much shit as she put up with lately from you, she needs this. Don't you want your woman happy?"

Warmth suffused Del. How had he known how badly she needed to be held and wanted?

Eric's face simply closed up.

No matter how much she'd love to stay in this moment with the lover who'd given her more consideration and pleasure than any other, she had to think about her marriage.

"Tyler . . ." she tried to protest.

"You're not giving up for him." Tyler punctuated the statement with a honey-slow slide into her pussy and a gentle thrust of his fingers into her ass. "You've given up everything in the last three months to care for him. The least he can do since he started this is to let us finish it."

Del melted. Her body felt so heavy and boneless, she wasn't sure she wanted to move. Then Tyler rocked into her, one smooth stroke after another. Sensations danced again. Her libido was like a car engine: Once revved, she was ready to race. It seemed like seconds before pleasure clutched low in her belly and another orgasm raced through her veins.

Before the burning pressure gave way to ecstasy, Tyler stopped, cursed, and withdrew.

"No!" she protested automatically. "Please don't stop."

Eric grabbed her face and forced her gaze to him. "You like him fucking you?"

She bit her lip, her own anger swelling. But unleashing it wouldn't solve this situation. "You started this."

"And now he's being an ass about it," Tyler asserted. "It's not all about you, dude."

Before her husband could reply, Tyler turned her into his embrace and perched her butt on the arm of the sofa. With impatient hands, he spread her legs impossibly wide, then surged back into her pussy.

Then he drilled his stare deep into her, somehow fusing them together. "I fucking need you, Del. Now."

His first thrust came hard and fast. And deep. So damn deep, Del swore she'd never lose the sensation of him being inside her. She groped behind her, trying to stabilize herself.

Before she could fall, Tyler reached around her waist and hauled her closer, spreading her legs even wider with his hips. He kissed her neck, her shoulder.

"Look at me," he commanded.

Helplessly, her gaze flew up to his, so green, so intent. In that moment, she could read him: his determination to make her feel good, the surprise at their insane sexual chemistry, the need to see her not just sated but happy.

He tucked a stray lock of hair behind her ear, then placed a lingering kiss over her mouth. Electric longing jolted through her body. For that fraction of time, it was just the two of them, and Del gave herself completely to Tyler.

Eyes closed, she threw her arms around his neck, trusting that he would hold her in place tightly against him. And he did as he eased in again and again, deep inside her, fusing their mouths together.

God, he was not just inside her now, but a part of her. She and Eric had been married for two years, and she'd had her fair share of college sex, but *nothing* had been more intimate than this. Tyler's hot breath against her lips, followed by the probe of his softly searching tongue. His sweat-damp chest smashed against hers, their hearts both pounding crazy fast in sync. Him clutching her backside and pulling her so close . . . No one else existed. It was just the two of them and the steadily rising tide of pleasure that threatened to drown her.

"Del."

Tyler's voice sounded damn near frantic. His deep, rapid breaths betrayed his excitement, and it spiked a thrill within her.

"Del!" he demanded.

"Yes. I'm here. Whatever you need."

"Jesus Christ, I need to be deeper inside you."

Suddenly, she wanted that, too. "You're as deep as you can go."

"No, damn it."

Unbelievably, his cock hardened even more. Her heart swelled with the thought that he needed her so much. She felt that need as he shoved a fist in her hair and pulled until her lips fit perfectly against his. Then he kissed her, hot, urgent, until she clutched at him and gasped into the hot cavern of his mouth.

"Fuck, yes," he swore against her lips. "Nothing has ever been better. Take all of me."

She nodded frantically.

"Say it."

"Give me everything."

"Come with me."

Del didn't think that was possible until he was shuddering and shouting, his entire body tense, his cock pulsing thickly inside her. His pleasure provoked hers. Desire broadsided her. She held her breath as a short, violent release stormed its way through her body.

"Tyler!" she screamed, orgasm ravaging her until she leaned limp and sated against his chest, her breathing slowly coming back under control as he cuddled her against him, a tender hand soothing her back.

Suddenly, clapping erupted behind her. Instantly, the spell was broken.

Del jerked her gaze around to see Eric slowly clapping, fury dripping from his expression. "I'm trying to decide if that was great porn or just a really fucking disloyal stab in the back." He gripped his chin in mock thought, then shook his head. "No. Actually, I know the answer."

"We gave you what you asked for here," Tyler bit out, holding her protectively, still buried inside her.

"Bullshit. You were supposed to fuck her at my direction, not cling to her like she mattered and make *love* to her."

Tyler had made something that felt a whole lot like love to her. She'd made love back with him at the end. Guilt swamped her.

Using his arms, Eric clambered off the couch, heading for his wheelchair. There was no doubt in Del's mind that he intended to charge Tyler and . . . what, pick a fight?

She glanced back at Tyler, meaning to warn him. He met her stare, his face tightening.

"Don't you dare regret this now, Del," he growled under the panting and huffing Eric made as he tried to work back into his chair.

Del winced. *Too late.* "You should go."

"I'm not leaving you here to deal with his shitty mood alone."

"H-he's just being a mean drunk. I can handle him." Tyler's mouth pursed, like he was going to get stubborn. She shook her head and gave him a gentle shove. "Please . . ."

Tyler cursed, then sighed. Slowly, he began to withdraw his softening cock from her. The second he pulled free, she noticed the copious wetness—and the pieces of latex.

The condom had broken. Her eyes bulged in dismay. Before she could release the gasp on the tip of her tongue, Tyler slapped a finger over her lips. She had no trouble reading his warning expression. *Shh. This will only piss Eric off more.*

And riling her husband more now would definitely make matters worse, so she gave Tyler a shaky nod, but . . . She had stopped taking the pill after Eric's accident. Tyler had to suspect that. Quickly, Del did the math. Her last period had ended eleven days ago. How likely was it that she was fertile now?

Her eyes slid shut, but everything inside her trembled. *Very.*

Tyler grabbed his T-shirt from the floor and used it to quickly wipe them both clean as Eric situated himself in his wheelchair. Then Tyler buttoned his jeans, wadded the shirt into a ball, and shoved most of it in his back pocket.

"You'll be okay?" he asked reluctantly.

"Fine. Go. I'll call you when he's calmed down."

He still hesitated, and Del knew he didn't like leaving her to Eric's wrath. She could handle it. She'd become all too used to his terrible moods since the shooting.

With a final caress on her cheek, Tyler stepped around her and got in Eric's face, leaning down, hands braced on the arms of his wheelchair.

"You going to fight me about this?"

"That wasn't what I asked for, and you damn well know it! Get the hell out of my house!"

"You're being a douche bag. I couldn't come at that angle, so I flipped Del around. And now you're pissed?"

"You didn't just fuck her. Admit it. And you weren't simply trying to come, but to shut me out. If I'd realized how badly you've got it for Del, I would have called Becker the Pecker."

Eric's assertion startled Del. Her husband thought that Tyler had feelings for her beyond friendship? No. She knew better.

Or she had before tonight. The way he'd touched her, cared about her pleasure and well-being, the way he'd kissed her . . . All that had been way beyond friendly.

She flipped a startled gaze over to Tyler. He wasn't denying Eric's accusation. Instead, he clenched his jaw and refused to look at her.

Oh God.

"Goddamn it, get out now!" Eric growled.

Tyler flinched. Del rushed over, placing a soft, reassuring touch on his shoulder, as she often had. But now everything was different. The feel of his bare skin under her hand swamped her with longing. They'd just had sex minutes ago. He'd given her five amazing orgasms. But it wasn't just about sex. She ached to be close to him, feel his arms around her. Why?

Suddenly, she wasn't too certain she wanted the answer. More guilt crashed over her. She'd agreed to Eric's request to save her marriage, not have great sex. Not fall for someone else. She had to put tonight out of her mind and focus on the man she'd pledged her life to.

Slowly, she withdrew her hand. "It's okay. Go. Eric and I have to work this out."

Tyler stiffened at her dismissal, no matter how soft. "Call me tomorrow."

She drifted toward the door. "Are you okay to drive?"

"I'll walk. Let me know if you need anything." He grabbed her hand. *"Anything."*

"Get your fucking hand off my wife and get the hell out the door," Eric shouted.

Del cringed. How could such a loving, giving friendship have gone so south in one night? She prayed that tomorrow everything would go back to normal. Would Eric be able to put this behind him, forgive and forget? And how would she ever look at Tyler again without remembering that feeling of being one with him?

She feared she never would.

"I'm sorry," she whispered to Tyler.

"No, *I'm* sorry. I fucked everything up." He drilled his stare into her, eyes so green and direct. "I just . . . I couldn't say no to having you."

Shock vibrated through her at his confession. He'd wanted her before tonight?

She was still grappling for a response when he slammed the door behind him.

In that moment, Del had never imagined that she wouldn't see Tyler again for two years or that she'd give birth to his son on her own. She only knew the profound sadness of someone really valuable leaving.

The second the door shut, Eric began shouting, "What the hell? You came for him *five times*! You've never let yourself go like that for me. What's that supposed to mean, that I'm not man enough for you? That you don't love me anymore?"

They'd argued all night, and as the hours slipped past, no

amount of reassurance had been enough for Eric because she couldn't deny that being with Tyler had fundamentally changed her feelings for him forever. In the days that followed, she'd cut off contact with him—at Eric's insistence—to try to save her marriage. In the end, she'd lost both men.

Del blinked, returning to the present, to Tyler's guest room and Seth's little grunt as he rolled over in his sleep. It was time—and her heart was breaking.

Before she remembered all the reasons that she'd rather stay in Lafayette with Tyler and Seth and enjoy life, rather than risk it, she rose from the bed, scrambled into her clean clothes, shoved on her shoes, grabbed her bag, and leaned over to pat Seth. Del wished desperately that she could kiss him once more, but didn't dare risk disturbing him. So she found the note she'd written earlier with Seth's care instructions and left it on the nightstand, then slipped out the window as silently as possible with a last glance back at the little boy. She hoped that father and son would forgive her someday—if she made it out alive. If not . . . at least she'd die knowing she'd done so trying to give her son life once more.

Chapter Six

JUST before dawn, Del parked her neighbor's run-down car in the long-term parking garage at the airport in New Orleans. She was exhausted, but she'd have to sleep on the plane back to Los Angeles. No time now. Still, second-guessing haunted her. Had Tyler discovered her absence yet? Was he angry or resigned? Would he be able to care for the son he knew so little about? She wished she could have left him more than a note. Would Seth be all right, happy? Regret weakened every muscle in her body with the need to run back to her little boy. She had to keep reminding herself that dealing with Carlson now gave her and Seth the only chance for a future.

After a long trek to the terminal, she made her way to the ticket counter. She'd stopped briefly at a twenty-four-hour diner on the outskirts of town for a cup of coffee and an egg. She was down to her last five bucks. It would have to hold her for now because she refused to ask Tyler for money. He'd already taken on caring for their son. That was more than enough responsibility for a man used to easy living and fucking even easier women at every possible opportunity.

At the café near the airport, she'd used a pay phone to call the airlines to book a fare home. It was heinously expensive since she was traveling last minute, but Glenda's car wasn't reliable enough to risk trekking back across the country alone. And she didn't have the cash for more gas.

To book her flight, Del had been forced to use a credit card. She prayed that Carlson's reach didn't extend all the way from Los Angeles County to Orleans Parish. Or that he wouldn't have a team of thugs waiting for her when she arrived.

Inside the mostly deserted terminal, the chill of the air-conditioning hit her, a relief after the sweltering humidity outside. A bleary-eyed airline rep manned the ticket counter. A check-in kiosk blinked nearby, clearly on the fritz. She chose another, trying to keep her head down and her face out of the security cameras, just in case. If Carlson had influence here somehow, she had no doubt that he could have her arrested on some trumped-up charge and thrown into a backwater jail to rot. The deeper she'd dug, the more she'd realized that he dealt with his enemies ruthlessly. She hadn't told Tyler the half of what she'd been through. He'd berate her for not coming to him sooner if he knew.

In a few moments, the machine spit out her boarding pass. The sliding doors behind her opened. An old lady with a cartful of luggage, pushed by a hunk of man wearing jeans and a low-slung cap entered. Dismissing them as a threat, Del turned toward the security line, dragging her duffel. The bleary-eyed TSA agent talked to a guy in a suit.

As she approached, another man sporting his Brooks Brothers look emerged from the nearby men's room—and kicked her instincts into high gear for two reasons: First, he and the dude talking to the TSA agent locked gazes and had a tense, seemingly silent conversation. Second, the air conditioner caught his suit coat. It flapped open just enough to see the shiny black semiautomatic in a shoulder holster.

A moment later, they both turned and headed straight for her.

If they were packing heat and in the airport's security line merely to board a plane, they'd be flashing badges and marching through, not looking at her.

So there was a good chance they'd come here for her, and they meant business.

Delaney looked around for an exit. The TSA agent watched raptly, like he might a good action flick. She spotted the old lady with the mountain of luggage standing at the ticket counter, deep in conversation with the agent. The man who'd been carting her luggage was nowhere to be seen. And her only means of escape was the glass double doors she'd entered through. She turned and darted for them.

The first of the suited-up guys looking stylish enough to star in a TV cop drama reached her quickly. He grabbed her arm. She felt something distinctly hard and metallic poke her ribs. "Not a peep, Ms. Catalano. Come with us quietly. We'd like to ask you a few questions."

His dark eyes were hard and challenging, as if he knew she was going to be a problem. As if he'd been warned that she didn't want to just die quietly. His partner's strawberry blond hair should have given him an Opie Taylor, "aw shucks" appearance, but a pair of flinty eyes and the hard set of his mouth made him look entirely menacing.

Del's instincts told her they had orders to kill her.

She resisted the tug on her arm, digging in her heels. "Who are you? What do you want? I need to see your identification."

Neither offered up a badge. The dark one just tugged on her arm again.

"No! You have no right to do this. I won't go with you. Anything you have to say to me can be said here."

"Let's not make a scene," Opie said to her. "Come quietly."

Oh, hell no.

Having been married to a cop and good friends with another, Del knew more than a bit of self-defense. Yes, the pretty bastard could shoot her, but she was guessing that he wanted her someplace private to kill her so that he didn't have to make a scene and do a lot of explaining later.

She nodded meekly. When he began to lead her away, she elbowed him in the gut. He grunted and released her, then she kicked Opie in the balls. After a rousing chorus of moans, she turned and punched the dark one in the nose, satisfied when he began to bleed. Opie grabbed her by the hair viciously, making Del's eyes water. But she stomped on his toes as hard as she possibly could. He released her instantly, muttering a foul curse.

Breathing hard, heart racing, she ran for the exit. For now, she pushed away the implications that she wasn't going to make her flight, wouldn't make it home to put Carlson away so she could get her life back. Instead, she focused on her deep suspicion that if pretty boy and Opie caught up to her again, she'd be hauled away—then silenced for good. Her only hope was to keep running.

As she hauled ass for the exit, dragging her duffel, Del prayed for a waiting taxi, but even if she could find one, the two thugs were hot on her heels. She could hear them over her pounding feet and pumping heart. She'd have no time to negotiate with the driver and store her luggage, much less make a clean getaway. Not that she had any money to pay her fare, either.

Now what?

A grunt and a splat behind her had Del glancing over her shoulder. Pretty boy was sprawled face down on the floor, gasping and flailing. Had he tripped? Opie was nowhere to be seen.

Del didn't know what had happened and wasn't about to the question her good fortune as she made her way back outside, bathed in the morning sunlight and New Orleans humidity. A taxi driver waited nearby, leaning against his cab, looking at her hopefully. It would be the most anonymous form of transportation—if she had cash. She was going to have to retrieve that ramshackle car from the garage and drive . . . where? To another airport? A bus station?

She'd figure it out later.

As she crossed to the parking garage, a man emerged seemingly from nowhere, peeling himself away from the shadows. She didn't get a good look at him before he glued himself to her backside and gripped her arm. She had no time to shriek or scream for help. He clapped his free hand over her mouth.

"Not a sound, angel. Let's make a nice, clean exit."

Tyler?

Slowly, he lowered his hand from her mouth but kept a hold on her arm, guiding her left. Del risked a glance over her shoulder. She could see Tyler's beefy chest and neck, his full mouth. Shadow concealed the rest under a familiar cap.

Relief flooded her. She shouldn't be so thankful. She shouldn't blindly put her trust in him to save her when he didn't know the situation. But instinctively, she already had.

"You helped the old woman in with her luggage?"

He nodded curtly. "You would have noticed me if I'd come in alone."

By blending in and giving himself a role, she hadn't given him another thought.

Then a terrible thought occurred to her. "Where is Seth? Oh my God! You didn't leave him—"

"I may have known I was a father for less than twenty-four hours, but I would never leave him home alone. Deke stayed the night with him when I took off after you. Kimber and Alyssa are watching him today, with a little help from Tara."

"I don't know them." It killed her to think of her baby with strangers. They didn't strike her as predatory or mean at all, but he was a defenseless child among many adults with seemingly interesting sexual proclivities . . .

"I do. I've trusted them with my life. They will treat Seth like one of their own. He's far safer with them than with us."

"You have to go back and take care of him!"

"No fucking chance. I'm with you every step of the way until Carlson is dead or behind bars. You're not getting more than five feet from me. No negotiations, no arguments. If you don't like it, Jack and Deke will be happy to help me keep you locked down in Lafayette while I put Carlson away myself. Your choice."

"I'm going! You have no right to take over or make decisions for me," she hissed.

"I'm making it my right."

Del didn't dare ask what that meant. It sounded possessive. Her belly flipped. "You don't get to do that! I'm a grown woman and—"

"Who almost got herself killed not five minutes ago. You're out of your element and in over your head. If you insist on coming with me, this is where I take over. You stand a much better chance surviving to raise Seth if you let me help you."

Tyler's words sank in. Del couldn't deny that he was right. It bugged the hell out of her, but she'd be stupid to insist that she had this under control. Clearly, Carlson's reach was farther and his methods more ruthless than she'd imagined.

Still . . . "This can't be your fight. What if Carlson kills us both? Then Seth has no parents."

"I won't let that happen."

What a male thing to say. "Is that you being arrogant or trying to make me feel better?"

Wrapping his arm around her waist, Tyler brought her even closer as he led her toward his truck. "It's the truth."

"Wait! My car is this way." She pointed across the garage in the opposite direction.

"Exactly." With another tug, he dragged her away from her neighbor's old compact.

A part of her was infuriated—at both him and herself for allowing it. Another part was simply relieved.

"What happened to the two goons?"

"I hit the one with the dark hair in the back of the head with a luggage cart. I tased the other and sat him on a nearby chair so that he looks asleep. I have their weapons tucked in my waistband."

He'd done all that by himself, without wasting a second or raising a ruckus?

Eric had always called Tyler a bad ass when they'd been partners, but he'd never been anything but teasing and kind with her. Del felt like she was seeing a whole new side of her son's father.

"How long do you think we have?"

"Before Carlson sends more assholes after you? Thirty minutes, tops. We've got to get on the road ASAP."

"On the road?"

"I'm driving you to L.A. We're going to put Carlson down together."

Del opened her mouth to object . . . but didn't have any new excuses to give him. Seth wouldn't be safe with them, and she had to believe that he was in capable hands. She'd be safer with Tyler by her side while she regathered her evidence, wrote her article, and put Carlson down.

The thing she feared for most now? Her heart.

Tyler shoved Del into his truck and down to the floorboard. She glared at him with confusion before he thrust a khaki green blanket at her. "Cover up. Security cameras are swarming. They'll catch us walking together in the parking garage. I parked in a very dark corner, so there's a chance they won't be able to see if you got in the truck. It has to look like you're not with me when we leave the airport."

He was right. With a nod, she crouched down and covered herself, thankful when he turned on the air-conditioning. The sun's zenith might be hours away, but the stifling Louisiana humidity was nothing this California girl had ever felt.

"Sorry," he grunted. Then he set a backpack on top of her.

It wasn't the lightest thing, but it wouldn't take long to get out of the airport. The extra cover would be more convincing for the cameras.

"It's fine."

The first few minutes were nerve-racking. A million thoughts raced through her head in the silence. Every bump in the road was magnified on the floorboard, as was the purr of the engine. Moments later, his phone rang.

"Yeah? I got her, Deke. Seth okay?" He paused. "Good. Let him sleep. Listen, get Tara up and to her computer. We need to find out exactly how Del might have been traced."

"My credit card." Del knew her voice would be muffled by the blanket.

"*What?*" From that tone, Del knew that Tyler had heard her and questioned her sanity more than her words.

"I waited as long as I could. I hoped that Carlson didn't know anyone in Louisiana."

Tyler sighed. "He can hire guns in a heartbeat. No more credit cards. They're too traceable. Did you hear that?" he asked Deke. "Right. See if Tara can prove that Carlson's been tapping her credit card records. Del?"

"Yeah." She wished she could see him, but it shouldn't be too much longer before they exited the airport—provided airport security hadn't picked up the entire altercation in the terminal and decided to hunt her down.

"Hang on and stay quiet."

The truck slowed. Her heart stopped.

The electronic window rolled down a moment later, and Tyler said, "Good morning."

"Hmm." The cashier made a noncommittal sound. "Is it? You're here early."

"Just dropping off someone for a flight."

"Two dollars."

After a rustling of bills, the window buzzed back up and the truck started moving again, picking up speed every second they rolled.

He lifted the backpack off of her, then tossed the blanket back a fraction. Cool air washed over her face, and she sighed with something between pleasure and relief.

Tyler jacked the phone back up to his ear. "Stay down another minute, Del. There are a few cops hanging around. Until we know who's involved . . ."

Don't trust anyone. That had been his and Eric's motto when they'd been together on the force.

The cab of the truck remained deathly silent except for her own breathing for the next few minutes. Finally, Tyler reached down and helped her into the passenger's seat. "Good. Now, tell me, do you have a copy of the police report about the bomb that exploded your car?"

"No. I didn't know who I could trust. I'd been asking questions at the precinct. I couldn't get anyone to help me. I thought about calling Eric, but . . . After the bomb exploded, I just grabbed Seth, borrowed a neighbor's car, and left town with nothing but the cash in my pocket. I stopped for a few supplies along the way and called an investigative reporter friend of mine, Lisa. She'd been helping me track you down. Once we pieced all the clues together, I drove straight to you."

"Right." Tyler's jaw tensed. "You don't know if it was C4 or a binary explosive? If it was an engine ignition or a remote detonation device?"

God, she'd seen the blast in her head a million times since it happened. Felt the shock, the roaring heat, heard the deafening roar of the blast. But she'd never picked the scene apart mentally with that much detail.

"Um, I don't know anything about explosives, so no idea what they used. I started the car with my key fob. As I turned to pick Seth up, everything blew up. Damn near vaporized it."

"Hear that, Deke? Yeah, I agree, sounds like it was rigged to blow when the ignition turned over." Tyler turned a serious gaze on her. "Do you remember anything else? See anyone unusual loitering? Notice that your car had been tampered with?"

"Nothing. It was early morning. There was no one on the street. The sun wasn't all the way up, so I couldn't see anything unusual about my car."

"Then what?"

"After the explosion, I screamed and stumbled back, shoving Seth to the ground. I covered him with my body. I got some scratches and bruises. He was okay, just scared. Oh, and it smelled terrible. A weird kind of . . . burned-orange-peel smell."

"Shit." Tyler gripped the cell phone even tighter. "Semtex, Deke?" He paused. "Yeah, run it by Jack. He'd know since he likes things that go boom. Let me know what he says. I'll call later."

With that, he hung up and turned to her. Whatever she'd said . . . Tyler's face more than hinted it wasn't good. "Tell me."

He didn't even pretend to misunderstand. "Semtex is the former Eastern Bloc's version of C4. It often smells like a burnt orange peel. None of the other explosives really leave a signature odor like that."

"Eastern Bloc?"

"Popular with the Russian Mob. They come up during your research?"

"No. From what I can tell, Carlson deals with street thugs and local drug dealers, not organized crime. Where would he get that kind of explosive?"

"From some really bad assholes. This shit is worse than I thought."

Del dropped her face into her hand. Suddenly, staying alive felt like something way beyond her ability. "How's Seth?"

"He's fine, angel. Still asleep. Kimber and Alyssa will be there to get him soon and take him for a playdate with their kids."

She nodded. Seth would enjoy having new friends and the chance to run around like a kid, not spend the day cooped up in a car. "Thanks."

Still, worry plagued her. What happened if they didn't catch Carlson right away? What happened if all her sources had dried up or refused to talk? She couldn't leave Seth indefinitely.

Or what if Carlson found him?

"I see that look. Stop worrying," Tyler warned. "Jack and Deke will never let anything happen to Seth. I swear it. Jack is a former Army Ranger. Deke was also military and did a little time with the FBI and still has connections all over the place. Seth couldn't be safer."

Those credentials did make her relax a bit. Her son was definitely safer with them. "If I thought for a second that giving up this story would make Carlson go away, for Seth's safety, I would."

"Somewhere along the way, you drew blood. You could have flown under Carlson's radar if you hadn't confronted him."

"I was hoping to catch him off guard and that he'd say something for the record that was incriminating."

Tyler just shook his head. "But since you did confront him . . . he'll do anything to prevent what you know from going public. Today demonstrated that."

"Since he destroyed all my latest notes, it's going to take some backtracking to put the pieces of his warped puzzle back together so I can prove what I know. Right now, all I've got is my word about a conversation I overheard, plus a thug willing to pin a crime on a respected member of the community—none of that will hold up in court. I did get a chance to back up some of my evidence a few weeks before the explosion."

Tyler sat up, hyper-focused. "In a safe-deposit box?"

"No." She bit her lip. He wasn't going to like her answer. "I put what I had at the time on a flash drive. I tried to think of the very last place that anyone would look for it. It couldn't be my house or office. A safe-deposit box seemed too obvious. So . . . I snuck into Eric's place." Tyler's eyes went wide, and before he could object, she plowed ahead. "Everyone in law enforcement circles knows our divorce was ugly. I figured if Carlson asked around about me, he'd never imagine that I'd hide my backup at Eric's. I put it where I used to hide anything I wanted to keep private." Even from Eric. Birthday cards from Tyler and her journal came to mind.

"When you called, he didn't respond. So you need to get in the house and retrieve your evidence. Any chance Carlson knows that?"

"How could he? People don't normally leave valuable items at their bitter ex's place."

"A bank might have been more obvious, but it would have been more secure."

"Until he found some trumped-up way to subpoena the contents."

Sighing, Tyler reached for her hand. "Yeah. This is all kinds of fucked up, but we're going to fix it, angel."

"You didn't have to come with me."

Tyler gritted his teeth. "Don't start that again. We're in this together."

Del knew that tone of voice well. Conversation over. He'd used it countless times before on suspects—and a time or two on Eric. That deep conviction rumbling from his chest always gave her the shivers.

"You're not the only one who wants to protect our son," he said softly.

And she loved that about Tyler. When he cared, he cared big.

"I understand, but I want to be clear: What happened last night in your bedroom can't happen again."

She didn't dare let him melt her resolve to keep distance between them. That kiss had been a huge mistake. They had a clear objective to take down Carlson and make Seth's life safer. Anything else just complicated the situation. Tyler, being a heartbreaker, made it all even more complicated. She'd never forget the breathless, sublime moments she'd touched him, had him deep inside her. They'd connected in a way she never had with any lover. But he'd taken a chunk of her heart . . . and then he'd moved on. That's who he was, and she'd be a fool to think that she—or even Seth—was going to change him.

"You want me to back off, keep my hands to myself?"

Even the thought of his hands on her made her belly flip. "Yes."

Tyler turned to her as the empty road flew past and the sun crawled up the sky. His green eyes gleamed. He sent her a cocky grin. "Don't hold your breath, angel."

* * *

THE morning passed by in a blur of tense silence and road stripes as mile after mile of back roads rolled by. They drove in a meandering path west as the sun rose. Tyler's cell phone rang off and on, but his terse, one-sided conversations made little sense. But she understood that they were meeting someone in Houston for an exchange. If Tyler intended to pass her off to someone else for safekeeping, she'd leave him in the dust.

Del didn't start the argument because he was strung really tight. He looked in the rearview mirror constantly. The police scanner tucked under his dash sputtered off and on, and he jumped to attention every time it did. She realized that he expected someone to be following them from New Orleans.

They hit the outskirts of Houston just before lunch. The morning rush had dissipated, but they still slogged through some heavy traffic. He stopped behind a gas station/mini-mart a few miles off the highway and told her to use the bathroom if she needed to. She did, keeping her head low around their cameras. On her way out, she longingly eyed the water bottles, but she was almost flat broke. And she'd be damned if she'd ask Tyler for anything more. He was already extending himself to help her. She refused to be a leech. When they got to L.A., she'd access the emergency fund she'd stashed in her garden.

Emerging from the little service station as traffic lazed by in the muggy air, Del came to a complete stop when she saw Tyler talking to a beautiful Asian woman with sleek curls brushing the top of her ass and a dress that wasn't much longer.

The woman spoke in animated hand gestures and a wink. Tyler grinned. An immediate stab of jealousy knifed her in the heart. Del took a deep breath. Tyler wasn't her man. He'd kissed her. So what? Apparently, he had a mad crush on his boss, Alyssa. Ex-boss. Whatever. Del knew that Tyler's heart wasn't hers, and that was for the best. Once this was behind them, they'd figure out some custodial arrangement beneficial to all and go their mostly separate ways. Tyler had always had a healthy sex drive and liked a lot of variety. Obviously, nothing had changed.

He caught sight of her and motioned her over. Swallowing the anger she didn't want to feel, she made her way to the duo.

"Del, this is May. Remember Tara, back in Lafayette, married to one of the Edgington brothers?"

"The redhead who isn't pregnant, right?"

"Yet. Logan is taking a land-based assignment in a few months. He'll fix that quickly, I'm sure. Anyway, he has a friend named Xander who sent May to help—"

"Seriously?" She grabbed his arm. "Excuse us," she said, dragging Tyler away from the beauty with the kohl-rimmed eyes.

"The fewer people who know what's going on the better," she pointed out. "I don't know Logan, much less his friend. And who is this woman? We're trusting her because she's a friend's friend's . . . girlfriend?"

He frowned, then wrapped an arm around her waist, the gesture meant to comfort. "I get it, but we don't have more appealing options. I'd trust Logan with my life. Xander is solid. This woman hasn't been told anything except to exchange cars with us. Carlson's goons will have gotten the license plate number to my truck from the security cameras at the airport in New Orleans. They'll be tracking a black truck with Louisiana plates and giving law enforcement my plate number. I guarantee you, if we'd stayed in the truck longer, we would have been pulled over on some bullshit charge and detained until Carlson could reach us. Since you bought a plane ticket, he knows your destination, angel. If you think he isn't watching I-10 like a hawk, you're deluding yourself. Now get in the car."

Del closed her mouth. Of course Carlson would have law enforcement on his side. For all she knew, he'd put out an APB on her. Did that make Tyler guilty of aiding and abetting? Was some crooked, small-town cop waiting just around the next bend for Tyler's big truck to appear so they could pull it over? She realized now that she'd only crossed the country unaccosted because Carlson hadn't known her destination, and he hadn't realized she'd be driving her neighbor's car. The kind widow had gone for a month to visit her daughter who lived overseas and wouldn't miss the little Honda for weeks.

But with her stunt this morning, Del realized that she'd killed their element of surprise and put them both in danger.

"Sorry. I didn't . . . think it all the way through."

"You're not used to thinking like this. Don't beat yourself up, angel. Get in the car, and let's go."

She nodded, then thanked May as she walked toward the sleek, gray Lexus sedan. She pulled the doors open, marveling at the new-car smell of the leather seats. Everything was pristine. The car probably cost more than she'd made last year. It was love at first sight.

Especially when she spotted the small cooler of water bottles sitting on the floorboard of the passenger's side. She grabbed one gratefully as Tyler climbed in and pulled away. He watched May drive off with his truck in the rearview mirror.

"You're giving her your truck?"

"The truck isn't important."

"You own it, right? It's worth a lot of money and—"

"It's not worth your life."

Del's heart flipped. He was so damn loyal. How could she not melt a little?

"May is taking it to a nearby garage, where it will stay out of sight. If everything goes well, I'll collect the truck later."

Del heard the note of finality in his voice. It was better if she stopped arguing. She didn't cede control of anything easily, but Tyler had a plan he'd apparently thought out pretty well. She'd been running for days on caffeine and adrenaline.

As they left Houston, they grabbed a fast-food lunch and headed toward San Antonio. The gentle rolling hills and greenery turned peaceful. The traffic tapered off to damn near nothing. The purr of the engine and the motion of the car lulled her to sleep.

She woke hours later to the sun setting. Her neck was stiff, and the landscape had given way to pure, flat desert. "Where are we?"

"About halfway between San Antonio and El Paso."

"Sorry I conked out on you."

"When did you last sleep a whole night?"

"Last week. Thursday."

Tyler reached for her hand. "You risked everything to bring Seth to me. I know things went to hell between us before, but I'm glad you trusted me."

Tears axed the back of her eyes, stinging. "He's the most precious thing in my life. Our parting may not have been great, but I knew you'd take care of him."

"I won't let you down, Del. My friends will give him the best care possible. And I'm going to take care of you, too."

How easy it would be to lean against him and let him handle everything. She did trust him. He would keep her safe and do a killer job investigating. He'd been a great detective, after all. But doing that would be so damn unfair to him. She'd upended his life after dropping a major bombshell on him. She had to pull her own weight. "You don't have to. I'm a big girl."

"Who's in over her head. Just let me handle everything." It wasn't a request. "Hungry?"

Del bit her lip and nodded. She'd prove useful as soon as they got to L.A.

In a little town with a population south of ten thousand, they stopped for a restroom and dinner break. They had limited food options. A rubber chicken sandwich and some fries later, they were back on the road. Del offered to drive. Tyler just shook his head.

Hours later, they pulled up into a dated motel off the highway in El Paso. Tyler unfolded himself out of the car. "Wait here and lock the doors."

He had to be exhausted . . . yet he continued to worry about her. "I'm fine. Go."

He grabbed a ball cap from the backseat and shoved it over his head, pulling the bill low. Then he disappeared into the hot, windy night. A few minutes later, he returned and, without a word, pulled the car around to the back of the motel.

"No one driving by will see this car from any road. I gave the manager a fake name and extra cash not to care." He exited the car, then grabbed her duffel from the trunk.

Inside, the room was painfully clean. Aging industrial carpet and stark white walls made it clear this wasn't the Ritz. She didn't care. There were two beds and a shower. She could kiss Tyler for making this happen.

But she wouldn't—for her sanity.

"Thank you." She shut the door and locked it behind her.

"No argument about not having separate rooms?"

Staying with him was a bit dangerous, since she was feeling so ridiculously vulnerable yet grateful, but . . . "No. Safety in numbers. I appreciate the separate beds."

"Damn, and I'd prepared my speech, too."

Despite her exhaustion, Del smiled. "Let's hear it."

"Probably not a good idea. I'd just planned to say that you weren't getting your own room. Separate beds is as much space as I'm willing to give you." He shrugged. "I'm not going to lie. I'd rather spend the night in your bed. In your body. I've missed you like hell, Del."

His words shocked her. God, she could even hear the longing in his voice, and it did something to her that wasn't good for her resolve. Cuddling up to Tyler all night, feeling the demanding press of his kiss, the hard thrust of his cock, waking up in his arms—it all sounded heavenly. But not smart. She was a mom now; she couldn't afford flings. And Tyler didn't do permanent.

"You can't say things like that. We can't do things like that. There's too much at stake."

"I knew you'd say that. It's just . . . the thought of you in danger makes me want to kill the motherfucker threatening you, then rip off every stitch of your clothing and take you in every way known to man."

Del swallowed, trying to absorb the impact of those words. They reverberated through her, pinging wildly, before finally rousing an ache in her chest and her pussy. She'd never known another man who could give her such pleasure, make her feel so safe. He was right there in front of her. The temptation to reach out and touch him damn near drowned her good sense.

But she had Seth and tomorrow to think about. And honestly . . . by the time Eric had encouraged Tyler to have sex with her, she'd been half in love with him. He'd been so steady, patient, kind during her ex-husband's recovery. Cutting him loose had hurt so badly. She didn't want to suffer it twice.

"Caveman much?" she joked.

"Always. You know that."

"Look, I already heard that you have a thing for Alyssa. I get why. She's gorgeous. I've never seen a woman that sexy. I know she's married, but . . . I'm living proof marriage doesn't always last. But while you wait for her, I won't be a substitute."

"Is that what you think?" Tyler approached, eyes narrowing. He ripped off the cap, then his T-shirt. He flung it to the floor.

Del swallowed hard. Dear God, she'd forgotten how overpoweringly masculine Tyler was. But now that he was half naked, that fact was front and center, evident in every bulge of his shoulders, every ripple of his abs, the veins running down his arms. Hard pectorals. Lean waist. Jeans hanging low on his lean hips . . .

He snapped, and she raised her stare back to his face, but Del was equally dazzled there, especially by the heat in his eyes. "Let's get one thing straight: You could never be a substitute for Alyssa. It was the other way around."

Chapter Seven

WHAT the hell was he thinking? Open mouth, insert ass. He'd blurted something so . . . true. Fuck. He'd been burying everything he felt for Del for two years. In an instant, she'd swept into his house and made him realize how damn much he cared about her. Still wanted her.

But Tyler sensed that, after everything that had passed between them—and whatever damage Eric's abandonment had caused—men, and him especially, weren't high on Del's to-do list.

But he wasn't letting her go easily or without a fight.

"Look, let's just . . ." Del sputtered, then looked away. "I'd like to call about Seth. I won't be able to sleep until I hear he's okay."

Everything inside Tyler wanted to argue. Or better yet, get her supine, get on top of her, and prove his point. But she was exhausted and scared. Now wasn't the best time.

"We can do that." He reached for his phone.

"Who has him tonight?"

Tyler tried not to wince. "Alyssa."

Before Del could comment, he punched the speed dial and jammed the phone to his ear. Alyssa answered right away.

"Your son is as mischievous as you are."

He couldn't help but smile as he turned the phone on speaker so Del could hear. "Yeah, well . . ."

"He's a bundle of energy and climbs everything. I'm not used to that with Chloe." Alyssa sounded somewhere between amused and exasperated. "But he's so sweet. He must get that from Del."

Del looked choked up, and Tyler wrapped an arm around her waist and whispered, "See, he's fine."

She nodded and leaned into the phone. "Hi, Alyssa. Thank you for taking care of Seth."

"The kids are having fun. Chloe has loved having a playmate, even if she's not sure what to do with plush trucks and toy airplanes." She laughed, the sound light and elegant.

"Seth is a climber, and if you have anything chocolate, he'll find it."

"Good to know. Luc keeps so many things in the kitchen. He's bound to have good chocolate here. I'll hide it. Can he have a little tomorrow?"

"If he eats his vegetables and tries a bite of everything on his plate."

After the women talked about Seth's naps and bedtime, Del pulled away from him. "Thanks again for everything."

Tyler watched with a frown as she disappeared into the bathroom and shut the door. He heard it lock, then the shower turned on. He sat on the edge of the thin mattress and shook his head.

"You still there?" Alyssa asked.

Turning the phone off speaker mode, he tucked it back against his ear. "Yeah."

"You okay?"

Del wanted nothing to do with him, and it hurt like fuck. "Sure."

Alyssa snorted. "Liar. What about Delaney?"

"She's in the shower."

"How is she holding up?"

"Exhausted and afraid. I'm doing everything I can to keep her safe and calm."

"I know you are." His former boss paused. "You want to tell me what's going on between you two?"

"Long story."

"That ends with you finding out fifteen months too late that you have a son. You had no clue?"

"None. She's a friend's wife. Well, ex-wife now—and ex-friend. I know that raises a million questions, just . . . not tonight."

Alyssa sighed. "How do you feel about her?"

Wasn't that a fucking ironic question? *Now* Alyssa wanted to know how he felt. It was just as well she'd never taken him seriously. Maybe she'd always seen through him and known he was trying to substitute her for Del. But why? They really weren't alike, except their backbone and determination to see something through.

His silence went on too long, and Alyssa broke it. "You're in love with her."

What the hell did he know about love? "I wondered for a while if I was in love with you, and you see how that worked out."

"No, dumb ass. I get it now. You latched onto me because I was unavailable. The more I said no, the harder you pursued. I thought maybe you liked the challenge. But you were trying to forget her."

Tyler closed his eyes. That sounded so painfully close to the truth. Great time to realize that his hard-on for Alyssa hadn't been about her at all. He'd buried all his hurt and yearning under lust. After all, Alyssa and all the girls at Sexy Sirens looked damn fine in corsets, thongs, and garter belts. But no matter how many Krystals, Jessis, Candys, or Aspens he fucked, he'd felt nothing but desire.

Not like the night he'd given every bit of his body and passion to Del. He'd been searching for that high again—for her—in every other girl. He'd come up empty.

Wasn't that a bitch?

The tangle of crap between them was deep and wide. They shared a son, and that mattered, but it didn't guarantee that Del was going to care about him beyond being her baby daddy.

"You going to marry her?" Alyssa asked.

The question blindsided him. The thought of marrying Del, of having her in his bed every night . . . His dick stood up, totally approving the idea. His heart beat faster. But he doubted she was in a rush to get married again. Besides, he knew exactly zero about being a good husband or father. His own had packed up and walked out when he was six. His mother had always said that he had no business getting married because he'd be just as restless and irresponsible. The way he'd moved from bed to bed since puberty, Tyler had believed her.

But Del was different. Not just sexy, though she absolutely was in a way that flipped every switch in his body. She wasn't just smart, but funny, tenacious, loyal. Perfect. If he were going to find one partner for life, he couldn't do better.

He probably wasn't going to get that chance. Even if she was willing to try forever, what if he wasn't cut out for a picket fence? How badly would he hurt her if he couldn't deal and left? She'd already been burned by Eric. Tyler couldn't risk doing that to her again. He refused to cause her pain.

But the idea of just being an occasional father to Seth and even less to Del set off all kinds of fury bombs inside him. And if he left her to raise Seth alone, didn't that make him the same kind of shithead as his own father?

"You're thinking way too hard." Alyssa sighed.

"Because I don't know how the hell to answer you."

"Do you *want* to marry her?"

"I don't know. How do you know when you're ready to marry someone? How do you know it's right?"

"You have to trust that, no matter what, you're going to be there for one other," she said softly. "So decide quickly if you can be her rock. If not, that girl is going to walk out of your life again and never look back."

* * *

THREE a.m., and he was wide awake. After learning about Seth, missing a good night's sleep, then driving the better part of eighteen hours, he should have been fucking exhausted. But no. His brain raced. Anxiety clawed up his spine. He hoped he and his buddies had been clever enough to elude Carlson's network until they could cruise into L.A. and put that motherfucker down.

And Alyssa's words kept turning themselves over in his head.

In the next bed, Del slept restlessly, her bare legs sliding against the sheets. Staring into the dark at her, Tyler could only think about two things: some career criminal being after her, and the fact that, even if the danger ended today, he wasn't prepared to let her go again. Both trains of thought made him ache to hold her. Protect her. Feel her safe and warm and luscious against him.

He probably should leave her alone, simply watch over her from his bed. But no one had ever accused him of being a gentleman. And he needed to start expressing now exactly how he wanted things between them.

Slowly, Tyler tossed back his covers and slid off the bed. Del thrashed in the middle of her bed, as if she'd gotten used to sleeping alone in the last two years. He smiled at that thought. Then it faded. What he was about to do might piss her off, but . . . she had all her defenses up, and until he found a way to get under them so she could at least consider how good they might be together, he had no shot with Del. They'd once been friends. Things had been good between them. Now, he needed to have her in whatever way he could, even if he simply held her.

He needed to start staking his claim.

Besides, as scared as she was trying not to be and as much as she worried about Seth, he'd bet she needed someone to hold her.

He lifted her sheet and slid underneath. Her body heat reached into him. Her personal scent, like sunlit cotton and springtime, comforted him. Tyler spooned her back to his chest, and closed his eyes, breathing her in. Holding her again took him back to the night Seth had been conceived, the hint of summer looming in the air, the sultry look of Del's flushed cheeks and wide eyes as she orgasmed. The regret on her face when she'd said she was sorry—the last words she'd spoken to him for two long years.

Her body relaxing, Del sighed, melting into him in sleep. He found his face in the crook of her neck and his palm on her stomach, thinly clad in a little black tank. She felt both familiar and brand-new. That night, he hadn't really been able to explore her. Did she like having her nipples pinched during sex? What did her pussy taste like when she came? How much would she blow his mind if he fucked her right now?

Three simple questions, and he turned hard as stone. He probably shouldn't . . . but Tyler couldn't stop his hips from pressing forward, into that sweet, slender ass.

Did she like being spanked? Would she enjoy anal sex?

A groan rumbled from his chest. Jesus, he had to stop this now, ease her into the idea of being with him so they could explore what might be between them, not to rattle her so much that she ran screaming.

Had Del missed him at all? Have any idea how many times he'd been in bed with a woman and wondered why they never felt as good as her?

Fuck. He needed to touch Del.

Tyler gripped her tighter and arched into her again, this time brushing his lips down her neck. Pleasure cut through him in a wide arc. In his arms, she shivered. Wriggled. Her breast was right under his fingers . . .

Damn, he was going to hell for this.

He inched his palm up just a fraction and . . . yeah, right there. He closed his eyes. Even through the thin cotton, Del's breast fit his hand perfectly, a bit heavier than he remembered. So damn lush.

Despite the heat of his palm, her nipple tightened. She shifted, her ass generating mind-blowing friction as she rubbed against his dick in her sleep. Del made his entire body throb, sent fire ripping through his veins. Shit, he might have to jack off in the bathroom to keep from attacking her in the next thirty seconds. Hell, he might even have to jack off twice.

Crap, he needed to slow down. Earlier, Del had emerged from the bathroom after her shower with tight, red-rimmed eyes. She'd refused to let him comfort her. He needed to show her—and himself—that he could be her rock. He couldn't accomplish that by feeling her up.

But she felt so fucking good, and he'd never wanted someone so damn bad. Just one touch . . .

Slowly, he slid his hand from the soft weight of her breast, down, down, until it slipped under the loose elastic of those shorts. His fingertips brushed over the flat of her belly, then—oh, holy shit. Her pussy. No, her bare pussy.

Tyler cupped his fingers around her flesh, parting her folds with one finger. Yeah, there was her clit, soft and slightly damp. He wanted his tongue there, lapping at her, making her fist the sheets and cry out his name. He pushed his cock into her ass again, knowing that if he didn't pull away, he'd wake her up and piss her off.

He'd rather get her off instead. She'd been so stressed and worried, she needed release.

Del shifted, backing up to him. Smiling at her unconscious gesture, Tyler grabbed her top leg and eased it over his thighs, spreading her open. Instantly, two of his fingers slid against her clit, gently stirring. It turned hard. Moisture seeped, coating his fingers.

It was a matter of time before Del woke. She was going to hand him his ass when she did. But he intended to enjoy this time with her . . . and help her realize that she enjoyed it, too. And make her feel good. He couldn't assure her a safe future right now, but he could give her a moment of pleasure.

He rubbed a pair of fingers across her hardening knot of nerves as he slid his other arm under her—and fondled the sweet curve of her breast. He brushed a thumb over her nipple, back and forth, as he swirled his other fingers over her clit. Moaning lightly in her sleep, Del arched up, into his hand.

"That's it," he whispered against her neck. "Let it feel good, angel."

The soft skin right under his lips beckoned. Tyler was way past resisting, and he swept kisses from the slender column, into the crook of her shoulder, where her scent pooled, driving him mad.

He reached below her clit, gathered more of her increasing moisture, then dragged it over the little bud of nerves. It pulsed under his fingers. Del's breathing turned hard. She wriggled against his dick again. Her arms flailed for a moment before her hand found his thigh. Her entire body tensed.

"Tyler?" she panted.

His fingers didn't stop plucking her hard nipple, rubbing that delicious clit in a light, now teasing circle.

He kissed her neck again, nipping at her ear. "I'm here, angel."

"I . . . Oh my God, I'm going to—"

"Come. Yeah." The thought made him even harder.

"No." But the word was a wail, a despondent cry of need.

Her body thrashed. More juice slicked his fingers, and she pushed into his hands, her breathing ragged.

"You're going to let me give you an orgasm." He didn't ask; he knew from her body that he'd taken her past the point of no return. She'd be pissed afterward . . . but he'd always lived by the motto that it was easier to ask for forgiveness than permission.

"Hurry."

He backed off just a fraction. He didn't want to rush her pleasure. It would grow bigger, feel better, if he kindled it slowly, letting it build and build and build.

"Soon." He nipped the back of her shoulder and moaned against her skin.

Del fought back, rubbing her ass against his cock again, streaking fire through his veins. If she kept that up, he was going to come in his shorts, like some teenager with a wet dream. Hell, Del *was* a wet dream.

Pressing the flat of his hand against her belly, he shoved up, grinding against her. She gasped, spreading her legs wider. Tyler took the opportunity to shove two fingers into her cunt.

She gasped, clamped down, then trembled around his fingers. That was also going to get her off too fast.

He withdrew, and she mewled in distress. "Damn it, Tyler."

"Soon, angel."

"You're a bastard. You said you wanted me to"—she gasped as his fingers found her clit again—"come."

Then she wiggled her ass against him, slow and sexy, intentionally lighting him up. God, he was desperate to get inside her, feel her sweet little cunt all around him, know that it was Del taking him, clawing into his back and calling his name.

For a long moment, Tyler couldn't breathe, so he just absorbed the pleasure mowing down every one of his better intentions.

They fell into a quick rhythm, Del gyrating back on his cock, then lifting into his fingers now circling her clit. Their breathing synced up, fast and shallow and loud.

"Tyler!" she all but begged.

And he could feel how distended her clit was, straining, jolting. She dug her nails into his thigh and cried out.

"Fuck, yes! Del . . ." He pushed against her, standing at the edge of a chasm of pleasure he couldn't wait to tumble into. He was going to soil his shorts, and he didn't give a shit.

Then it hit. Fire danced up his cock. The base of his spine tingled. His balls turned tight and heavy. He exploded. Under his hand, Del tensed and whimpered, her hips bucking, drawing out her own pleasure and his until it made his whole body seize. Until he gave himself over completely. Warm jets of semen shot between them, coating his belly and her back where the tank top had ridden up. It made him twelve kinds of primitive to be glad that if his seed couldn't be inside her, at least it was on her.

Moments later, their heavy breathing stopped. Del stiffened and pulled away.

Now it was time to pay the piper.

"What the hell were you doing?" She wrenched away.

Tyler resisted the urge to point out that she'd been complaining thirty seconds ago that he was withholding her pleasure. Big guess, but it would only piss her off more.

"Getting close to you and making you feel good."

"Why?"

Because I think I want you for longer than a road trip, and I need to give you a reason to feel the same. Hmm. Maybe that explanation would have to wait.

He rose, flipped on the bathroom light, and grabbed a cheap washcloth from the towel rack and ran hot water over it. Wincing, he shucked his shorts and wiped himself clean, then rinsed the scrap of terrycloth and wrung it out. Stark naked, he crossed the room to Del, all wrapped up in the sheet and looking at him as if he'd lost his mind.

She judiciously avoided looking south of his face. "I told you earlier not to touch me."

I told you earlier not to hold your breath . . . "Who else is going to clean your back?"

Del hesitated, then scrambled out of bed. "I'll take a shower. I have to clean my clothes anyway."

When she would have walked off, he grabbed her arm. "Don't. I made the mess. Let me clean it up."

With one hand, he pushed her shorts down her legs until they hung around her thighs.

Fuck, she wasn't wearing any panties, and her pert ass was totally bare.

Before that thought could roll through him and awaken his libido again, he yanked her tank over her head.

She shrieked. "I have to be naked for this?"

"It'll work better if I can actually get to your skin." He swept the damp cloth over her back, into the sexy hollow at the base of her spine, over the firm globes of her ass. He'd take any excuse to put his hands on the sweet flare of her hip and run a finger up the shadowy line bisecting her backside, where he was pretty sure no man had ever taken her . . .

"That's enough." She pulled away.

Prickly. Okay, he'd stepped over the line. He'd meant to comfort and release her. Instead, he'd almost molested her. If he wanted to ever touch her again, he was going to have to downshift, go slower. With her, that was so hard. "I didn't mean to upset you, but it felt damn good to hold you. I'm not going to apologize for something I don't regret."

Del grunted as she stripped off the shorts and grabbed a towel from the bathroom. She tucked it around herself as she made her way to her duffel, picking through the garments. He rinsed out his shorts, throwing a little soap on them. The silence was tight and awkward.

"I didn't hurt you, did I?" He frowned at the thought.

"Of course not."

"So you're mad because I touched you without permission or because you got off?"

"Because we don't need this complication now. Someone is trying to kill me, and—"

"Not right this second. The only person in the world who knows exactly where we are is Alyssa. You're safe." He walked toward her, as naked as the day he'd been born. "So tell me what this is really about?"

"This—us—isn't a good idea."

"Why? When did I ever hurt you?"

Guilt crossed her face. "You didn't. I probably hurt you by shutting you out. And I know it's not fair of me to paint you with Eric's brush, but you were best friends. I'm just not ready to be . . . involved again."

"So no one has been taking care of your needs, Del?"

"I can take care of myself."

"Yeah? Who's going to hold you, make you feel desirable, protected, and adored?"

"I'm too busy to worry about any of that. Divorce and parenting by yourself sort of kills the sex drive."

"Yours seems to be working fine now."

"Bastard!" She yanked a pair of panties and a T-shirt from the heap of her duffel. "I can't believe you want to talk about my sex drive before you ask about the birth of your son. But it's you, so I should."

"Oh, we're going to talk about Seth, too. I want to know everything I missed in his life. But let's finish one conversation before we start another."

"That's easy. This conversation is over."

"And you're pissed off at me, why? Because I made you feel something for me that you're afraid of?"

"No," she insisted.

Tyler knew he'd hit a nerve but shrugged. "If you say so. Let's see if you'd be less angry if I got you off with my tongue."

Del gasped. When he reached for her, she hustled into the bathroom and slammed the door in his face. By the time she emerged again a few minutes later, all covered up, she looked composed and pristine. He supposed now wasn't the right time to mention the love bite he'd accidentally left on her neck. He smiled.

"Are we going back to sleep or are we driving?" Her tense face and posture warned him to back off.

That wasn't his style. "We're talking. I told you that we're doing things my way this time. I think you needed to be held. I damn sure needed to be closer to you. The thought of you with some killer makes my blood run cold. The way you've been stressed is not good for you. Sue me for caring."

"There's a difference between caring and feeling me up."

"Maybe I don't know the difference. It's not like I have a lot of experience with wanting more from a woman than a simple fuck."

"You don't feel that way about me. We were friends. You're confused because of Seth."

He curled a hand around her neck, breathing onto her soft lips. "Don't tell me what I feel. How the fuck would you even know? I put myself out for Eric that night, not just because he asked but because we both wanted it. For days, I waited for you to call me afterward. You never did. I was his best man at your wedding. I was your friend. No one saw fit to tell me that you were pregnant or getting divorced. It slipped your mind to find me before you went into labor? Or you just didn't give a shit about me?"

"Oh God." Guilt tightened her face. "Is that what you think? Of course I cared. Because of that night, Eric realized that the feelings I'd been having for you weren't totally platonic."

Tyler froze. She'd wanted him before they'd made love?

"Oh, don't look surprised." Del frowned, and he wanted to kiss her. "For the next week, I tried everything I could think of to calm him down, to convince him to reach out to you and discuss it. He forbade me to call. Normally, I'd tell him to go to hell, but I was trying to make the marriage work . . ."

And his partner in crime fighting and best friend had cut him off cold—all over the wife Eric hadn't lifted a finger to love or cherish. That motherfucker.

"But I always meant to call you."

He wanted to believe it, and something in his chest jolted at the thought that she might want him, too. "I tried to text you about a week later."

Regret flitted across her face. "While I was out one day, Eric bummed a ride and went to the wireless store. He traded in my phone and got me a new number. When I flipped through it, all your contact information had been deleted, along with every picture I had stored of you."

So Eric had been a jealous bastard and done everything possible to come between them. Because he'd wanted to repair things with Del, or just because another man had challenged him for a place in her heart? And Tyler bet that once he'd gone to Lafayette, Eric had directed all the anger about his inadequacy at Del, making her feel guilty and miserable.

At the time, Tyler assumed leaving L.A. to wrap up his case in Lafayette would give them the space they needed. When Del hadn't returned his messages, and Eric had answered him in monosyllables, Tyler had stayed in Louisiana and tried to convince himself that he was in love with someone else while drowning his hurt in sex. That had been his worst move of all. How much different would everything be now if he'd admitted then that he wanted Del and had pursued her?

He sank onto the edge of the bed. "What happened next?"

"We both tried to make it work for a while, but we never really talked about . . . that night. With every day that passed, he just sank deeper into anger, then depression. It was like the first few weeks after the shooting, but worse. He began to drink. A lot. The positive pregnancy test was just the final nail in the coffin."

"You left then?"

She pressed her lips together, hesitating. "Eric asked me to leave."

Tyler jumped to his feet. "The son of a bitch threw you out when you were pregnant? He knew you had no family, nowhere to go."

"I found a place after a week in a motel." She shrugged. "It was for the best."

Fury boiled inside Tyler, hot and insidious. The guy hadn't always been a true and faithful husband, but Tyler had thought that Eric would at least ensure her well-being. What a prick.

So, all alone, Del had gone through, what? Morning sickness, her body changing. He'd been around Kimber and Alyssa through their pregnancies. They'd complained about peeing all the time, backaches, swelling ankles, food cravings and aversions. Deke and Luc had catered to their every whim, taken over responsibilities so they could rest. Who'd taken care of Del through all of that? When she'd gone into labor? When she'd come home with a newborn?

"I'm going to beat the fucking hell out of him."

Tyler realized that he hadn't been much better, hanging out in Lafayette, up to his eyeballs in Jack Daniel's and pussy. Guilt serrated him.

What else had he expected? He could hear his mother's voice, *Like father, like son . . .*

"Don't." Del sounded tired. "It won't solve anything. If it helps, I didn't go through everything alone. Eric and I were together, signing the papers so he could buy my half of the house, when I went into labor. He took me to the hospital. He actually stayed through the delivery. He's not a terrible person, just insecure. At times, he took it out on me. You know the shooting totally changed him."

Eric had seen *his* son brought into the world. Tyler wondered what he'd been doing that night. Cracking skulls and fucking some stripper?

"I'm so sorry. I knew that you could be pregnant and—"

"What? You didn't really have a way to reach me. I didn't expect you to be psychic."

No yearning, no anger. Nothing. Goddamn it, he'd rather have her blame. "Didn't you wish, at least once, that the father of your son was there to help you or hold your hand?"

"It's over and done, Tyler. I'm okay, so don't waste your time feeling guilty. Let's move forward and end this shit with Carlson. Then you can go back to you life, and I can go back to mine."

"And then what? I'm supposed to pretend that I don't have a son who needs a father?" *Or that his beautiful mother seems determined to raise him without me?*

"Right now, it's the middle of the night. You're just supposed to go to sleep."

Without another word, she crawled back in bed. Tyler did the same, but sleep wouldn't come.

Damn it, he didn't want to let this go. But even if she was willing to make a life with him tomorrow, what did he know about being a good husband and father? How could he convince her that he'd figure it out and be ten times the man Eric had ever been when he wasn't completely sure himself?

Chapter Eight

By six that morning, they pulled back onto I-10. In Phoenix, they stopped for lunch and another car exchange, again courtesy of Xander, via some gorgeous blonde who looked ready for a stripper pole. This time, Del didn't say a word as Tyler transferred her duffel into the back of a nondescript white SUV and thanked the woman. Then he climbed into the vehicle, and they took off again.

Del sank back against the plush leather seats, listening to the heavy alternative rock banging through the speakers. She peered at Tyler from beneath her lashes, trying to make heads or tails of him.

"You can let me do something, you know. I'm not helpless."

He stopped at a light and turned his heavy gaze her way. "You brought my son into the world and raised him alone for fifteen months. You drove the two of you safely across the country with a madman on your tail. Helpless is the last thing I'd call you."

His words made her glow. "Then why are you taking responsibility for everything? The Tyler I knew would have brought the beer, but . . ."

"I would never have thrown the party." He surged ahead in the traffic, merging on the freeway. "I know. You've handled everything up until yesterday. I'm going to take care of you now."

Del stared. Something had changed about him. She liked it—more than she wanted to. And she was incredibly relieved. Of course, she needed to stand on her own two feet and be strong for Seth . . . but for this brief moment, it was so nice to lean on Tyler's broad shoulders. He'd fed her, kept her safe, even taken care of her sexually. She was almost ashamed to admit how much she'd needed that orgasm—and how badly she'd wanted it from him. For those blissful minutes, she'd felt close to him again.

Afterward, she'd directed all her guilt at him. Regret now weighed her down. Del knew that if the blame belonged to someone, it was her for being unable to resist Tyler. She knew who and what he was. He never turned down a willing female. They had so much unresolved between them. It was natural that he'd come on to her.

She could never make the mistake of thinking it meant anything important to him.

Still, once the orgasmic high had faded, Del realized that her life would become horrifically empty once Tyler was gone again. Yes, he made noise about sharing something in the future, but the Tyler she'd known wasn't cut out for marriage and kids. Despite his changes, he might never be. Alyssa's strippers called him Cockzilla with good reason. As much as she cared for Tyler, she'd never want him to put himself in the uncomfortable position of being a husband simply because he felt obligated. She'd only end up hurt when he left her or strayed. Best to solve her problems, then keep her distance. Let Tyler be the eternal bachelor he was meant to be.

"Thanks. I'll be able to take care of things again once we've dealt with Carlson."

"First, we have to convince Eric to let you back in to retrieve your flash drive."

Del sighed. How could she explain this? "He doesn't hate me.

He was really angry for a while. Once he started rehabbing in earnest and his ability to walk returned, he seemed better. I think that if I explain why I snuck in, it'll be okay. He might not love me anymore, but he wouldn't want me dead."

But there was a possibility he'd be pissed. Or he might not care at all. Del really didn't know. It was a gamble. Everything right now was.

"The motherfucker better help you, or I'm going to open his skull with my fists."

She reared back. In the hotel room this morning she'd sensed hostility from Tyler toward Eric, but this was obvious. As tight as they'd been, like brothers, it stunned her a little. If he'd been in Eric's situation and felt like he'd been cuckolded—

No. She realized. Tyler would have never used Eric as a sexual crutch and asked his pal to fuck her. Tyler had always been more pigheaded and had more gumption. He would have used his words, his hands, even toys to get her off and give himself something to look forward to. Hell, even his tongue, as he'd suggested this morning. The thought gave her a guilty tingle. But Tyler would have never folded and given his woman away to another man.

That's one thing that had helped Del accept her divorce from Eric. She'd lost respect for her ex-husband that day. She'd wanted to help him in his recovery, take an active part in saving her marriage. But after it was over and the blame started, she realized that she didn't feel the same about Eric anymore. His petulant anger diving into depression and vicious outlashes made her see a part of him that she'd never seen—and couldn't live with.

Things always happened for a reason. That night had happened to show her Eric's true colors and to allow her to have the most precious person in her life, Seth.

As Tyler flowed with the traffic on the freeway heading west,

Del stared out at the road, which gradually thinned back into empty desert.

"Tell me about your friends in Lafayette," she asked into the silence. "You seem close."

"It snuck up on me, but yeah. I went to Lafayette for a case, and I went to work for Alyssa as part of my cover. Through her husband, Luc, I met his cousin Deke, Deke's brothers-in-law, Hunter and Logan, and Deke's business partner, Jack. They're all great, stand-up guys. We've been through a lot together, protecting some of their wives from stalkers and assholes determined to hurt them."

She frowned. "That sounds dangerous."

"They have dangerous jobs. They've always had dangerous lives. We've got the adrenaline-junkie thing in common."

Del knew that about Tyler. He'd never played anything safe. "Your friends also have some . . . interesting sexual preferences."

"Caught that, did you?" He smiled. "Deke and Luc are total cavemen. The rest are into BDSM."

"BDSM?"

"Bondage, dominance, sadomasochism."

Del sat back in her seat, shock and confusion pinging through her—along with unexpected heat. "Like restraints, whips, and chains? They hurt their wives?"

"Just a little pain to enhance the pleasure. As Jack is fond of saying, it's more about the mind fuck." Brow cocked, he shot her a speculative glance. "What do you know about that stuff?"

"I've heard of it." Not for anything would she tell him that the thought of Tyler tying her up and having his wicked way with her made her ache. "You into that now?"

"I've picked up a thing or two listening to them. Interested?"

"No," she lied.

"Then why are your cheeks flushed?" He grinned.

"You're hallucinating."

Tyler's hand slid across her cheek before she could pull away. "Definitely flushed. Interesting . . ."

"Shut up and drive."

He laughed, but Del had no doubt he was filing away the observation. "I will . . . for now."

Damn, his playful side had always gotten to her. Her own nature tended to be far more serious, and Tyler had always done a good job of reminding her to laugh and enjoy life a little. It had been so long since she had anything to laugh about.

The sound of the phone ringing suddenly filled the SUV. Tyler grabbed it and glanced at the number, all business again. "Jack, what've you got?"

After a long pause, Tyler spoke a series of monosyllables, and Del lost total track of the conversation. Instead, she stared out into the desert, the late afternoon sun beating down relentlessly. A few minutes later, Tyler hung up with a ripe curse and turned to her.

"Tara dug around. Your credit card purchases are definitely being tracked by the DA's office, through the pretense that you have an outstanding warrant. What is that about?"

The gravity in his tone hit her with anxiety. "I don't know. I have an unpaid speeding ticket. That's it."

"Carlson is trumping it up to reckless driving. The warrant says you're a danger to others."

"That's ridiculous!"

"I think there's more than you're telling me. Jack has the same theory I do. When a bad guy wants to off someone, they don't usually start with something as flashy as a car bomb. Because then it's obvious someone is trying to kill you and the police tend to look at that crime a lot more seriously. That wasn't Carlson's first attempt, was it?"

"No."

Tyler raked a hand through his hair, clearly exasperated. "Why didn't you tell me that sooner?"

"I wanted you to watch Seth, not get involved with the case. I knew if I said more, you'd jump into the middle of this mess, exactly like you have."

"I was always going to get involved, Del. You were kidding yourself if you thought otherwise."

"I didn't need you to be responsible for me, just Seth. Just for a little while."

"I'm taking care of Seth by taking care of you. He needs his mother."

She wasn't going to win this argument.

Delaney sighed. "The first incident, though I can't prove it, was nearly being run over while crossing the street one evening. I literally dived onto another car parked on the street. If that car hadn't been there, I think he would have followed me onto the sidewalk to run me over. Then a few days later, I went to the bank. When I came out, a thug with a gun tried to hold me up. But he didn't seem interested in the three hundred bucks in cash I had in my purse, just in shooting me. I kneed him in the balls and clocked him in the jaw as hard as I could. Then I ran. He shot at me. When I close my eyes, sometimes I can still hear the bullet whizzing right past my left ear. The next day, someone broke into my house. Thankfully, Seth and I weren't there. They didn't take anything, but they trashed the place."

"Fuck, Del . . . You should have told me sooner."

"I thought I could get the story written, expose Carlson, and get him put away before he got me. The morning the car bomb exploded, Seth and I were packing up to stay at a motel. I turned on the car with my fob to get the air conditioner going, then I'd planned to strap

Seth in and load up the car." Tears hit the back of her eyes when she thought about all the danger she'd unwittingly put her son in. "I keep thinking . . . what if I'd strapped Seth in first?"

"Hey." Tyler reached for her hand. "You didn't. Don't cry. It's okay. You did the right thing, coming to me. We're going to fix this. If you think for one second that Jack, Deke, and I are going to let this fucker get away with terrorizing you and threatening my son, you don't know me."

She knew Tyler . . . and she didn't. He'd definitely seemed to have changed. He'd always been funny and on the protective side, but now defending her was like a code to him. A mantra. He meant every word he said, obviously committed in a way she hadn't seen before.

With watery vision, Del sent a grateful glance to Tyler. "Thanks."

"I don't want you to thank me. I want you to live." He wiped away the tears on her cheek. "Jack and Deke did some prodding and got ahold of the police report detailing your car bomb. It was definitely Semtex, a quarter-pound directional charge, under the dash. So Carlson has connections to some bad people. Angel, you shouldn't be involved in this." He gripped the steering wheel tighter. "Xander is flying to L.A tomorrow. I want you to go back to Lafayette with him. Take care of Seth. I'll deal with this."

"I can't. I think Carlson has a lot of dirty cops in his pocket. So I'm not expecting any help from that end. Carlson won't go away without public exposure. My editor at the paper is just waiting for this story. *I* have to do the legwork and write it."

"But Seth needs you."

"He needs to be safe even more. You can't write this story, only I can. So I'm going to do it, then go back to my son. Besides, I'm not leaving you to clean up my mess and risk yourself."

"You are one hardheaded woman. Jack swears that a good

spanking is one hell of an attitude adjuster. I'm beginning to see his point."

"You're not touching my ass—or any other part of me."

He sent her a lazy smile that did crazy things to her pulse. "Angel, I wouldn't take that bet if I were you."

Del swallowed. Yeah, she wasn't sure that was a wise bet at all. Within a few short days, she'd gone from being certain that temptation was the very last thing on her mind to almost craving the feel of Tyler's skin on hers, his lips demanding her surrender, as he drove deep inside her. How long could she really resist? And did she genuinely want to?

She cleared her throat. "So what's the plan? Are we rolling into L.A. tonight?"

"No. We'd get there late. You're tired, I'm tired, and I'll bet Carlson has a whole network of people on the lookout for us. The closer we are to his turf, the more dangerous it is. We need to rest and have a solid plan. You've got to get in touch with Eric, too. We need that evidence you stashed at his house."

And that fact really pissed Tyler off. Unfortunately, he was right.

It was early evening when they pulled into a little motel just inside Palm Springs that had seen its heyday forty years ago. They exited the air-conditioned SUV under a sign that advertised COLOR TV and SWIMMING POOL, then approached the sprawling blue-stucco structure surrounded by desert and palm trees. Tyler pulled a baseball cap low over his face.

Del frowned. "Why here?"

"It's off the beaten path. It's not a chain, so I can pay cash. There's parking around back, but no road behind us. Someone would have to be deliberately looking for us here to find us. And I don't think that's going to happen."

No, it didn't look like anyone would come here voluntarily.

Tyler opened the door and stepped inside, body taut, eyes

watchful. He glanced at her over his shoulder. "Wait by the vending machine. Keep your back to the guy behind the counter. We don't need witnesses or security cameras."

She didn't argue, just filed in behind him, head down, and made her way to the soda machine humming in the corner. Within a few minutes, Tyler had secured them a room. He grabbed her arm and led her back to the car.

"Good news. Our room is upstairs. There are two nearby stairwells that lead to the parking lot, a service elevator next door, along with roof access from the balcony. If Carlson is coming, I don't think he'll be able to muster enough guys to block four escape routes before we can blow this joint."

Del nodded gratefully. She would have chosen a nice hotel in the middle of a tourist area, hoping to blend in. She would have never considered where the parking lot was situated in relation to the road or how many escape routes the room might have.

"Thank you."

"Don't thank me yet. You're not going to like our accommodations." With a nod, he ushered her inside, then locked the door behind him.

As she looked around, her stomach tightened. "There's only one bed."

One lumpy, king-sized bed decorated with a vinyl tufted headboard, cracked with age, and a turquoise bedspread with bright yellow flowers. Cheap wicker furniture that had seen better days, a fading mural of palm trees along the bathroom wall, and cracked off-white tile flooring rounded out the look.

"To get the bonus safety features I mentioned, we had to compromise."

She scowled. "I'm not sleeping with you."

"Yeah, you are, at least next to me, where I can keep you safe. We'll decide about sex later. My vote is yes because I'm done tiptoeing around the fact that I want you damn bad. I'm pretty sure this is the only chance I'll have to convince you that something about us works, so if I have to be ruthless . . ." He shrugged. "I have no problem with that."

Del's jaw dropped. She should be pissed off. And she was trying to be. But she found something so compelling about Tyler's desire. He wanted her and he refused to deny it. She couldn't refute the ache flaring in her again. She hadn't missed sex in almost two years, and here he was, making her need and want it in a way she never had.

"For now, I'm going to take a quick shower. Call to check on Seth, if you'd like." He tossed her his phone. "When I get done, we need to find some dinner, buy a few supplies, and exchange our car again. Xander will call to set it up."

With that, he disappeared into the bathroom. Del sank onto the bed, disquiet dawning. Tyler had never come after her with all his seductive prowess. For years, she'd watched him turn it on other women, always somewhere between envious and grateful. As much as she wanted him now, resistance was going to be brutally difficult.

Was it worth the effort when they'd only be together for a few days? Whatever he said, Tyler would likely go his separate way when this mess was over. Instead of pushing him away, maybe she should seize the opportunity to feel like a woman again, to feel loved, put closure to this chapter of her life.

Biting her lip as she considered the question, she turned Tyler's phone over in her hands and opened his contact list. She scrolled and scrolled and scrolled. Lots of females, first name that usually sounded artificial and overtly sexual with a phone number only. Jazmine, Krystal, Angelique, Chastity—yeah, right—and even a Lexxxie. Del rolled her eyes, trying to ignore the jealousy blazing through her. Tyler wasn't hers, and he never would be. She couldn't afford to lose sight of that fact.

Finally, she came across Alyssa's contact info and dialed. The woman answered almost right away. "Hey, Ty. Figure your shit out yet?"

"It's not Tyler."

"Delaney? Hi."

"Hi." She didn't want to resent the woman he called friend, that he'd clearly wanted—and slept with?—at some point. The woman now watching over her son. But she couldn't help it. "How's Seth?"

"Great. Kimber brought Caleb over to play with Chloe and Seth. They are having a great time. Magically, she's keeping the boys from fighting. He seems really happy. He misses you at bedtime, but we've all done our best to comfort him."

Tears speared her eyes again. She'd been strong for so long, but one thought of Seth sad or in need brought her to the brink. That's one thing she hadn't seen coming before giving birth, the power of a mother's love for her child. She'd never known anything so pure and unconditional. For that alone, she was so grateful to Tyler.

After they chatted for a minute, Delaney ended the call. If she and Tyler were going to have a plan before they reached their destination tomorrow, she needed up-to-date information.

Digging through her purse, she found the disposable phone she'd bought on the road and dialed Lisa, one of the paper's investigative reporters. They'd been working together for just over a year. Lisa was wicked funny, but more importantly, she was razor sharp when it came to digging for dirt. That's exactly what Delaney needed right now.

"Del, is that really you?"

"Yeah. I'm fine. I should be back in L.A. by tomorrow."

"And Seth?" Lisa sounded all kinds of worried.

"Fine. I miss him, but he's better off being out of town with friends. Tell me what I've missed."

Lisa's voice dropped. "The lid is about to blow here. If you have any intention of stopping Carlson, you better do it quickly. Rumor is, he's got some shit on the DA. Apparently, the esteemed Mr. Reed likes to swing both ways, and Carlson is threatening to publish pictures of him and a barely legal boy together in a park. And they aren't throwing a Frisbee."

Shock doused Del. "Seriously? Mr. Family Values and Church?"

"Isn't it always the ones you least suspect? But you haven't heard the worst. It's likely that Carlson will be appointed to replace him until the next election."

Del nearly dropped the phone. "As sneaky as he is about getting positive press, it's unlikely he wouldn't be elected."

"Bingo."

"Oh my God."

This changed everything. If she couldn't get this story published before he became the district attorney, she feared he'd have too much power for her to take him down via a mere newspaper article. Hell, for all she knew, he could have her thrown in jail and Seth taken away.

Fear lashed her.

"How much time do I have?" Del whispered.

"A few days, maybe. A week at most. I've been staying on top of this for you, just like you asked. Sorry I don't have better news."

"Thanks for letting me know," she said woodenly.

But Del's thoughts raced. If she didn't succeed, what would happen to her and Seth? Every time she turned around, Carlson proved all over again how ruthless he was. He'd already tried to have her killed more than once. She was the only one standing between him and power. He wasn't going to stop.

"You sound rattled."

To say the least. "Don't worry about me. Just keep your ear to the ground."

"What's your next move?"

Del sighed. "I'll have to try calling Eric again. I tried while I was heading out east. Somehow, I'll have to explain that I hid part of my evidence on a flash drive and stashed it at his house."

She hoped that conversation didn't go badly. They'd managed some civil conversations since their divorce. If he had a new girl-friend and was getting laid, he enjoyed rubbing it in her face. If he wasn't, well, Eric had proven during the divorce that he was fabu-lous at serving up a cocktail of acid and guilt. She'd known when she hid the flash drive at his house that she'd have to retrieve it sooner or later. She'd simply hoped that time would continue healing him, and they'd be on better speaking terms.

"Keep me posted. I think he's been out of town. Newspapers are stacked in front of his house, at least when I drove by there on my way to work this morning to check for you."

Maybe that explained why he hadn't been answering when she called the house. At least she hoped that was all. She had to get back in the little Craftsman quickly. She'd simply sneak in again, but with everything going on, Eric had a right to know that someone might hit his house. But she also had to keep him and Tyler from coming to blows. Hmm. Maybe she should meet Eric by herself . . .

"Please let me know if you hear anything else."

Lisa agreed, and they hung up.

And Del saw her future teetering on extinction. So much was riding on these next few days, her ability to navigate Eric, get this story written, and dodge killers. She thanked God that Seth was safe and away from the danger, but every moment she couldn't talk to him, she worried something terrible was happening to him. If some-one hurt him because of her . . . Guilt choked her.

Tears began to flow. God, she hated being weepy, but fear did that to her.

Del wished she could undo the day she'd confronted Carlson with everything she knew. She'd wanted to provoke him into admitting something. Be a hard-hitting investigative journalist. She'd been determined to show the world what ruthless scum he was.

Naïvely, she hadn't counted on him being this violent, and now she and Seth might pay with their lives.

* * *

TYLER emerged from the bathroom to see her set her phone aside. Then she dropped her face to her hands. Her shoulders shook with sobs. She was dead silent. Her pain was a blow to his gut.

"What's wrong, angel? Is Seth all right?" He put a hand on her shoulder.

She jumped up and pressed a hand to her chest, quickly wiping away her tears. "He's fine. It's just that . . ."

Del stopped talking, her gaze grazing his face, then moving down his chest. The air conditioner kicked in, and he felt the rivulets of water cold on his skin. Once more, her gaze dropped to the little white towel wrapped around his hips. In the next instant, her cheeks flushed rosy. Her lips parted breathlessly.

His cock stood at attention. If she liked what she saw, Tyler wasn't above using that to his advantage, but not until she calmed down.

"Don't look at me like that, angel, unless you want me to accept that unspoken invitation and take you to bed. I'm trying to be a good guy here and find out why you're upset."

Del looked away, cleared her throat. "I was just talking to an investigative reporter I work with, Lisa. She helped me find you. She's been keeping an eye on the situation in L.A. while I've been gone."

Tyler stared. What the hell was she thinking? He didn't want to yell and upset her more, but damn it. "Did you tell her where we are?"

"No, just that we'd be there tomorrow."

Tyler breathed, trying to calm himself. "I know you're trying to help, but I don't like this. I know nothing about this woman."

Del turned imploring eyes on him. "She's my friend, I promise. You asked me to trust your friends. Now I'm asking for the same."

"We should have discussed this first."

"I'm trying my best." The angry tears that stabbed her eyes only made him wince with pain. "There wasn't time. At the end of the day, it's *my* problem. And now we have a bigger issue. Carlson is about to be named district attorney." She explained everything Lisa had divulged. "If I can't take him down before that happens, he's going to find a way to shut me up for good."

Tyler wrapped his arms around her and dragged her against his chest. "I won't let that happen. Do you hear me?"

"He's got contacts everywhere and—" Tears overcame her again, and she swiped at them angrily.

"Aw, angel, don't cry." He brushed a tender hand down her hair, kissing the top of her head.

"I'm scared. I need to be strong, but . . ."

"It's okay," he whispered. "Lean on me."

"You're already done so much."

In the last two years? No. The way he looked at it, even if he wasn't crazy about her, he owed her like mad. The excuse of needing to pay up kept her close—a bonus that would buy him time with her.

"No worries. Whatever you need."

She chewed on her bottom lip and looked at him with wary blue eyes that silently begged. "Hold me."

He wrapped her up tighter, all but drowning in her sweet scent. "You got it."

Tyler would love to do a whole lot more, but as upset as she was, now wasn't the time.

Del placed a hand on his chest, then backed away to meet his gaze again. "Kiss me."

His heart stopped. "You're sure?"

Slowly, she nodded. His hormones flew off the chain.

She was fragile; he had to remember that. No tossing her to the bed and devouring her. No ravaging her lips, violating her pussy, or making her take every bit of the hunger he felt for her.

Fuck. How was he going to manage that? He knew a shitload about getting a girl off. Not so much about comfort. But for her, he'd do his best.

Taking hold of her shoulders gently, he let out a calming breath and cupped her face, resting his forehead to hers. "Angel . . ."

He laid his lips over hers, a soft press, a sharing of breath. Reverent. Connected. Tyler felt her all the way to his core. The moment was endless, effortless. He could simply breathe her in all night.

But she wanted more. Needed it, he knew.

He laid his mouth over hers, gently nudging her lips apart, then let her take the lead. Del grabbed his shoulders with a desperate gasp and surged against him, thrusting inside his mouth with a moan. Her fervency ripped away his restraint. Tyler grabbed her, met her, took her in greedily. Crap, he wanted to soothe her, but he couldn't stop himself from trying to consume her in one fiery kiss.

Everywhere, they were entangled—arms, tongues, heartbeats. He clasped her hair tightly in his fingers, keeping her right where he wanted her. She felt so perfect to him. How the fuck could he ever let her go again?

Tomorrow, she might hate him, regret whatever happened next, but she needed something from him. He wouldn't turn her away, even if she just wanted to be held. The first time he'd touched her, he'd done it at Eric's request, trying to push aside how badly he burned for Delaney. But even then, he'd wanted to give her what she'd needed. Right now, he'd think not of his throbbing dick, but only of Del and how he could ease her.

With a sharp intake of breath, she pulled away, chest heaving as she stared. Her eyes were so damn blue and resolved.

"Tyler?"

"Yeah?" He panted.

Please, God, don't let her push him away.

She whispered, "Will you . . . make me forget everything?"

Chapter Nine

EVERY word Del spoke tingled through Tyler's body. He clenched his jaw. "I only know one way to do that, angel."

"Please." She tugged at his towel and brushed her soft lips against his neck.

Lightning shot down his spine.

An instant later, he eased her back and pressed her to the mattress, staring at her through the shadows. Need and insecurity, fear and vulnerability—they were all over her face, and it damn near broke his heart.

Maybe she and Eric would have divorced, eventually. But he'd certainly helped the situation along, unleashing all his buried feelings for her that night. It was at least half his fault that she'd been alone for the last two years. No fucking way was she going to be alone tonight.

Tyler wrapped his arms around her and captured her mouth under his. Sweet. Always so sweet. Open and ardent and tasting like soft woman. From the second he'd torn away the veneer of their platonic friendship and kissed her two years ago, he'd searched for this sense of connectedness with every other female he'd touched.

As he sank into the kiss, he wondered if he'd ever find it with anyone else. His road seemed to lead back to Del.

Tomorrow was far away, and he had no idea if he was truly built for the long haul, but he'd stay with her and love her well until this road ended.

Pulling back, he cupped her cheek. "God, I've missed you."

A little smile lifted her rosy lips for a moment, then the frown came back. Damn, she was working hard to fight tears.

"I missed you, too. I wanted to talk to you so badly so many times."

Her words were like a stab to the chest. He didn't want to blame her; he hadn't tried hard enough to get over his hurt and pride and stay with her. Her rejection had stung like a bitch, and he'd gone off to lick his wounds. Now he knew that she'd been through a lot, but he looked at all his wasted time and wanted to punch a fucking wall.

"Why didn't you? I was aching to hear from you."

"I . . ." She shook her head. "I didn't know what you'd say. I wasn't anything like the girls you dated. I know me asking you to leave that night hurt you. Part of me wondered if you'd take Eric's side, since you two were so tight. I guess I didn't want to burden you."

What the hell? "I would never have skipped out on you when you needed me."

"You're different now. It's clear you're more . . . solid." She shrugged. "I think at the time I felt incredibly guilty for betraying Eric in my heart. And I was most afraid of hearing that you'd done it for Eric and didn't want me anymore."

Her confession shocked him, and fire charged through his veins. "I know the guilt. I felt it, too, for making love to you because I wanted to for reasons beyond Eric asking. But regardless, we gave him exactly what he wanted. Don't ever forget that or take the blame on yourself."

"I've worked hard to get to that realization, too."

"I felt guilty because I wanted you too much." He swallowed. "I still do."

After a breathless pause, Del wrapped her arms around his neck and lifted her mouth to his. She didn't have to ask him twice. He angled his head and nudged her lips apart, opening her wider to him, sinking deeply to drink in that addictive taste of hers and the rightness flowing between them.

Refusing to waste another second, he tore off her T-shirt, exposing her delicate shoulders, narrow rib cage, so-soft skin. Tyler kissed his way down her jaw, her neck, nipping at her lobe, loving the way she turned her head to give him greater access. She clutched him, keeping him close, and moaned softly.

The sound went straight to his cock. Tyler closed his eyes. He wanted to pin her beneath him, taste her until he felt her pleasure on his tongue, then force his cock into her so he could drown deep inside her. He wanted to do every nasty, possessive thing to her that he'd ever imagined.

But now wasn't the fucking time to unleash his inner caveman. She needed comfort.

With a ragged sigh, he propped himself on his hands, lifting his body off her. *Slow, dumb ass. Go slow.* "You okay? I'll back off."

"No." She panted, reaching for him. "More."

Did she know what she was saying? He eased down onto her again. "How long has it been?"

She bit her lip. "Since the night we conceived Seth."

Shock blanched him, but a possessive fever rolled right behind it. It didn't matter that she'd been married to someone else. He was the last man she'd taken into her body. And right now, he burned to keep it that way.

Mine.

No way he could go slow now.

Tyler covered every inch of her, pinning her to the bed as he gave her a blistering kiss. He pressed her mouth open wider, demanding she take more. Del opened sweetly, accepting the ferocity of his desire, which only made him rage hotter. He wrapped one arm around her waist. The other worked the clasp of her bra. In seconds, it melted away. He tore it from her body and flung it across the room.

Del gasped and moved to cover herself. Tyler wasn't having any of that. He grabbed her wrists and pinned them to the bed, glancing down at the lush press of her breasts against his chest, her beaded nipples searing his skin.

"Don't," he growled. "I'm going to get my mouth on those, angel. I'm going to roll them around on my tongue, suck and kiss and lick them until your pussy is soaked and you're scratching at my back."

"Oh God." Del's voice wobbled.

Yeah, she was finally starting to get the idea that he wanted her fiercely. And she still didn't completely understand. But she would.

Slowly, she arched up, offering herself to him so beautifully.

"Fuck, yes."

Keeping her wrists pinned, he slid down her body until his lips hovered right over one of her nipples. Rosy brown, plump, puckered. Her clean feminine scent was strong here, and he inhaled. That hint of sunlit cotton on her skin, along with musky female, drugged him.

He could have started gently, kissed the side of her breast, tongued its swell. Fuck, no. He opened his mouth over her nipple, sucking it in fiercely, pressing it between his tongue and the roof of his mouth before nipping at it with his teeth.

Del gasped. "Tyler . . ."

In her voice, he heard surprise and pleasure. That was green light enough for him. He did it again, swirling his tongue around the luscious tip, toying, torturing, swelling it. Then he pounced on the other and did the same.

Beneath him, she thrashed but didn't fight his hold. Her little sighs, gasps, and moans went straight to his dick. Her skin flushed; those gorgeous blue eyes were dilating. She liked being manhandled.

That realization ripped away what little restraint he had.

He needed more control, wanted her immobile, where he could do anything and everything he chose. A glance at the headboard had him cursing. Nothing to tie her to there, and he knew from their conversation earlier that she fantasized about it. Those pretty flushed cheeks had proven her denials false.

Tyler had never been much for bondage. He could take it or leave it. Del was different.

Flinging himself to his feet, he prowled around the room, searching, seeking . . . He wrenched open the closet doors and found exactly what he needed.

"Tyler?" Her voice shook.

He grabbed the two aging, overbleached bathrobes the hotel had provided from the closet, then tossed aside the hangers. As he dropped the garments on the bed next to her, Del frowned.

Yeah, she didn't get it. But she was going to real quick.

With impatient hands, he tore into the first robe, pulling the tie completely free from the garment. He did the same to the second.

Let the fun begin.

He gripped the two terry-cloth strips in his hand and stalked closer. Del's pretty eyes grew round.

"W-what are you going to do?"

Tyler might think she was nervous if her nipples hadn't gotten harder.

He just smiled and tore through the snap and zipper of her

capri pants, then shoved them down her thighs. She wore a little blue thong with a small, silky bow right above her pussy. The cotton was faded and comfortable and damn near transparent.

Enough to see that she was bare and lovely.

"Take them off for me or I'll rip them. Your choice."

She blinked, hesitated. "What's going on?"

"Not quick enough." He grabbed the little panties in his tight fists.

"Wait!" On wobbly legs, she stood. He didn't give her a spare inch of space, but kept her wedged between him and the bed as she lowered the thong down her hips.

Tyler took over, forcing them past her thighs, to the ground. Then he threw them across the room, thinking that they really belonged in the trash. Damn things had been in his way. He was beginning to see that they'd always be an unwanted barrier between him and—he looked down and lost his mind, staring at Del's perfectly bare pussy.

God, he couldn't wait to have that.

He guided her back to the bed. "Give me your wrist."

Slowly, warily, she extended it to him. She wasn't exactly sure what he was up to, but she trusted him, and it was beautiful. Suddenly, he began to understand Jack's, Hunter's, and Logan's quest to push their wives' boundaries. It wasn't just to please them, but to know how fully those vibrant women would surrender because they loved and believed in their men. The push-pull he felt now only seemed to reinforce his bond with Delaney.

Tyler wanted more.

Silently, he looped the tie around her wrist, then rested her arm back against the bed, near her shoulder. With his other hand, he grabbed her thigh, spreading her legs wide to get his first full look at her cunt.

Fuck. So wet, already swollen. Pink, perfect. Beautiful.

"You want this." His stare drilled into her as he willed her to answer.

"Yes. I shouldn't, but . . ."

"Fuck shouldn't. This is about you and me and what feels good. I'm going to silence that destructive little voice in your head spouting this 'shouldn't' crap." *And make sure you don't worry about Seth, danger, or death anymore tonight.* "I'll give you something much better to focus on."

Del's breath caught. The edge of fear was getting to her. The anticipation. He was loving dishing out the dominance and making her tremble.

Tyler looped the bathrobe belt around her thigh, then pulled on both ends, forcing her wrist down and her knee up at her side.

"Give me your other wrist," he demanded.

Understanding dawned in those pretty blue eyes. Del realized that he intended to spread her wide open and immobilize her completely.

He waited a second, breath held. He was asking for a lot of trust after everything that had passed between them. His heart chugged, and desire gnawed at him viciously while she worked it through in her head.

Finally, she held her free hand out to him, looking right into his eyes with all the trust in the world.

That giving expression sizzled right down to his dick.

Tyler didn't hesitate another moment before he wrapped the belt around her delicate wrist, then reached for her knee, opening that leg to her side, and knotted the fabric there. Now, she was wide fucking open, each arm and leg attached, resting at her sides. The restraints lifted her hips to him perfectly. God, he wanted to pounce on her that second and lay claim to her sweet flesh—seduce her into wanting only him.

He forced the urge down for a second. "Is anything too tight? Hurt?"

"No." She sounded breathy, looked flushed, as she gazed at him softly, with need.

Clenching his fists, he forced logic for one more minute. "Any requests before I take you in every way known to man?"

Her breath caught. That pretty little tongue swiped across her lips, then she looked down his body, lingering on his hard cock, before her wandering gaze made it back to his face.

"Just one," she whispered. "Can you make the knots tighter?"

Oh fuck. Six little words, and he was at the brink. She wanted to be more completely under his control? "Absolutely."

He made a mental note to thank Jack and the Edgington brothers later for their frequent conversations about handling the pretty, willful women in their lives.

Tyler bent to his knots, tightened, rechecked that she still had circulation. "Move your hands and ankles. Anything too tight now?"

She shook her head, her eyes silently begging him. "Nothing."

"Then get ready, angel. I might be done with you by dawn. Maybe."

Del barely gasped in a single breath before he was on her again. He pushed past her lips to taste the deepest recesses of her mouth, gripped her hips, and shoved his cock right against that pretty pussy. God, she was so wet and bare, he could feel her sliding all over him, coating him with her cream. He ground against her. It had been good this morning, feeling her lush curves all against his cock, but this . . . Fuck, he was going to lose his mind.

Tyler tore his mouth from hers to stare down at her. Oh yeah, she was still with him, jagged breathing, pleading blue eyes. How had he never gotten the upside of bondage before?

Because he'd never wanted to keep someone open for him, and him alone, like he wanted with Del.

Tyler inched down her body. Her plush breasts waited for him, so soft, topped with hard, swollen nipples. He took the unspoken invitation and circled one with his tongue. God, those were good. He loved the scent of her, the flavor. She groaned as he shifted to the other, thumbing the hard tips, nipping at them, gratified when she whimpered his name.

"I like this. Mmm." He swiped his tongue along her abdomen, loving the way she shivered. "I remember my first night in Lafayette the week after I left your house. I had an empty apartment and a full bottle. I missed you . . ."

It was the first night he'd let himself masturbate to the thought of her. But not the last—not by a long shot. He always saved her for the times he was too drunk to remember that Del had thrown him out of her life. Even so, she'd still affected him like no one else.

"I fantasized about doing this."

Tyler slid farther down her body, bracing himself between her thighs. She was slick and succulent. The tangy-sweet scent of her went straight to his cock. He glanced at her, wide-eyed and restrained, before dropping his gaze again.

Lowering his weight to his elbows, he eased her folds apart with his thumbs. Her clit looked tight and red. Needy. She clenched, and Tyler salivated at the thought of his tongue, his dick, working into that tight little spot.

"I'm going to eat you up, angel."

She drew in a trembling breath. "Please . . ."

Fuck, he couldn't wait another second. He bent and ran the flat of his tongue from her hole slowly, slowly up to the hard berry of her clit. With a little moan, he swirled his tongue around it, his thumbs keeping her open wide.

Del stiffened as she cried out. Her entire body went taut. A glance up at the rapid pulse beating at her neck told him that her heart was racing.

He loved the idea that he'd already driven her to the brink of orgasm—and that he could keep her there and build on her sensations for as long as he wished.

With that thought, he dove right into that sugar-slick flesh and gorged on her, sliding his fingers inside her cunt, probing, testing, searching . . .

"Oh my God!"

He found her G-spot. Leisurely, he rubbed at it with firm fingertips as he took her clit into his mouth. With every second, her skin flushed rosier, her body grew more tense, her breathing more ragged.

"Tyler. Tyler . . ." She sounded desperate. Her long fingers closed into fists.

And he loved it.

He swiped a thumb across her clit, toying, keeping her on the edge. But no way was she going over before he was ready. "You like my tongue on you?"

With a devilish grin, he demonstrated again.

Del gasped. "I've never—" She clenched her fists, swallowed hard.

"Never what?" he prompted.

"Come like this."

Eric had never done this for her? No man had? Damn if that didn't motivate him to make her scream with pleasure.

"Oh, angel. I'm not letting you get away until you do." He gave the pad of her pussy a playful tap.

Her whole body twitched. Around his fingers, she clenched in need.

Then Tyler set about to prove that he wasn't all talk. He bent between her legs again, his hands at either knee, prying her apart even more. She hissed and arched, both protesting and begging.

He couldn't wait to give her this experience. And he controlled it completely. The way she'd put herself in his hands turned him on. Hell, everything about her did. No way would he let her down. Tyler intended to take very good care of her.

Latching onto her pretty, wet clit, he dove in, already addicted to her flavor, her pillowy-soft flesh that swelled with every swipe. God, she was like heaven, and responded to every touch with a gasp, a wriggle, an arch. He loved every offering of her passion.

Nothing about this experience was normal. He wasn't trying to get her off fast so that he could get his cock into her and get back home to his big screen or so she wouldn't be late for her "dance" number around a pole. Nothing else was in his head except making her feel good and giving his all to ensure that she wanted him.

"Tyler . . ."

Now her breath came fast and heavy. He smiled, staring up at her as he lashed her with his tongue again. "I'm right here. You going to come for me?"

He had no doubt she would. Every muscle in her thighs was taut. Her clit twitched. The power of holding her pleasure in his hands gave him the biggest rush.

With a smile, he plunged two of his fingers right against the sensitive spot deep in her pussy again, then sucked the hard little bundle of her nerves into his mouth. Within seconds, she screamed his name, then began jolting wildly. Tyler stayed with her, riding her to the very edge of her climax, milking every moment.

When she went limp and sighed, Tyler untied her and eased off the bed to grab a condom out of his jeans. Yeah, he was assuming. Or hoping, anyway. But if she said no, he'd respect it—and keep trying to convince her they were good together.

After donning the condom, he slid back onto the bed, right between her legs. He grabbed a thigh in the crook of his arm and started kissing his way up her body, lifting her leg with him, opening her to his seeking cock.

Spreading soft kisses around her breasts, he sucked in her nipple, savoring the plushy-hard texture with a moan. Delaney wrapped her arms around him.

"I'm going to get inside you, angel. Make you feel good."

"Hurry, or I'm going to roll you on your back and take over," she panted.

Later, yes. Much later, he'd indulge in the visual of her straddling his hips, taking every inch of his cock inside her, breasts bobbing, hair flowing, face racked with pleasure.

But now, he needed control.

"That's not a threat. That's a great idea." He grinned. "We'll get to it. But first . . ."

He pushed his way inside her.

Dear God, she was a tight, wet heaven, gripping him as she spread kisses across his face and neck. No way could she take him all in one thrust, and he stopped trying to fight his way in.

"Hey, angel, relax. We're going to get there." He kneaded the muscles of her hips and lower back with his fingers, slowly feeling her give way and let go. He pushed in a bit farther, pausing when she tensed and gasped.

"There's more?" she squeaked.

More than she probably wanted to know. "Just a bit. We've done this before. We were good together the first time."

"Yeah." She sighed.

Nuzzling her neck, he smiled against her skin, then eased back languidly. He took her free leg into the crook of his other arm and spread her even wider. It would keep her from being able to tense up too much, and he didn't want to hurt her. Just make her feel so damn good. And happy to be with him.

Once he spread her completely, he slid in slowly, like butter melting over a hot stack of pancakes. Finally, he pressed deep, deeper—all the way in. Del cried out, but it wasn't in pain, thank God. Her skin flushed rosy. Her nails dug into his shoulders as she arched up to him.

Fully seated, Tyler released his hold on her thighs, then wrapped his arms around her, cradling her. He took handfuls of that luscious ass into his palms and tilted her up to his cock as he pounded down.

On the first stroke, her eyes flew wide open, deep blue pools of wonder. She grasped at him, lips parting.

"I've got you," he promised.

Slowly, she nodded, then arched up, taking him a fraction deeper. Del didn't just feel good, she felt important. Perfect. He'd had so much sex in the last twenty years. Skanky sex, sweaty sex, forgettable sex, indoors, outdoors, under water, in a car, on a boat, on a plane, on a train. Hell, he could rhyme better than freaking Dr. Seuss when it came to all the places he'd fucked someone.

But the one and only time it had really meant anything . . . that belonged to the woman under him.

Tyler brushed the hair from her face and fused their lips together, shuttling inside her over and over, feeling her body tense, build, reach out for another orgasm. He closed his eyes, intentionally filling her with long, deep strokes that awakened both her G-spot and all the nerves he nudged around her cervix.

"Touch your clit for me," he whispered, propping himself on his elbows to give her room to maneuver.

Del reached a slender hand down her belly—then stopped. "Really? You want me to touch myself while you're inside me?"

"Is it going to get you off?"

"Probably." She bit her lip, eyes closing shyly. "I'm really sensitive there."

He grinned. "Get your fingers on your pussy, angel."

She didn't hesitate again, just slid her fingers between them and started rubbing that little sweet spot with slow, gentle strokes. He filled her, deep, sure thrusts, one after the other, that rasped over all the dark, sensitive corners inside her. With every thrust, she tightened until she forced him to take shorter, faster strokes, dig right at those nerve-laden spots that had her gasping once, twice, as she wrapped her long legs around his hips and thrashed under him, silently begging for release.

"Do you want to come?"

"Yes." She sounded as if she'd run a marathon and stroked her clit faster. "Please!"

"Now," he growled the command at her, feeling his own pleasure creep up his spine and tingles gnaw their way through his belly.

An instant later, her entire body jolted, and she let loose a guttural cry. A rosy hue flared across her cheeks. God, she was so fucking beautiful. Tyler fought to stave off his climax. He wasn't ready for this to end. For the last two years, he'd been floating through life. In Lafayette, he'd found the place he now considered home. He'd found the friends he knew would always have his back.

But he'd been missing Del, trying to fill her void with anyone he possibly could. He knew now that no one else would do. And he couldn't keep from releasing the need boiling inside him.

Del held him tightly, her pussy gloving him perfectly, squeezing and pulling him in. Pleasure suspended him seemingly in midair. The tension reached its zenith until he didn't breathe, didn't hear, didn't think. He simply felt Del—then released everything he had inside her in an outpouring that exploded through him, damn near overwhelming him. Tears stung the back of his eyes, and his throat closed up. He clutched Del tighter.

Under him, she clung to him, sobbing softly. He brushed the dark strands from her rosy cheeks and dried her tears. "I'm here."

She nodded but closed her eyes against him. "Don't do this to me. Just . . . go."

Fuck, her dismissal was frustrating, but not surprising. She'd known him for years as a player. Her first impression of his life in Lafayette wouldn't have changed that. He'd gotten her pregnant and left before she could tell him. She'd been through a messy divorce and birth all by herself. And now he'd worked his way right back into her panties. Naturally, she was cautious and questioning how long he'd be here for her.

Withdrawing from the warm clasp of her body, Tyler disposed of the condom and grabbed his towel. "Del . . ."

She shook her head and rose, clutching the sheet against her. "I'm going to shower."

Before he could reply, she'd darted across the room and closed the door. *Shit.* How ironic was this? All the times he'd fucked and run, leaving some female most likely wondering how he felt about her. Tyler winced. Now he knew that feeling. And it sucked.

He sat on the bed with a sigh. What the hell did he do now? Go with his gut and pursue her? Did he have more staying power than his old man, or had his mom been right all along?

Tyler could still hear his mother and the bitterness that dripped from her every word. She would get drunk and tell him how much like his father he was. After a while, it had become the background noise that filled his childhood, but Del was bringing it all back. Was he like the old man? Destined to ruin everyone around him?

He had no clue, and he certainly didn't have time to deal with his past boo-boos now. He'd call his mom at some point, tell her about Seth . . . but not today. Now, he had to focus on Del and what was happening between then. He wasn't calling the old bitch and letting her crawl in his head now.

With a sigh, he picked up his phone and dialed.

Jack answered on the first ring. "You okay there?"

Define okay. "Since we got out of New Orleans, it's been pretty smooth sailing. Xander's contacts, while scantily clad, have been helpful. But the asshole trying to kill Del is about to be named DA." Tyler filled Jack in. "See if you can dig up any dirt on him."

"Will do."

"And Del's got this friend, Lisa. I didn't get a last name. Here's her phone number." Tyler prowled through Del's phone until he found her last call and repeated the digits to Jack. "Del says this is a friend who's been helping her. I just want to make sure she checks out. If not, we might have a very unwelcoming party once we hit L.A. tomorrow."

"I'll look into her and get back with you in a few hours."

"Thanks, man."

"You sound tired."

Tyler sighed, rubbing at gritty eyes. "Fucking exhausted."

"You've trekked across half the country in two days, been shot at . . ."

"Yeah." But that wasn't really the problem. Tyler tapped nervously on the phone with his thumb, then decided to go for broke. "How did you convince Morgan that you were the right one for her?"

"Whoa, that's out of left field."

"Sorry."

"That's okay. To be honest, I was relentless about getting Morgan into bed. But then I fucked up, and I had to grovel a lot. Ultimately, I had to put the decision in her hands. I couldn't force her to trust me a second time."

Tyler squeezed his eyes shut. Jack was right, but that was the last goddamn thing he wanted to hear. Del wasn't ready to believe that he was into her for the long haul. Hell, despite the way he felt, *he* wasn't even sure. She had too much on her plate for him to expect her to sort it out now.

"You in love with Del?" Jack asked.

How the hell could he answer that? "Never really been in love. I don't know."

"What about Alyssa?"

"A very beautiful crutch."

Jack paused. "You tried to use her and all the other strippers to avoid thinking of Del?"

"Pretty much."

"Well, damn." Jack sighed. "I'm going to owe my wife something from Tiffany for being right—again."

"About my feelings?"

"Yep. She knew right away that you loved Del and that you were going to go after her."

Tyler sat back. Morgan had seen that? "What if I'm not good for her? I've got a lot of feelings for Del, but I've never tried the long-term relationship thing. Even the word used to give me hives."

"Picture the rest of your life without Del and give me a one-word description of it."

"I can't decide between bleak or pathetic," Tyler admitted finally.

"There you go."

He raked a hand through his hair. "But I know fucking nothing about loving a woman for the rest of her life."

"Think I knew anything before I married Morgan? I had subs, not girlfriends. The most bonding I did was a slave to the wall, never a woman to me. Thankfully, once I earned Morgan's trust again, she had most of it figured out. Follow your gut. Once you win Del back, work with her. Listen. Together, you'll find the answers."

Jack made it sound so easy. Tyler hoped his buddy was right.

* * *

AS they drove with the rising sun at their backs, Del tried not to look at Tyler. She'd only remember waking up in his strong arms and feeling genuinely safe for the first time in weeks. She tried to forget how badly she'd wanted to snuggle up to him, kiss him awake . . . and see where the morning led them.

Stupid. Of course, Tyler would have sex with her. He had a lot of sex, and none of it meant anything to him. Putting her heart out there with him just didn't make sense. Tyler was a great guy, but when it came to monogamy, she didn't think he was built for more than a night or two. And was she really ready to jump back into the relationship pool? She knew all too well how one minute everything could seem great, then in the next . . . anger, accusations, blame, heartache. Signing up for that possibility again simply didn't hold any appeal.

"You're not drinking your coffee." He glanced down at the fast-food cup full of java.

"It's like battery acid eating away at my stomach. No, thanks."

"You didn't eat, either." Tyler sighed, rubbed his forehead. "We should talk about it."

"No, we shouldn't. Unless you just want me to bolster your male ego, then I'll admit that you were great and rocked my panties. Thanks."

"I don't give a shit about my ego."

"That's right. You've had plenty of girls over the years tell you how good you are in bed. Dozens? Hundreds?"

"I didn't count, and stop trying to make what happened between us impersonal. You mean something to me, Del. I wouldn't fucking be here now if you didn't. If you're trying to protect yourself by acting like it doesn't matter, you can do that. But it matters to me, and I'm going to prove it."

Shame stung her cheeks. She was being a bitch and hurting Tyler's feelings. Del didn't know why he was trying so hard to convince her that he cared about her. Because she was Seth's mother? Because he felt guilty? Or because she really did matter?

"I'm sorry if I hurt you. I just can't chase Carlson, worry about Seth, and think about my love life now. I'll admit you're spectacular in bed. I'd be lying if I said I didn't want you again. I'm more than willing to be your lover until all this crap is over. Just . . . don't talk to me about emotions. Whatever you think you're feeling, it's the situation, not me. You'll get over it and move on. So let's just enjoy each other now and not worry about the rest, all right?"

Tyler opened his mouth, looking like he was going to object, when Del's phone, sitting in her lap, rang. They both glanced at the display, and anxiety gripped her when she saw an all-too-familiar number pop up.

Chapter Ten

"E<small>RIC</small>?" Del's voice shook.

Tyler's gut tightened. She'd been trying to call her ex-husband to get the flash drive she'd stashed in his house, but it rubbed Tyler the wrong way that Eric thought he could call Del and expect her to answer after the terrible way he'd treated her.

"Put him on speaker," Tyler murmured.

She hesitated, then complied, hitting a button.

"—the fuck are you into?" Eric was ranting. "I come home from a week in Cancun to find a bunch of messages on my answering machine from you that abruptly stop three days ago. After my flight landed at LAX, I called in to the precinct to check in. Some of my buddies tell me your car exploded. I came home to find my house has been ransacked. Not robbed, but torn apart. What do your panicked messages, which they listened to, by the way, have to do with this?"

Del sent him an alarmed glance. Tyler knew that she was thinking the same thing he was: What if whoever broke into Eric's had stolen her flash drive?

She clutched the phone, looking angry and nervous. "I didn't do anything to your house while you were gone. I've been away. I had to leave town after the car bomb."

"When did this start? The guys at the precinct said you were gone by the time they arrived on the scene to find your car was damn near ash. They have no idea who's behind this. From your voice mails, I'm guessing you do. What's going on? Why didn't you tell me sooner?"

"We're no longer married. I'm not your problem anymore. I just called you for one small favor."

"To hell with that, Del. If someone is trying to kill you, tell me. We may not be married anymore, but damn it . . . I want to do something. Is the asshole who's trying to kill you the same one who broke into my house?"

"It's complicated."

He huffed. "Since I solve crimes for a living, I think I can figure it out."

Del looked at Tyler, her expression a silent question. He shook his head. No telling who was onto her connection with Eric. Better not to talk more specifically until they were face-to-face. If Carlson had anything to do with Eric's place being trashed, the culprits could have just as easily planted listening or surveillance equipment.

"It's not safe for me to talk right now."

Eric hesitated. "I understand. The kid okay?"

Tyler gritted his teeth. He should probably shut up, but . . . "My son's name is Seth, and you can stop barking at Del."

Eric didn't say anything for a long moment. "Tyler? When the hell did you meet up with Del? Are you sniffing at her skirts again?"

Not "Hi, old friend" or "How have you been?" It rubbed Tyler entirely the wrong way. "Don't be a stupid motherfucker. She needed help. I'm helping her. Are you more concerned about what I might be doing with your ex than the fact that someone's trying to kill her?"

"Fuck you!"

"Stop it, both of you!" Del insisted. "Eric, Seth is fine. My personal life is no longer your concern, so let's please keep this civil. I only have one favor to ask of you, and it won't take too much of your time. Can we come by in a bit? I'll help you pick up."

"We? So you and my former best friend are a couple now?"

"No."

"Yes," Tyler said at the same time, then glared Del's way. "Definitely yes. I care about her and I'm going to keep her safe, since you're too busy running off your mouth. That's all you need to know."

"Tyler . . ."

He heard the protest in her voice, and it just pissed him off all over again. But they had to deal with Eric first.

End that, he mouthed to Del, pointing at the phone.

Her mouth tightened. Yeah, she didn't much like being told what to do. Tyler understood, but there was more than pride at stake here.

"So can we come by later?" She spoke into the phone.

Eric hesitated, and Tyler had no doubt his former friend wanted to refuse. "*She* can come."

"Get your head screwed on straight, man. Someone is trying to kill her. I'm not in a hurry to see you, either, but if you care an ounce for her, you shouldn't want her running around unprotected."

Tyler could almost hear Eric gnashing his teeth.

"Fine," he snapped finally. "What time?"

Since they were still out in the middle of the desert, it was going to be a while. "We'll call you."

Moments later, they hung up. Del clutched her hands in her lap, looking ready to explode.

"Spit it out," Tyler demanded.

Like she'd just been waiting for a sign, Del lifted her head and looked at him like he'd gone mad. "Seriously? You know Eric almost as well as I do. Everything you said to him was like waving a red cape in front of an enraged bull's face."

"He isn't going to treat you like that."

"That was an improvement! He called Seth a kid instead of a brat. He didn't tell me to go fuck myself or that I deserved whatever mess I'd gotten myself into. You told Eric to get his head out of his ass and stop thinking with his pride. You need to do the same. This crap you're pulling isn't helping. We need his cooperation to search the house. I hid the flash drive really well. Hopefully, it's still there, but we won't ever find out if you don't stop the verbal equivalent of lifting your hind leg and pissing on me like a fire hydrant."

Tyler tried to swallow down his rising fury. The crappy thing was, she was right. He was being overprotective and possessive. Eric couldn't hurt her through the phone. But he didn't like her talking to the asshole, didn't like remembering that his former buddy used to sleep curled around her, kiss her awake, join her in the shower each morning—then put on his uniform and cozy up to badge bunnies all day.

Del deserved better. But above all else, she had to stay alive. Which meant that Tyler needed to stop being an ass and focus on the flash drive.

"Sorry. I don't want to see him hurt you again."

Her face softened. "Thanks. Sometimes, you can be a great guy."

"I can be a great guy for you." The words were out of his mouth before he could stop them.

Melancholy tinged her smile. Regret. "When I was pregnant, I used to wonder what it would have been like if we'd met under different circumstances. You know, if I'd never married Eric, and you two weren't friends. Would we have had any connection or would I have just been another girl you tapped and forgot?"

"You're not the kind of girl I can forget, Del."

"Because we have so much history, and it's all just tangled . . ."

"Because it's *you*. You're what attracts me, not the fact that you're Eric's ex-wife or the mother of my son. You're sassy, smart, funny, and honest."

"I'm not the only woman in the world like that. I'm sure you've done a few and probably just never talked to them long enough to learn about them."

Tyler gritted his teeth. "They weren't you. What is your fascination with my sex life?"

"C'mon, Tyler. We both know that I'm one of many. Yes, Seth puts me in a slightly different category, but—"

"Bullshit!" He pounded on the steering wheel. "Is that the crap you tell yourself so you won't care too much about me?"

She frowned. "I just . . . know you. I've known you for years. I'm not expecting that sleeping with me or being a father will make you be a different person. I'm just being realistic."

"I've changed."

"In some ways, yes, you have. But according to the conversation I overheard you having on the patio with your harem, you're having anal sex with Alyssa's strippers in the dressing room regularly, causing them to catfight onstage about you. That sounds like the same ol', same ol' to me." She shrugged. "Whatever. Like I said, I don't expect to change you."

Tyler felt heat creep up his neck and face. She had a point, but she didn't really know how he felt on the inside. "You're not going to believe me if I tell you I marked time with them but always wanted you."

"You're right." Her smile was faintly apologetic. "Be reasonable, Tyler. I've known for years that you're a playboy. I see that something about you is different now, but if you're really trying to convince me that you're a whole new person, I need more than forty-eight hours to believe it. And if not . . . really, it's okay. I'm not asking you to be different."

Frustration carved up Tyler's composure, but he grabbed a ruthless grip on his temper. "But I think I am. So I'll be here for you, day in and day out. You'll get it eventually."

She cocked her head at him and laid a gentle hand on his arm. "I think you really believe that at this moment, but the first gorgeous Latina who walks by you with cleavage and a lush booty . . . I'm pretty sure I know what's going to happen. You don't have to pretend to be something for me that you're not. If you'll just spend some time with Seth and let him get to know you, that's all I ask."

But Tyler wanted more. He couldn't dispute everything he'd done before Del had walked back into his life. And he couldn't convince her with words in just a few short hours that she was different to him. Only time would do that. Tyler didn't know how much of that he had.

Wouldn't his mother be laughing now, if she could see him? Even she would doubt his staying power in a relationship. He might never have had any before, but this felt different. He felt tethered to Del, and it may not make sense, but he knew if the strings connecting them were cut, something in him wouldn't survive it again.

But to Del's point, she needed time. In the midst of danger and crisis wasn't the best moment to expect her to notice or believe that he had become a different man.

Gripping the wheel with one hand, he tangled the fingers of the other in her hair, bringing her close to him. "I'm going to give you everything you need and want—and more. I promise you that. Just give me time to prove it."

*　*　*

A few hours and another vehicle exchange on the outskirts of L.A. later, they rolled up in front of her house. Her former house. She'd loved this little Craftsman but lacked the money to buy Eric's half in the divorce. He'd come up with the cash somehow, so she'd signed away her rights and turned over the keys. The money had given her the down payment on a new condo, allowing her to get a fresh start with Seth. It had all worked out.

But coming back here was always like visiting a haunted house. So many memories. Some good, like Eric carrying her over the threshold with a smile. Some not so good, like the morning her pregnancy test had come up positive. There'd been the barbeques and holidays with friends and family. There'd been the nights Eric had come home hours after his shift ended, looking utterly spent, and when she'd needed his attention, he'd merely flopped on the bed and fallen into a deep sleep. Del turned her gaze away from the little house.

"You okay?" Tyler grabbed her hand and squeezed.

She nodded. He was trying to help, and she had to lay off him about his past. It was really none of her business who or how many women he'd slept with. The jealousy was misplaced and pointless. He still slept around a lot. That was Tyler. She agreed that in some ways he'd changed, but so much that he was suddenly the model of fidelity? That wasn't likely, but it didn't matter. They were here to stop Carlson, not rekindle anything. Seth had to come first. Tyler wanted to protect and help her; she needed to be grateful for that— and stop wishing that, maybe, they could have more.

"Fine. Let's go."

Tyler ducked out of the sedan, climbing the steps up the hill beside her, heading for the door. He wrapped a beefy arm around her waist.

She sent him a rueful stare—but she'd be lying if she said she didn't like his protectiveness. "You don't have to do that."

"Yeah, I do." And he clearly wasn't going to budge.

"Eric isn't going to hurt me."

"Do we really even know him anymore?" His face tightened. "I'm not taking a chance."

Maybe Tyler had a point. In truth, she felt more secure, and maybe Eric would dial down the volume on his asshole meter if he knew someone would defend her.

As they reached the door, she knocked softly. Eric unlocked the bolt and ripped the door open, his dark eyes glowering in a newly tanned and freshly rested face as they popped back and forth between her and Tyler. His gaze settled on Tyler's palm curled around the curve of her opposite hip.

"You've got a lot of nerve," Eric spit at Tyler.

"I'm not the one who told my friend to fuck my wife, then got pissed off when they both liked it. You cast her out onto the street when she was pregnant and you never fucking called me once to tell me she was going to have my son. What kind of miserable bastard does that make you?"

Eric flushed. "You don't know all the details."

"I know enough to know she's better off without you."

Del stepped between them. Clearly, seeing her with Tyler brought out all of Eric's insecurities and anger. She had to try to soothe everyone's anger or this was going to end badly.

"Guys, stop. So you're never going to be great friends again. Fine. But let's bury the hatchet so we can all stay alive. I'd rather not stand on the porch and scream out all our secrets."

At her reminder, Eric lifted his head and looked around at the surrounding houses. He had to realize that Mrs. Morris next door, the crazy cat lady, was hanging on every word. Who knew if the perpetrators who'd broken into Eric's house were nearby, listening.

"Get in," he snapped, grabbing her by the wrist and hauling her inside. Tyler had barely cleared the threshold when Eric slammed the door behind him and locked it again.

Del eased from the foyer into the living area, sinking into the familiarity of the house, its antique rocker, the sleek leather sofa. The ceiling beams stained dark, their vintage pendant lights hanging, shedding warm light on the brick hearth. He'd kept all the modern lamps and accessories in brushed nickel she'd selected, which had been the perfect fodder for the house's character and charm.

But the rest of the place looked like a tornado had hit it.

Broken glass littered the floor, along with a slew of papers in nearly every color of the rainbow. The globe on the mahogany stand that had once belonged to his grandfather had been toppled over. The drapes were strewn across the floor, a puddle of fabric and splintered wooden rods.

"Oh my . . . This is terrible. I'm so sorry," she murmured. "How did anyone get in? You're always careful about keeping the place locked up."

"We'll talk about it in a minute." Eric turned his glare on Tyler, then shoved him into the kitchen. "Thirsty?"

They'd already proven that imbibing together led to trouble. "No, we just need to talk to you. Let's sit in the living room."

"Well, I need something to drink." He shoved at Tyler again, who looked like he was itching for a fight, too.

He'd done some really awful things to her, like throwing her out when she was pregnant, but he'd been hurting and lashed out. Del felt a bit like she'd started it. He'd been fearful of never walking again, relying on his wife to stay with him through better or worse, in sickness and in health. Instead, she'd succumbed to his best friend. Yes, Eric had asked, but he hadn't asked her to enjoy it so much. He hadn't asked her to fall half in love with Tyler. He especially hadn't asked her to get pregnant. At a time when she should have been focused on him and helping him recover, getting him past his anger at fate, she'd shoved him into a deeper pit of despair.

Clearly, he hadn't worked through all those issues. And now, she'd brought violence to his door, then followed it up with a reminder of the breaking point in their marriage. Talk about a post-vacation letdown. He had a right to be angry—and her guilt kept piling up.

"It's three thirty," she pointed out, hoping to keep him on task.

"Which makes it past five o'clock somewhere." He reached over her to grab a glass. "Wine?"

"No, thank you," she murmured.

She noticed he didn't ask Tyler if he wanted anything. He just slammed the cabinet door, then reached in the pantry for the liquor. Tyler leaned against the refrigerator, keeping his back covered, and watched with narrowed eyes. Suspicious eyes. They exchanged a glance. Eric was up to something; they could both feel it. Best to get what they came for, then clear this place.

"I actually just came by because I left something here a while ago for safekeeping."

He frowned as he poured a shot of whiskey and downed it. "Before the divorce?"

This was where her explanation would get tricky. "No, after."

Eric hesitated, thinking, pouring another shot. "You let yourself in with the spare key on the patio without my permission?" He didn't even wait for her to confirm. "Why?"

"I've been working on a story, an exposé. I can't say a lot now, but it's really big. The person I'm writing about caught wind of my investigation. I had some of my research on a flash drive and hid it here a few weeks back, just in case. I didn't think anyone would suspect that I'd keep anything valuable at my ex's house. I never thought they'd hit your place. I'm really sorry."

"You hid evidence in my house without telling me and dragged me into this shit unwittingly, but you won't cough up who or what you're investigating? Is that right?"

Del winced at his bitterness. "It's safer if you don't know."

Eric's dark gaze slid over to Tyler.

"But you dragged him into it? Because you trust him more or care about his safety less?"

As he tossed back the second shot and swallowed it, that question dropped between them like a bomb loaded with a ton of TNT. Either reply had the potential to turn this downright ugly. She bit her lip.

"No answer for that, huh?" Eric drawled, pouring a third shot. "How about I help you? You ran to him first because you trust him to help you, no matter how pissed he might be at you about the br—" He looked sideways at Tyler. "About Seth. How long was it before you let him back in your pussy?"

She flinched. Del thought of lying, but Eric would see through that fast, and being dishonest would only make the situation worse.

"He's already fucked you?" Her ex-husband laughed bitterly, then sucked back his third shot of whiskey. "God, I'm a stupid ass. Of course he did. My old pal fucks anything that moves, and you itched to take him for another ride, didn't you? You tracked him down so he could shove that big, prized cock of his right into your cunt—"

"Shut your goddamned mouth," Tyler growled. "Now. Before I shut it myself. You begged her to have sex with me that night, just like you begged me to fuck her. We had never crossed the friend line before you suggested it. Don't shove your baggage on us. Shit happened. If you couldn't handle it, you shouldn't have asked."

Eric threw his hands in the air. "You know, you're right. I should have realized you two were hot for each other. I should have thrown you out of my life the minute I suspected you had a hard-on for my wife."

Before she could sputter a word, Eric charged Tyler, grabbing something from his back pocket. Handcuffs. Del tried to sputter a warning at Tyler. But with the refrigerator at his back and a wall of cabinets beside him, he had nowhere to go.

Eric hooked one cuff around Tyler's wrist with a decisive click. Tyler punched him in the jaw with his free hand. Despite Eric's head snapping back, he maintained focus and yanked on the cuffs. Tyler stumbled, close enough for Eric to snap the other cuff around the handle of the refrigerator, tethering Tyler in a blink.

Del gasped.

Like an animal of prey, Eric whirled on her and began stalking. A terrible smile spread across his face. At six feet two inches and with an active life, he was a wall of solid muscle. No way she could outrun or outfight him. Apprehension tightened Del's stomach. What was he up to?

"Are you trying to intimidate me? Because this is stupid. Just let me get what I came for, then we'll leave."

Eric shook his head, his shaggy, dark hair moving with him. "I haven't gotten what *I* let you come for. That night he fucked you—" He nodded over at Tyler. "I saw a whole other side of you, babe. I saw a very naughty vixen. You'd have given him anything that night. You'd have let him come down your throat or shove his dick up your ass—all the things I never got out of you. I saw you come for him over and over. And I had to watch you not only take pleasure but demand it. I was fucking helpless to do anything."

"You touched me," she reminded him.

"And you screamed his name when you came." Bitterness streaked across his dark features, the kind she hadn't seen since early in their split. "You put on quite a show. Do you know what that did to me?"

Del could imagine. His self-confidence had never been the best.

The resulting quirks were sometimes hard to live with. But every-thing had been much worse after the shooting.

Eric raised a dark brow at her. "Now, we're going to put on a show for him."

His words sent panic thrumming through her body. She didn't like the sound of that at all. "Don't touch me."

"Stay the fuck away from her," Tyler demanded, yanking so hard on his cuffs that the refrigerator rolled a few inches across the floor.

But it wasn't enough. With Eric squarely blocking her path to Tyler, she couldn't get to him. Even if she could run fast enough to escape her ex-husband, she wouldn't leave Tyler here to take his wrath. She had to stand her ground and get them both out of this.

"I'm not going to hurt you, babe. I just want to make you come while he watches."

Eric had never been particularly good at bringing her to climax when they'd been married. And this now was nothing more than a power trip, one he wanted to take to salvage his pride. He didn't really even want her; he just wanted to rub Tyler's nose in her or-gasm. After everything that had happened during their breakup and her pregnancy, the thought of Eric touching her again made her stomach pitch and roll.

But she wasn't terribly surprised. In fact, she should have seen this coming. Eric had always looked for validation in everything. His lack of self-confidence sometimes drove him to take stupid risks. That's how he'd been shot in the first place, trying to play the hero without adequate backup.

"You better not fucking touch her!" Tyler shouted, jerking against his restraints.

"What?" Eric asked, all innocence. "You don't think it'll be great fun to watch the woman you love get off at the hands of another man?"

"It's not going to happen, Eric." She crossed her arms over her chest, shooting him her sternest look.

He stalked closer, and Del had nowhere to go. She held up her hands to ward him off, but that was like hoping a butterfly net would stop a barreling semi.

"Sure, it is. I want to get my tongue on your pussy, Del. How does that sound, Tyler?" Eric tossed a triumphant glare over his shoulder at his former friend.

Hell no. She had to put a stop to this now.

Del pulled her cell phone out of her pocket. "I don't want this, and I don't want you, Eric. Are you planning to rape me? Really?"

He cocked a brow. "Since you basically cheated on me when I was crippled and wasn't sure I'd ever walk again, don't you think you owe me the chance now to prove that I can flip your switch as much as he does?"

After throwing her out because she was pregnant? After divorcing her in nothing flat, despite the fact that she'd taken care of him for months? His insecurity and feelings of inadequacy had been understandable, given how fast and hard she'd fallen for Tyler that night, but he'd pushed them together, and she couldn't change it now. Her bigger question was, why the hell hadn't he gotten over it in the last two years?

"It's not like you want me back," she pointed out. "Our marriage fell apart in six short weeks. It's over. You're not going to make me come, and I'm not going to let you try." She focused on her phone for a second, then sent him a warning. "Come a step closer, and I'll call nine-one-one."

That only made Eric laugh. "Which one of my friends will respond to the call? You think they're going to help the adultering whore who broke my heart and the traitor who knocked her up?"

His words sank in and made her feel all kinds of sick, but Eric was right. No one who responded to her distress call would believe her or lift a finger to help her.

"Don't even think about it," Tyler growled.

He yanked on his cuff again, but there was no way he was getting free. The handle of the refrigerator was built seamlessly into the unit and made of solid steel, as were the cuffs. He cursed, then turned to riffle through the nearby drawers for the cooking knives. They were empty, and he struggled to tear them out of the cabinets, to no avail. She realized now that the counter had been cleared of the blender and other heavy knickknacks Tyler might have thrown or used as weapons. When he wrenched open the cabinet above, all the glasses had been removed. Eric sent his former friend a terrible smile.

Del's stomach plummeted, cramped. Eric had clearly put some thought into this plan. God, now she was actually terrified. How far would fury and insecurity push her ex-husband?

An awful feeling of vulnerability set in. Panic. After the shooting, Del had quickly learned that, when angry, Eric was capable of hideous insults that he may or may not regret later. Now that he was healthy and mobile again, she suspected he was capable of much worse than hurtful words. And that he was bent on some sort of revenge.

"If I ever meant anything to you, please don't touch me." Del heard the pleading note in her voice, and as much as she hated to show weakness, she hoped it penetrated the thick shell of his rage.

It didn't. He just came closer and gripped her wrist, tugging on it to drag her to him. "It's because you meant something to me that I'm not giving up."

Bullshit. This was about Eric's pride, about hurting Tyler. About losing out. Whatever love he'd felt for her had died long ago.

"You look so pretty, Del. I've missed you." He wrapped his free arm around her waist and ground his erection against her stomach, tried to nuzzle her neck.

Apprehension soaring, she pushed at him. "Eric, don't."

"Get your hands off of her, you motherfucker!" Tyler shouted, yanking again on the handcuffs. The refrigerator rattled across the hardwood floor. Blood trickled down his wrist.

Del's heart lurched in her throat. Tyler was going to hurt himself getting free. And given the fury thundering across his face, he would kill Eric—and enjoy every minute of it. If Carlson became DA and got wind of the fact that Tyler was trying to help her, the corrupt bastard would make sure that Tyler went down hard. Being convicted of murdering a cop never came with an easy sentence.

"Calm down, Tyler." Her voice shook. As frightened as she was, panicking wasn't going to help either of them. She had to keep him from doing his worst.

"Fuck that!" He strained against the cuffs. But the two feet separating him from Eric might as well have been a chasm.

"Relax, babe," Eric murmured in her ear, spreading kisses across her jaw, heading toward her mouth. "I just want to kiss you, make you feel good."

No, he just wanted to flaunt her to Tyler.

She shivered. Familiarity mixed with her fear. A huge part of her was furious, even felt betrayed all over again . . . but even now, guilt clung like frost to a window. On the surface, her marriage had ended because Eric hadn't been able to handle the sexual favor he'd asked of his wife and his best friend. But deep down, they'd divorced because she had been more in love with Tyler than her own husband after that night—and Eric had known it. It would be easy to lay all the blame at his feet—but not entirely fair. She'd played her role.

"Eric, don't . . ." She almost couldn't look at him. "This isn't going to solve anything. What's done is done."

He took hold of her face and forced her stare into his. The anguish and lack of self-confidence there wrenched at her heart. Since she'd gone, she knew he worked too many hours and drank too much when he was off duty. She'd heard that he plowed through dozens of women, as if trying to prove that he was no less appealing than Tyler.

Fighting Eric physically was futile. Since regaining his mobility, he'd clearly been working out. He'd never been in better shape. Her only choice was to try to fend him off with words. And if she could give him any peace, maybe this would stop and they could all move on with their lives.

"Babe . . . Did I—I matter to you? Really?"

There was his painful insecurity. He hated it, and the vulnerability always made him so angry that he got mean. She had to talk fast. "Of course! I married you. I lived with you. I bought a house with you. I took care of you when you were shot. I loved you."

"But you never once responded to sex with me the way you did to Tyler that night." Self-doubt clouded his eyes.

"It doesn't matter anymore," she tried to argue. "What we had is over."

"Because of him. And I hate the way we ended, babe. I want to remember what you feel like again." Eric bent toward her.

His gaze caught hers, fused her stare with his as he came closer, closer. Before she could shove him away, he pressed their lips together, then nudged her mouth open and dove in. In the background, she could hear Tyler growl, his handcuffs rattle against the stainless steel. But the nervous roar of her heartbeat filled her ears. Eric tasted like whiskey and desperation. Aversion filled her, and she tried to wrench away, wishing she were anyplace else. But he couldn't stay in this emotional limbo where he both wanted and hated her, where he seemed determined to punish all of them for the past.

Del pushed against the hard granite of his chest, dying a little inside. Two years ago, she would have been so grateful for any sign that he didn't hate her. Now, everything inside her rebelled. She pushed again, but Eric didn't notice, merely dragged her closer, fitting his hard body against her curves and moaning into her mouth.

"I'm going to make you come, babe. It's going to feel so good."

No chance of that happening. She gave him a little shove.

"Del! Goddamn it, no!" Tyler shouted.

When Eric tried to take her mouth again, she bit his lip. He yelped, and she broke away.

"What the hell are you doing? You want to play rough? Is that how you like it now? Fine by me." Eric licked at the little cut she'd made in his lip and began to unbutton his shirt, looking at her with nasty promise in his eyes.

Her belly flipped, turned. Nerves set in, but she forced herself to try to stay calm. Both men were damn near rabid with anger. If she lost it, too, this was going to get ugly fast. Tyler getting in the middle of it was only challenging Eric more and making him ratchet up faster. She gave Tyler a little shake of her head. He had to understand that they'd get nowhere finding the flash drive or healing their past unless Eric could get some confidence and closure.

"It's not easy to watch, is it?" Eric gloated. "Seeing me kiss her? Wait until I put my hands and lips all over her, then get my cock deep inside her and fuck her breathless. How furious and helpless do you think you're going to feel then?"

Chapter Eleven

FUCK *no*. His inability to help Del brewed a raging fury in Tyler that he felt to the very core of his being. "You begged me to have sex with Del. I didn't ask for this shit today."

"When you demanded she come for you repeatedly, then knocked her up, you absolutely did," Eric assured.

"Eric . . ." Del protested. "I don't want this. You're forcing me. If we were any other two people, you'd arrest the bastard for what you're doing to me now."

His former friend just shrugged, seemingly determined to prove something to everyone in the room, especially himself. Del sought to defuse the situation, but the way he'd worked himself up, Tyler doubted that saying anything to the stubborn bastard was going to do a damn bit of good.

Eric freed the last of his buttons and shoved his shirt off his shoulders. He'd always been in good shape, but now his body was leaner, harder, roped with more muscle. Bigger. Del's breathing turned ragged. Her eyes went wide with fear.

Anger pumped through Tyler's veins. Dread kicked him in the stomach. Again, he yanked on the cuff. The refrigerator was heavier than a motherfucker, and it screeched across the hardwood floor another inch or two. His wrist throbbed like a bitch. Drops of blood burned their way down his forearm. He didn't care. Whatever it took to get to Del.

"Come here, babe." Eric brushed his knuckles across her nipples, tweaking one hard enough to make her whimper.

"Get your fucking hands off her," Tyler demanded, grabbing both handles of the refrigerator now and trying to drag it close enough to kick Eric's ass. The heavy-duty plug tethered to the wall prevented him from going any farther.

And Tyler couldn't unsee the way his former friend manhandled her, the way she struggled against him futilely. The vision burned into his brain. A violent urge to pound Eric into the ground roared through him.

Then the bastard upped the stakes and yanked off Del's shirt in a few swipes of his hand. She screamed and shoved at him, fighting the panic dawning on her face. "Eric, don't. Please. Listen to reason. This is wrong and you know it."

"No means no!" Tyler roared.

Eric ignored them both and clawed her bra off, even as Del fought, kicking and slapping. In seconds, she stood half naked, backing away. When she tried to cross her arms over her bare breasts, he grabbed her wrists and held them together at the small of her back, forcing her to arch closer to him.

"None of that," Eric chastised her. "Give me everything you gave him."

"No," she shouted. "I don't want this! How many times do I have to say that?"

"Give me a chance. I'll change your mind." Eric cradled a breast in his hand, and a fresh need to kill crashed through Tyler. "God, I missed these. You've always had pretty tits."

"Goddamn it, stop now!" Tyler roared. "Or I swear I'll kill you."

She sent him a glance that begged for his silence. Del wanted him to shut up and let her handle it? That went against every protective instinct he possessed. He knew she'd be dead if she didn't get her hands on that flash drive, and Eric, the jealous bastard, wasn't about to let her search for it until he got his pound of flesh.

His former pal didn't respond to the threat, merely shifted so Tyler would have a great view of him pinching Del's bare nipple. "You didn't stop that night when I wanted you to. Instead, you fucked her more. I think I'll take a page out of your book."

He'd barely processed that stab in the back before Eric lifted her breast and bent toward it. Del cringed, screamed, and pushed at him with all her might. Tyler saw red.

Fuck, he'd give anything to spare her this, to be able to fight this battle for her. Del needed him, and he'd never imagined that Eric would force his point or try to heal his own inferiority complex this way. Tyler wouldn't make the mistake of underestimating him twice.

Her ex-husband came after her again, going after the sensitive tip of her breast she'd managed to keep from him. She pushed hard at his chest. "Stop, damn you!"

"Listen! The difference between that night and now? I wasn't forcing her," Tyler ground out. "I would never hurt her."

Eric caressed her shoulder. "I wouldn't, either."

"Don't you think she'd be running out the door now if she didn't need your help? Call it what you want, but she said no. If you go any further, it's rape."

Eric merely grabbed Del's arm tightly, forcing her to be still, and licked her nipple, dragging his tongue across the tip, throwing every ounce of possessive fury to race through Tyler's veins. Del looked ashen, shaken as she punched at him.

Tyler didn't bother to fight the urge to rip Eric limb from limb. He lunged, dragging the refrigerator across the floor with a screech another few inches, pulling the cord from the wall. "I'm going to annihilate you into so many pieces, they'll need tweezers to find all the parts."

"But first, you'll know the joy of watching the woman you love coming for another man."

As Eric backed Del against the counter so she had nowhere to retreat, he took her nipple back into his mouth. He tore at the snap of her pants. Even as Del shoved at him, he yanked her zipper down, jerking everything, including her panties, around her hips. Then he thrust his hand between her legs.

Del screamed and fought, but it only insinuated the bastard's fingers deeper in her folds.

"You're not wet yet," Eric chided. "Stay still. Let me fix that."

"What part of no don't you understand?" She sounded damn close to hysterical, and Tyler had to fight back another wave of fury. "You're angry and feel betrayed. I understand." Del squeezed her thighs together, trying to dislodge him. "But I do *not* want this."

"You will."

"I won't!" She sobbed. "It's over, done. We're divorced. I didn't *reject* you. We grew apart and put an end to the marriage. Just move on."

As Eric shook his head and rubbed in slow circles around Del's pussy, frustration poured hot acid fury all over Tyler. He growled and kicked at the refrigerator. God, it hurt to watch them, especially when tears began to run down her cheeks. Another mountain of impotent rage crashed through Tyler, like the bowels of hell had opened up and poured in pure molten fury.

"We can't go back in time," she pointed out. "And you can't force me to want you."

"Look at me." Eric tangled his free hand in her hair and yanked, snapping her head back. Del's eyes flew open, and he pinned her beneath his furious, dark stare. Violence poured off him.

Tyler feared there was a good chance Eric would leave Del violated and broken if he didn't do something fast. As much as he hated to give Eric the satisfaction, Tyler gladly swallowed his pride.

"You wanted to hurt me, make me jealous? Angry?" he challenged Eric. "You got it. You win. Watching you touch her is like having my insides gnawed on and spit out. It's fucking torture. You hate me, not Del, so stop hurting her, and let's settle this like men."

"No, Tyler!" she protested.

Eric paused, clearly listening. "Go on . . ."

"You want the chance to beat the shit out of me? Take it now. Don't be a coward and hurt the woman. Come fight me like a man."

Eric cocked his head. Some part of him was tempted. But then he turned his focus on Del again, as if he knew Tyler would hate seeing her mauled way more than having a black eye.

"I'd rather touch her. Come on, babe," he murmured.

Del recoiled, her expression filling with resolve. "I'm sorry for the way things turned out. I'm sorry if what happened between me and Tyler makes you feel rejected." Then she shoved Eric's hand away from her pussy and finally got enough space between them to knee him in the balls. He doubled over and grunted out in pain. Tyler would have clapped if he could have.

"Del . . ." Eric groaned.

"I'm sorry for a lot of things, but I'll never be sorry for defending myself. Don't ever fucking touch me again."

Eric growled and grimaced as he tried to stand upright again.

She yanked her panties up, wriggled into her jeans—then slapped his face. "I won't let you use me to drive Tyler over the edge. Eric, you manipulated me, then took your anger out on me and abandoned me when I needed you most. I'll never trust you with my body again. Stop your pity party. My feelings have nothing to do with your looks or prowess. You showed me in a million different ways that you didn't love me. Blaming me for your request and the consequence of it was the worst. Just . . . move on. If it makes you feel any better, Tyler and I aren't planning any sort of happily ever after. We're just trying to keep Seth and me alive."

Eric winced, blinking at her in shock as he continued to cup his gonads. "You don't need to fuck him to stay alive."

"No, but I need reassurance and human contact from a man I trust."

Tyler was damn proud of the way she stood up for herself and told Eric exactly why he was a douche bag. But the tears filling her eyes—and the dispassionate way she reduced their relationship to irrelevance—stabbed Tyler right in the chest.

"He's the first person to hold me since the divorce," Del went on. "I know you can't say the same."

Eric looked away, guilt all over his face. "Goddamn it, Del. Why him?"

"Because he never once let me down," she whispered. "Because he would never do what you just did."

"Fuck." Eric blinked, frowned, as if finally realizing that he'd done something terribly wrong. He eased back into the nearest kitchen chair, folding his big body into it with a sigh and dropping his face into his hands. "I guess I deserved that. I never meant to hurt you . . . But you bruised my pride."

"You bruised my trust." Once it seemed clear that the fight had gone out of Eric, she reached for the rest of her clothes and yanked them on. "When we were married, I wanted to love and believe in you so badly, and when you turned your back on me for honoring your wishes . . . you crushed me."

"I didn't know how to handle what happened." His face tightened, a deep frown settling between his brows. "I expected it to feel like I was with you again. Instead, it was like watching you reveal what was really in your heart."

"Tyler made me feel beautiful and treasured that night. With all the anger you'd blasted at the world after your shooting, I hadn't felt that in a really long time."

Eric whipped a stunned stare up to her, as if she'd stabbed him in the heart again. The acceptance settled across his face. "I'm sorry. I loved you in my way. Maybe that wasn't how you needed to be loved. God, I'm so fucked up. So damn angry." His face crumbled, and he looked as if he might cry. But he manned up and swallowed the tears down.

With a frown, Eric waved a hand in the air. "Go. See if you can find what you're looking for, then leave. I can't do this anymore."

Solemnly, Del nodded and approached Eric. "That makes two of us. Get some professional help. Find someone you can truly love. Handcuff key?"

After a moment's hesitation, Eric fished it from his pocket and set it in her palm.

Tyler watched her make her way to him, then fit the key into the hole. He breathed out. It wasn't a sigh of relief. Anticipation thrummed through him, making his heart race, his fists clench. He was going to destroy the fucker now—and he couldn't wait. But the closer Del got, the more she looked pale and terrified. "Angel?"

She met his gaze, her blue eyes watery. "I'm fine."

But she wasn't, and a renewed ferocity consumed Tyler. "Bullshit. He hurt you."

Closing her eyes, he saw as Del tried not to reveal how much Eric's rough treatment had disturbed her, but it bled through. It wouldn't be enough to leave Eric battered and dead on the floor. Tyler wanted to tear the asshole up into small, unrecognizable pieces. Whatever it took to keep her safe.

"I'll be fine," she murmured. "Are you all right? You're bleeding."

He glanced at his wrist. "It's nothing. Let me loose. Let me at the son of a bitch."

"No." She turned the key and freed his wrist, leaving the other cuff attached to the refrigerator.

"I'm going to tear him limb from limb." He took a ground-eating step toward Eric, menace charging through him.

Del grabbed his arm tightly with both hands and tugged. "Be smart. Don't do it."

His entire body shook with the need to dismantle Eric. Rage gnawed at him. His fists clenched. His heart pumped.

"If you touch him, they'll throw the book at you," Del pointed out. "And if you go to jail, what happens to me and Seth?"

They probably died. *Fuck*. And if he disrespected her wishes, was he any better than Eric?

Tyler gritted his teeth and dragged her into his arms. God, she felt good here, and he wanted to eliminate Eric because he couldn't stand the thought of seeing Del hurt or threatened ever again. But in this case, she was right.

That didn't stop the adrenaline from coursing through his system like a drug, revving him up. He was jagged, on edge. How the hell was he going to make her feel safe while taking the top off his frustration? He needed to either fight or fuck.

"All right. I won't touch him." *Yet*.

Emotional overload hit Del. She melted against him, trembling in his arms. Tyler did his best to manage his raving frustration and pulled her closer, where she'd be safe. But over her shoulder, he glared with blatant hostility at Eric.

"Thank you," Del breathed.

She shouldn't thank him yet. His restraint was only going to last for so long.

Tyler eased her back and thumbed the fresh tears from her face. "Let's find your flash drive and go."

He almost choked on the words. He really just wanted to kill the motherfucker, but Del needed his comfort and protection more than he needed to unleash his temper.

She gave him a watery smile and slipped her hand in his. The trust she showed him now, especially after Eric had abused hers so wretchedly, floored him.

Squeezing her hand, Tyler let her lead him through the house. They stepped over broken glass, around toppled furniture, their feet wrinkling papers beneath them. Finally, at the end of the hall, they entered one of the spare bedrooms. Del had used it for an office at one point. Now, it held Eric's weight equipment, all scattered across the floor.

She trotted over to the closet and opened the door. The house had been built in the 1920s, and the tiny closet was almost nonexistent. The dark hardwood floors gleamed, and Del knelt and shoved her fingernail into a little ridge in the floorboard, popping the wooden plank up with the first yank. The board clattered to the floor as she stuck her hand inside the little hidden cubby.

A moment later, she froze and looked up at him with wide eyes. "It's gone."

* * *

AS soon as they left Eric's house, Tyler folded Del into the car and pulled out his phone. Shit, she looked shell-shocked. Devastated. And his need to pound on the person responsible nearly pushed him beyond reason. He didn't fucking know how to make this better for her. Eric claimed he didn't know anything about her flash drive. Didn't even know she'd ever hidden anything in that spot. He'd had some work done to the floors last month after the hot water heater had leaked and caused some flooding . . . right around the time Del had hidden the little device. And of course, someone had broken into the house. Anything could have happened. Anyone could have taken it.

Tyler didn't like this shit. The urge to kill Eric still rode him hard. It had taken everything in him to leave the fucker alive. Now, dread gripped Tyler as well.

He grabbed Del's hand. "We'll figure this out. Who would have broken into Eric's house? I doubt it was random or a simple burglar. You told your friend Lisa that you'd hidden the flash drive here?"

"Yes. I know what you're thinking, but I can't imagine that she'd betray me."

"No one ever wants to imagine that someone they trust would willingly hurt them, but we have to look at every possibility. Who else knew where you'd hidden your information?"

"No one. Carlson must have decided to hit Eric's place on the off chance that I'd hidden something there."

Maybe. Maybe not. He'd keep working all those angles.

"I was trying to be clever, but Carlson's mind works a lot more deviously than mine." Del sighed tiredly. "Every bit of my research is gone. I'd been sketching a timeline, keeping track of contacts I'd made. I can probably remember some of it, but not phone numbers and exact dates and . . . I'd even started drafting a story. I never imagined that he'd blow up my laptop *and* that I'd have to start from scratch. That will take longer. I don't know if I have that much time before he's named DA."

"You didn't back up at the office?"

She shook her head. "A colleague had his work stolen about six weeks ago. He was working late at night, and some goons came in, roughed him up, and took everything he had on his story. The paper is supposed to be instituting new security procedures, but they haven't implemented them yet. So I didn't dare leave my stuff there."

And home wouldn't have been any better. In fact, Tyler bet if they went by her place now, they'd see that it had been violated, too. This fucker Carlson was thorough and seemingly one step ahead.

She blew out a deep, troubled breath, looking exhausted. "Maybe Seth and I should assume aliases and move out of the country. If I stay, there's no way Carlson won't hunt us down eventually and kill us. I don't want to be always looking over my shoulder."

Del covered her face with her hands. She didn't sob aloud or shake with tears. But Tyler felt her desperation deep in the gnawing of his gut. He swore under his breath, even as he wrapped an arm around her. A deep sense of possession gripped him. No fucking way was she simply going to disappear. If she needed protection, he'd give it to her.

"Don't worry. I'm going to help you."

"I can't ask you for more. You've already dropped your life to help me, been so supportive . . ."

"There's no asking. It isn't negotiable. I *will* help you. You and Seth will be safe. Put that worry from your mind for now. You start thinking about who you can talk to in order to rebuild your story. I'll see about making sure we have a safe place to stay for a while. Now, how much did Eric hurt you? Do you need to go to the hospital?"

"He scared me and hurt my feelings more than anything. I . . ." She blinked away fresh tears. "I feel betrayed. I loved him once. If I hadn't talked him down, I don't know how far he would have gone."

No question in Tyler's mind that Eric would have pinned Del to the floor and done his worst. He didn't even know the bitter, vindictive bastard Eric had become since the shooting—and the divorce. Just thinking about it made him violent again.

"Don't worry," Tyler whispered. "Deep breaths. Sit back. Let me handle this."

With a soft touch, she reached up and cradled his jaw. "I've been alone for so long, it's nice to have someone to lean on. I'll miss this."

When she'd gone. That was her intimation. Tyler tightened his jaw. Yeah, fuck that.

As if she had no clue that his tension was escalating, Del leaned back in the passenger's seat. Tyler started the car, and a soft ballad drifted from the speakers, and though he hated the song, he didn't touch the radio. If it brought her peace, he'd deal.

As he flipped a U-turn and gunned the car down the street, he looked back and saw Eric watching them from the front window, his gaze following until they turned out of sight. He gripped the wheel with white knuckles, wishing it was the asshole's neck.

Reaching for his phone, he punched in Jack's number. His pal and new boss answered on the first ring. "What's up?"

"The flash drive is gone."

"You saw the ex?"

"Yes."

"Think he's involved?"

Tyler hesitated. Del likely thought Eric was just lashing out. But Tyler couldn't rule out the possibility that Eric was trying to sabotage her story, or worse, get her killed, for his vendetta. "Possible."

"Is he dangerous?"

Now, Tyler didn't skip a beat. "Very likely."

"Can't talk? Del near?"

"Exactly."

"I'll add him to my list of people to look into. You might have another problem. Del's friend, Lisa? She's had a bit of trouble with credit cards. She's awfully fond of Nordstrom, Coach, and Prada. Has had a few maxed-out credit cards for a while. Transferring one balance to another card for lower interest rates, blah, blah, blah. She paid most of that off this morning, to the tune of thirty thousand dollars. I want to know where she suddenly got the money."

Tyler wanted that answer, too. "Any record of interesting phone calls?"

"Nope. Squeaky clean. But that just means there may be a non-traceable, prepaid cell somewhere in the mix. I'll keep running it down. There's an answer, and I'm going to find it."

Great. Another fucking traitor. That made Tyler's mood even peachier.

"Anything else?"

"Digging into Carlson has been interesting. A lot of chatter. A lot of rumor and innuendo. If I had to bet, the guy is crooked as a dog's hind leg. There's a whole lotta people around him either toe-ing the company line or saying nothing at all. I don't like the way it smells."

"Me, either. Especially since someone broke into Eric's house and trashed the place, but apparently didn't take anything, except maybe her research."

Jack hesitated. "Who knew you were going to see him?"

Tyler was intensely aware of Del's eyes on him and couldn't say a damn thing.

But Jack was intuitive, as always. "Let me guess, Lisa?"

"Yep." He'd bet she'd sold Del out to Carlson for thirty grand. Tyler didn't like where this conversation was going. His frustration ratcheted up another notch. "We've been in this car too long."

"I was just going to suggest a change of vehicle. Xander is on the ground in L.A. now. I'll have him call you to arrange something. Got a place to stay?"

No, and night was coming in a few hours. Del was exhausted and needed somewhere she could feel safe. "We could go to a motel."

But Tyler didn't love the idea. Carlson would expect that in L.A.

He had too many eyes and ears in this city. Motels were public. It would be too easy for Carlson to get a dirty judge to issue a warrant for their arrest and a SWAT team to come after them.

"I don't think that's wise," Jack said. "If you've got eyes on you . . ."

Clearly, Jack was thinking right along the same lines, and Tyler wasn't about to put Del in more danger.

"Any other suggestions?"

"Leave it up to Xander. He's from that neck of the woods. Money can buy you a lot of security, and Logan says he has a shitload of it."

"I'm not looking for a handout or a babysitter, just a little help."

Jack laughed. "Xander likes playing at the edges of this dangerous shit, so if you want his help, you're going to have to suck it up and take it all."

Just fucking dandy. "All right. We'll try to find someplace to lay low until he calls."

The line went dead. For all Jack's good-ol'-Cajun-boy routine, he still had a lot of Special Forces and suspicious bastard in him. Tyler related.

He tossed the phone on the dashboard, aware of Del's stare. "Now what?"

Before he could shove his rage down again and find an answer, his phone rang. PRIVATE CALLER displayed.

"What?" he growled into the phone.

"Tyler?" a man asked.

"Who wants to know?"

The man on the other end of the line laughed. "All you sons of bitches are cautious. It's Xander."

He relaxed. The cavalry had arrived—damn quick. "Yeah. Thanks for the vehicular assistance across country."

"No sweat. Your truck is making its way back to Lafayette as we speak. May likes driving it. She'll drop it off with Alyssa. I guess they know each other."

"Really?" Tyler frowned.

"Same profession, at least once upon a time."

In other words, they'd both been strippers. "Thank May for me."

"No worries. I have something really special in mind."

Tyler heard the playful lechery in the other man's voice. "Great. Spare me the details."

Xander laughed, something robust and genuine. "I'm not great at sharing anyway. Ask my brother. But that's another subject for another day. Tell me where you are and what you need."

"A new car. A place to stay, if you've got one. We have to start tracking down some people and information."

"Done." Xander didn't hesitate. "Can you meet me at the little regional airport in Santa Monica in thirty minutes?"

Tyler gauged the number of miles to the destination versus the traffic. "Yeah."

"Perfect. I'll see you then."

"Since we've never met, how will I know you?"

"You got a pretty girl with you?" Xander asked playfully.

He gnashed his teeth and gripped the phone. "Yeah, but I don't fucking share at all."

Xander laughed. "I'll find you."

Ending the call, Tyler frowned. He had no idea how to take the bastard. A prankster or a player? With a shake of his head, he tossed his cell back on the dashboard. God, more shit. It all just pissed him off.

Del's brow furrowed. "That didn't sound like it went very well. How well do we know this guy?"

"Jack says he's rich, knows L.A., and has connections."

"What is he, a drug dealer?"

"Logan wouldn't make friends with a criminal, guaranteed. He's as true-blue as they come. Xander apparently helped him save Tara from something really dangerous before they were married, and they're tight. Logan says he's a stand-up guy. I have to guess that Xander likes yanking people's chains a bit."

"Great."

They spent the next few minutes in silence, Del using Tyler's phone to send Alyssa texts to check up on Seth and finding that all was well. Knowing that seemed to calm her. He was glad one of them was coming down from the rush. Tyler still felt like a ticking bomb.

"Thank you," she began. "For everything you've done. You didn't have to—"

"Stop there." Tyler sent her an unyielding glare. "Yes, I did. It's your problem, and Seth's problem. Therefore, it's my problem. Because I care. Don't act like I'm doing you a huge fucking favor. I want to take care of you, and you know it. I'm trying to prove it. After watching Eric damn near molest you, I'm not really in the mood for the distance you're trying to put between us. You say you just want to fuck until we sort all this out, and no way am I turning that down. But don't pull this overly polite shit and try to keep walls between us."

"But—"

"No," he growled. "Remember, we did it your way two years ago and it was a huge clusterfuck. It's my way now. And if you don't stop, you're going to find out exactly how possessive and insistent I can be. As it is, I'm fighting my inner caveman. After watching Eric put his hands all over you, it's all I can do not to go back and beat the fuck out of him. Or stop the car right now, strip those annoying clothes off of you, and get you underneath me." He pulled the sunglasses down to the bridge of his nose and looked at her with a blatantly masculine demand. "Your pick."

* * *

DEL blinked, then blinked again. *Holy hell*. This was affable, laugh-a-minute playboy Tyler?

"I—I . . . Neither."

"*Buzz!* Wrong answer. Try again."

"What is the matter with you?"

"You really have to ask?"

No, she supposed she didn't. The situation with Eric had been beyond tense. Tyler might be laid back most times, but apparently he had a big ol' alpha streak, and she'd just run smack into it. He was edgy, his thumb tapping rapidly on the steering wheel.

"You're awfully . . . aggressive."

"Welcome to the real me. When you were married to Eric, you saw the pal, the prankster. You saw the guy who didn't take much seriously because I didn't have anything to be serious about. I still want to have fun, but when it comes to you, I'm serious as a fucking heart attack."

His words should scare her. But it felt so good to be so wanted. It was probably temporary. He'd never been a forever kind of man. If she let him, he'd screw her out of his system. That was probably for the best. She couldn't imagine trying commitment again.

"Tyler, we said we would just . . . be together while this stuff is going on."

"No. You suggested that. I never agreed. I walked away once because you asked me to. I told you, I won't do it again."

Del saw the signs for the turnoff to the airport. She grimaced. "When have you ever thought about settling down with one woman in your life? You, who nailed a different woman every night, some-times more than one? You used to get drunk and talk about your daddy running off. Your mother told you that you're just like him—

and you agreed. You can't be hearing your biological clock ticking since you have a son. So what's with the sudden change of heart?"

Tyler gripped the wheel. He looked mad. Madder than mad, actually. "Maybe I don't want to buy into the old bullshit anymore. So my mom thought I was a deadbeat. I can't prove that she's wrong. But there's a huge difference between marrying a girl straight out of high school that you knocked up and wanting a woman who makes you feel whole. Even when everything between us was supposed to be bad and wrong two years ago, I felt a connection to you. A . . . completeness. I'm beginning to realize that I've never given another woman a chance because they weren't you. I'd built rituals around you, Del, like Tuesday tacos and Sunday afternoon movies, not because I loved the cuisine or the flicks, but because I loved—"

"Don't say it." Del's heart pounded. She shouldn't, but she wanted to hear the words. God knew how badly she wanted the father of her son—and the lover in her fantasies—to care about her. "You're mixing up friendship and protectiveness with anything more lasting."

"You don't know shit about how I feel. But you keep telling yourself that if it makes you feel better. I'll be right on your sweet ass, tackling all your misconceptions until you believe me."

Before she could get a word in, Tyler released her and swung the car into the asphalt lot, shoved the car in park, then hurtled out the door.

Del ran to catch up with him, blinking like she was seeing him for the very first time. And maybe she was. "I didn't mean to hurt your feelings. I'm sorry."

He stopped, then backed her against the trunk of the car. "You're making me crazy. I need you. I need to know that you're safe. I need you naked now, with those pretty blue eyes all wide and dazed, your sweet thighs spread, and my name on your lips."

She swallowed. Tyler made that sound way too appealing. The

bottom fell out of her stomach, and she dug her fingers into him, trying to figure out how things had gotten out of hand so quickly. Before she could say a word, he propped his foot up on the bumper of the car and leaned in. No mistaking his erection, long and thick behind his zipper. Then he fisted her hair and gently pulled, positioning her lips right beneath his. He devoured her, no pleasantries. Just all possession and heat. And she melted against him with a moan.

She was probably setting herself up for heartbreak, given her skittishness since the divorce and the number of women Tyler had taken to bed. She couldn't forget the times he'd said that he'd rather cut off the protruding parts of his body with a dull, rusty knife than commit to one woman. What had changed about him, really? And why, when he touched her, did the craving dig in? Her brain shut down—and her heart took over. Every time he touched her, Tyler made her feel like not only the most important woman but the only one in the world.

This time was no different. She wrapped her arms around his neck, knowing it wasn't smart, knowing she'd probably wind up alone and hurt . . . but she couldn't bring herself to care. It would be easy to tell herself that she needed a balm after Eric had made her feel dirty and used. But it was more than that. Way more. The first time Tyler had kissed her, she'd felt a zing all the way to her soul. Some part of her had been overjoyed when she'd learned she was pregnant because she'd known she'd have a part of Tyler forever.

Damn, she had it bad for him.

He angled his head to get deeper into her mouth. So hot, so single-minded. Delaney felt every nerve in her body light up in anticipation. When he cupped her breast and thumbed her nipple in the middle of the parking lot in broad daylight, she couldn't find the will to care. He was a drug to her system, and she was addicted.

"I can't get enough," he murmured against her lips. "I'll never get enough. Every time I taste you, I only want more."

"Well," said a masculine drawl behind them. "Unless you're trying to attract attention or you'd like to get arrested for public indecency, you need to save it until I can get you a room."

With a gasp, she broke away from Tyler and glanced around him to see the familiar face of one the richest, most notorious, and most gossiped about playboys in Los Angeles.

"Xander Santiago?" She gasped, then turned to Tyler. "This is Logan's friend? He's your idea of laying low?" At Tyler's nod, she shook her head. "We're doomed."

Chapter Twelve

XANDER didn't try very hard to suppress a grin as he held out a hand to Del. "Nice to meet you. I guess you've heard of me?"

Who hadn't? Anyone who lived around here knew all about the money—and the exploits—of the infamous Santiago brothers. Tyler could hardly believe *this* was Logan's buddy from a Dallas BDSM club. Then again, if Xander was into tying up women and spanking them, he'd have a more difficult time keeping a lid on that in this city, where everyone knew his face. With a private plane, the middle of the country and relative anonymity was just a few hours away.

"Of course I do. My name is Delaney." She shook his hand. "I'm an L.A. native."

The other man smiled at that, his hazel eyes sparkling with mischief under his sleek brows and two-hundred-dollar haircut. Tyler had no trouble understanding why he'd had so many women all over the country willing to help him out. Besides being sinfully rich, Xander was a good-looking SOB and a natural flirt. Tyler fought the urge to punch him in his perfect face for caressing Del with his stare.

Gritting his teeth, he watched as Xander raised her hand to his lips. "Los Angeles has some incredibly beautiful women."

"Many of whom are taken. I'm Tyler." He inserted himself between Xander and Del and sent the guy a don't-fuck-with-me glare.

"What a shame." Xander looked around his shoulder at Del and winked.

Del raised a delicate dark brow. "I'm also a reporter."

In a lightning-fast move, Xander backed away from Del. His playful grin fell away.

"I've never written about you," she clarified.

"Keep it that way," Xander demanded. "Let's go. I've had a brief conversation with Jack about your situation. Being seen in public might be risky for you now. Carlson may be able to track your movements through security or traffic cameras. Normally, this place is monitored, but this is a small commuter airport, and I managed to arrange for a ten-minute camera . . . malfunction."

He'd covered the important angles. Tyler had to give him that. But after watching Eric maul Del today, he'd be a lot happier not to have to fight off Xander, too.

A moment later, a pristine black limousine pulled up. A beautiful woman with pale hair in a professional twist and a skirt so short it was nearly illegal exited the vehicle and opened the back door for them. "Mr. Santiago."

"Karissa." Xander nodded as he approached and dropped a hand on her ass. "Nice to see you."

The driver's expression didn't change, but her body softened. She leaned closer. Clearly, the guy got around a lot.

Tyler grabbed Del's hand and led her inside. A moment later, he transferred their few pieces of luggage and other personal belongings into the limo and abandoned the car. He climbed in to find Xander handing Del a glass of champagne.

"What the hell are we celebrating?" Tyler asked.

Xander's mobile phone began ringing. "That you're about to disappear until you're good and ready for Carlson to find you."

"You know him?" Del demanded.

"Not personally, but nothing I hear is good. I've got my network digging." Xander pressed a button on his phone with a sigh. "Javier, I've been on the ground for less than twenty minutes. What?"

Tyler did his best to zone out on Xander's conversation. He looped an arm around Del's shoulders and pulled her into him. They sank together into the buttery leather seats. The anonymity that the tinted windows provided should have made Tyler relax a little, but the need to pound something or someone was still jacking with his mood.

Fuck, he had to put a lid on it. Del didn't need more aggression now.

"You okay?" he whispered to her.

She nodded. "Long, tough day."

"I'm here for you, whatever you need."

Del turned and slanted those blue eyes at him, dark like an endless sea. He fought back the urge to tear off her panties, plant his head between her legs, and make her come until next week. She looked a bit like she wanted to argue about his commitment—or lack thereof—again, and Tyler steeled himself, tamped down his anger. Did she not understand that after the showdown with Eric and getting a sweet taste of her mouth, he was on an adrenaline high?

"No," Xander insisted into the phone. "You don't need another liter of vodka. You need to get your head out of your ass. Christ, it's barely five o'clock in the afternoon." He paused, listened. "I know that I'm your brother, not your fucking keeper. But you have to accept that. Francesca is gone, and I'm sorry. But she was bad for you. You need to move on."

The bite in the other man's tone made Tyler look up. So Mr. Perfect didn't have a perfect life after all.

Xander grimaced with concern and gripped the phone. "I'll be there in an hour. Just . . . don't do anything. Promise me." He breathed a sigh of relief. "I'm taking you to Látigo tonight. No arguments. You'll learn some self-discipline, even if I have to shove it down your throat."

Látigo? Tyler knew enough Spanish from working for the LAPD to translate. It meant whip. Did that mean Xander intended to take his brother to a BDSM club? To train him as a Dom? He'd learned enough from listening to Jack, Hunter, and Logan over the last two years to suspect so.

The call ended, and Xander pocketed his phone. "Sorry."

"Everything all right with your brother?" Del asked. "I've read about his wife's disappearance. Has anyone seen her since that security footage captured her in Aruba?"

"Do you want to know as a reporter or a friend?" Xander challenged.

"She's just a kind person asking a question because she gives a shit," Tyler growled.

"I would never betray someone trying to help me stay alive, especially for a story." Del laid a gentle hand on Xander's.

Tyler tried not to see red and rip her away, then rearrange Xander's face beyond all recognition. That response might be overkill for the situation. Maybe.

"Not all of your brethren share your scruples." He sipped his champagne, then grimaced and set it aside. "Francesca was a headcase and a bitch, and Javier was too busy to rein her in, so she ran wild. He seems dead inside, and I don't know how to save him. But that's my problem. You have enough of your own."

Xander pasted on a stiff smile, and an uncomfortable silence filled the car as the limo driver headed east on I-10.

"Where are we going?" Tyler asked. He realized that he didn't sound terribly friendly, but he was having a hard time reversing that. The day had been awful. His mood was worse, and he needed to have Del all to himself, even if he did nothing more than cuddle her and reassure himself that she was safe and okay.

"I recently purchased a little place for some privacy. It's got nice views of the city. The deed is in a corporation's name. It keeps the press away." Xander leveled a stare at Del. "So even if anyone manages to connect you two to me, no one will be able to guess that you're there."

Again, he had all the angles covered. Tyler had to respect that.

Xander withdrew his phone again, dialed a number, and in less than three minutes, made the security cameras at the facility disappear for the next two days. Tyler wished he could pull that trick out of his bag. Money talked, and he supposed that since Xander's bank account equaled a small nation's GDP, he could probably shout with a bullhorn all day long.

Through the ever-heavy L.A. traffic, they wended their way up the 405 freeway, then disappeared into the very high-rent district, up in the hills. It wasn't long before a big wrought-iron gate opened. Lush bushes and flowers, along with well-placed trees, obscured whatever building lay beyond. Tyler had a feeling from the swank of the address alone and the size of the houses that this place would be anything but little.

The limo surged up the private driveway until a huge building came into view. The place was purely old Hollywood with a modern twist. A golden-hued stucco design with high arches, graceful porticos, and a shitload of windows. Palm trees, a lawn manicured within an inch of its life, and a natural stone fountain in the middle of the circular drive all screamed wealth. Del shrank back against him, looking a bit daunted. Hell, he'd grown up in a rusted trailer with a sagging floor and a single mother who chain smoked. What was he doing here?

Keeping Delaney safe. Tyler tightened his arm around her.

Xander tossed him a key. Tyler caught it in his fist.

"It's an old hotel that's been converted into eight units. You're in the penthouse. I've got to go deal with my brother," the other man said, clearly not looking forward to it. "Make yourselves at home. I'll check in with you as soon as I can."

"Thank you," Del said. "We'll get out of your hair quickly."

"Take all the time you need. I don't keep much of a staff here, just a part-time maid. She can cook in a pinch. I'll bunk with my brother. He probably needs the company. And if he gets on my nerves too much, the family house has sixteen bedrooms. I'm sure I can find one to suit me." Xander smiled faintly.

"I hope all goes well with Javier. Maybe a pep talk will—"

"He doesn't need a pep talk. He needs an intervention, and I'll have to find at least one other person on this planet who doesn't think he's a ruthless cutthroat and actually gives a shit if he lives before I can stage one." Xander sighed. "Stay safe. Call me if you need anything."

"Thanks, man." Tyler shook Xander's hand, but only because he hadn't tried too hard to seduce Del.

The driver opened the back door, and before Tyler could climb out, the woman had removed their bags from the trunk. Key in hand, Tyler hauled them inside, Del in tow. The limo, with Xander inside, pulled away.

Tyler paced during the slow, silent elevator ride to the top of the eight-story building. It was either that or rip Del's clothes off and impale her on his wretchedly hard cock. The thought just made him harder. Damn it, she didn't need to be attacked twice today.

Fresh off the elevator, he approached a wall covered in natural stone. He dragged their luggage across the floor lined with rich, dark hardwoods, then inserted the key into the lone door. A moment later, the latch gave way, and he pushed inside.

Tyler's jaw dropped. The hardwood floor extended into the unit, but the rest of the room was a stark, modern white—the walls, the plush sofas, the cushy throw rug. A pewter side table, a dark wicker ottoman, a brushed silver statute of a half-naked woman, her head thrown back in passion, filled the space. Yeah, there was a flat screen TV nearly as big as the wall itself, and in the distance, he saw a dining room and a kitchen, but the main attraction in this room was the nearly solid wall of windows that overlooked the city. The views were sick and went on forever. The place had to have cost millions.

Outside the French doors, a shaded terrace lined the back of the house. A mission-style table with chunky chairs and a built-in outdoor kitchen made the perfect place to enjoy the infinity edge pool. Wow, must be nice to finish laps and look out over the Wilshire District, see the city at work and play. It sure beat the hell out of the crappy apartment he'd had when he'd lived here.

"Oh my God," Del breathed behind him. "Is it wrong that I want to swim in that pool?"

"No." Hell, if she was getting in the water, Tyler wanted to get in with her—and do a whole lot more than swim.

Damn it, he had to stop thinking about sex. It wasn't going to happen tonight. She needed some time, and he needed to get that through his thick skull.

"We'll swim tonight, if you want."

"I didn't bring a bathing suit."

And just like that, Tyler got even harder. If his T-shirt wasn't covering that up, it'd be fucking obvious for sure.

"Another reason to wait until dark. Cuts down on the possibility of any sort of aerial surveillance."

"Didn't think of that." She looked shaken. "I should focus on the case, anyway. I need to spend some time jotting down all the details I can remember so I can go back to some of my key informants and interview them again."

Bright, driven, dedicated—everything about Del just made Tyler want her more. "Are you up for that?"

She shrugged. "I have to be."

Good point.

"I'll be right back," he murmured and took the luggage down the unit's main hallway.

After a quick glance through the rest of the rooms, Tyler found one guest bed and bathroom, a fully stocked home gym, a home office, and a locked door on one side of the hall. On the other, a master suite, complete with the most opulent bathroom he'd ever seen and more endless city views. He set their luggage in the room. She might want to sleep alone, but that wasn't happening. He'd do his damndest not to touch her until she was no longer shaken by Eric's rough treatment, but he wasn't leaving her in another room without protection.

Ambling back down the hall, he found Del standing in front of the windows, her arms wrapped around her like she was cold. She stared out into the afternoon, her profile looking pensive.

Tyler walked up behind her, wanting so badly to touch her, wishing her shirt would melt away with his touch and leave nothing behind but her beautiful bare skin. He dug his fingers into his thighs. "Hungry?"

"No. I peeked in the kitchen. I don't see the maid, but the fridge is stocked, if you are."

He was, but it could wait. "You look dead on your feet. I know the case is important, but why don't you lie down for a few minutes? Rest. There's a huge bed and blackout drapes. I'm sure the thread count on the sheets is probably north of a million."

A little smile lifted the corners of her lips. Fuck, he wanted to kiss her again. No, that wasn't it. He wanted to possess that mouth. Own it. Have the right to take it in whatever way and at any time he wanted. He blew out a breath.

This whole "sex for the duration" thing wasn't going to work. Tyler saw no scenario in which he walked away from Del at the end of all this and left her alone to raise their son. His mother might have believed deep in her bones that he was the kind of man to abandon his family, like his own father. But he didn't want to be that same scumbag. And he didn't want to let Del go, leave her free to fall in love with another man who would put a ring on her finger and plant more children in her womb.

Oh fuck, even the thought of it made him violent. Not that he'd been far away from that feeling since leaving Eric's.

"What are you going to do?"

Bleed off some of his pent-up energy and frustration. "I think I'll go pound the treadmill and the weight machine down the hall."

Del turned to him, wearing a little probing frown that made him feel like she was trying to crawl into his head. "Would you hold me, Tyler?"

His entire body tensed at her suggestion. Of course. The problem was, would he stop there? Somehow, he had to find the fucking will.

"Sure." He wrapped an arm around her waist, filtering his other hand into her hair, as he held her in what he hoped was a gesture of comfort—and kept enough distance between her body and his pike-hard dick.

"How's your wrist?"

Hell, he hadn't thought about it since they'd left Eric's. He lifted his arm and glanced. The blood had dried. It would leave a nasty scab and a shitty scar for a while, but he'd deal. "I'll wash it up later."

"You were worried about me," she whispered.

"Of course. I didn't know what the motherfucker was going to do to you. He's not the same guy I was partners with."

"Eric came on strong and acted like a total ass. I— It surprised me," she admitted. "It all seemed so surreal. I never imagined that the man I married would actually hurt me."

"Yeah? He strapped me to the refrigerator and made me watch him paw you. I wanted to kill the son of a bitch. I still might."

"Then . . . I kicked him in the balls, and it was like shutting down his penis turned on his conscience. Or like the pain finally pierced through his anger. I still don't understand."

"I don't, either, angel. I'm just glad you fought back, and that he didn't do more." And all this talk wasn't going to help her forget. He opened his arms to her. "Come here."

Del burrowed closer to him, nestling right against his erection. She froze. He closed his eyes. *Busted.*

"Your entire body is . . . tense."

Tyler tried to take a deep breath and relax. The last thing he needed to do was scare her. She'd had enough of that today.

But the tension wouldn't ease. Tucked in the corner, he saw a sleek, marbled wet bar. A new bottle of Cîroc vodka sat on the counter. His name was all over that. Tonight, after she'd gone to bed . . . Yeah, that was his. A five-mile run on the treadmill, a quick session or two with his hand wrapped around his dick, and that bottle might bring him down enough so that he didn't pounce on Del the second she got supine. At least he hoped so.

* * *

TYLER backed away from her, and Del frowned. He was so tense, he was pinging. Jumpy. Hard everywhere.

"Where can I settle you before I hit the treadmill?"

She started to tell him not to bother before she realized what Tyler was saying without saying it. He'd been tense since the encounter with Eric. He was buzzing with leftover adrenaline. After a lot of action on the job, Eric had often wanted to run, fight . . . or fuck.

Swallowing, she stared. That was it. He needed to release this tension, and he was willing to put that aside and take his aggression out on the home gym, rather than risk upsetting her. Something inside her melted.

Yes, she had to resume work on this case today, but Tyler needed her right now. After the way he'd turned himself inside out to help her since she'd shown up on his doorstep, she wanted to give to him in return. And she wanted to replace the ugly memory of Eric's pawing with Tyler's touch.

"How about the bed?" she suggested.

She saw a muscle in his jaw tic, but he nodded, then gestured her down the hallway. Del walked slowly, aware of his hot gaze all over her backside. Purposely, she swayed her hips as she made her way into the master bedroom. Maybe she should be more afraid of being near a man as keyed up as Tyler after Eric's crap earlier today, but she knew Tyler would cut off his arm before hurting her.

A huge king-sized bed dominated the space, done up in cream and chocolate, with a floor-to-ceiling studded, padded headboard towering over the bed. Two sleek nightstands flanked the bed, their modern lines almost stark, but the warm tone of the wood saved the room from being sterile.

In the corner, a big barrel-backed chair in a welcoming gold tone rested, framed by more warm wood. Del turned away from Tyler, peeled off her T-shirt, and draped it over the back. A quick flick of her hand later, and her bra dropped to the ground.

Behind her, Tyler sucked in a breath.

God, the tension in the air between them was thick and buzzing. It flew across her skin, hovering, leaving tingles dancing all over her body. Her blood sang. Already, her panties were embarrassingly damp.

Tyler did this to her every time. Made her feel desired, womanly. Whole and perfect.

She reached for the snap of her jeans. Suddenly, he was behind her, grabbing her wrists in a grip just shy of painful.

"Don't," he snapped.

Del looked at him over her shoulder. His face was taut, mouth compressed. A vein bulged in his temple. He crowded her personal space, and no way she could miss that erection against the curve of her ass.

She locked gazes with him, looking him right in the eyes. "Come to bed with me."

His nostrils flared. His grip tightened a fraction. "You don't know what you're inviting."

"You're on a ledge. You need to come down. Let me give you what you need."

Instantly, he released her and turned away. "It's a bad idea, and I don't want a pity fuck."

"I don't pity you, Tyler. I desire you."

He shook his head and stared out over the city, resolutely not looking at her. "Don't think that spreading your legs for me is some sort of Band-Aid for my foul mood. I want you, too, but not like this. Not after what Eric put you through. Let me bleed off this frustration some other way."

She didn't reply, just doffed her jeans and panties.

Del doubted Tyler could fail to hear the rustle of her clothes. His stance squared, his ramrod spine straightened further. Even with his feet slightly spread apart, nothing about the way he stood looked casual. He was keeping himself together with a teeny thread of self-control. She wanted all that passion unraveled and directed at her. She wanted to ease him, be what he needed. Now wasn't the time to examine why. If she did, it would probably scare the hell out of her. For now, it was enough just to be here for him.

On quiet feet, Del made her way across the rich Berber carpet.

She grabbed a handful of Tyler's T-shirt and pulled slightly, revealing that place where the cords of his neck smoothed, then flared again into the bulge of his shoulder. She put her lips there. He tensed even more beneath her mouth.

"Tyler . . ." she breathed.

He clenched his fists. "After what Eric put you through, you deserve tenderness. I can't be gentle right now."

She nipped at his ear and pressed her breasts against his back. "Come to bed."

"Jesus, Del!" Tyler turned, backed away. "I'm telling you flat out that . . ."

His voice trailed off as his gaze trekked all over her body before settling between her legs. He swallowed hard, then met his stare. The look he drilled her with was so hungry, her pussy tightened. Need throbbed.

She pressed a hand into her fluttering stomach, then eased it down, down, until she settled her fingertips over her clit and rubbed in slow, soft circles. Tyler's gaze latched on, unblinking, transfixed. Burning.

For once, Del felt not just sexy but powerful. She had no doubt this man wanted her badly. Sex with Eric had been erratic and often somewhat meh. Most times, when she'd instigated, he'd blown her off with something between dismissal and annoyance. Not so with Tyler. She was getting to him. And when he unleashed his dark side . . . The thought made her shiver.

"Please, Tyler." She closed her eyes and tossed her head back, slowly driving herself insane with a teasing touch.

He ate it up with his stare. Del could feel his gaze fused to hers. She dared a peek at him. His fists were clenched, his breathing ragged. He looked ready to explode.

"Fuck!" Tyler bellowed as he took a ground-eating step toward her. He grabbed her wrist and pulled her hand away from her clit. "If I hurt you, you goddamn tell me."

She nodded.

"Promise me," he demanded. "Say it out loud."

"Of course. I—"

Del didn't get a chance to say more before Tyler shoved her wet fingers into his mouth. He licked, groaned—and it broke open everything he'd been holding inside.

He lifted her and lunged to the nearest wall, shoving her against it. "I've got to have your pussy, Del. It's mine. To taste, to fondle. To fuck. Mine."

Those green eyes of his drilled into her, and her heartbeat tripped, then picked up speed. Her nipples beaded. He seemed to be waiting for some response, so she nodded. In an hour, she'd be her own person again, and he'd back off. But now, she'd be what he needed.

Primal satisfaction crossed his face. His nostrils flared. Then he reached down and wrapped an arm around each of her thighs and lifted her up, back sliding against the wall.

"Tyler?"

"Mine," he growled in answer.

The next thing Del knew, he'd hoisted her thighs over his shoulders, wedging her back high against the wall. He aligned her pussy with his mouth. His intentions became crystal clear.

In this position, she had no leverage, no way to move. No control.

"Tyler."

He didn't reply. Instead, he swooped forward and latched onto her wet flesh, his tongue unerringly flicking her clit. Del gasped. Sensation wound through her instantly, hot, drugging. She felt so alive and aware. He gripped her so tightly, she wondered if she'd bruise. The two days' growth of whiskers on his cheeks abraded her inner thighs with every plunge of his tongue. His breath on her folds was hot, rough as he latched onto her, totally unrelenting, and ate her like a ripe fruit, nipping at the flesh before licking up the drops of nectar that flowed freely.

Her orgasm built so quickly. He hadn't kissed her, hadn't touched her anywhere else. Before this, she would never have believed that she could be this aroused this quickly without more seduction. But the absolute insistence in Tyler's demand ramped her up. Her thoughts clouded over as more pleasure rushed in. She gasped, flattened her hands against the wall, and let it happen.

When he speared his tongue inside her, Del couldn't help but clamp down on him.

"Come for me." He laved her clit, then shoved his tongue deep again.

The disparity of sensations, the stimulation of so many nerves nearly at once, sent her spiraling closer to release.

She wailed as everything built. Her legs stiffened, her breathing grew erratic, and under it all, she was weeping, dying. This orgasm was going to roll over her, harsh and insistent, and leave her shaken to her core. But Tyler wanted it now. Demanded it. Del was helpless to do anything but give it to him.

The tension rose, tightened. Everything between her legs throbbed with need. Then Tyler nipped at her clit and sucked it into his mouth again mercilessly. She let go with a scream.

Waves of pleasure crashed over her like lightning, fierce and mind robbing. Del's cries echoed through the big penthouse, filling her ears in an endless stream of desire that left her panting and spent.

Tyler wasn't about to slow down. Her orgasm didn't pacify him at all. If anything, it revved him up more, and he ate at her with even more hunger.

"Again," he demanded.

"I—I can't. Oh God." Her womb continued to pulse with every flick and caress of his tongue.

"Bullshit." Everything about him told Del that he intended to prove her wrong.

"Too much. Too fast," she panted.

"Take it," he growled. "Tell me to go the fuck away or take it."

"Don't go." She'd die if he left her now.

Without hesitation, Tyler lapped at her again and again, and his unrelenting attention to her clit became a pleasure so sharp, it was almost pain. She balanced on the edge, whimpering. Del reached out for something to claw, but he'd positioned her so that she was powerless to move or do nothing except allow his head between her legs, his tongue on her aching flesh. She could only feel. God, no way she could avoid that.

The sensations he forced on her grew, multiplied. They ratcheted up higher than anything she'd ever imagined, much less felt. Every breath, every lick of his tongue, every scrape of his teeth magnified inside her. And still she hurtled toward ecstasy with no end in sight.

She let loose a keening cry. "Tyler!"

"That's it, Del." Primal satisfaction rang in his tone. "You've swelled so sweetly. Like eating a ripe fucking peach. Feed me more. Come again."

Her body stiffened, jerked. She slapped the wall behind her, flailing helplessly as the pleasure rolled over and over her. It coiled inside her so tightly, her stomach cramped. She whimpered again. But there was no way she could resist his command.

The orgasm didn't just seize Del; it flattened her. Devastating. Destructive. The breath left her body. Her heart roared, stopped, then started beating hard and deep. And the pleasure of it, dear God . . . She gasped, then screamed until her voice gave out. And still she cried out silently, nails clawing the wall. The ecstasy gripped her ruthlessly, shaking her body, stunning her.

Finally, the pulses slowed, giving her a moment to catch her breath. Thoughts gradually returned. Del felt exhausted, heavy and boneless.

Tyler trembled as he shrugged her legs off his shoulders and set her on her feet. She didn't have to worry about supporting herself, though. He pressed her against the wall and grabbed her face in his hands, locking her stare onto his.

The need she saw screaming there made her heart jump and something that felt too much like desire pulse behind her clit again.

She didn't bother begging for mercy. He wouldn't have any, and she'd invited him to do his worst. Right now, that's exactly what she wanted.

He tangled his fingers into the hair framing her face, then slanted his mouth over hers, taking complete possession, tongue plunging deep. She tasted herself on his lips, along with his frantic desire. With their lips fused together, he inhaled sharply, as if he could breathe her in, while he gripped her tighter. Her nipples chafed against his T-shirt, and she felt drunk on the euphoria of two massive orgasms and the promise of more.

She wrapped her arms around him and clung. Tyler took and took, devouring her, grabbing her ass, and pulling her tightly to him. He pumped his cock right against her mound, rhythmic and hard. Instantly, Del felt empty. Her sex clenched with the craving to be full of him.

She dug her fingers into his shoulders, tiny whimpers of need escaping her as she raised her legs around his waist and ground against that monster erection of his.

"I'm sorry." His voice sounded rough, like someone had ripped out his voice box, ran it through a blender, then shoved it back in.

"F-for what?"

Tyler didn't answer. He merely tore her limbs away from him, grabbed her by the hips, and turned her around. Before Del knew what was happening, Tyler jerked her to the bed and bent her over the mattress. She heard the rasp of his zipper, the rustle of denim, the rip of foil. He shoved his fingers into her hair, fisting at her nape, and lifted her head. No way Del could miss his hard cock sliding between her thighs as he leaned over her. "Last chance. Do you want me to stop?"

Chapter Thirteen

"N-NO." Delaney couldn't keep her voice from shaking. "I want you. Inside me. Please."

Tyler nipped at her earlobe, then shoved her hair out of his way and pressed kisses up her neck. "Even a please. So fucking sexy."

The pleasure evident in his voice suffused her with longing and a strange sense of pride. He wanted her. Yes, he'd had sex with a lot of women, but everything about his behavior told Del that the intensity of his want was totally new even to him. Until now, he'd always loved 'em and left 'em. Yet he'd told her over and over that he'd be by her side. She doubted that he'd ever said that to a woman before.

Del didn't know why he'd gone so far out of his way to help her. Maybe he had more feelings for her than she'd imagined. God, she feared that she wasn't just falling in love with Tyler again, but plummeting. She didn't know where she'd bottom out and find stable ground.

"Now," she pleaded.

Del wriggled her hips back at him, and he hissed in a breath. His fist tightened in her hair.

"Take me, angel. Every fucking inch I've got. It's all for you."

He positioned himself at her weeping entrance and pushed in, a steady, forward drive that made her flesh burn as she rapidly stretched to accommodate his thick cock. He bumped against her narrow walls, stopped. Del tried to relax and let him in, but he felt huge. He was barely inside her, but the fire and yearning to have him fill her made her whole body tighten in anticipation. Nothing felt like taking Tyler deep.

"Angel, let me in. Fuck." His palm trailed fire down one of her hips. "Please."

Del took a deep breath and tried to focus on relaxing and releasing her muscles to open herself up for him. Tyler pressed in again, this time sliding smoothly into her farther, deeper, faster, until his hips rested against her ass and he filled her completely.

"Ah, yeah. That's it. Like a hot knife through butter." He tightened his grip on her and groaned. "All wet and all mine. Aren't you? Tell me you're mine."

His demand made Del clench down on his cock. But it also went straight to her heart. She nodded and whimpered.

"Say it," he whispered. "Say it for me now, and I'll make you feel so good."

The admission he sought to extract was a just a mirage, but the fantasy of having Tyler all to herself, of him wanting her to be exclusively his, was too sweet to resist.

"I'm yours," she choked out.

"That's right, angel," he breathed in her ear. "I've ached for you all day. I'm dying to see you come again, this time on my cock."

The burn of his desire turned her on. She wondered if he'd ever been this intent or possessive before. What they shared was supposed to be just sex, but it felt far deeper. His every touch and word seemed designed to bind them together. But she knew he might not be truly ready to jump in and be a full-time husband or father. She might never be ready for the commitment thing again. So she'd accept some money from him for Seth's college fund someday. And she'd take this irresistible desire now.

When he withdrew, Del held her breath. She wasn't disappointed. He thrust in again with slow, ruthless power, awakening every nerve ending of her slick sex. She whimpered, clutching the covers in her fists. God, he'd barely gotten inside her, and the burning urge for climax was already disintegrating her. No other man had absolutely mastered her body the way Tyler had.

"I need more!" she panted.

"In good time, angel. I'm not racing through this. No way. I'm here to stay, and I'm going to wring every drop of pleasure from you. I'm going to pound you until you scream again and again. After I've come, I'm only going to want to do it all once more."

Conviction rang in his tone. He exuded something so primal and male as he demanded total surrender from her. Beneath him, Del trembled and shuddered.

He withdrew almost completely from her body again before driving deep once more. His thrusts were controlled but remorseless. Then his fingers cupped her mound possessively, honing in on her clit. She gasped.

"Perfect, angel. You're all tight and wet around me. I'm never giving this up, you know that? I'll do whatever it takes to get inside this pussy every day and give you so much pleasure you'll never think about walking away from me again."

God, when he said things like that, Del wondered how she'd ever work up the will to let him go. She should probably write off his words. They were spoken in passion, after all. But the woman inside her who yearned for him wanted to lap those words up greedily.

As his fingers swept over her sensitive clit once more, Del melted. If he kept touching her like this, how the hell would she ever disentangle herself from Tyler once the danger had passed? Having not just someone to lean on these last few days but a man she genuinely trusted had been nothing short of a godsend. He'd taken so much off her shoulders and put them onto his own, for no other reason than to keep her safe and make her feel protected. How could she not appreciate that? Not fall for that?

But what would happen once they returned to real life? She'd still be a mom and busy reporter in Los Angeles. He'd still be doing who knew what in Lafayette . . . and probably nailing a bevy of easy women. They'd never work, no matter how tantalizing the fantasy.

Tyler caressed his way up her body until his hands cupped her breasts, fingers toying with her nipples. He leaned over her, as if he wanted to join not just bodies, but skin, breaths, souls. Del closed her eyes.

In and out, he moved with ruthless control—and maximum devastation. Every stroke into her body awakened more nerves, and the ramp-up to orgasm began to overtake her body, shut down her thoughts.

He thumbed her nipples, and they beaded for him. She felt the blood rush through her body like a heady cocktail. And just like if she were drunk, the sensations overloaded her. Nothing mattered in this moment but Tyler and connecting with him.

"I feel you everywhere," she whimpered. "God . . ."

"Good, angel." He kissed his way up her shoulders, to her neck. "I feel you, too. Every fucking perfect bit of you surrounding me. Are you going to come for me again?"

With anyone else, that would have been practically impossible. With Tyler, it was inevitable. It was like her body was hardwired to his, like he knew all the right buttons to push. Like every touch between them was magic.

No sense in teasing him or drawing this out. He had to feel the way her sex clamped down on him. Her breathing turned erratic again. She reached behind her and clutched at his thigh.

"Yes. I don't know how, but . . ."

"Because we're good together, angel. Always have been." He brushed rough palms down her body again, then settled his fingers over her clit once more. "Give me everything. I need it."

No way could she deny him. The pleasure surged and grew, seizing and spiraling. She couldn't breathe, couldn't think, couldn't stop herself from letting go.

Del didn't just come undone in his arms, she shattered. And Tyler was there to catch her, holding her together with his embrace and his growled encouragements.

"So good, angel. Oh, fuck yes. That's it. No one feels like you."

Every emotion inside her poured out, spilled over onto him. She grabbed his arm, held it to her chest like she never wanted to let go, and rode out the wave of her pleasure.

When it was over, she felt raw and hollow and frighteningly exposed. Del could almost feel her heart reaching out, trying to attach itself to his. She took a deep breath and reminded herself that her feelings were hers and hers alone. Regardless of what he said—or even believed at the moment—Tyler had never been built for forever. He'd changed, no denying that. But how could he become the sort of man who suddenly practiced fidelity in a handful of days?

God, she had to protect herself. She had to find some way to keep from falling in love so deeply that once this was over and they parted ways, she wouldn't be a flattened, crushed shell.

She wriggled away and made it across the bed, turning over to plaster on what she prayed looked like a cheery smile. And Del hoped like hell he couldn't see that, inside, her heart was on the verge of breaking.

* * *

THE uninhibited bliss of Del's climax slid over Tyler's senses, and he clenched every muscle in his body to keep himself from following her over. The urge to join her in ecstasy was so strong, but he wasn't done with her, not even close. He wanted to spend half the night inside of her—at least.

But the second her orgasm swept past, Del moved away from him. Not just physically—across the bed wasn't that far—but her guarded eyes, her body language, the way she crossed her arms over her chest and curled her legs in front of her, hiding that sweet pussy from him—it all had him gritting his teeth. And if that smile was any more plastic, the folks at Tupperware would pull her aside for a chat.

Distance. Tyler recognized what she was trying to put between them immediately. He'd played this game with countless other women once they'd bored him. He knew how to read the signals. She'd probably be willing to do whatever it took to get him to come quickly—then she'd end all intimacy between them and try to act like this didn't mean anything.

Bullshit.

"Come here," he demanded.

Del frowned, a furrow appearing between her dark brows. "I'm right here, silly."

"Back where you were, angel. Right in front of me, bent over to give me that pretty pussy and ass. Where you can't hide from me."

She froze. "I—I'm not hiding."

He raised a brow at her. She was a terrible fucking liar. "Then you won't mind coming back here and giving yourself to me again."

Del glanced at his dead-serious face, the hard rise and fall of his chest as he took deep breaths and struggled for calm, then down to the hard stalk of his cock that stood tall and thick and beyond ready.

Patiently, he sat back and watched her decide. Finally, she crawled back across the bed to him, then stopped without turning around. "Do you want me on my back?"

Tempting, but . . . "No." He wanted her absolutely vulnerable, where she couldn't see what he was doing but would have to simply trust him.

She bit her lip. Tyler saw her tension rise. He made her nervous. She had good reason to be. A faint smile fell across his mouth. He wasn't playing her bullshit game. He planned to get closer than ever and make her feel him in a way she never had. So she'd never again doubt that he meant to have all of her, now and always.

Still, she hesitated. "I'm, um, sore."

Stunning that she'd lie simply to put distance between them. Definitely, he had to fucking address that now.

"I'll keep that in mind. Turn around, Del."

She swallowed. "Can't we take a shower? It will ease my muscles, and I can, um, suck you."

Nice offer, but far more impersonal than what he had in mind. "Either come back here, in the position I've indicated, or tell me what the hell is really bothering you. Because I haven't fucked you enough to be sore. When I have, you'll feel it."

Del hesitated, debated, then took a breath to steel herself. Then she turned around, bent over, with her ass exposed and her pussy looking all swollen, wet, and vulnerable.

Knowing a bit about Xander, Tyler suspected he'd find exactly what he needed in the nightstand drawer. Silently, he padded over and opened it. *Bingo!* Grabbing it quickly, he stood behind Del again. She looked over her shoulder at him with vulnerable blue eyes.

"Talk to me, angel."

She blinked, and the look was gone. "Nothing to say."

More crap. There was plenty left unsaid, and if she didn't want talk now, they'd get to it soon.

In the meantime . . . Tyler unscrewed the cap on the tube in his hand and squeezed out a healthy dose of lube, realizing this could backfire on him in a major way. They hadn't discussed anal sex, and she had no experience with it. But he had more than enough to know that no act was more intimate. She'd be allowing him where no other man had been. And she'd feel every inch of him inside her, all through her. She wouldn't know how to counter the pleasure or put up barriers between them. He'd strip away all this fronting and get strictly to him and her and whatever she was trying to hide.

He slathered the lube on his cock with one hand, then grabbed her hair in his fist with the other. "I told you we were going to do things my way. I want this. I want to give this to you. I want you to feel it because I intend to make sure this is unlike any experience you've ever had. And when it's over, we're going to talk, and you're going to tell me whatever is in that head of yours that you're hiding from me."

Before she could deny it again, he rubbed the rest of the lube on his fingers across the untried rosette of her ass.

Finally understanding, Del gasped. "Tyler, I don't—"

"You haven't yet," he corrected. "But you will. Because you can, and there's no reason to hold back from me, angel. I'm going to make it so good for you."

To bring his point home, he pressed one finger into her back entrance. She gasped. Her hips wriggled. Trying to seat him deeper or dislodge him? He wasn't sure, but the result was that his entire finger slid all the way into her hot depths.

Fuck, she felt beyond hot and tight. He wasn't going to last long once he got his cock in there, but it was going to be one sweet ride. Nothing ever felt like Del, and knowing that he was the first—and the last—man to take her this intimately was going to blow the top of his head off.

He withdrew for a moment, then pressed two fingers inside her ass. Del didn't gasp this time. She moaned, a little involuntary animal sound of pleasure.

"It's going to feel even better when it's my cock back here, angel.

You think you feel every touch now? Just wait. I'm going to fuck you so deep and slow, there's no way you're going to be able to deny the pleasure. You'll absolutely feel every inch of me, totally joined with you."

And he was going to use every weapon he had to get under her defenses, strip her bare, and overcome her objections. As far as he was concerned, he'd tear down a cement wall with his bare hands to get to her. Whatever emotional barriers she was trying to erect now should be no match for his determination.

Slowly, he slid his hand out of her hair, caressing his way down her spine, circling her waist, before he slid over her belly, then between her thighs to rub her tender, swollen flesh. She might be slightly sore, but more than anything, she was needy. Her cunt wept, and when he put his fingers over her clit, her body leapt to life, bucking. She tossed her head back, and the spill of her dark hair across her skin, almost to her ass, turned him on even more. Everything about this woman—her intelligence and determination, the way she loved his son unconditionally, the fact that she represented home for him—all made her downright perfect.

With his right hand, he lined his cock up with her little rosette and gently pushed in until his head began to breach her tissue.

"Tyler." Her body went taut, and she was already clawing the sheets.

It was nerves, not pain. He hadn't tried to push past the tight ring of her muscle. Yet.

"Relax, angel. I'm not going to hurt you."

She was panting. "You're big. And you're going to get too deep."

Tyler heard the fear in her voice, and he caressed her hip, trying to gentle her. "Yeah, I'm going to get deep. Very deep. But there's no such thing as too deep, angel." He pressed his hand into the small of her back. "Arch for me."

She succumbed to his demand, and he focused on his cock

sinking into her body. He parted the cheeks of her ass with his fingers and watched her body slowly accept him.

Finally, the thick ridge of his flesh encountered the barrier of her tight muscles. Tyler pressed his thumbs across her tense lower back, then caressed her hips again. "Relax. Just take a deep breath and push out."

To entice her, he brushed his fingertips across her clit again. She gasped instantly and arched a bit more. The action opened her up just enough that the head of his cock slipped past that tight ring. After a little scream of panic, she gasped long and low. Fuck, she was like a burning vise, pressing in from all sides with a heat he'd never known.

Forcing himself to move slowly, he penetrated her, sliding down, down, down into the tightest recesses of her body. Beneath him, her head thrashed, and she clawed at the sheets.

"Hurt, angel?" He paused immediately and waited, swirling a little friction against her clit to keep her pleasure high.

"Yes. No. More. God, more!"

A feral smile stretched across his face, and he finished burrowing his cock in her backside. A giant rush of air filled her lungs. Her body tensed as she screeched out in a sound of pleasure unlike anything he'd ever heard.

"It's okay, angel. I'm in. All the way in. Now it's just going to feel good."

She nodded frantically. "Now! Please. More. Everything."

Del was completely with him, thinking only about the pleasure coursing through her body, not about protecting her heart. He wasn't about to risk hurting her, so he couldn't fuck her too hard, but he'd definitely give her something to scream about.

Tyler picked up the pace a bit, experimentally withdrawing and plunging into her. Tight. Silken. Perfect. And all his. He draped his body over her back. The sheen of perspiration across her skin merged with the sweat beginning to dampen his. This wasn't going to be a simple, gentle ride. The more she felt, the more she'd fight. The more he'd have to hold on. And he was determined to do exactly that.

He circled her clit with his fingers again and settled his chin in the crook of her neck so he could whisper in her ear, "Angel, I'm going to stay right here, keep after you so deep and hard until you come for me like you never have. You're going to take me here, just like this, until you let go for me."

Her panting grew rougher.

"Understand?" he prompted.

"Yes. Yes!" she screamed as he put a bit more force behind his thrust.

Jesus, the pleasure staggered him. Lightning shot down his spine. Electricity gathered in his balls. Inside, a perfect storm of need, possessiveness, and love brewed. He wanted to claim her, mark her, leave her—and every other man on the planet—absolutely no doubt who she belonged to.

He worked his fingers a bit faster over her clit. Del responded, thrusting her body back at him, taking his cock even deeper in her ass. God, he couldn't stand it. He absolutely needed more of her, needed her against him.

Tyler stood tall, lifting her torso upright until her back rested against his chest. Her nipples stabbed the air, and he trailed a hand up to them, pinching one, then the other. Instead of trying to get away, she reached behind her and clasped her hands around his head, sinking her fingers into his hair.

With a last brush against her nipples, he latched onto her hip and drove into her even faster, even deeper. "Take me. Every bit. All the way inside, angel."

"Yes." She gyrated back on him, and the slap of their flesh together was frantic, intimate. "I need more."

He pumped inside her in a measured, relentless pace and watched her skin flush, her muscles begin to tense and quiver. Her breathing grew erratic. Another brush of his fingers over her nipples told him they were harder than he'd ever felt. Her pussy was so swollen and dripping.

As much as he wanted to just lose himself in the pleasure, now was the time to press his advantage.

"Just when you think we're done here, I'm going to fuck you again. And again. Until you admit that we're good together and beg me to never stop."

"Yes. God, yes." She turned her head to press frantic kisses across his jaw.

"Not just sexually," he growled. "We're good, period. We've got something, and it's more than lust, angel. Isn't it?"

Del thrust back on him again. "Please. Don't talk. I just need . . ."

"You need *it*? Or you need *me*?"

She nipped at his neck, then pinched her own nipples. The sight nearly undid Tyler. Goddamn, everything about her was so beautiful, so sexual, yet so familiar and sweet. He'd always been able to walk away from anything or anyone. He'd done it once for Del because she'd asked him. Never fucking happening again.

No matter how much it killed him or how much restraint it cost, he had to show her that he meant business. He froze and clutched her hips, not allowing her to move. He was still lodged deep inside her, but not moving, not touching her sensitive little clit, now so hard it was a ticking time bomb.

"Tyler!" she screeched, her body bucking frantically.

"Answer the question," he growled in her ear. "Is it just sex, angel? Or is it me?"

"Why are you doing this?" she demanded, trying to gyrate on him, sliding her fingers over her clit.

With one hand, he grabbed her wrist and held it away from her body. With the other, he exuded an iron grip on her hip, keeping her still.

"That cheap orgasm you're trying to steal isn't going to make you feel half as good as I can, and you know it. Answer the fucking question."

Her pants turned to sobs, and the starch left her body. Tyler had to hold her to keep her against him, keep his breath in her ear to remind her that he wasn't going anywhere.

"You, damn you. It's always you. Is that what you wanted to hear?"

The accusation in her voice was a knife to the chest, but she'd been completely honest. Tyler had no doubt about that. Now that he'd wrung the truth from her, he had to please her, gentle her, complete her.

"Yeah, angel. It's always you for me. From the first minute I touched you, it was always you. Every other day and every other minute, I was marking time. No one else ever meant a damn thing. But you haunted me. The moment you knocked on my door in Lafayette, you sealed your fate. There's no way I'm letting you get away from me again." He might not know a damn thing about commitment firsthand, but he wasn't letting his mother's bitter voice crawl up in his head and fuck this up. He was determined to work it out and keep her. "Now move with me."

Tyler withdrew slowly and inched in once more, his pace maddening. Beneath him, Del released a string of short, stuttering gasps, each one higher-pitched than the last. Her body tensed again.

He slid his fingers over her clit again. "We're going to come together. And you're not going to hold anything back. Afterward, you're going to fall into my arms and kiss me with all the emotion racing through you. I'm going to kiss you back with the same intensity."

Then he lowered her to the bed, covering her body with his

own, and shoved a pillow under her hips. Tyler gripped the edge of the bed and used his grip as leverage to fill her in agonizingly slow, deep strokes. Under him, Del melted, and he linked the fingers of one hand with hers, splayed across the mattress. The other hand, he fitted against her clit. Every stroke into her rubbed that bundle of nerves into his hand.

Soon, her gasps became sobs. She tightened under him, around him, moving recklessly with him, taking him completely. There was nothing between them now but shared breaths, passion, heartbeats, unspoken emotion, and the glittering promise of satisfaction.

"Give it to me, angel. Come for me."

She shook her head. "It's too big. It's going to wipe me out."

"I'll be here for you," he crooned. "Give yourself to me."

He pushed into her again. With every breath, he got behind each thrust. He poured everything he felt into her, held nothing back. Against his hand, her clit hardened unbearably. She stood at the edge of the cliff and held her breath, just waiting for the right touch, the perfect penetration. Tyler was right there with her, feeling the electric tingle of orgasm brewing in his balls, everything inside him gripping, coiling. Motherfucker, this was going to be huge.

"Now!" he demanded.

And he plowed into her hard, deep, fast, no stopping, no holding back, no mercy.

Under him, Del cried out, a guttural moan that sounded torn from her chest. She jolted, shuddered, and clamped down on him in a long, strong pull of muscles around his cock that sent him hurtling into a pleasure so intense, Tyler couldn't hear anything but the roaring of his heart. The switch flipped inside him, and he unleashed the last of his restraint, releasing jet after jet of semen. Spots danced before his eyes, and his entire body stiffened as he emptied everything he had and was inside her.

Finally, he found his ability to breathe. His mind kicked back online a few seconds later, and he found Del shuddering and sobbing underneath him.

Fear kicking him, he gingerly withdrew and threw the condom in the nearest bin. Then he rolled Del into his arms and looked down at her with a frown of worry. She wasn't hurt, but her blue eyes were a sea of pleading. Tears ran down her cheeks.

"Tyler . . ." She clasped her arms around his neck.

"Angel." He scooped her against him and held her tight.

He'd undone her utterly. Now he had to put her back together.

Still struggling to get his breath under control, he fused their lips together and let her have all the emotion roiling around inside him. The sated exhaustion, the reverence of a man who knew he'd been blessed by someone special, the silent promise to love and protect her, the determination to never let her go.

Beneath him, she opened and accepted. Everything he gave, she took, then gave back all that was in her heart: her confusion that he'd stripped her so bare, her fear that it meant more to her than him, her gratitude for giving her a pleasure so profound there weren't words to express it. And love. Yeah, there it was. Under all the complicated tangle of flavors in her kiss, there was the grim acceptance he'd been looking for. She wasn't ready to trust him totally with her heart yet. But she was going to roll the dice with him, give herself, and hope that he didn't let her down.

Now, maybe, they had a chance.

* * *

THIRTY minutes and a long, hot bath later, Tyler deposited her back in the bed. As he held her in the silence, she felt the gravity of the moment. If he'd meant this afternoon to be a bonding experience, he'd succeeded. Even now, she could still feel him deep inside her, where no man had been, laying claim to her body. She could still feel the avalanche of pleasure burying her. And as she lay across the bed and curled up beside him, she could feel the care in his touch.

And Del was forced to admit that Tyler had real feelings for her, more than she'd believed him capable of.

So, what came next?

"You're thinking too hard," Tyler whispered. "Just . . . let it be."

Del winced. She'd always tried too hard to plan her future, know where every path in front of her was leading. Age and wisdom had taught her that sometimes that just wasn't possible. Now was one of those times. But it still frustrated her.

"Why? You forced me to feel."

"Because we're a team. We're fighting Carlson together. We're Seth's parents. We're lovers. I want more, and I think you do, too. We owe it to ourselves to be honest. You were hiding."

"Of course I have feelings for you. I'd think that would be obvious. I trusted you with our son, with my life, with all my secrets. I tried to keep the rest to myself. The you I knew two years ago would have never wanted more than that."

"Time away from you has made me see things differently. I lost you once. Not happening again."

She absorbed his vow in shock. He really, really meant that. "Tyler, what's this about? You care, but it's not like you're in love with me."

"You sure about that?" His green stare burned into her, daring her to disagree. If she did, he was fully prepared for another battle that would be just as wholly and ruthlessly waged as the last one.

Del hesitated. If he'd challenged her on this subject yesterday, even an hour ago, she would have confidently said that whatever Tyler might be feeling was temporary. Now . . . He hadn't merely had anal sex with her; he'd told her with his body how much he wanted to be with her, to claim her and make her his. And now he

was saying it out loud. Maybe . . . maybe he did love her, at least
a little.

Was she ready for that?

Her breath caught. A part of her desperately wanted to believe
him. The rest of her was scared shitless.

He sighed and held her tightly. "I get that you're gun-shy. I'm
asking you to believe something that would have seemed impossible
two years ago. After all this time apart, your bitter divorce, becoming Seth's mom alone . . . I get it. But if you care for me at all, can't
you take a chance on me? If you don't, won't you always wonder
'what if'?"

Tyler had her there. Del remembered all the months she'd been
pregnant and wondered what Tyler would have thought of her expanding body, of the fact the life he'd planted there was growing
inside of her. She remembered all the nights she'd stayed awake with
Seth when he was an infant, and she'd wondered if Tyler would be
proud of their son. She'd yearned for the man's love and approval
then. Nothing had changed—except that she'd grown comfortable
with this icy, walled-off heart beating in her chest.

Staying frozen was safe; was it really going to make her happy?

She clasped her hand in his. "You're right. I just need time."

Tyler hesitated, then folded her against his body, trying to
smile. "All right. Since I have you here, whatever shall we do?"

Chapter Fourteen

AFTER a quick shower, they made love again, once by the bedroom window overlooking the city as the sun went down. Then again, as they slipped into the pool after dusk and looked at the lights of L.A. glittering like somewhere far away and magical. Xander's "little place" became their paradise. They fed one another tidbits out of the refrigerator, opened a bottle of very expensive champagne and drank it, then fell into bed together again and gorged on the love growing between them, hour by hour, minute by minute.

Tyler was almost afraid to hope. Del had been through a lot in the last two years, largely because he'd been thinking with his hurt, not his heart. He'd heeded her dismissal and walked away from her. Now, he planned to stay right by her side, no matter what she said or did.

As their breathing returned to normal, he wrapped his arms around her and let her melt on top of him, brushing his hand down her spine.

"Tell me about Seth, angel." He pressed a kiss to her swollen mouth. "I've missed so much. I want to hear everything."

She blinked down at him, frozen.

Tyler rolled over, putting her beneath him. "I'm not going to hurt him or take him from you. I just want to know about him."

A moment later, she relaxed and nodded. "I know. I've just been his only protector for so long . . ."

"I'll keep him safe now, too. I'd lay down my life to do it. I love him."

She frowned, seemingly puzzled. "I know you'll protect him. That's who you are. But you barely know him."

"I felt the bond right away. He's my son. *Our* son. That means everything to me."

She sent him a tremulous smile that made everything in his chest tighten and ache. She wanted to believe . . . and she was afraid. It was frustrating, but not surprising. Eric had done a hell of a number on her. But, God, she had no idea how hard and fast he had fallen for her again. And he was falling deeper still. No stopping it.

"Seth was born almost two weeks early, on Valentine's Day. It was cold that day, rainy. I'd left work early to meet Eric so we could sign the papers giving him my half of the house."

"Where'd he get the money?" Eric had often complained about being broke.

She shrugged. "He got some settlement from the department for getting shot. I'm sure his parents gave him the rest."

Probably so. To the parents of a big Italian family, their only son could do no wrong, and Mr. Catalano had done pretty well in the restaurant business.

"Go on." Tyler prompted.

"I hadn't been feeling right all day long. I'd had faint contractions since the middle of the night, which wasn't unusual. But I was tired and feeling really . . . down. I wondered if this was the last time I'd see Eric, and I'd hoped we could be civil. But he hadn't seen me in almost three months, and now I was so pregnant that he couldn't ignore it. He took one look at me, and his eyes got so cold."

Tyler squeezed her hand. "Fuck him. Get back to Seth."

"Just after we signed the papers, my water broke. I couldn't afford an ambulance, but I couldn't drive. Eric took me to the hospital. I think he knew then how afraid I was, and he stayed with me. I dilated pretty quickly, then stalled out at six centimeters for a while. I was exhausted, but I'll always be grateful to Eric for staying there to feed me ice chips and massage my aching muscles."

Yeah, he probably owed Eric some gratitude, too, if he'd made Del's time giving birth to Seth a better experience. But that took a big person, one capable of a lot of forgiveness. Tyler wasn't sure he had that in him just now, not mere hours after Eric had handcuffed him to the refrigerator with every intention of raping Del and making him watch.

"Anyway," Del went on. "The doctor came in at about ten that night when I started dilating again. After that, they administered an epidural, and Seth with born just after one in the morning."

"I'll bet you were exhausted."

"Yeah." Tears filled her eyes. "But I'll never forget hearing his first cry. It was a healthy wail, so loud that it made the doctors laugh. I heard one of the nurses say that he was just beautiful. They weighed and measured him, eight pounds, four ounces, and twenty-two inches. Then they laid him on my chest." She drew in a shuddering breath. "I felt so complete. I felt as if God—and you—had given me this beautiful boy to help reward me for all the dark days I'd been through."

And he'd missed every bit of that. He hadn't heard his son's first cry, hadn't been able to hold Del's hand as she'd pushed their son into the world. He'd missed Seth's first tooth, his first steps . . . all because Eric had contrived to keep them apart. Tyler's own hurt had been too great to swallow his pride and follow Del. Yeah, he was furious with Eric. But he was angry with himself most of all.

"What kind of infant was he?" He brushed damp tendrils of hair from her flushed cheek.

She smiled, and Tyler was sure she'd never been more beautiful to him. It was like a kick in the gut, and with every passing moment, he knew he belonged with this woman. He had to convince her somehow that he wasn't her past coming back to haunt her but that her future had finally arrived. He had to convince her that he wasn't going to turn on her, change on her. That she could trust him.

"Hungry." She laughed. "He ate constantly. I breast-fed as much as I could, but it wasn't enough for him, so I augmented with bottles. He was so healthy and big. He weighed nearly thirty pounds at his one-year well visit. He's always at the top of the height and weight charts. And smart. Just a few weeks ago, he figured out how to open the drawers to my desk and climb up to get to the jar of chocolates I keep there. I came back into the room from doing laundry and found him sitting on the desk, the jar empty, and chocolate smeared all over his face."

Tyler laughed. According to his own mom, he'd been a bundle of mischief, too. He wished he could prove to her that he could, in fact, be the kind of husband and father who stayed. When this danger was behind them, maybe . . . he'd contact her, tell her that she was a grandmother, see if she wanted to meet Seth. But for now, he had to let her bitterness go. Her words no longer had the power to hurt or haunt him.

"Was it very hard trying to take care of him by yourself?"

Del hesitated, closed her eyes. Then she sent him one of those too-bright smiles, and he knew she intended to put a cheerful spin on the topic.

"The truth," he demanded.

Her face fell, and her eyes glossed over. "Yeah. He didn't sleep through the night for nearly six months, which means I didn't sleep. He was colicky nearly every evening. I didn't love the day care I had him in, but it was close to work and all I could afford. He got very sick his first Halloween, and we spent it in the emergency room, me fearing the worst. The sitting and pacing all alone while they ran tests . . ."

Behind her back, Tyler clenched his fists. She'd needed him, and he'd been cock deep in women he hadn't really given a shit about because he'd been licking his wounds. He didn't totally regret going to Lafayette. He'd found friends who felt a lot like family, and he knew without hesitation that they'd do anything for him. They were doing it now, safeguarding his son. He'd do anything for them, too. That network of people, even if they didn't know it, had seen him through some lonely times. Del had had no one.

"I'm so damn sorry, angel. You'll never have to worry about being alone again."

"The last few days have been intense. I have to think about everything when Carlson isn't breathing down our necks. Let's just see how we feel when this is over." She pushed him off and rolled away, turning her back to him, then grabbed the TV remote and flipped it on.

Goddamn it, she was afraid. Tyler gritted his teeth, trying to remember that happily ever after hadn't worked out for her before. That she needed time and patience. But those were two things he didn't have much of.

Suddenly, Del gasped, turning white as a ghost. She trembled, her eyes wide.

Tyler focused on the screen, showing a sunny afternoon—then a body bag being wheeled out on a stretcher of a little kitschy retro cottage. A reporter filled the picture next. "The body of thirty-one-year-old Lisa Foster was found early this afternoon. According to authorities, this was definitely a homicide, but they're declining to give further details. At this point, they have no leads and no suspects. Neighbors are shaken."

An older woman looked into the camera and dabbed at her eyes with a tissue. "She was a sweet girl, always had a smile and a wave. She didn't have any enemies. I can't imagine who would want to hurt her."

A cold slither of dread went through Tyler. "Your friend Lisa, from work?"

She nodded sharply. "Oh my God. How . . . Why . . . ?"

Tyler edged closer and wrapped his arms around her, pressing his chest to her back. "Angel, I think she may have been up to her eyeballs with Carlson and his goons."

"No!" she burst out. "She wouldn't do—"

"I think she did what they asked for a lot of money. She was over thirty thousand dollars in debt last week. As soon as you told her that you were headed to Eric's to retrieve your flash drive, someone broke into his house. Now, it's missing. Around that same time, she magically paid off all her credit cards. And now she's dead. You got another explanation?"

Del looked over her shoulder at him, mouth gaping open like she wanted to argue. Then resignation crossed her face, and she knew she couldn't. "She sold me out?"

"I think so. I'm sorry. I know you trusted her."

She clapped a hand over her mouth, like she was trying to hold in a scream. Then her eyes went wide, and she gasped. "Oh my God. Lisa is the one who helped me track you down in Lafayette. What if she told Carlson that? Seth!"

"Did you tell her where we've hidden Seth?"

"No. I—I think I just said that he was staying with friends." She trembled.

"Shh." Tyler stroked her back. "Carlson wants *you*, not Seth.

He'll only step that far out of his jurisdiction if his back is against the wall. His power and his backup is here, and now you're on his home turf. Besides, even if he knew my address, he's not going to find Seth at Deke or Luc or Jack's homes. He's fine. I'll text everyone and tell them to be on the lookout, just in case."

"Thank you." She nodded, then broke his embrace and hopped to her feet. "Why is it that I always let people in my life who are destined to hurt me? Eric. Lisa. Maybe you. Did I have such a drama-free childhood that I unconsciously seek assholes determined to rape my trust?"

Tyler winced. He could see where she'd think that, but he had to set her straight fast. "No. You're a kind, trusting person, and sometimes scumbags take advantage. You're not wrong; they are."

Defeat slumped her shoulders. "It makes me wonder who else I've naïvely trusted that I shouldn't. I know nothing about your friends."

"They're solid, angel. You've talked to Alyssa or Kimber every day since we've been on the road. Seth is fine. Xander put us up here. We're safe. Jack and Deke are doing everything they can to help behind the scenes. We're going to work this out. I swear." He scrambled to his feet. When he gathered her close and stroked a hand down her hair, her shoulders began to shake. Tyler murmured, "Don't talk to anyone else from work, not until we can vet them."

She gave him a shaky nod. "I need to talk to Seth."

"I saw a laptop in one of the bedrooms. I'll see if I can get it up and get Skype running. Alyssa has an account. You might be able to video chat and *see* Seth."

"Really?" The hope in her eyes was almost painful. No doubt, she missed that little boy. Tyler ached, too. For the chance to comfort her. For the chance to know his own son.

But now wasn't the time for sentiment. Now that Carlson was leaving a body trail, there was work to be done.

"Sure. Why don't you put on some clothes and grab yourself a glass of wine while I set the computer up?"

"Thank you. I'm stunned and terrified and probably more numb than I will be tomorrow, but you . . . make everything better for me." She put her arms around him and drew him close.

Tyler felt a hundred feet tall. Those words, a measure of her growing trust and caring, gave him a whole lot of fucking hope.

"My pleasure." He kissed her lips softly.

She darted into the bathroom to toss on her clothes. Tyler yanked on his pants, grabbed his phone from his pocket, and made his way to the home office across the hall. He had Jack on the line before he'd even sat down.

"There's a body." Tyler explained what he'd heard on the news.

Jack cursed. "Why pay her, then kill her?"

"I have to think that she'd outlived her usefulness somehow."

"Carlson wouldn't want to leave her as a loose end indefinitely, but something happened. Maybe the thirty thousand was a down payment for more information," Jack surmised.

"Or maybe Lisa grew a conscience and threatened to talk." Tyler raked a hand through his hair. "Anything is possible."

As long as he and Del stayed here in Xander's posh cocoon, they were safe. But they couldn't nail Carlson from behind these secure gates. At some point, they'd have to start making moves. Already, they'd wasted time eluding goons and dealing with Eric.

"Fuck," he ground out in frustration.

"Sometimes," Jack offered, "the best defense is a good offense."

"I was just thinking that. I've got to go after this dirtbag where he lives and breathes. Without the flash drive, Del is trying to remember all the pertinent facts so she'll know where to start, but I've got to figure something out fast. They're going to come after her. Or Seth."

"Seth is perfectly fine. Put that worry out of your head. He and

Caleb are becoming fast friends, except when Chloe is in the room. Then it's an all-out battle to keep the pretty girl happy."

Despite the tension, Tyler laughed. Chloe was such a girly-girl, already well versed in batting her eyelashes to get her way. Or like her mother, she toughed things out until she got what she wanted. If this trend continued, his son and Deke's would spend years bowing and scraping to the princess.

From across the hall, he heard a soft sob, and Del's murmurings, as if she were giving herself a pep talk. Reality intruded.

"We've got to catch this fucker. We're running out of time. I can feel it."

"Agreed," Jack said. "Deke has been talking to some of his contacts at the FBI. Apparently someone over there has got a file on Carlson, but we have no idea what's in it yet. Xander has a hundred bankers who will bend over backward to get or keep his business. He's looking into any money trail. Carlson's wife and brother both seem to deal with large sums of money periodically, but no details yet."

"Fuck. No one who has that much shit going on around them can possibly smell sweet."

"As soon as we get anything solid, we'll call you."

"Make it fast." Tyler started the laptop on the desk with a heavy sigh. "Del is reeling from her so-called friend's murder. But that won't last long. Soon, she'll go on a rampage, all furious about what's happened to her life, Seth's life, her friend, the community . . . you name it. I'll have a hard time restraining her then."

"I recommend nylon cords securing her to your headboard and a swift spanking. It might not stop her for long, but it will get her attention."

Tyler was beginning to see the wisdom of that. Despite the hours he'd just spent inside Del, his dick stood up at the suggestion.

"Sounds good. I'll ring you if anything happens."

He ended the call just before Del entered the room, chin held high, all that mahogany hair swirling around her shoulders. She didn't wear anything enticing, just a pair of jeans and a gray tank top. But Tyler had the sudden urge to tear all that off, tie her to the bed, spank her ass red, just like Jack suggested. Then get deep inside her—stay inside her—until the danger passed.

God, he should have been sated, but instead, he only felt hungrier. The difference between lusting after a woman and truly loving them, he guessed. Whatever it was, he liked it and refused to let go.

"It'll take me another few minutes to install Skype."

Del nodded, then held up her prepaid cell. "I've thought about the case. I know a few people I can call to start recreating my evidence. When I talked to them a few weeks ago, several were really interested in taking Carlson down."

Tyler nodded. "Why don't you give me all the background on the case before you go jumping in? What do you remember being able to truly verify and what were you still working on?"

"Yeah, I think this conversation is probably overdue." She sighed. "What I'd been able to piece together was that Carlson had struck a deal with Double T, who runs the 18th Street gang. He'd look the other way when their cases came to trial. Felony possession would only be entered as a misdemeanor, and sentences that should have ensured hard time ended with probation or community service. In one particular case, a street dealer got pissed at a customer who tried to stiff him. He shot and killed both the customer and a four-year-old playing in the yard next door. Community outrage didn't seem to mean a damn thing. The guy stayed in jail while his case came to trial. He was found guilty, but only given three months. As soon as the verdict was read, he was released for time already served and given a small fine. That's it! Earlier this year, a similar situation with an MS-13 member netted the assailant a sentence of over three hundred years. In the case of the 18th Street gang, the guy trying to buy the drugs didn't have a weapon. The kid certainly didn't, either. What should have been two counts of at least second-degree murder was reduced to involuntary manslaughter and given the lightest sentence I've ever seen."

"Shit." Tyler didn't like the way any of that sounded. There'd be danger at every turn, both from authority and in the streets. The gang would protect Carlson and their livelihood using their brand of violence. The scum ADA's reach was far longer than he liked.

"I've also heard that some arrests that should be made aren't," she said.

Tyler's head snapped up. "You think Carlson's got dirty cops on his side, too?"

"Yeah. I had a source just before the car bomb who was ready to talk to me and name names. Lobato Loco is from the 18th Street gang, second in command. He was trying to convince Double T to break the deal with Carlson. Lobato Loco thought that Carlson wanted too much money for his protection. Double T refused to end the agreement. Lobato Loco was pissed."

"And willing to talk. Let's start there. Call this guy. See if he's still willing to name names."

Del nodded. "That's what I was thinking. I'm just not sure I still have his number. I'm afraid it blew up with my notes, or I'd have been on the phone with him days ago."

Tyler glanced at her and bit back a curse. She looked exhausted, nearly ready to fall down. He hit a few keys on the computer. "Call Seth. Let me find something for us to eat, then we'll get back to work."

"I'm not hungry." She moved to the computer eagerly, already putting his suggestion out of her mind.

He slammed the laptop lid shut. "I didn't ask; I'm telling you.

This case is going to be ugly, and it's going to take a lot out of you. It already is. Eat a meal. Keep up your strength."

"You're being bossy." She glared at him.

"Get used to it. I'm also right."

"Fine." She rolled her eyes, but he saw a hint of a smile there. She might rebel against his care for show, but she liked it.

He prowled toward the kitchen on bare feet and was scrounging through the refrigerator when his phone rang. PRIVATE CALLER displayed again.

"What's up, Xander?"

"You two lovebirds settling in?"

"We're fine."

"Am I interrupting anything?" He sounded almost hopeful.

Tyler didn't know whether to laugh or beat the guy's face in. "Not at the moment."

"Damn, I usually have better timing."

"How's Javier?" That ought to stick in his craw.

Xander's sudden silence bled across the line. "The same, with his head still mostly fermented. So I've been spending my time more productively, digging for shit on Carlson. This is interesting. I obtained all of his financials about two hours ago—"

"How?" Bank records were notoriously hard to get unless you were law enforcement. Granted, Xander had contacts, but . . .

"Easily. I would have had them sooner if I hadn't had to rip a bottle out of Javier's hands and send him off for a sobering shower. Dumb ass. Anyway, besides being an ADA, which doesn't pay for a family of three to live in the kind of luxury he does, he also has a business called Communications Redirect. It's supposedly a multi-million-dollar-a-year business and the source of most of his income. Their website talks about the latest in personal communications, so I stopped by their 'corporate headquarters.'"

"Yeah?"

"It's a storefront in a strip mall in a lousy part of town," Xander said. "Know what they sell? Beepers. When was the last time you saw a beeper?"

"God, ten years ago, at least. No cell phones or mobile hotspots?"

"Nothing of the sort. And this corporate headquarters had one employee. She barely lifted her head at me enough to say that they weren't taking on new customers at this time."

"What? Who the fuck says that to a potential customer, especially in these economic times?" Tyler sighed as the truth hit him. "Unless your business isn't legitimate."

"That's my thought, too. Nor can you make millions and millions of dollars a year selling old technology to no one."

"So he uses the business to launder the money he gets from his scam with the 18th Street gang."

"Precisely. I'll fax you over all the financials I've got. I also had my driver take some discreet pictures of Communications Redirect. It won't prove anything except that something odd is going on, but it's a start."

"That's more than we had. Thanks, man."

"My pleasure. If I get more, I'll let you know. In the meantime, take care of that pretty girl. You never know how valuable she is until you don't have one."

Did he speak from experience, or in riddles, just to piss him off? Tyler shoved the question aside. He had bigger fish to fry.

"Believe me, I know exactly how valuable she is."

"Damn, I was hoping you were stupid," Xander teased.

Or was he teasing at all?

"I appreciate all your help. Now leave us the hell alone." Tyler hung up, grabbed a few things from the kitchen, and headed back to the office down the hall.

As he got closer, he heard Del's high-pitched, singsong conversation with their son. Her baby talk did something to his heart. She loved that boy and didn't try to hide it in the least. That amount of loyalty and love was somehow a huge turn-on.

Seth gurgled something back, and Del waved. Tyler stepped behind the computer to see Luc bouncing Seth on his lap, Alyssa bustled around in the background with Chloe.

"Everything okay?" he asked.

"Great," Luc responded. "Your boy is a healthy eater."

"So I've heard." Tyler turned his attention to Seth. "Hey, little man."

Seth smiled wide, like he understood, then shoved part of a crumbling biscuit in his mouth.

The exchange opened up his chest and poured more love in. Shit, he wanted to be with Seth right now, able to pluck the little boy into his lap and tickle him or talk to him. He had to start finding ways to ingrain himself in the toddler's life because he intended to be a father—and a damn good one.

"You want to talk to him for a bit?" Del asked.

"Yeah." He almost choked on the word.

"I'll go in the other room to start making my phone calls."

Tyler nodded as she said good-bye to Seth, then walked out. He turned his attention to the little screen in front of him. "So my boy is being good?"

"Yeah. He's really fun. A little temperamental."

"I wonder who he gets that from?" Alyssa called out with a grin from the background.

When Seth looked away for a moment, Tyler gave her the one-fingered salute.

"Our biggest problem is getting him to sleep," Luc admitted.

"Is he ready for bed now?"

"Yep. Fresh diaper, full belly, the whole nine yards."

An idea crossed Tyler's mind. When he'd been a little guy himself, he'd spent a few precious weeks a year with his grandmother. Unlike his own mom, she wasn't displeased with her lot in life, didn't smoke all the time, and hadn't preferred party life to parenthood. And he remembered one thing that had comforted him more than anything else.

"Put him in his playpen and set the laptop just outside, at eye level, will you?"

Luc frowned and groused about the amount of work Tyler was causing him, but he complied. There was a lot of bouncing and muffled sounds as Luc dragged the laptop through the house and into a guest bedroom. With a brush of a soft hand over Seth's hair, Luc laid him down in the playpen. Seth started wailing immediately.

The chef set the laptop on a little stool and leaned down in view of the webcam. "Are you sure about this?"

No, but he had to try. "Sure."

With a shrug, Luc got out of the way and pointed the built-in webcam at Seth's little face, currently turning red from all his exertions.

Tyler did the only thing he could think of. He began to sing.

* * *

DEL paced the kitchen, grabbing a few spare grapes from the refrigerator. She was so tempted to call her boss, Preston, and find out what he knew about Lisa's murder. But she didn't dare. At this point, she didn't know who she could trust, and she had to focus on tracking down people would could help her implicate Carlson and make all this go away.

Eric might be a source of information, but no way was she going there again. She didn't hate him for what he'd done; in a weird way, she understood. He'd always had a lot of pride, and she'd trampled over his by being "unfaithful" and enjoying Tyler's lovemaking so much. He'd always been a golden boy and didn't know how to process such a slight. But his hungry ego wasn't her problem, and no matter how badly she needed some phone numbers to get started on her quest, she'd have to start somewhere else.

Just before the car bomb had destroyed her phone and all her contact information, she'd received a voice mail from Lobato Loco. Maybe she'd saved it. The phone was gone, and it was a long shot, but the only possibility she had at the moment.

Dialing her cell phone's voice mail number from Tyler's phone, she retrieved her messages, including one from Lisa that had her near tears. She'd been one of her closest friends for two years, always there when she needed something. Del could always use more money, but she didn't understand how Lisa had simply sold her out, knowing the people paying her would more than likely kill her.

She closed her eyes and deleted the message.

Two more incidental messages, and she heard what she needed. A muffled, hurried voice with a heavy Latin-American accent rambled on about Double T, Carlson, and all the "shit going down." He didn't leave his name or any details, but she'd figured out his identity based on the information he'd left. And he'd left a phone number for a restaurant in the Pico-Union district—a little hole-in-the-wall burger joint. He instructed her to call back on Thursday between seven and ten p.m.

Del winced. She was over a week late, and who knew if he'd talk to her anymore or if anyone there would even know to expect her. Still, she dialed.

On the seventh ring, a woman picked up and greeted her in Spanish. She knew only enough of the language to be dangerous.

"*Se habla Inglés?*" she asked hopefully, because that was about the extent of her Spanish.

"Of course," the heavily accented voice on the other end of the line answered.

Crap, how did one ask for a known gang member over the phone? "I received a voice mail from a man asking me to call here. I'm a reporter for the *L.A. Times*. The man didn't identify himself but said he had information I needed and he was willing to share."

The woman started sobbing and babbling incoherent curses in Spanish. Del recognized a few street terms that made her wince.

"I'm sorry if I've caused a problem. I'll call back."

"No, it is not you who causes the problem, yes? It is my son."

"Your son? Is he called Lobato Loco by all the other . . . homies?" God, she hoped that asking the question wasn't going to upset this woman more.

"That name is *estúpido*! Esteban was a good boy until all those others come around. Now he gets into all the guns and the drugs."

"I understand, señora. Is there another way I should reach him?"

The woman sniffled and rattled off ten digits. "This is his phone number."

Del jotted it down, thanked her, and ended the call, then ran for the office in the back of the massive house—and stopped abruptly to find Tyler singing into the computer, his rich baritone voice a deep, soothing presence in the room.

He lifted his head to stare at her and stopped abruptly.

Gripping the doorframe, she blinked, stared. She'd had no idea Tyler could sing so beautifully, such a haunting, gentle lullaby. "What are you doing?"

"Seth is asleep," Alyssa's voice sounded over the computer before he could answer. "That's amazing."

"Thanks." Tyler flushed. "Glad I could help. We'll call again tomorrow." He quickly severed the connection with Alyssa, looking almost embarrassed. "What? It's just a song."

No. To Del, it was much more than that. He'd been singing their son to sleep, trying to be a father to Seth, even though they'd barely met and were over a thousand miles apart. A fresh bolt of love ripped through her chest. If she'd had any hope of getting through this tough time without losing her heart altogether, it had just died a fiery death. She closed her eyes.

"Is something wrong?" He pushed out of the chair that rolled across the floor. "Del?"

She blinked. *Focus, damn it!* "I have the number for my informant inside the 18th Street gang, someone who might be able to give us some information or proof—someone who can help us."

Tyler smiled and patted his lap, indicating that she should sit there. "You're brilliant. Let's call."

Chapter Fifteen

THREE rings later, someone answered the phone. *"Bueno?"*

The heavy beat of Latin dance music pounded in the background, and Del could hardly hear. "Esteban?"

"Quien habla?" he barked.

Del thought he asked who was speaking. "I'm the reporter from the *Los Angeles Times*. You called and left a message a while ago?"

"Sí. I did." He paused. "Took you long enough."

Del was aware of Tyler hanging on her every word. He looked ready to grab the phone out of her hand and rip the guy on the other end a new one.

"Someone put a bomb in my car, and it exploded in front of my eyes. I've been shot at, escaped across the country and traveled back, and spent a lot of time just trying to stay alive."

On Esteban's side of the line, Del heard rustling. The music began to fade. Then she heard a door squeak once, twice, followed by blessed silence in the background.

"Carlson knows about you," Esteban said. "You still want to take him down? You still want that information?"

"Yes." *Desperately.*

"I got everything you need, names, details. If I get rid of him, then business goes back to usual, yeah? Meet me at midnight at Desnuda. It's on Ninth. I'll be inside the club, near the front."

Del had no idea where or what that was, but she figured she could find it. "Sure."

"Come alone," he warned.

"I'll be bringing a . . ." She stared at Tyler, trying to decide what to call him. She didn't really want to define her complicated love life for a stranger. "Friend."

Tyler's expression didn't change, but he froze. Then he looked away.

Damn, she'd upset him.

"He better not be a cop," Esteban challenged. "Or there are consequences, you know?"

"He doesn't even live in this area." Del didn't mention that Tyler used to be an LAPD Vice detective. At this point, she had to pray that they'd never seen him before or Esteban was likely to cut her cold.

Esteban let it go. "Wear tight jeans and red shoes. You look *hermosa*, yeah?"

Del thought that meant "pretty." "I'll try."

"Order wine at the bar. You'll stick out for sure." He laughed.

But she feared the joke was on her. Still, she didn't have much choice but to agree.

As soon as she hung up, Tyler frowned. "I don't like it."

"I don't, either, but what are our more appealing options?" She shrugged. "None. Until midnight, I need to keep working. Let me see the computer, please."

Tyler stepped away, letting her sit. The seat was warm, and his scent lingered everywhere, soothing her, even as her thoughts whirled and she longed to throw herself into his arms. Instead, she forced herself to concentrate on the task at hand.

"I need to send an untraceable e-mail. Any idea how?"

"Why?"

"I need to test Preston and find out if I can trust him. If my boss is at all in league with Carlson, I'd rather know it now than when it's too late.

"Untraceable e-mails aren't my area of expertise, but I know someone who can help." Tyler called Deke. In less than five minutes, Deke had walked them through the process. Tyler gestured in her direction. "Type away."

Quickly, she began composing an e-mail to her boss. Then stopped. "I need to talk to Xander."

Tyler looked like he really wanted to object.

"It's urgent," Del assured.

With a curse, he handed over his phone. She flipped through the numbers and found the record that said PRIVATE CALLER. When she dialed, Xander answered on the first ring.

"Everything okay, Tyler?"

"It's Delaney. If I wanted to . . . misdirect someone who might be playing for the dirty team to somewhere in town that's being watched and has security, where would that be?"

"Cautious little cat, aren't you? I like that," he drawled. "Jot this address down. It's a warehouse I own. Round-the-clock surveillance with state-of-the-art equipment. Logan and his brother, Hunter, made sure of that."

"Perfect. Thanks! I owe you."

"Hmm. Careful, or I might come around to collect."

Tyler ripped the phone from her hand. "Over my dead fucking body. Back the hell off."

With a laugh, Xander hung up.

Del rolled her eyes as she typed quickly. "He only does it to annoy you. It doesn't mean anything to him."

With a snort, Tyler sat on the edge of the desk and stewed.

She put the warehouse's address in the e-mail to Preston, claiming that's where she was hiding, then asked about any information he might have on Lisa's murder. All done, she hit send. If he or a group of thugs showed up at the warehouse instead of answering via e-mail, she'd know that Preston was dirty. Now, all she could do was prepare for the coming night and hope that her upcoming chat with Esteban was the big break she needed.

* * *

TYLER hated this whole plan. Going to visit a gangbanger on his home turf when they had no idea what they were walking into? Something like suicide, he feared. But no, he didn't have a better idea. While Del showered, he had to fucking call Xander again because Del didn't have any red shoes, and it was too risky to walk into a well-lit public place to shop. There'd be a lot of security cameras there. And who knew how many dirty cops Carlson had and if their beats included the mall?

He managed to force another few bites of food into Del before he hopped in the shower and readied himself for the meeting to come. He'd feel better with firepower and backup, but that wasn't in the cards. Then Xander rang the doorbell.

Tyler pulled it open to find the man dressed casually in jeans and a clearly designer shirt. He dangled a pair of red fuck-me peep-toe pumps in one hand and had a duffel bag slung over his shoulder.

"Thanks for picking the shoes up." Tyler reached out to take them.

"Not so fast." Xander stepped into the house. "Javier is so predictable it's making my head hurt. He was a complete disaster at Látigo. We'll try again tomorrow night. In the meantime, you're my ticket out of boredom."

"You think you're coming with us?"

"Yes." Xander smiled wide. "I have experience with Desnuda and the guys who roll there. I can help. And I come bearing gifts." He held out the shoes.

Del walked down the hall just then and grabbed them. "Oh my God, they're beautiful."

"They're Christian Louboutin. Enjoy!"

"These are crazy expensive. Did you just have these hanging around?" Del frowned.

"No. I shopped. I tried to imagine the shoes you'd look sexiest in naked and bent over—"

"Shut your fucking mouth," Tyler growled.

Xander just laughed. "I brought you presents, too. Happy birthday."

"My birthday is in September." Tyler gritted his teeth.

"Then happy fuck-off day." Xander shoved the duffel bag in his midsection.

As Tyler grasped it, the metallic sounds of the jostling contents told him immediately what lay inside. "Hardware."

"A lot of it. A nice collection of semiautomatics, a sniper rifle or two, a few hand grenades—though I hope it doesn't come to that since Desnuda is a decent club—and even a Corner Shot."

Tyler gaped. As much as Xander got on his nerves, Tyler kind of loved the guy in that moment. "Wow, money really does buy everything."

"Mostly." Xander shrugged. "The rest . . . I'm still figuring out how to get."

Unable to imagine anything Xander lacked or wanted for, Tyler shrugged. "Are we ready?"

Del nodded. "Yeah. I'm ready to go anywhere in shoes this fabulous. Thank you so much."

She closed the distance between her and Xander and placed a kiss on his cheek. Xander wrapped his arm around her waist, looking like he hoped to bring her in for a big, juicy kiss. Tyler wasn't having any of that.

He grabbed Xander's shoulder, pinched hard on the nerve, then slammed him back into the front door. "Straight up? I appreciate your help, and we wouldn't be doing this well without you. But that doesn't mean I'm going to let you touch my woman." Tyler got in the other man's face and forced him to meet his stare. "Are we clear?"

"Tyler! Stop!" Del insisted, gaping at him in shock.

"That you're a caveman? Absolutely. She'll come to her senses soon and find me irresistible." Xander shrugged free and winked at her.

Gritting his teeth, Tyler let him go. If not, he'd risk really pissing Del off. And given the bastard's grin, Xander knew it.

"I've got a car outside," the billionaire said. "Let's go."

Tyler slung the bag over his shoulder, then grabbed Del's hand. Following Xander, they made their way out into the night air. It was crisp and light, with a hint of a cool breeze. Xander stopped beside a sleek black Audi so new it didn't yet have license plates and opened the door for Del.

She bypassed the open door and climbed in the back. Tyler grinned as he slung the duffel onto the floorboard and eased into the passenger's seat where Xander proffered the door open.

"Shithead," he muttered, and slammed the door.

Within minutes, they were off, heading out of the hills and down into a seedy part of town. Clusters of older homes merged with liquor stores and pawnshops, flashing lights, ladies of the night, and drug deals going down everywhere. They parked in a shadowed lot behind an old stucco building. As Tyler tucked a couple of the Glocks into his waistband at the small of his back, he watched Del. He didn't like the dark surrounding them or the cautious, tense expression on her face. Xander didn't seem to notice as he grabbed a pistol, tucked it away, and led them around the side of the building, to the front door, painted a garish red. Tyler glanced behind him and stared at the club's sign, then winced at the neon dancing woman edging red panties down over her ass.

This wasn't a nightclub; it was a strip joint.

Xander stopped them before they could enter. "I'm going to walk in first, get the lay of the land. They've seen me here before, so I won't stand out. If there's anything wrong. I'll call. If you haven't heard from me in five minutes, the coast is clear."

As much as Tyler wanted to object, the plan made sense. Del nodded.

The minute Xander disappeared inside, Tyler wrapped his arm around her waist and dragged her into the shadows, just in case Lobato Loco had sold her out, too. He wished he could tell her that they didn't have to do this, but that would be a lie. Her life literally depended on this, and there was no way around it until they could prove how dirty Carlson was.

Del stood stiffly against him. "I'm way out of my element. I don't like it."

"I'm here for you. I'll keep you safe."

Gnawing on her lip, Del nodded. She looked so nervous, and Tyler just wanted to wrap her up and hide her away. It wasn't in the cards.

After five minutes, they hadn't heard from Xander, so Tyler led her into the club. It wasn't upscale in the least, and he wondered why a billionaire came here for kicks. The music was loud, and everything smelled steeped in alcohol, with a slight tinge of musty underneath. A pretty Latina woman danced on the stage, wearing only a spangled thong. She dragged a sheer red scarf back and forth, across her hard, rosy brown nipple. Seen it, fucked it. Not this particular woman, but after a while, women like her were all the same.

Rolling her eyes, Del eased over to the bar and ordered a white wine. The bartender looked at her like she was crazy, but shrugged and poured her a glass. She looked around the room then and spotted Xander, who looked engrossed in the journey that red scarf was taking around the stripper's body.

Tyler approached her, and he felt Del's tension as she scanned the room for her contact. He glanced at his cell phone. They were still a few minutes early. Maybe Lobato Loco wanted to make a big entrance.

"We should sit toward the front, someplace visible so he sees you when he comes in."

Del clearly didn't like it, but she nodded. Together they found a table in the front corner of the room. She crossed her legs, and those red shoes were like a beacon in the club. No way any man entering could miss those long, slender thighs and those shoes so provocative, they were an X-rated invitation all their own. Tyler sat closer to her, threw an arm around her shoulders, wanting every bastard in the joint to know exactly who she belonged to. Behind them, he could almost feel Xander laughing.

Five minutes slid into ten. The woman with the scarf was replaced by a naughty nurse, then a cowgirl who made chaps look downright indecent. A few years ago—hell, two weeks ago—he would have grinned and whistled, coughed up a twenty, and hoped for a little action later. And how fucking pathetic was that? He'd been using sex like a drug so he didn't have to confront how lonely he'd been without Del.

At the twenty-minute mark, Del had finished sipping her wine and was looking around for her contact. Still nothing—except the painted-up beauty who'd wielded the scarves earlier headed in their direction. She wriggled her curves in between him and Del.

Then she straddled his lap with a lascivious smile.

Del backed away, her brows raised and her mouth open with annoyance. The dancer thrust her breasts in his face and wriggled down on his lap. Tyler reared back and closed his eyes. This had to be Xander's work, and he was going to throttle the asshole.

He grabbed the dancer by the hips. It took him a few moments to stop all her gyrations and unplaster her from his chest. Undaunted, she grabbed his face and smothered his mouth with her too-red lips.

Tyler wrenched away. "I'll give you a hundred bucks just to go away."

She paused. Her come-hither glance fell away, then she shrugged and held out her hand. Snarling, he pulled bills out of his pocket and thrust them into the dancer's hand. "The guy who hired you? He's loaded. Absolutely stinking rich."

The dancer smiled wide, then planted another kiss on Tyler's mouth, this time in gratitude. He pushed her away again and set her off his lap with a grimace. God, she smelled like booze and sweat and other men. He'd done a hundred girls who smelled just like her, and it had never bothered him before. But it bugged the shit out of him now, and he knew the cause: Del.

He looked over at her chair. Empty. *Fuck*.

He jumped up and looked around the room. She wasn't hard to spot, trolling the room, looking around for her contact. Xander had an eye on her, but Pimphead Warbucks was a lover, not a fighter. Tyler doubted he would be able to save Del if she needed help.

Throwing his chair aside, he stormed after her, catching up to her mid-aisle. He grabbed her arm. "What the hell are you doing?"

"Looking for Esteban." She wrenched free of his grip and crossed her arms over her chest, refusing to look his way.

Tyler gritted his teeth. "It's not safe or smart for you to do that alone."

"You were occupied."

"I didn't invite her to dance on my lap."

Del rolled her eyes. "From what I saw, you weren't trying terribly hard to make her leave."

Tyler's ire rose. "Xander pulled that shit on me."

"I know." She kept strolling, looking everywhere but at him.

"I paid her to go! Seriously?" He planted himself in front of her. "You're going to be mad because a woman I didn't want danced on my lap?"

Del stopped, pondered. "I think I have to. I didn't pay much attention to the other women around Eric when we were married. I thought he loved me, and their attraction was one-sided. So I let it slide. But after a while, a healthy twentysomething man not having sex with his wife for months . . . I can't prove that he cheated on me, but—"

"He did," Tyler admitted.

Fidelity would always be a concern of hers if he didn't come absolutely clean. Now wasn't the best time, but Esteban was looking like a no-show, and putting this off only left Del with a festering wound. As soon as everything was out in the open, he could reassure her that he wasn't the same guy he used to be—and he definitely wasn't Eric.

She sucked in a stunned breath, looking pale, as if the truth had flattened her. But she didn't deserve more lies. *In for a penny, in for a pound . . .*

"I was seeing this one girl in particular. We didn't have anything special, just a good time. But then I realized that Eric was . . . with her, too."

"Destiny." Del's face closed off.

He hated like hell to hurt her. "Yeah. She wasn't the only one."

"Damn it!" she exploded. "I knew it. Deep down, I knew it and didn't confront him."

Some of the patrons turned her way. Attracting attention wasn't a good idea, and he had a feeling that Del was too overwrought to hold all her fury in. When he tried to take her hand to lead her outside, she wrenched it away.

"Don't touch me."

Tyler scowled. "I'm not Eric, Del. I didn't lie. I didn't cheat on you. I never would."

"You fucked every girl who moved, even after having sex with me. And you, one of my best friends, didn't tell me that my husband was being unfaithful. Why? Because it didn't occur to you that it was an issue? I'm leaving."

She stalked off, forcing Tyler to follow. Out of the corner of his eye, he caught Xander frowning, then beating feet to the door. He could accuse the bastard of a lot of things. Thankfully, being stupid wasn't one of them.

Xander pushed outside first. Del followed, shoving the big red portal out of her way, leaving it to fly in Tyler's face. With a curse, he slammed it against the wall and jogged until he caught up with her. "Think about what you're doing. You're supposed to be meeting a contact who will give you information you need to make all this danger go away."

She stomped her pretty Christian Louboutin pumps onto his toes, and he reared back, clutching his injured digits with one hand and glaring at her. "What the hell?"

"You think I don't know that? Esteban is now thirty minutes late. I doubt he's coming." She pulled out her cell phone, punched a few buttons on her prepaid cell, and shoved it up to her ear.

"Del . . ."

She turned her back on him.

A long minute later, she stabbed a finger at the buttons again and pocketed the phone. "He's not answering. Maybe he's spooked. Or in the middle of a big deal. I don't know. I'll call him again tomorrow. All I know is that right now, I want to get in bed and sleep. Alone."

"Goddamn it, Del!" He turned her to face him again, ready to have it out.

Xander whacked him between the shoulders. "As entertaining as this little lovers' quarrel is, I think we're being watched. I've got a bad feeling. If this contact didn't show, maybe someone else will appear in his place—and it might be one of the bad guys."

That possibility washed over Tyler in a cold surge. He'd been too fucking tied up in his own drama to keep his head clear. As soon as he realized his mistake, he heard a gunshot out of nowhere whiz right between him and Del and strike the building. Stucco kicked up, then crumbled onto the sidewalk. They all ran, and Tyler drew his weapon, hoping like hell that they all made it to the car alive.

* * *

DEL could literally feel her legs shaking out from under her as she sprinted around the side of the club toward Xander's car. Tyler popped off a few shots back. The men flanked her, ready to pick her up or help her, but she was determined not to be a detriment in platforms, no matter how pretty. Hard not to be scared as hell as more bullets whizzed past, coming dangerously close.

Shooters started coming from the opposite direction on foot, too. Somewhere in the dark parking lot, there were dangerous men with guns, intent on killing her.

She, Tyler, and Xander were all creeping low, ducking bullets, dodging shooters in between cars. Del's heart pounded; terror ate at her. She hoped like hell that she got back to Seth alive. Beside her, Tyler reached out and grabbed her hand, as if telling her to hang on. As if underscoring that he was there for her.

She should be blazingly pissed at him now for keeping Eric's infidelity from her for all these years. But right now was about life or death.

Del squeezed his hand in return.

A few feet from the car, Xander deactivated the locks. The alarm chirped and the lights flashed. The shooters immediately darted closer; Del could hear their footsteps pounding against the pavement. It was going to be a footrace to the car to see who got there first—and if anyone died.

Tyler reached the car first, opening the back door as he shot at the gunmen, then all but threw Del inside. As Xander dove into the front seat and started the car with a button, Tyler scrambled in, covering her body with his own.

"Go!" he shouted to Xander.

But the other man was already peeling out of the parking lot with a ripe curse. "What the fuck happened?"

Del's heart beat so hard she felt sure it would fall out of her chest. She'd barely caught her breath when she heard Tyler say, "Somehow, Carlson must have figured out where we were going to be. Maybe Esteban was a setup."

"Maybe. But why not send thugs into the club?" she asked, pushing Tyler off of her.

He eased away reluctantly. "Too visible?"

Xander sped down the mostly deserted streets and nodded. "If he's up for appointment as the DA, even temporarily, he has to keep his nose reasonably clean. Everyone is going over his records with a fine-tooth comb right now. He must know that you don't have enough hard evidence now or you'd have already written your story. It's possible he's trying to scare you off more than kill you."

"I doubt it," Tyler disagreed. "Those were real bullets."

"In this neighborhood . . ." Xander trailed off. "It wouldn't raise too many eyebrows."

"Agreed. But if Carlson was behind this, and they'd managed

to kill us, we wouldn't have been the first innocent bystanders to become victim to seeming gang violence. It would have been tragic, but not unheard of. And not worth much of an investigation. If they'd gone into the club and caused a scene, it could have raised a red flag, especially if there had been lots of collateral damage." Tyler cursed, clearly not liking it.

"I'll have to track Lobato Loco down again and feel him out. Maybe it wasn't a setup. Maybe something spooked him." Or he was dead. But Del hated to think about that. Not only did she not want someone else dying for this story, she had no leads if this homey bit the dust.

Damn, it was cold in here. She trembled, gathering her arms around her, huddling to keep warm. Tyler was right there, arms around her.

"Del?"

She shook her head and pushed him away. "I'm fine."

He refused to be put off. "You're having trouble coming down from the adrenaline."

Yes, and he knew the signs. "I'll be fine."

He put his arms around her again and stubbornly stayed. It felt too good to push him away.

Within moments, Xander dropped them off at his lovely "little place" in the hills and helped them into the house. "Damn, there went that car."

"Something happen to it?"

"If Carlson's goons didn't identify me, they can identify a new Audi with temporary plates. And I just bought it today." He sighed glumly.

"It's a car," she pointed out. "You were shot at. All things considered, wouldn't you rather save your ass than worry about a car?"

"Yeah," he conceded. "To be safe, I should swap out."

Del frowned as she watched him jog back to the Audi. Suddenly, the garage door opened, and he pulled the car inside. Thirty seconds later, he backed a red Mercedes convertible out, window rolled down.

"Much better. Now I can get home without worrying about being pulled over and questioned. Besides, this is a sweet ride, too."

You think? Del sighed. Some poor woman someday would have her hands full with Xander.

"What if security or traffic cameras picked you up, and the police come to your door?" Tyler asked.

Xander raised a brow. "I *dare* them to try to arrest me or hold me for questioning. Carlson might be dirty, but he's not stupid. He knows I can call a press conference faster than he can spit. It would be a PR nightmare."

Tyler nodded, and Del agreed. Carlson was smart enough to leave Xander alone.

"You leaving?" Tyler shoved his thumbs through his belt loops and stared.

"Yeah. I shouldn't turn my back on Javier for too long. Call me if anything develops."

With those words and a jaunty wave, Xander burned rubber out of the driveway and sped down the private road.

Tyler shut the door, and the evening rushed back to Del. What the hell had gone wrong? She turned it over and over in her head, trying to understand how Carlson could have traced her through Lobato Loco if the gangster hadn't sold her out. Their only common point was one phone call. She took out her cell phone, stared.

And a cold wave of suspicion crashed over her. She dropped the phone onto the coffee table with a gasp.

"What?" Tyler demanded, running over to her.

"I think I know how Carlson tracked us down, but now I'm worried."

Tyler frowned, thoughts turning, then suspicion narrowed his eyes. "You called Lisa with this phone before her murder."

"Yes. If they got this number, they could trace who else I've called, including Lobato Loco."

She turned up to him with a lost stare. She was a fluff reporter, for God's sake. All this subterfuge and danger was over her head. She didn't know how to cope, how to compensate. What the hell was she supposed to do?

"Before Lisa's murder. I—I don't remember who else I've called with this phone. What if I called someone in Lafayette and—"

"Relax. You haven't." He grabbed the phone and looked back through her call history. "All clean. We just need to ditch the phone."

She gave him a shaky nod. "I'm scared. Really scared."

"I know." Tyler leveled a grave stare at her. "When you started this investigation, did you know you'd be starting a shit storm?"

"Not really. I thought I'd fly under the radar. I never believed he'd really take me this seriously. I write about baby showers and dog shows. I had no real proof, just a supposition based on a conversation I overheard."

"You must be damn close to the truth. And you work for the most important paper in his city, angel." Tyler sighed. "There's nothing more we can do tonight. Let's just . . . try to unwind. We need to go to bed."

He was right; it was late. Her fear warred with her anger. He could not only keep her safe but make her *feel* safe. Del always felt protected in his presence. But damn it, he'd kept the knowledge of Eric's indiscretions a secret. She was furious and wondered what the hell else he'd keep from her in the future if she let him. It might not be rational, but that was how she felt.

"I know. But I want space. Can you just . . . let me spend some time alone for a while?"

His mouth flattened into a grim line. "You're still angry with me?"

"No. Yes." She paced. "I'm hurt that I wasn't important enough for you to tell me the truth. That you didn't realize how much I valued fidelity. Of course you didn't. What am I thinking? It's you I'm talking about."

Tyler darted after her and grabbed her arm. "What the fuck is that supposed to mean?"

"Like you should have to ask? When have you ever been faithful to any woman?"

"I've never made a promise to any woman, ever. I've never had a reason to be faithful. And I've never made a habit of spending time with a woman who would have given a shit about my fidelity. Except you. I'm making you a promise here and now. As long as you're with me, I won't ever touch another woman."

She reared back and stared at his rapt expression. Those green eyes of his penetrated her, tearing away what little protective armor she had. He pulled her closer. Del fought . . . but not very hard.

God, when he said things like that, it was so tempting to believe him. And if he turned out to be a liar, how much would it hurt?

"I don't know what to say. Your past—"

"Is the past. Stop letting it hang you up. When you've got no one to care about and nothing else in your life, playing Lothario and nailing hot girls fills a void. For a while. But when you're with someone who means everything, you realize what a stupid, pathetic existence it was. I can say it over and over to you, but words won't convince you." He raked a hand through his hair. "I get it. Eric burned you. You think I condoned his behavior. Should I have said something? Probably. But every day, we hit the streets together. He put his life in my hands; I put mine in his. At first, I rationalized that if I was the kind of partner to stab him in the back, it would damage the partnership. My first allegiance then was to him."

Del looked like she wanted to argue and throw it back in his face. But instead, tears welled in her eyes as she crossed her arms over her chest. Damn it, he was right.

"After the shooting," he continued, "I didn't see the point. Destiny and all the other faceless girls were in his past by then. We didn't know if he'd ever walk again, much less have an extracurricular sex life. Letting him heal and having you take care of him while he did were the most important things." Tyler sighed. "Then came . . . that night."

Del closed her eyes. "Don't say anything else."

"Fuck, I'm not keeping quiet anymore. Being with you was like finally watching the sunrise after decades of dark. I could *see* what life was supposed to be. I'd felt it, touched it, held it close. Then I fucking had to let you go because you asked me to. Don't think the truth didn't cross my mind in that moment to tell you about every one of the girls he'd been fucking since almost the day you were married. But I knew I'd be spilling for my selfish reasons and that you didn't need my shit right then. I'd planned to sit you down in a day or two and come clean. My allegiance had shifted from my friend to the woman I loved. But then you were gone from my life."

His words crushed Del. He'd given her so much information, she didn't know what to process first. His poetic admission about how important she'd become to him? The fact that she'd hurt him by letting him go to try to reconcile with her douche bag ex-husband? Eric apparently having far more lovers than she'd imagined? The fact that Tyler had admitted straight out that he loved her stood above all those, and she trembled.

Del believed him. How could she not? But did three words guarantee that he could love *only* her? Tyler had never been a one-woman man. Not that he couldn't change—he had in some ways— but trusting in the constancy of his feelings . . . After everything she'd endured with Eric, how was she supposed to just open herself up again without time and healing?

But if she didn't put her faith in Tyler, what would they have together?

She let out a sob.

"Fuck this," he growled.

Before she could understand what he meant, he bent and thrust a shoulder in her midsection and stood again. That quickly, Del was over his shoulder in a fireman's carry, and he was strutting down the shadowed hall toward the bedroom.

"Put me down. Damn it, I don't need a caveman."

Suddenly, he dropped her on the bed, then covered her body with his own. He was hot and hard everywhere. Del trembled.

"You need a firm hand. You need to be restrained and spanked. And then you need for me to make love to you until you can't see straight, until you understand how goddamn serious I am and that I'll never let anyone come between us again."

Chapter Sixteen

UNDER the hot weight of Tyler's body, Del panted, stared. She froze under the gravity of his words, but inside her heart took off like a rocket.

"I—I don't . . ."

"Know what to say? Care?" he shot back. "I'm done talking."

Suddenly, the rough hands that pinned her to the bed were on her, moving down her body, pulling at her clothes, flipping her over to lie on her stomach.

In seconds flat, Tyler stripped her bare—except the red shoes. She should be indignant. He'd picked her up like a sack of potatoes. But she was already wet and aching. And so hopeful that he meant even a word he'd said.

Then he hauled her across his lap and braced one of his forearms into the crook of her knees. The other anchored her at the small of her back. "I'm sure if I searched this place, I could find a whole room full of perversions because that's how Xander rolls. But I don't need nylon cords or wooden paddles to get my point across."

He really meant to spank her? She froze, but a traitorous ache took up residence right between her legs.

The question had barely cleared Del's thoughts before she felt the first whap of his hand across her ass. She yelped. Pain bubbled across her backside, but tingling followed. Then heat.

"Fuck," Tyler groused. "I need light."

He leaned over to the nightstand for the lamp. Del knew his grip wasn't as sturdy in those moments and that she could probably wriggle free. But she needed him. Not just for sex, though that would likely be mind-blowing as always. She needed to see how insistent he was, how far he was willing to go to prove his point. So she waited, breath shallow.

A second later, soft golden light bathed the bedroom. Tyler sighed and palmed her ass. "You're already pink. Fuck, that's pretty."

He pressed his palm into the small of her back and took another whack at her ass, sending a new shiver of sweet pain and heat through her body. "That's right, angel. Listen to me, feel how fucking much I want you. You're going to stay here and take me until you believe it. Then we're going to talk. You're going to nod and tell me that you love me, too. Then we're going to nail Carlson's ass to the wall."

Tyler made it sound so easy to open herself to him, body and heart, to admit how she felt. But even if she didn't, he saw right through her. He knew she loved him. And he knew they had to stop Carlson before the bastard stopped them.

"No arguments?"

"I don't know how to just believe that you'll be faithful. I want to, but . . ."

He turned her so that she rested on her side, her breasts against his chest, her head now on his shoulder, back cradled by his strong arm. He delved into her eyes with a stare so open and searing, more of the fear and ice inside her melted.

"I know, angel. You've been through a lot. I'm asking you to take a big leap of faith. But don't assume that I won't be faithful before you've even given me a chance. We owe it to each other. To our son."

Del gulped. Yeah, she had no defense for that.

Suddenly, sobs racked her body. The rest of her walls crumbled down, and she threw her arms around Tyler's neck. He gripped her tightly, holding her crushingly close. And she didn't care. The sounds of his breathing and heartbeat filled her ears, but he said nothing. The moment was timeless, endless. So deep. Words couldn't possibly fill it.

Instead, she raised her face to his, layered her mouth across his lips, and kissed him with everything exploding from her heart. Swift, deep, ravenous, she took him. And he responded in kind, grasping at her as if she was a precious treasure he would never let go, sinking into the kiss again and again. His heartbeat quickened against her chest, in time with hers. Del melted into him.

That wasn't close enough for Tyler. He laid her across the bed and followed her down, his lips searing across her cheeks, her neck, down to her breasts, suddenly tight with need. His lips closed around one nipple and sucked hard.

Electric desire shocked Del. She arched up. "More."

"I'm going to give you more, angel," he murmured, switching to her other breast. "I'm going to be at you until you can't think about anything except the way we feel together."

They should talk about this more. She should really have her head clear before she fell into bed with him. He'd take this to mean forever. But her heart urged her to grab him and accept him. They could sort out anything else later. For now, this felt right.

"Please." She was whimpering.

And Tyler was loving it. He pressed his lips over hers, thumbing both of her nipples in firm strokes that only made the gaping gash of need inside her grow. She thrust her hips up at him.

He didn't wait an instant before he accepted her invitation.

Tyler reached behind him and yanked off his T-shirt, revealing slabs and ridges of golden muscle. He was taut everywhere, veins standing out strong. Primal, perfect male, intent on having her. Del shivered.

Then he tore off his jeans, shoved them around his hips, and plunged into her with one demanding stroke. She gasped and spread her legs wider to take him.

"That's it," he breathed as he wrapped his arms around her and clutched her ass to tilt her up, then set up a rhythm of relentless strokes, slow, deep. Every one rubbed against that sensitive spot inside her as he entered. As he filled her completely, he roused nerves deep in her cervix—a sensation she'd never known before him. And he ground his pelvis against hers, nudging the nerves of her clit.

Del couldn't find her breath. Every muscle in her body tightened, and rapid heartbeats coupled with the thick honey of arousal soared in her veins. She clutched Tyler, knowing that she'd never felt this way about any man. At every turn, he surprised her. He'd protected her, despite the total upheaval of his life. He tried to build a relationship with the son he barely knew. Even now, he tried to claim her like some primitive warrior of old, using his body and the pleasure he gave to brand her as his. And God help her, she didn't think she would ever be whole without him again.

If she ever wanted to be happy, she was going to have to throw herself into his arms, put her heart at his mercy, and love him with her whole being. If he betrayed her . . . then she'd know. But she refused to walk away a coward.

Pleasure coursed through her now. Del dragged her lips up his neck and bucked into Tyler's thrusts.

Within seconds, her body was aflame. Ecstasy breathed against her skin, about to overtake her, and Tyler was too attuned to her not to know it.

"That's it, angel. Come for me."

He didn't have to ask twice. The ache deep in her pussy grew, tightened. She could actually feel the rising tide of orgasm overtake her just before it exploded like a skyrocket, sending her soaring high and fast. She clamped down on his cock, still deep inside her.

"Yes," he groaned, his body tensing above her as he tried to breathe through each stroke and prolong her pleasure.

But it was costing him, and the way he clamped his eyes shut told her more than anything how much the effort tortured him.

That wasn't going to do. Del wanted him to feel as good as she felt. She shoved him to the side, urging him to roll to his back. He played along until she was seated above him. Tyler's gaze fastened on the heavy sway of her breasts.

"Now I'm really fucking glad I turned on the light. You're beautiful. Move with me, angel."

He set a leisurely pace, scraping that thick cock of his across every nerve endings he'd already stimulated. Despite her recent climax, the crescendo to pleasure was inexorable. Determination firmed his jaw as he plowed up into her, going even deeper than before.

Del had thought to turn the tables on Tyler, make him lose his self-control. But here he was, ratcheting her pleasure up again. And here she was, helplessly falling into the fray of need until she screamed out in a gush of release and clutched him with her arms, legs, sex. Still, he just kept pumping into her until one orgasm became another, then a fourth, until she couldn't count anymore.

He pressed kisses across her face, then lingered on her mouth. "I will never want anyone more than I want you. I could do this all night with you and still want you the next day. Angel, please give us a chance."

Del absorbed his words. He'd unraveled her, turned her inside out, and all that was left was the raw woman who bled and feared . . . and hoped. Tears fell down her cheeks, even as another orgasm clawed its way through her and left her speechless.

So she simply nodded.

As if that had turned on some switch inside Tyler, he shoved his cock into her rougher, faster, grabbing her hips and looking her right in the eye. "Come with me. Yeah?"

It astounded her that she could. She could barely move at that point, she'd been so drugged by the pleasure. But she managed to nod, then clamp down on him in a thundering climax harsher and more demanding than all the rest. She screamed until she lost her breath, her voice—and still the ecstasy racked her. It turned up a notch when she felt Tyler jolt, then the wet jet of his semen blasted deep inside her.

With a long, low growl, he filled her again and again with his pleasure and his seed, clutching her. The growl became something like a moan. Then his body went completely limp underneath her.

Their hearts thundered together. Breaths mingled. And reverent silence filled the rest of the room. Something had happened here. She'd given a piece of her soul to Tyler that she'd never be able to take back. It scared the hell out of her.

Walking away from him scared the hell out of her more.

"Angel," he breathed. "God, you're perfect. It's never been just sex with you. It's like . . . melding. I only wanted to get deeper inside you and never leave."

"Yeah." She didn't have prettier words, just a fresh batch of tears at the touching way he'd described their lovemaking. "It's like my body knows how much you mean to me."

"I'm sorry I didn't tell you sooner about everything . . . the past."

Del swallowed. The stark honesty on his face couldn't be a lie.

He meant every word he said. His apology and his sincerity choked her up. Could this man get any more perfect? "I know."

Relief filled his expression, and he burrowed his face into her neck, breathing her in. "I want to hold you all night."

It sounded heavenly . . . except they were going to need a change of sheets if they didn't get up soon.

Then their situation struck her. She gasped. "You didn't use a condom."

"I'm clean," he offered immediately, then peered closely at her. "You're not on the pill?"

She shook her head. "No reason to be."

He hesitated, then nodded. "You're right. No reason at all. Seth needs a brother or sister."

That quickly, Del felt his cock growing, lengthening. She gaped at him. "Tyler, we—"

"We're going to be good parents to the boy we have. Don't you want more children? I do."

"When all this danger is over, we can talk about it, but I—"

His strokes grew deeper, longer. "I'm not letting this mother-fucker dictate my future. We're going to get him, and when we do, we'll celebrate. If you're pregnant again, we'll celebrate even more. Angel, please. I want to be with you every step of the way this time. I want to make you utterly mine."

Damn, the picture Tyler painted was so seductive. He made it sound heavenly and ridiculously simple, like all she had to do was lay back and let him love her until nature took its course and a new baby to love grew in her belly.

Reality intruded. Carlson could even now be on their asses. They were still in danger, and until this slimy bastard was caught, none of them were safe. That wasn't her only objection. She wasn't terribly old-fashioned, but she'd just gotten divorced last time she'd given birth. This time she wanted to be married and settled.

Still on top, Del disentangled herself from Tyler and pushed off the bed before he could grab her. "Now isn't the time to be careless or make rash decisions. I need to think about this."

Confusion racked Tyler's face. "I love you. I love Seth. I want our family, and I want it to grow."

"Right now, we don't even live in the same state," she pointed out.

"And neither of us can rent a moving van and fix that?" He raised a tawny brow at her.

She flushed with something between anger and shame. "We can. Like I said, this is happening awfully fast. I knocked on your door in Lafayette a handful of days ago."

"I've loved you for years. You love me. I think you've loved me for years, too. I'm not letting anything come between us again. What else is there to know?"

Del couldn't answer that. But she felt like her life was on fast-forward. She didn't know how to cope. The most prolific playboy she'd ever met now talking about forever and babies and commitment just didn't compute when she was still rattled from danger and mind-bending sex.

"Just . . . let me sleep on it, okay?"

His face closed over. "Sure."

She'd hurt his feelings, and that hadn't been her intent. All she'd needed was for him to slow down a bit and let her breathe.

On silent feet, she padded over to Tyler and wrapped her arms around him. "I love you. I'm not walking away again, I swear."

"Good. I'd just come after you." He relaxed a bit and enfolded her into his embrace, placing a soft kiss on her mouth. "Take a bath and get ready for bed. I'll see if I can find out if your phone has been traced and if there's anything new on Lobato Loco."

"Thanks." She squeezed his hand. "For everything."

Tyler nodded, slapped on his jeans, and walked away.

* * *

DAMN it.

Tyler stomped into the office across the hall from the master bedroom, slammed the door shut, threw himself into his chair, and shoved his head in his hands.

Real smooth, fucktard. She got shot at tonight after finding out her ex-husband was cheating scum, and you want to make babies. Want to hunt for unicorns and rainbows next?

He was angry, not just at himself—but at the fear that coursed through him. The last time Del had been sweet but distant after sex, he hadn't seen her again for two years. No fucking way would she get that far from him again. She was *his* now. Was always going to be his. Once all this shit with Carlson was over, she'd stay his. There'd be time for more babies then. Oh, and she'd probably want to get married first. *Duh!* He probably should have mentioned that.

The "M" word that had once made him break out in shivers and hives now had him smiling. She'd look gorgeous walking down the aisle toward him in white lace with Seth beside her and all their friends around him. Of course, he liked the picture better with her sporting a baby bump. Guess that made him a caveman after all.

Right now, he had to get his head out of his ass. He couldn't possibly hope for that future if he didn't untangle this danger. Despite the clock reading something like two in the morning, Tyler resolved to press on. There was a reason Lobato Loco hadn't shown up, and Tyler wanted to know why.

First, he had to solve the problem with Del's prepaid cell. Wincing, he called Jack. No doubt, his new boss would love the oh-dark-thirty wake-up call.

To his credit, Jack answered on the second ring and didn't sound remotely sleepy. "Tyler?"

"The shit is hitting the fan." Tyler explained what had happened at Desnuda.

"That's a lot of shit." Jack agreed with his assessment.

"How can I tell if Del's calls are being monitored?"

"You can't, and it doesn't matter. You need to dump that phone."

"It's the only number Lobato Loco has for Del," Tyler argued.

"He's either a traitor or he's dead. In either case, he's useless to you."

Tyler raked a hand through his hair. "That's going to kill her. We've got nothing else."

"Xander's money trail is interesting, but inconclusive. It looks shady, but . . ."

"Doesn't prove a damn thing. I don't know where to turn. She needs something, Jack. She's a strong woman, but being away from Seth, being in this much danger, it's too much upheaval. It's killing her. I'm worried."

"God, you're so in love with this woman." Jack laughed. "The girls here are already planning a wedding, you know?"

Despite the grim situation, Tyler smiled. "Tell them to make it sooner, rather than later. I don't want to wait."

"Will do. Get some sleep for now. Deke is supposed to have a follow-up with his guys in the FBI later today. Maybe they've dredged something up. They sounded real eager to talk."

With that, Tyler disconnected the call. The computer hummed in front of him, and he opened the lid, checking some local sites and blogs to see if there were any news or warrants following the shooting at Desnuda.

The flash of Del's e-mail at the bottom of the screen caught his attention. She had a new message.

Jumping up, he found her soaking in the tub, looking frail and exhausted. But when she opened her eyes, the look inside them was fierce. She was totally committed to ending Carlson and—he hoped—getting on with their future.

"You have a new e-mail. You should come check it, just in case."

She didn't ask questions or protest about being tired. Del just rose, water dripping from her body like some Venus. Inch after inch of creamy skin looked rosy, and he could see the marks of his possession on her body—whisker burns, faint bruises, swollen nipples and mouth. She couldn't look more gorgeous, and all he wanted was to sink back into her body and love her again.

Adjusting himself in his jeans, Del watched with a raised brow. "Again?"

"Always," he promised hoarsely.

A blush rushed up her cheeks as he helped her out of the tub. It took a lot of restraint to let Del cover herself. Right now, nailing Carlson was more important than nailing her. At least that's what he told his dick.

She tossed on a fluffy robe they'd found on the back of the bathroom door, and Tyler took her hand. Together, they padded across the hall. Wordlessly, Del sank into the chair and concern crept across her face. As she put her fingers to the keyboard and accessed her mail, she looked tense, ready for flight. He cupped her shoulder in a show of silent support.

"It's from Preston," she murmured.

"Before we read whatever he's said, we should know if he tried to go to the warehouse you misdirected him to."

Del sat back in her chair, leaving the e-mail closed and waiting. "You're right. I have to know whether I can trust him."

Tyler picked up his cell and called Xander again. God, as often as he'd been reaching out, the asshole was likely going to think it was either a joke or a come-on.

Xander answered, panting. "Yeah?"

Something laced his voice, not sleep. Not exhaustion. Something happier, something— Shit, it was satisfaction. "Am I interrupting something?"

"You've got lousy fucking timing."

Tyler winced and paced across the room. "You didn't have to answer."

"I do if you're dying, right? Spit it out."

"Did anyone try to hit your warehouse tonight?"

"No," he ground out. "Not even a mouse stepped foot on the premises. I looked into it before I . . . settled in for the night."

"She anyone we know?"

Xander laughed. "Well, let's say now I know what's under the red scarf and thong."

Tyler couldn't help but grin. "Thanks, man. Um, carry on."

Xander didn't even bother to reply, just hung up.

Tyler set his phone down and turned to Del. "Looks like Preston might be in the clear. It's not one hundred percent . . ."

"Nothing is," Del agreed. "But if he'd been working for Carlson and had a supposed lead on our location, I think he'd have followed it up quick."

"Especially after everything went south at Desnuda."

With a nod, Del opened the e-mail. Her gaze flew across the screen, her eyes getting wider and wider until she gasped.

"What?" Tyler demanded, his gut clenching.

"Oh God, Lobato Loco is dead—at the hands of his own gang."

"What?" Tyler scowled, then demanded. "How do you know?"

"Preston says that after he finished answering questions for the police about Lisa's murder and identifying her body, they dropped him off at the office so he could get his car and go home. On the office's stoop, he found a box and a note that proclaimed Lobato Loco a *rata*."

"A rat. Okay, but why do you think he's dead?"

"Because"—her voice trembled—"they sent the note along with his head."

The bottom dropped out of Tyler's stomach. Del looked pale as a sheet, and when she looked up at him, eyes frightened and mouth trembling, he nearly jumped over the desk to take her into his arms.

"Tyler . . ." She looked so damn scared that it broke his heart.

"Shh, angel. We knew they were terrible bastards. We're still here alive, still safe."

"But for how long? He's not going to stop coming after me, and I have no evidence to expose him. I can't keep running forever."

Thoughts buzzed through Tyler's brain. He wanted this fucking bastard gutted. Carlson needed a hole in his skull, and Tyler wanted to spit in it before he fed the son of a bitch to the fish. It went against his every instinct to give up. But he'd been a cop. Del was a mom, a reporter. She had no experience with this relentless danger, and it was wearing her down.

"If you want to, we can. You, me, and Seth can go someplace totally new. Jack will help us change our identities. We can get married, start a totally new life. Carlson will be looking for a single mom, not a family. He'll never think to look for us in BFE, Oklahoma, or wherever you want to go."

She blinked, looking up at him through wet lashes. "You'd do that for me?"

"What?"

"Give up . . . everything. Your job, your friends, your past and future?"

His offer surprised her? He grabbed her arms and dragged her body against him. "Angel, I'd do anything for you. When are you going to get that?"

Her mouth opened like she wanted to say something, but the silence dragged on. Instead, she threw herself into his arms and clung.

Del needed an anchor, and Tyler was not only happy to oblige, he was thrilled. She was leaning on him, trusting him—coming to him and needing him.

More tears fell as she looked at him, and the love on her face made his heart go boom. Jack was right; he was so in love with this woman, he'd never recover. And he never wanted to.

Moments later, her hands were at his zipper, and his jeans were sliding down his hips. He hadn't bothered with a shirt, figuring he'd just be going to bed.

He kicked his pants away and looked up in time to see Del peel the robe off her shoulders, leaving her to stand alabaster perfect by the room's faint light. Her eyes looked feral, hungry, and so needy.

Craving torqued in Tyler's chest, and his cock stood up, harder than it had been all night. Del didn't gently layer her mouth over his, but attacked it, urgently forcing his lips apart and running inside. She moaned, not merely like she liked kissing him, but like he was vital—her shelter from the storm. He wanted to be that and more for her.

Del stunned him when she shoved him back into the desk chair and mounted him in a flash, legs straddling his hips. The head of his cock flared against her entrance, and he felt her soft flesh, already wet, grasping and clenching above him.

Fuck, he wanted her so badly, he couldn't breathe. But he felt compelled to point something out. "Angel, no condom."

She ignored him completely, sinking down on his shaft with a long moan that ripped into Tyler's self-control. Still, he held off. In Del's head, this wasn't about forever or babies or anything other than needing to feel safe and alive. He had to relax and let her ease the terror bubbling inside of her. If that was sex . . . well, he wasn't going to complain.

And if she sported that baby bump before the wedding, he'd just grin.

Tyler grabbed her hips. "What do you need?"

"You." She gyrated on him frequently. "Just you. Please. Now."

"Always, angel."

"Hard and fast."

She was really asking him to make her forget, even for a while, that everyone around her was dying. Tyler was happy to oblige. He pressed his cock deep into her. "Take me, angel. All of me."

With a gasp, she nodded frantically as he filled her again. And again. And again.

Fuck, the friction was almost a burn. Deep, so tight. The pleasure seared, not just because her pussy gloved him so perfectly but because Del needed him. Because she wasn't just opening her body to him. This was love. This was trust. He'd never gotten off on those things before, but with every pump of his cock into her body, he could feel her giving way, giving herself over to him. Giving him everything.

He was going to come.

"Angel?"

"Don't stop." Her muscles around him began to ripple, and she increased the pace of her thrusts. "Please . . ."

An invitation to totally let go and give her everything in return. No way was he turning that down.

Tyler gripped her hips even tighter and unleashed the blazing ache in his cock, now tingling at the base of his spine. He shoved all the emotion choking his throat and clogging his chest into the kiss he seized her lips with. He filled her in every way he could in that moment, and when she shouted into his mouth, he gave over the last of his control again and flooded her deep with his seed.

God, he couldn't love her more.

He lifted his head and brushed her damp tendrils away from her face. "Angel—"

"Don't say anything now. We have a lot to sort out, especially if I get pregnant again. I know what I said earlier, but I needed to feel you now."

"I understand," he said gently.

"And I need a goddamn plan. Two people have died simply for coming into contact with me. I won't be the cause of any more murders. Let's put a stop to this now."

Chapter Seventeen

DEL awakened the following morning wrapped up in Tyler's warm embrace, tangled in the soft blankets of the big bed they shared. And the damn ringing of her disposable cell phone.

She opened an eye and realized the sun had risen, but it was still fairly early. The clock confirmed that it was just minutes past eight a.m. Who would be calling her little throwaway phone? She'd given the number to no one. Nearly everyone she'd ever called with the number was dead. Unless Carlson himself was calling her. The possibility chilled her.

Scrambling out of bed and across the room, she grabbed the phone off the dresser, pressing the speakerphone button so Tyler could hear, too. Just in case. "Hello."

"Del? It's Eric."

Oh shit! She'd forgotten that she'd called her ex-husband on this phone. He might not be her favorite person in the world, but she wouldn't wish the sort of death on him that Lisa or Lobato Loco had experienced. Despite all the sunshine and warmth in the room, she shivered.

"You shouldn't talk to me on this number. It's been compromised."

"I'll be quick, and if something happens, I can defend myself."

"I'd rather not risk—"

"I have your flash drive," he said grimly. "I want to talk to you about what's on it."

Del froze for a long moment, then her heart began to pound. Eric had her evidence. If she could recover it, she'd have a jumping-off point for saving herself and Seth. This nightmare might actually come to an end. Then she frowned. "How did you get it?"

"I'll explain everything when you get here."

Suddenly, she felt Tyler's heat at her back, heard his breathing in her ear. Del turned at his grip on her elbow.

"You are not going there again," he whispered.

"Why don't we meet for breakfast somewhere?" Del suggested. "Is that little omelet place around the corner from the house still open?"

"You and I both know that what's on this flash drive shouldn't be discussed in public. It needs to stay as hidden and safe as possible."

Eric made a valid point, but Del wasn't about to give in. "Remember what happened the last time I came to the house? I'm not in a hurry to repeat the experience."

"I was an ass, and I'm sorry," he said through gritted teeth. "I won't touch you. I give you my word. But if you want this back, I want to talk to you first, make sure you know what the fuck you're getting yourself into. Ten o'clock, sharp."

Del opened her mouth to argue with him when she realized Eric had hung up. She punched the END button on her phone with a curse. "Bastard!"

"I don't want you going over there." Tyler had no compunction about voicing his opinion. "No fucking way."

"If I want the flash drive back, I have to go."

"He didn't say that you had to go alone."

Del pondered that statement. She'd feel personally safer taking Tyler, but Eric seemed to have a lot more animosity toward his ex-friend than his ex-wife. If Tyler hadn't been there last time, Eric would have yelled and made his point, but she doubted he'd have touched her against her will. That whole show had been for Tyler's benefit. Was bringing Tyler this time like bringing a powder keg to a roomful of sparks?

"Whatever you're thinking, no." Tyler shook his head and crossed his beefy arms over his chest. "I'm going. That's final."

"I need that flash drive, and I suspect that you'd just make a bad situation worse."

"Fuck," Tyler muttered, then raked a hand through his hair. "I don't trust him. If you go without me, that leaves you vulnerable. He's got a plan. There's some reason he's giving you the flash drive now. He's got a price in mind, and I'm pretty sure I know what it is. No."

Del caught onto his insinuation. "You think he's going to want me to have sex with him?"

"If touching you would hurt you, I think he'd be fine with that. If it will hurt me, even better. And he knows it would eat me up inside."

Wincing, Del had to admit there might be a kernel of truth there. "But if I bring you—"

"Then I'll go in, guns ready. I won't go ape shit sitting in this house or some car down the street, wondering if you're safe." Tyler paced the room. "But something about this whole situation isn't adding up. Where has the flash drive been since we asked for it? Why did he read it? He says he wants to turn it over, but what's in it for him?"

She'd wondered some of the same things. Eric was generally the sort of person who didn't do anything without some personal benefit, and hanging on to the flash drive for a few days so he could read it, just to give it back, didn't make a lot of sense.

"If he's read it and thought about it, he's had it for a while." Her gut instinct was telling her that.

"Agreed. Maybe he had it all along. Was that break-in even real?"

"Or a cover story? I don't know."

"Why would he try to cover up the fact that he had the flash drive?" Tyler mused. "To get more time with it? See what you're into?"

That was the logical explanation, but why? Del wondered if there was more to it. She tried to take a step back and look at the bigger picture. How would he have found out that she'd kept the flash drive there? If he'd had it for weeks, he wouldn't have needed to hang on to it. So he'd just recently found it. What had made him go looking for it? When they'd spoken on the phone before going over there, she hadn't told him what she was looking for. The only people she'd told were Tyler and Lisa. Tyler would never tell anyone. Lisa . . . had probably blabbed to Carlson for thirty thousand dollars. Which meant . . .

"Eric is in bed with Carlson," Tyler proclaimed into her silence.

"I was just coming to the same conclusion." Her voice shook. "Oh God."

If her ex-husband would really sell her out to someone so ruthless, was she walking into a trap? Would he even blink when they killed her? Eric was a cop, damn it. Wouldn't he protect her? Maybe not. He'd done nothing when Lisa and Lobato Loco had been viciously murdered. What did it matter to him if his ex-wife, who was in love with his former best friend, got the ax, too? And Eric hadn't told Tyler not to come. In fact, he had to know that Tyler would accompany her. What was that rat bastard hoping for, a twofer in the murder department today?

Something inside her crumbled. She'd once loved that man. Hadn't the frequent cheating been enough for him? Or did he think that she and Tyler deserved to die because the sex they'd shared two years ago had resulted in a beautiful little boy? Because it had meant something to them and they'd fallen in love?

"I think he intends for both of us to die," Del said solemnly. "How did you figure it out?"

"He's the first person you talked to with your disposable cell, yet the only one who isn't dead. He suddenly found the flash drive . . . None of this shit adds up. We've said that Carlson has to have dirty cops to make this work. I guess that means dirty Vice detectives, too."

Tyler would probably be furious for asking, but she had to know. "And you knew nothing about this?"

"Fuck, no!" he exploded. "Toward the end of our partnership, Eric acted oddly at times, and I clearly should have asked more questions. But I didn't know anything. I may have bed hopped a lot back then, but I would never have allowed that corrupt shit. And I sure as hell wouldn't line my own pockets to let criminals get away with drug dealing and murder. You know me better than that."

"Yeah. I thought I knew Eric, too," she said softly.

Dragging a hand down his face, Tyler sighed. "You've got to be really confused, angel. But I swear to God, I would never accept money from a slime like that. And I'd never let anything happen to you."

Tyler took her in his arms, clutching her tightly, and Del didn't resist. She needed an anchor in this storm of lies, deceit, and intrigue. And he was perfect—solid, supportive, unwavering.

"I'm sorry," she murmured.

"I won't lie and say I love it, but I understand feeling burned by people you trusted. The question is, what do we do now? If Eric is on the take from Carlson, we have to expect that he's sold us out.

This is going to be dangerous. And before you say a word, you aren't going to Eric's alone."

As much as Del wanted Tyler removed from danger, she had to think of Seth. He needed parents. She couldn't bear the thought of leaving her baby all alone, and the odds would more likely be in their favor if she took Tyler along.

"All right. But we're going to need help."

"Agreed." Tyler nodded. "We can't contact the police for help. They're either going to be corrupt, Eric's buddies, or both."

"And we have no evidence to prove our suspicions yet, so . . ."

"We're going to have to come up with a plan B. I'll use the computer to call back to Lafayette. Take my phone and call Xander. Get whatever resources you can. I'll do the same."

With a solemn nod, she grabbed his phone and meandered toward the kitchen. She wasn't hungry, but they'd both need strength for the trial to come. She tried to push aside the betrayal making her chest tighten and ache. How could the son of a bitch who had once promised to love, honor, and protect her turn her over to the man who would celebrate her murder?

Shoving the thought away, Del called Xander. He picked up right away. "This had better be good."

She winced at his growl. "My ex called. We're supposed to be at his house at ten. I think we're the lambs he's leading to slaughter. And we can't call the police. You must have bodyguards or something. Would you be willing to lend them to us for a few hours?"

"They all suck ass. I escape them constantly, except one. Expect a knock on your door from Decker McConnell in less than an hour. Former Special Forces who went to work as a field agent for the CIA. Deep cover. Tough bastard."

"Don't you need to talk to him first?" She frowned.

"I pay him to be ready at a moment's notice. Sit tight. I'll be there soon."

"Oh no. Please don't—"

Click.

Tyler strolled into the room, and Del turned, frustration shredding her composure. "The bastard hung up on me. He's sending a guy, and as soon as I tried to point out to Xander that it wasn't safe for him to come along, too, he hung up."

"Maybe that's just as well. Jack and Deke said it might take a couple of hours to track down some of their former army buddies who live in this area. By then, this is over."

Yes. And Del hoped this meeting didn't become a bloodbath.

"They've also called some connections at the FBI." He shrugged. "Maybe something will pop there. C'mon, angel. Let's shower and get ready to do this."

Del dug in her heels. "I have to talk to Seth again . . . Just in case."

She shoved back tears and regarded Tyler with an unflinching stare.

He scrubbed a hand down his face. "You don't have to go to Eric's. I'll go alone. I'll tell him that he scared the hell out of you last time you came by and—"

"No. I have to get my evidence back if I want a future. He wants to talk to me, and I know he's not going to hand it over until I do. Just let me talk to my son one last time."

"*Our* son." Tyler led her across the hall to the spacious office and the computer.

She sent him a sad smile. "I'm not used to that yet."

"Get used to it."

As Tyler sat at the computer and initiated the online video call, she whispered, "I'd like to. Right now, I can't help fearing this is the last time Seth will see me and that he won't remember me if—"

"Don't you dare finish that sentence. You are not going to die, damn it."

Del pressed her lips together. "We don't know that for certain. Eric might be leading us right into a trap. We can only do the right things and hope for the best."

"Hey," Luc said casually into the computer. "All okay there?"

She exchanged a glance with Tyler, who said, "Yeah."

"No," she corrected. "I'd like to see Seth."

Luc went on alert. "What's wrong?"

Tyler cursed under his breath, then sighed. "Jack's got the details. I think this thing is coming to a head this morning."

Del watched as understanding, then quiet acceptance, dawned across Luc's face. "I'll go get Seth. Earlier this morning, he saw Caleb take a stuffed animal from Chloe. When she started crying, Seth grabbed it away, handed it back to her, then pushed Caleb on his ass."

That sounded like her little boy. A moment later, his smiling baby face filled the screen. She tried not to cry, but she was so proud of him, already exhibiting such strong qualities—intelligence, a sense of fairness, a willingness to defend those weaker than him. She only hoped that if things didn't go well today he eventually understood her decisions.

"Hi, little man."

"Ma ma ma." He lunged forward and reached out for the screen.

A pang of love welled up, filled her, mixed with longing and pain. A sob racked her body, and Tyler's arm went around her immediately. She sucked the tears back. Being strong for Seth now was imperative.

"Hi, Seth," Tyler said into the webcam. "How's our big boy today?"

He gurgled and reached for the screen again. Luc held him back with a big hand across his little belly.

"This kid is strong," Luc commented. "He likes spinach, too."

"And sweet potatoes."

Luc grinned. "Did you know he loves Cheetos? He ate nearly a whole bag of Chloe's little munchies when he was supposed to be napping. I shouldn't be surprised that he crawled out of the playpen and remembered where we'd stored the stuff."

Tyler smiled like he was proud. "Sounds like something I would have done at his age."

It did. Del grabbed his hand. Then she realized there wasn't much left to say. "Kiss him for me, please."

Luc nodded. He looked like he wanted to tell her that everything was going to be okay, but no one could assure her of that. He simply nodded and placed a soft kiss in Seth's pale hair, patting his little shoulder. "He knows that you love him."

"Tell him I love him, too," Tyler asked, then swallowed. "I'm going to try to update everyone when I can. If you haven't heard from us by four o'clock your time . . ."

Tyler didn't finish that sentence. He didn't have to.

With a nod, Luc wrapped protective arms around Seth. "Anything else I can do for you?"

"Pray." Del's voice trembled.

"Absolutely." Then Luc looked at Tyler. "Take care of you and yours."

With a nod, Luc was gone. After the screen went blank, Del desperately wanted to collapse into Tyler's arms. But now wasn't the time. They had barely over an hour to get ready, plan, and cross town.

Stiffly, she rose and made her way across the hall, into the bathroom. When she started the shower and pulled off her clothes, shivering, Tyler eased into the bathroom behind her and pulled her against the solid warmth of his body. He was naked, too, and every inch of his hard frame blanketed her back.

Threading his arm around her waist, he kissed the top of her head. "We'll get through this together, angel."

Having him close was such a comfort. Funny how a few short days ago she was certain that Tyler would be another drive-by in her life. She'd drop Seth off, solve all this herself, then pop back in and pick up her son, no muss, no fuss—and above all, no emotions. Now, she couldn't imagine facing this danger without him. By herself, she wasn't sure she had any chance to survive. Tyler would move heaven and earth to keep her safe.

Delaney more than loved Tyler Murphy; she'd wrapped her heart, soul, and life around his so quickly. Even with this black cloud hanging over them, she relished the feeling of connection to the one man she'd never forgotten.

She opened the shower door and eased in. Tyler climbed in right behind her. Wordlessly, they embraced under the spray, a long moment filled with warm water, beating hearts, and utter stillness. They were saying good-bye to one another, just in case the worst happened. No words necessary. They both knew. They both felt the solemn moment and didn't spoil it with chatter.

A moment later, Del backed against the cold tile wall and held out her arms to Tyler. He came to her silently. Maybe the look in her eyes told him what she needed. He just nodded and lifted her, holding her thighs over his arms and bracing her against the wall. With steam rising from the hot spray and their deep breaths filling the space, Tyler probed her pussy with the blunt tip of his cock. The moment he found her open and slick, he pushed her down, surging up into her tight walls.

One thrust became another, then a dozen, then she lost count. The only thing she knew was Tyler's deep penetration, the burn of his flesh against her already sore sex, but she welcomed the sensation. It reminded her that she was alive, could hurt and need. It reminded her that she could feel.

Del wrapped her legs around his hips and used whatever leverage she could to wriggle and bounce. Her nails dug into his shoulders. Her mouth found his, slanting over that hard slash to invade and silently tell him that she'd never wanted anything or anyone more than she wanted him.

His thick fingers dug into her hips, and the sensations spiraled. A heavy ache settled behind her clit, mixing with the pleasure-pain of his possession, scraping up her swollen channel and the friction of his flesh rubbing her little bundle of nerves repeatedly. It was too much—the pleasure, the love, the need to experience this moment to the fullest. Del crested over the edge, careening into a dizzying ecstasy that made her cry his name, into a significant love that utterly reshaped her.

With a long, low groan in her ear, he followed her into pleasure, and she felt the warm spray of his semen jet deep inside of her. Del closed her eyes. She hoped she lived long enough to find out if all the unprotected sex they'd had in the last twenty-four hours brought them another bundle of joy. It had only taken once before, and suddenly she wanted to have Tyler's child again, experience everything from morning sickness to college graduation with him.

Slowly, Tyler disentangled himself from her and placed a reverent kiss on her shoulder. "Let's clean you up."

She nodded, but every time she reached for the soap or loofah, he slapped her hands out of the way and washed her himself. Long, soft sweeps of his palms over her abdomen, lingering low where he felt the few stretch marks she'd gotten from carrying Seth.

"I'll bet you were so pretty pregnant. I wish I'd seen it."

Del wished he had, too. She wished she could have both shared the experience with him and had someone to lean on. But rather than dwell on what she couldn't change, she tried to lighten the mood. "Only if you like a beached whale."

His gaze was so green and intent, it almost hurt, especially when that look admonished her. "You're beautiful, no matter what. To me, you always have been."

Probably not 100 percent accurate, but Del smiled at his kindness. Then he set her under the spray. With the utmost care, he proceeded to wash her hair, his strong fingers rubbing her scalp, easing away last night's grime and a bit of this morning's tension. Del melted against him.

"Have you always been like this with lovers?" Because that wasn't how she'd heard it.

He paused. "I didn't act like I cared about any of the other women because I didn't. It took me doing without you for two years to realize how much I loved you."

"I've been numb for two years. I feel like I'm finally alive again because of you. Even if today doesn't end well, I want you to know how much that means to me."

Finally, they couldn't stall anymore and left the shower, drying slowly, both lost in thought. Tyler pulled his clothes on first, just as someone pounded on the front door.

"Showtime," he sighed. Then he pressed a kiss to her forehead, grabbed one of the guns Xander had given him the night before, and headed to the front of the house.

Del put on the rest of her clothes with trembling fingers. By tonight, she'd either be a free woman or dead.

* * *

TYLER wrenched open the estate's heavy front door. Xander stood wearing something clearly *GQ* and designer, looking perfectly unconcerned and unruffled. Behind him, a big motherfucker straight out of a *Rambo*-esque movie stood as still as a statue, black hair military cut, blue eyes scanning his surroundings, on the lookout for any sign of trouble.

Xander looked Tyler over with a critical eye. "Nice. You're going to a major sting wearing a T-shirt that says 'Cops have bigger guns.'"

"I'm probably going to end the day killing someone if I'm not killed myself. So I don't really give a shit if I meet with your fashion approval." Tyler stepped back.

Xander and the stranger entered the house, the former looking around for Del, the latter just looking for threats.

"Del okay?" Xander asked, staring down the hall.

"Almost ready. She's nervous."

With a nod, Xander strolled into the living room. "Understandable. How's she going to hold up?"

"She'll come through. Del is tough." Tyler would bank on that.

"Good." Xander turned to the big guy behind him. "This is Decker McConnell. I told Del about him on the phone. I'd give you a full list of his credentials, but then I'd have to kill you."

Tyler stared at the soldier. He looked like he'd seen his fair share of action. "You packing?"

"Always."

"Seen combat or been in a firefight?"

"Yep, on four continents." McConnell had a voice that sounded more like a deep rattle of gravel. Under that neck-to-toe black and Kevlar, he likely had more than a few nasty scars.

"Hand-to-hand?"

"Black belt in three martial arts, former military boxing and wrestling champion."

Impressive. "Nervous? You seem jumpy."

McConnell cut cold eyes over to him. "Anxious to stop the fucking pillow talk and get on with the action."

Tyler heard that. He looked back at Xander. "Yeah, he works."

"Thanks for the vote of confidence," McConnell said like he didn't give a shit. "You got a plan?"

"I'm going to go in with Del. We need to have some sort of recorder. Plan A is that Eric gives us the flash drive and we go away. But I don't think that's going to happen. I believe Eric is dirty as hell, and I'm expecting company. I want to catch anything he might say on audio or video and see if we can use it to build a case against Carlson. If you can sneak into the house and watch our backs, our chances of survival go up immensely."

"I figured you'd say something like that," Xander drawled. "Hi, Del."

Tyler turned to see her coming down the hall. She wore jeans and her gray tank top, a pair of sneakers, almost no makeup. She still managed to look stunning. He turned back to the other men. Xander wore a comforting smile, one Tyler hadn't believed the bastard had in him. McConnell looked at her with a seemingly flat stare, but Tyler sensed the guy's interest. It didn't set well with him.

It was probably high school of him, but he brought Del close and threw his arm around her waist. "You ready?"

She hesitated, then nodded. "As I'll ever be."

Damn, she looked nervous. Tyler swore he'd do whatever it took to keep her safe.

"I've got something that might help you, Del." Xander turned and looked expectantly at McConnell, who shrugged a black backpack off his meaty shoulders and foraged inside until he withdrew a gorgeous buttery leather Coach bag.

"Wow." Del's eyes widened. "I saw that bag in a catalog. It was ridiculously expensive. You can't keep giving me gifts."

Annoyance curled through Tyler's gut. "She's taken, shithead."

Xander rolled his eyes. "Such a caveman." He faced Del and explained, "It's special. I bought it and had it outfitted with the tiniest surveillance camera the technology division of S.I. Industries, my corporation, makes. It's installed in one of the grommets. See?"

When he pointed to one of the purse's studs, Del leaned down and stared. Tyler did the same.

"I don't see anything." Del sounded confused.

"Me, either."

"That's the point." Xander beamed like a kid who'd put one over on his teacher. "It's got a tiny wireless transmitter sewn into the lining. It's almost a real-time feed of whatever you're filming to my laptop. If Eric or anyone else says anything incriminating, it's going to be captured on film instantly."

Del reached out and took the satchel-style bag in her grasp. "Which way do I need to point it?"

"As long as you keep this side pointed away from your body, you're good." Xander pointed to the purse's side with the Coach insignia mounted.

Tyler didn't like any of this, but as much as he hated to admit it, Xander had a good idea.

"Anything else?" the billionaire asked.

Del looked Tyler's way, and he would have given anything to take that look of fear from her face. Instead, she just shook her head.

"You take the Audi in the garage," Xander instructed. "I'll ride with McConnell in the black SUV we brought."

Another good call. "That way if Eric is watching, he doesn't see uninvited people in the car."

"Exactly. Let's go."

They all hopped in their respective cars, and Tyler tried to ignore the silence, so thick with tension. Instead, he held her hand and ran the plan through his head over and over, looking for any way in which this day didn't end without him killing Eric or Eric killing him. So far, he hadn't been able to find one.

A few minutes before ten, they entered Eric's kitschy little neighborhood. Del grew visibly more nervous, and Tyler squeezed her hand. "Angel, you're going to have to calm down. Eric will take one look at you and know that something is up."

She blew out a deep breath and shook her head. "I know."

Tyler parked the car just past Eric's house, where no one could watch them through the windows. "All you have to do is keep your wits about you and that purse pointed toward Eric. Ask him a few leading questions. I'll do the rest."

"What if he's not alone?"

Yeah, Tyler suspected they could be walking into a den of killers, bent on shooting them right between the eyes in the first thirty seconds. "I think I've got an idea. You let me worry about that, okay?"

Del nodded. "I trust you."

Finally, it was ten o'clock on the nose. Tyler opened the car door and emerged into the sunny Southern California morning. On the passenger's side, Del did the same. They crossed the street, and Del rang the doorbell.

Chapter Eighteen

Eric cracked the door a few seconds later, and Tyler, standing in the shadowed corner of the porch, watched, his gut tightening. His former friend looked Del up and down, but there was something in his eyes. Eric was tense. Tyler frowned. If he only wanted to return Del's flash drive, why would he be nervous?

Unless, as he and Del had feared, Eric wasn't alone.

Tyler's blood began to run cold. He reached for the Glock tucked into his waistband and stepped forward. Eric sent him a nearly imperceptible shake of his head, then peeled his right hand away from the doorframe and brushed his fingers across his ear.

The gesture had been one they'd worked out long ago, when they'd first become partners. It was their silent signal for "get backup!"

"Come in, Del." Eric grabbed her arm and began to draw her inside.

No fucking way was the asshole who'd cheated on her and nearly raped her going to take her inside the house alone with danger afoot. Tyler was ready to throw down to keep Del outside, where she might have a chance of surviving. Once she went in and that door shut behind her, Tyler didn't know how much he'd be able to help her.

Eric sent him a pleading stare, his face so tense, body rigid.

Del turned back to him, and Tyler felt her hand on his chest. The gesture silently asked him to stay away, begged him to keep silent so he didn't alert whoever waited in the house to his presence.

Tyler's mind raced. If he went in with her, they'd train guns on him and strip him of his weapons. He had to get his emotions under control. As much as he hated it, if he stayed outside, he had a better chance of helping Del. He and McConnell could take the stealth approach and blindside these motherfuckers.

"If anything happens to her, you're a dead man," Tyler murmured.

Eric nodded just enough for Tyler to see the acknowledgment.

"Hi, Eric," Del said almost too brightly. "You have my flash drive?"

"Yeah, come in." Eric opened the door for Del to enter, then shut it in his face.

Tyler waited to hear him engage the dead bolt. Eric never did.

Hmm. The paranoid bastard had never failed to lock doors and windows. Ever.

With his heart pounding furiously, Tyler slinked along the shadows of the porch and overhang, until he reached a row of hedges that separated Eric's driveway from the neighbor's. He crawled through them, then emerged to sprint over to the black SUV parked across and down the street. As he approached, Xander lowered the window.

"Let's go." Tyler looked at McConnell, not bothering with pleasantries. "Eric took her in the house. He's got company. The front door is unlocked, but knowing Eric, his 'company' is hanging out in that part of the house. There's a back door and a bedroom window we may be able to crawl through. Since he tipped me off, I'm hoping he was smart enough to unlock them. We'll have to sneak our way in and eliminate whoever's there."

"Stealth and killing, my favorite kind of mission." McConnell let himself out of the SUV, now carrying an M4 carbine assault rifle. Tyler could almost bet the big guy was loaded to the gills with other weaponry. But Tyler was prepared, too—a couple of Glocks, a wicked knife, a grenade, if necessary. If Carlson had the balls to show up to this meeting, it could only mean that he wanted Del dead. If that was the case, no way was the fucker getting out of this alive.

Together, he and McConnell made their way across the street, avoiding the view from Eric's windows, just in case. They crawled along the far side of the house, then leapt the cinder-block fence. Almost soundlessly, they landed in the side yard, where there was nothing except an air-conditioning unit already chugging away against the day's promised heat.

Without a sound, Tyler pointed toward the back of the house. They ducked under the windows to avoid being seen by anyone who might happen to be in the bathroom or back bedroom. Plastered against the back wall, he directed McConnell to the French doors on their left. Then he pointed to himself and the bedroom window back to the right.

With a terse nod, McConnell began to prowl away. Tyler grabbed his arm. "No matter what, you save her."

"I will. But get your dick out of your pants or this rescue will be a fucktastic disaster," he growled, pulled free, and edged toward the patio doors.

Cursing under his breath, Tyler crept toward the window and began easing it open. Eric had definitely prepared in advance for company and unlocked it. Did that automatically mean Eric was on his side? Or just that he was anticipating another way to trap his ex-partner. After all, if someone was as dirty as Eric, what was a little murder among enemies?

A quick glance down the little flagstone patio proved that McConnell had already made his way inside without incident. Tyler crawled inside the sloppy but unoccupied bedroom. The door was ajar, but he didn't see anyone lying in wait for him in the hallway, either. What the fuck was Eric up to?

Prowling through the house, Tyler focused on disposing of any bad guys and watching for treachery. He had to hope they weren't too late to save Del.

* * *

ERIC led her inside, through the foyer, then into the living room. Immediately, she saw a gangbanger with a big gun—and her blood turned to ice. Eric had set her up to come here and discouraged Tyler from entering with her. To remove her protection or give Tyler time to mount a stealth attack? Del didn't know. That terrified her. So did trusting her ex-husband.

The thug promptly patted her down, lingering a little too long over her breasts. He wasn't big, but the gang tattoos and AK-47 made her take him really seriously. She saw two more similar goons at the back of the living room, one leaning against the wall separating the living room from the kitchen. The other lingered at the entrance to the hallway. She recognized him from photos as Double T, the leader of the 18th Street gang.

And on the sofa, just as comfortable as if he was at home, sat Carlson in a charcoal gray suit with a pristine white shirt. His salt-and-pepper hair looked perfect. He wore a cat-who-ate-the-canary smile. Fresh terror gripped her belly.

She whipped a furious glare up at Eric.

He didn't flinch, and she wondered if trusting him would turn out to be her fatal mistake. For a second, she closed her eyes and said a prayer for Tyler. She was at peace with the fact that, if she wasn't here to be a mother to Seth, he would see to their son.

"Hello, Ms. Catalano. Or do you prefer your maiden name now that you and the good detective here are divorced?"

She'd retained her married name for her byline, since her readers knew that. For legal purposes, she'd gone back to her maiden name so she would match Seth. She doubted, however, that Carlson really wanted that scoop. "It doesn't matter."

"Probably not," he agreed amicably.

"People know exactly where I am, so if anything happens to me, there will be questions and folks all up your ass."

"That's why I have the good detective on my side. He can make so many things go away and, over the years, has proven remarkably apt."

Eric *had* been dirty. For years? Del turned to Eric, betrayal bleeding through her all over again. He refused to meet her gaze.

Over the last two years, he'd shocked her. Rejecting her, cheating on her, dismissing her when she discovered that she was pregnant. She'd never imagined that he was the sort of cop who'd not only turn the other cheek at crime but facilitate it. His new betrayal kicked her in the gut.

"So tell me, what possessed you to go on this witch hunt for me?" Carlson drawled, like he didn't have a care in the world. "I'm just a public servant doing my job."

She snorted. "Yeah, unless it interferes with you taking bribes on the side. The public shouldn't be made to accept more gang and drug crime just because you want a fatter wallet."

"You can't prove any of that."

"Actually, I think I can," she bluffed. "I talked to Lobato Loco in depth before you had him killed. He told me *everything*."

Carlson exchanged a quick glance with the thug leaning against the kitchen wall, then recovered his smile. "It's the word of a dead criminal against mine."

"He had audio recordings of some incriminating phone calls," Del lied. She had to because she couldn't think of another way to get him to talk enough about the incident to incriminate himself. If he did, Xander's purse camera would record everything.

The ADA's face changed instantly. "What do you mean?"

"I know about your deal. You lay off the 18th Street gang, and they give you kickbacks from their drug trade. Lobato Loco gave me some recordings outlining the details before you had his head chopped off. It's over."

"Really? If that's true, why haven't you written the story yet? Why are you here, desperate to retrieve your flash drive?" he smiled smugly.

"Who says I haven't written the story?" She raised a brow. "Maybe it simply hasn't run yet."

"I think you're bluffing. I don't think you can prove anything."

Del shrugged, feigning a confidence she didn't feel. "Even the hint of this kind of scandal would be really bad for someone on the fast track to becoming DA. There could be a lot of questions asked, maybe an investigation . . ."

Carlson hesitated, clearly stifling his anger. He tapped the toe of his expensive Italian leather loafers against Eric's hardwood floor. "This is all nonsense. I'm sure we can work something out."

Del wanted to spit in his face and tell him that she'd never compromise with a skeevy bastard like him. But with three armed goons watching her every move, that wasn't her wisest course of action. Besides, she not only wanted to prove Carlson's guilt, she wanted to walk out of this house alive. Pretending to cooperate would help.

"What did you have in mind?"

"Drop this ridiculous witch hunt, and I'll make it worth your while."

"Meaning?" she drawled. "How will you do that?"

"I'll surprise you."

She snorted. "You already did. You blew up my car!"

"I'm not aware of that." But his too-innocent expression said otherwise.

"Bullshit. Drop the act."

Del bit the rest of the angry words on her tongue. Trying to bully him into confessing wasn't going to get her anywhere. She was going to have to call his bluff. Her heart pounded. She might be shaving time off her life with this tactic, but as soon as she'd seen the goons with the guns, she'd known this wasn't going to go down pretty.

"Fine. You're an angel," she conceded, then turned to Eric. "Can I have my flash drive?"

His eyes widened at her, his expression asking her if she'd lost her mind. *Probably so.*

"The flash drive is no longer in one piece. Such a pity," Carlson cut in. "But it contained so much aimless speculation about my associations and finances. I wouldn't want that misconstrued."

She snorted. "I was invited here to recover my flash drive, and in the ensuing two hours, it's been destroyed? Eric wouldn't have done that, so I have to assume that you mangled my critical information so that I wouldn't leak it to the public. If you have nothing to hide, why go to all this trouble? Why are you here at all?" Into his silence, she rolled her eyes. "Whatever. If my flash drive is no more, I have no reason to stay. I'm leaving."

Maybe that would force his hand.

Del turned toward the door, angling her purse toward the ADA. Carlson was off the sofa and had a harsh hand wrapped around her elbow in an instant.

"Not yet," he murmured. "My . . . associates want to have a private conversation with you."

When he nodded in Double T's direction, Del got a quick picture. The gunman would take her into the bedroom, shoot her, then Carlson would spin it so he came out smelling like a rose. He had the connections to make that happen, including Eric.

She had two choices now: fight, or keep talking and hope that her death wouldn't be in vain.

"You've outsmarted me. I've got to hand it to you. Somehow, you've anticipated my every move. Before Double T and I have that private chat, will you at least tell me, if the information I had on you was all just speculation, why are you having me killed? Why did you have my friend Lisa murdered and Lobato Loco beheaded?"

Carlson waved a hand. "I'm sure I have no idea what you're talking about."

"C'mon. Level with me. If I'm going to be dead in the next five minutes, why does it matter if you tell me the truth?"

"I don't owe you anything," Carlson told her coolly.

"True. But I admire your genius." She stroked his ego—and nearly gagged on the words. "I mean, you've fooled and eluded everyone for years now. That's a real feat. And I'll bet you've had to keep it mostly to yourself. Since I'm disposable, what harm is there in telling me? I mean, if curiosity is going to kill the reporter, at least assuage mine."

It wasn't working; she could tell from his mulish expression. She'd try to prick his vanity instead.

She frowned. "Oh, or did I misread the situation? Was this someone else's idea and you're just reaping the benefits of their genius?"

Carlson paused, a muscle twitching in his jaw. Then he looked at the gangbanger who'd patted her down. "Did you check her thoroughly?"

The goon nodded. "She's clean."

The asshole's gaze fell on her purse and narrowed. Del gripped it, doing her best to breathe through the fear and act like nothing troubled her. Quickly, he grabbed it, rummaged through it, shoving her stuff this way and that. Satisfied, he threw it on the ground at her feet.

"You want a story, honey. I'll give you your story since you're going to be dead in the next five minutes. After I'm done talking, I'll let Double T take you back to your ex-husband's bedroom and put a bullet in your brain."

Del glanced at a smiling Double T and tried not to panic. She had to stay calm if she wanted to bring Carlson down.

"Don't think for a minute that this was someone else's idea," Carlson growled. "No one knows exactly how to manipulate the system like I do. No one is better at it than me, you stupid whore."

"You had someone plant the bomb in my car." She didn't ask; she knew.

"Of course. You were becoming tiresome, digging into my affairs and my finances. The intent was to end you quietly." He sent a look of displeasure to the thug against the kitchen wall. "Someone didn't get the memo."

Euphoria swept through Del. She might die for this, but Carlson had already said enough to incriminate himself. Still, she didn't just want to nail him for conspiracy to commit murder or accessory to murder, she wanted him to go down for fraud, money laundering, racketeering, bribery . . . the whole nine yards. She glanced at Eric, wondering if he'd go down, too. He looked shell-shocked.

I didn't know, he mouthed. About the car bomb, she supposed. Would it have made a difference if Carlson had told him? Maybe. Del could see the panic and anger on his face. He might be a douche, but he didn't want her dead.

She couldn't linger on that now. She had to get Carlson to admit as much as possible on tape.

"It took me a long time to piece together your system of funneling drug money from the 18th Street gang to your dummy company, Communications Redirect. You sometimes used your wife's interior design business or your brother's car dealership, which kept me guessing. You were clever, spreading it around like that. What was the cut you took from the 18th Street crew, five percent?"

Carlson scoffed. "As if I'd settle for such a paltry amount or go to that much trouble for mere pennies. I take fifteen percent, and I earned every bit of it. Besides, I used a portion of that to pay others, like your ex-husband."

Her disappointment must have been all over her face. Eric sighed, his shoulders drooping. "I know what you're thinking. I'm . . . sorry."

"You cheated on me, accepted bribes from scum. How far would you have gone the other day if I hadn't kicked you in the balls?" He didn't respond, and Del's anger grew. "What is wrong with you? You are *not* the man I married. You're not the man I thought you were."

"Yeah, I'm kind of discovering that, too. When we were married, I just wanted . . . more than I had. Carlson made me an offer. I took it. I liked the girls and the cash. The more I had, the more I craved. I'd finally gotten kind of happy right before the shooting. Then one fucking bullet changed everything. All my anger was magnified. I . . . don't even know what the fuck happened to me after that." He sounded miserable, his voice full of self-loathing. "Maybe I just went bad."

He hadn't always been, and she felt sad for him. But he'd made his bed. And this wasn't about her baggage with her ex. She had to get the dirty ADA to keep incriminating himself.

"How much money have you made in this scheme, Carlson?"

"In the last three years? Millions. Every year just gets more lucrative."

God, the whole thing disgusted her, but she'd gotten her story. Xander should have all that footage captured. Now, she had to hope that Tyler could help her or find some way to escape.

Del struggled for something to ask, anything to live a few minutes longer and try to find a way out of this. Maybe Tyler and McConnell had a plan. Tyler wouldn't let her die without giving his all to rescue her. No matter what, he would have her back. She had to buy him more time.

"Does your wife know?" she asked Carlson.

"Of course not. Marbella is beautiful and likes everything lovely. She leaves all the finances up to me."

"Your brother?"

Carlson nodded. "We often used his shipments of new cars to make deliveries. His reputation as a very legitimate businessman is invaluable. No one suspects a thing."

Del turned to Eric. "And how much did *you* make?"

"Babe, don't do—"

"I am *not* your babe. After everything you did to screw up our marriage and my life, and you owe me the courtesy of one answer. How much money did you make?"

He sighed. "A couple hundred thousand dollars. I used the money from Carlson to buy you out of your half of the house."

So she'd unwittingly taken drug money. Damn it, that pissed her off even more. "Bastard! And now you're just going to let me die?"

Eric turned pensive but said nothing.

"After I'm dead, I hope the fact that you've left a little boy motherless keeps you up at night."

"Touching," Carlson sneered. "I think we're done here. I'll be leaving the house shortly and calling the office so there will be witnesses to the fact that I had nothing to do with your murder. In ten minutes, I'll be long gone, and Double T can end your miserable life. Detective Catalano, you will call nine-one-one and say that you've just arrived home to find your ex-wife dead in your bedroom. It will look like a tragic suicide, because she pined for you terribly and no longer wanted to live without you. I'll have Detective Hines in Homicide smooth it over."

Del sucked in a breath. Carlson laid out the details of her death like a man would talk about the weather. Little inflection, no importance. Just follow a career criminal to her death and have her legacy be that of a troubled woman unable to move past her divorce.

That just couldn't happen. Where was Tyler? What if he'd been captured or injured or couldn't get into the house? Fear tore through her belly. If that was the case, it was up to her to save herself and make sure he was all right.

Across the room, Double T impatiently gestured for her to join him at the entrance of the hallway. Del opened her mouth to argue, but it went dry. And arguing hadn't freed her yet. She had to keep her eyes peeled and look for an opportunity. If she was alone with one man instead of four, she stood a better chance, despite his AK-47.

On wooden feet, Del took a step forward. Inside, she felt numb, almost dead already. But her heart pounded, her blood roared, her thoughts raced—all screaming that she was very much alive. She watched Double T, waiting . . .

The goon leaning against the kitchen wall smirked as she passed, then he called to Double T, "Don't have all the fun with *la chavalona* without me, *vato*."

Double T laughed and grabbed her arm. "Don't take too long, or I'll already have wasted her."

* * *

PRESSING his back against a wall farther down the hall, Tyler had to count to ten to restrain the urge to kill the motherfuckers. He was going to tear the bastards limb from fucking limb, and that included

Eric. His former friend had given him the means to save Del, but hadn't done anything else to contribute to the effort. It hurt like hell to realize that if he'd paid more attention to Eric's behavior before the shooting, this entire shit storm might have been avoided.

Of course, that would mean giving up Del and Seth, but he'd do it gladly if it kept them alive.

Footsteps resounded down the hall's hardwood floor, one set sure and impatient, the other a frantic scramble without rhythm, accompanied by feminine moans of pain, and then the sounds of someone being dragged.

Definitely, Tyler would kill the sons of bitches. But for this to work, McConnell would have to be at the top of his game.

As the thug carrying Del stomped passed him, Tyler jumped out from around a corner and gouged the fucker in the back of the neck with the blade. He dug it into his spine, severing the cord and killing him instantly. Del backed away with a gasp as Double T began crumbling to the floor. Tyler shot her a warning glance as he caught the gang thug before the sound of his fall echoed through the house.

He pointed to the bathroom door, hoping that Del understood. She did and opened the door quickly to avoid the telltale creak. Moments later, Tyler deposited the homey in the big claw-foot bathtub. Slowly, soundlessly, he drew the shower curtain shut, concealing Double T's body.

Shooing Del out, Tyler nudged her into the master bedroom. "Crawl out the window and around the side of the house. Don't go out the back gate. It makes noise. You'll have to climb the fence, but Xander is—"

"I'm not leaving you here alone."

She looked gorgeous and stubborn, and Tyler wanted to argue, but they didn't have time. He should have known she wouldn't bow out. Instead, he handed her one of his Glocks and his phone with a sigh. "You know what to do. McConnell should be watching my back. Text Xander. Tell him to make sure Carlson doesn't escape out the front."

Then Tyler turned to creep down the hall and finish this.

She grabbed his arm. "There are two more of Carlson's goons out there, one against the wall between the living room and the kitchen, the other near the front door."

"Thanks, angel." He cupped her cheek.

"I don't know what Eric will do. Please come back to me in one piece."

"Eric can either get on board or take a bullet between his eyes. His choice."

"I love you." She clutched his arm tighter.

"I'm going to come back and love you in return." He pressed a hard kiss against her lips, then he prowled toward Eric, Carlson, and the gangbangers.

With his back hugging the wall between the hall and the living room, he angled his head to look into the kitchen. McConnell had wedged himself into a shadowed corner. Tyler nodded, and Xander's bodyguard sprang into action, making his way to the back door and rattling the handle.

It could easily sound like someone trying to escape.

Carlson barked, "Check that out. Manny, back door. And Huero, master bedroom."

Tyler heard two sets of footsteps pounding across the living room floor, drawing closer. He waited, breath held for Huero to hit the hallway. Once the homey rounded the corner, out of Carlson's view, Tyler slit his throat clean. With little more than a gurgle, the punk went down. It was sad; this kid looked barely over eighteen. But he'd been willing to help kill Del, and that's all Tyler needed to know.

He dragged the dead gangster to the tub, tossed him on top of Double T, and left the bathroom. Fuck, there was blood all over the floor and all over his shirt, but he'd worry about that later.

"Manny, what the hell is going on?" Carlson barked. When he didn't receive an answer, he called out again. "Huero?"

Dead silence. Literally.

After a quick prowl to the end of the hall, Tyler peeked into the kitchen. Sure enough, McConnell had taken out the last gun-wielding asshole without losing his breath. In fact, Xander's bodyguard looked relaxed enough to prop up his feet and have a beer while he waited for the next confrontation.

Tyler smiled. McConnell was as advertised. Holy shit, this might work.

"Damn it, answer me!" Carlson demanded.

Not gonna happen. Tyler smiled.

The ADA growled, a deep sound of frustration. "They're probably too busy getting some pussy and not thinking about the fact that Hines having to cover up a rape will make burying all this more difficult. You have a gun, Catalano?"

"Always." Eric walked across the room, and a moment later, Tyler heard the sounds of a cartridge being loaded into a pistol.

"Good," Carlson said with approval. "Go kill the bitch. Didn't she cheat on you? That should make this fun."

Tensing, Tyler waited, breath held, to see what Eric would do. A moment later, he heard the cocking of the gun. "I've done enough to Del. I won't do that."

Tyler froze. Had Eric finally decided to grow a set and do the right thing?

Carlson just started laughing. "Don't point that at me. I *own* you. If you cross me, I could kill you outright, but that would be too easy. I think I'd rather see you in prison. How long do you think you'd last before the members of 18 and other *Sureños* find out you double-crossed them? What do you think they'll do then?"

Low fucking threat, but a real one.

"I've done a lot of your dirty work for the last two plus years," Eric said. "The way I look at this, my life is toast no matter what I do. I fucked it up, and that's no one's fault but mine. Del was only trying to do the right thing, and I'm not going to kill her for it. I loved her once."

"Boo-hoo." Carlson mocked. "Listen to your stupid bullshit. The 'right' thing is whatever I tell you to do. Don't grow a fucking conscience now." He sighed impatiently. "I'll go get Huero out of the bitch's pussy and kill her myself."

Heavy footsteps stomped across the hardwood floors, toward the hall. Tyler tensed.

"Stop!" Eric demanded. "You're not touching her."

A moment later, Tyler heard a tumble and a crash, then the clank of metal. He peeked around the corner and saw Eric wrestling with the suited-up Carlson, pinning him to the ground. The ADA grunted and struggled, but Eric held him down with his hands around the fucker's neck. Glass from a broken lamp littered the floor. Eric's gun had skittered a few feet away.

With a gesture to McConnell telling him to stay put, Tyler charged out of the hall, into the living room, his footsteps never making a sound. He'd kick Carlson's ass, pray Eric didn't double-cross him, and leave McConnell in place. If Carlson headed up the hall, McConnell would ensure the fucker didn't get far. Either way, no one was going near Del.

As Tyler darted into the living room, Carlson managed to roll Eric to his back and punch him viciously in the jaw. Eric wasn't frozen for more than a second, but it was long enough for Carlson to lunge for Eric's gun.

"Put it down!" Tyler shouted, pointing his Glock at Carlson.

The bastard whipped his head around, eyes narrowed as he rose to his feet. "The bitch's lover. I should have realized that she wouldn't come alone."

Unblinking, Eric stood, looking relieved.

"You should have," Tyler drawled. "I'm ten steps ahead of you, asshole. Everything you said to Del earlier? Recorded and transmitted. Already being distributed to the FBI and every news outlet in the state as we speak. I expect the feds soon. I think they have a few questions for you. It's over. Put it down."

Anger contorted Carlson's face.

The fucker was planning, and Tyler wasn't having any of it. "I'm not even going to count to three before I put a bullet in your skull."

With a sigh of defeat, Carlson began to lower the gun. A moment later, he leapt behind Eric, using him as a human shield, and pointed the gun against Eric's spine. "I can make sure I damage his spine for good this time if you don't let me walk out of here. Or you can try to kill me, but you'll have to kill him first."

Motherfucker. Tyler thought furiously, knowing he had seconds at most to save Eric and stop this from becoming a clusterfuck. But Eric came to the rescue, elbowing Carlson and ducking, giving Tyler an open shot.

Carlson fired and hit the middle of Eric's back—just as Tyler fired, and his bullet connected with the bull's-eye between Carlson's eyes.

Eric collapsed to the ground, groaning and cursing as Carlson fell, already dead.

It was over.

Chapter Nineteen

A WEEK later, Tyler found himself on his back patio, kicking back with a beer, surrounded by his buddies' wives—just like the night Del had stormed back into his life.

Today, she was glaringly absent. The only reminders he had of her now were his son and his memories.

After Carlson's death, the LAPD Internal Affairs and the FBI had escorted Del away, presumably to answer a million questions about the ADA's scheme, examine her evidence, and launch a full-scale investigation. No doubt they wanted to see how deep the scheme went and who else they could indict. Tyler had done everything in his power to stay by her side. She'd only kissed him softly and told him that she was okay and would call soon.

Tyler had let her go reluctantly, thinking they'd be separated for a day or two at most. He'd gone with the LAPD, as had McConnell, to give their statements. The camera Xander had placed in the Coach bag he'd given Del had captured virtually everything and made the case remarkably simple.

The following morning, Tyler had received a text from Del asking him to go back to Lafayette and take care of Seth. She swore she'd be out to talk soon. He'd tried to call her back minutes later, only to receive a recording that her phone was out of service. That quickly, dread had settled into his gut. Was she okay? Was the FBI being hard on her for some reason? Or, was Del backing away from him?

Tyler didn't want to believe that all her avowals of love had been fleeting, but after seven days without a word from her, fear had turned to anguish. Being heartbroken the first time hadn't been a cakewalk. This time . . . it was fucking tearing gaping holes in his chest that he didn't think would ever heal.

"Del writes a hell of a story." Tara slapped his copy of the *L.A. Times* on the wrought-iron table. "She'll win awards for this article."

The rest of the women agreed, and Alyssa picked the paper up to scan it again, cuddling Chloe.

Yeah. Tyler had already read it four times that morning. Del had used her words to paint a vivid picture of Carlson, his crimes and deceptions, along with the cost in taxpayer dollars and lives. No doubt her boss would ask her to stay and make her a featured reporter—everything she'd always dreamed of. He feared that she'd try to sweep back into his life long enough to take Seth back to Los Angeles and leave forever.

The thought that she'd want him to do without her and their son was absolutely agonizing.

Seth bounced on his lap, and Tyler sent the boy a smile. The one bright spot these dark days had been his son. He'd really bonded with Seth over the past week and wholeheartedly admitted that he loved the boy with every bit of his heart. Yesterday, he'd even worked up the nerve to track down his mom. She'd remarried a great guy and lived in Phoenix now. She'd been really thrilled to hear that she had a grandson and asked to meet him. She'd wished him all the happiness in the world, like all that bitter crap she used to spout at him under the influence of Boone's Farm hadn't existed. He'd told her that he'd call back and see what they could work out. But for

Seth's sake—and his own—he figured it would be good for his mother to meet his son.

Taking Tyler's smile as encouragement, Seth slapped his open palms on Tyler's chest and squealed. Tyler looked down to find little greenish handprints on his favorite shirt.

"You probably don't want to know what that is." Kimber winced.

He silently agreed. The shirt would wash, and it was a small price to pay for having this precious time with the boy, given how many of Seth's other days Tyler had missed out on—and how many more he might miss in the future if Del decided to sweep in and return to L.A.

Through his bittersweet sadness, Tyler grinned and shook his head at the toddler's chubby impish little face, then scooped him up, heading for the kitchen. After a quick wash of the boy's hands, Tyler headed back out to the patio.

"Avocado," he drawled. "Seth climbed up to the counter and grabbed it. I'll bet he had a ball squishing it between his fingers and painting my kitchen cabinets."

Kimber tried not to laugh. "Caleb does stuff like that all the time. You really can't turn your back for a minute."

Tyler hadn't had much experience with parenting or kids until now, but he was quickly figuring out how right Kimber was.

May had become June, and the weather bordered on sultry now. Dusk approached and the cicadas chimed in, vying with the sounds of the croaking frogs.

Alyssa set the paper down, then turned to Tara. "So Xander is in your guest room and driving you crazy because he's trying to avoid the press in L.A.?"

She nodded emphatically. "Since the article spelled out how helpful he was in bringing Carlson down, he's been bombarded. Apparently, he doesn't like being called the James Bond of billionaires." She giggled. "And because he's Xander, he's driving me crazy. I know when he pokes fun at me that he's just teasing, and I can mostly take it. But the groupies . . . His phone never stops ringing. He disappeared four times yesterday, each time with a different girl. I didn't know he even knew anyone in Lafayette, much less had met enough girls to get laid multiple times a day, every day." She sighed. "Remind me to clobber Logan next time I see him. I'd beat Xander silly, but besides servicing his apparent harem, he's clearly going through a tough spot with Javier."

"Learning that your wife is dead at the hands of the lover you didn't know she had can't be easy on Xander's brother," Tyler pointed out.

Five days ago, the police had found Francesca's strangled, bloated body. Xander wanted to be with his brother. He'd said as much. But the press was swarming around him now. No way would Javier get any time alone to grieve if Xander went back to L.A. So he waited here, chomping at the bit, taking out all his frustration with a constant barrage of mindless sex. Tyler understood. The situation would be kind of funny if it weren't so sad.

"I can't believe the prick who killed her just dumped her body in the ocean," Morgan chimed in, stroking her growing belly. She and Jack were anticipating a September baby. "Have they found him yet?"

"No," Tara answered quietly. "There's a huge investigation going on, but until they learn the identity of the man she was with . . ."

Nothing so far. Tyler figured it was only a matter of time before the authorities learned the identity of Francesca's murdering lover, but the fucker was clever and had a monthlong head start.

Kissing her daughter's downy head, Alyssa looked Tyler's way. "What about Eric?"

"He's lucky. The bullet missed his lungs by a millimeter. He's going to be fine physically. He's trying to cut a deal with the DA now. I think they're offering him immunity in exchange for the names of everyone else he knows that Carlson roped into his scam."

Before leaving town, Tyler had visited Eric in the hospital. They were never going to be friends again, and Eric had a lot to work through. They'd talked. Eric had apologized. After seeing the damage he'd nearly wrought on Del by touching her against her will, he'd started taking a hard look at himself—and Carlson. It hadn't taken long to figure out that the dirty ADA had been trying to kill her. He'd snatched the flash drive out of Del's hiding place when he'd figured out that Carlson wanted it bad enough to trash the house, but instead of giving it over, he'd read it and realized that Del was living on borrowed time. So he'd set up the meeting between her and Carlson, then done everything possible to ensure that Del lived. The visit had been enlightening. Eric seemed to finally understand that he was truly responsible for his actions. That was a start. He'd also agreed to stay the hell away.

"So . . ." Alyssa slated him another stare, this one really direct. "Hear from Del again?"

Other than one text in which she'd told him that she'd come soon? "No."

And he didn't fucking want to talk about it. They'd only try to find some bullshit words to console him, some "if you love her, set her free" crap that made his teeth grind.

He loved her and he wasn't ready to let her go, not unless she looked him in the eye and told him that she didn't love him. He had feelers out to track her down now, and the second she slipped onto his radar, it was goddamn for sure that he was going to run her to ground. They would have a long talk about the future. He wouldn't let her leave until he was absolutely convinced that she didn't want to be with him.

Because he wanted to be with her for the rest of his life.

"Sorry," Alyssa murmured. "Given any thought to coming back to work at Sexy Sirens? All the girls really miss Cockzilla."

Tyler had to repress a grimace. He hadn't gone more than a handful of days without sex in years. In the past, a seven-day drought would have had him climbing the walls. Today? Sure, he wanted sex, but only if the kisses were Del's. Only if the body he pushed into was hers. Only if the nails in his back and the cries of passion in his ears belonged to her.

"No. I'll hang with Jack. You can find a bouncer anywhere. My skill set is better suited to his line of work."

Alyssa cocked her head, studying him. Tyler felt like a bug pinned to a board.

"What?" he demanded.

"You are head-over-heels, one-hundred-percent completely in love with this woman. I'll have to tell Jessi and Skylar that you're off the market. I think they might actually cry," Alyssa drawled.

"Fuck off," he groused, then remembered his son was still sitting in his lap and winced. Seth was young at fifteen months, but would probably start repeating everything he heard soon. Tyler knew he was going to have to watch his mouth.

Morgan looked at her watch, then across the table at him. "I think it's great that you're in love with her. You're too good to be alone."

"Tell that to Delaney." Tyler sighed. The waiting was getting tougher every day.

Just then his back door opened, and Jack Cole appeared. "Tell her yourself."

When the other man shifted out of his way to cross the room to his pregnant wife, Delaney came into view. She stood, staring, wearing a pair of rumpled capri pants and a brown T-shirt that made her eyes shine incredibly blue. She looked pale and tired. And above all, she looked uncertain.

"Hi." She waved, biting her lip. She glanced at the others, then clenched her hands in front of her as she stepped onto the patio.

"Ma ma ma!" Seth darted off of his lap and toddled across the floor to Del.

She met him halfway, arms open, and engulfed him in a big hug. "My little man! Oh, Mommy has missed you. Sweet boy . . ."

As Del pressed kisses to his little face, she looked ready to cry with the joy of holding her son again. Tyler was conscious that she'd barely greeted him, had almost been unable to look at him. Even now, he could feel Alyssa, Kata, Kimber, and Tara's gaze on him, assessing, probably pitying him. *Fuck.*

Jack approached him a second later, startling Tyler.

"I talked to Del yesterday. She only wanted to know two things: how you and Seth were, and if I'd pick her up from the airport today. She asked me to keep it a surprise."

"Mission accomplished," he muttered. He couldn't be more stunned by Del's presence here if he tried.

Seth placed a sloppy kiss on Del's chin, and she laughed. Tyler scrubbed a hand down his face as he watched the love flow between them. Yeah, he knew he couldn't force her to stay with him, make a family with him, if she didn't love him anymore. But damn it, he'd thought she'd at least try.

He shut his eyes. They stung. No, they fucking hurt, like someone was taking tiny pickaxes to them. Damn it, he would not cry.

Forcing the tears back, he fixed his gaze on Del again, trying to decide what to do next.

"If you keep staring at her like that, you're going to scare the hell out of her," Jack pointed out.

"Like what?"

"Like you can't decide if you want to tear into her for not contacting you again over the past few days, or just fuck her into next week."

Tyler grunted. "Both."

"Fair enough." Jack shrugged. "Just . . . remember to listen before you pounce—either way."

Probably good advice. Jack had been married for a few years now, so he probably knew something. For all of Morgan's submissive tendencies, Tyler knew she'd beat the hell out of Jack if he behaved like an asshole.

"Let's go, *cher*." Jack helped Morgan from her chair, making sure she had her center of balance under her before wrapping an arm around her waist and leading her to the door.

At the threshold, Jack turned back to Tyler with a sly smile. "Oh, you can thank me later."

With that, they were gone. Kata and Tara scrambled to their feet and departed, as well.

After greeting Del and a few quick hugs for Seth, Kimber looked between him and Del. "You two look like you could use some time to talk. Why don't I take Seth with me so he can play with Caleb?"

Del didn't object, and after Tyler and Del both placed a soft kiss on their boy's cheeks, Kimber picked Seth up and left, too.

Alyssa lingered. She rose to her feet slowly, staring at Del like a protective parent might stare at her daughter's slimy boyfriend. Del lifted her chin and stared back.

"I hope you're not here to hurt him," Alyssa said to Del. "He's been through enough."

Tyler cringed at her words. Yes, he'd been pining, but Alyssa had basically announced it. *Shit.*

She didn't wait for Del's answer, just walked out, leaving them alone. Tyler stared, his gaze fused on Del, petrified that if he blinked, she'd be gone again. But he had no clue what to say. If he opened his mouth, he had a bad feeling that he'd unload all his worry, frustration, and pain out on her. Jack had advised him to listen, so he figured he'd better at least try.

Del swallowed nervously and sat in Alyssa's vacated chair. "You okay?"

No, I'm fucking terrified. But he simply nodded. "All right. I've been better."

"Hard to deal with Seth all by yourself?"

"No. He's been . . . the best part of this week. I've loved getting to know him, seeing him every day. I—" He choked. "I need that."

Del bit her lip again and hesitated, as if trying to decide what to say. "So this week was hard because . . . ?"

Tyler shook his head. "What do you want from me? An admission that I've been miserable without you? Okay, you've got it. I missed you. I love you. I'm not letting you or Seth go without a fight. If you're going back to L.A., I'll go, too. I'm pretty sure the department would hire me again, and I'll do whatever it takes to prove that—"

She threw herself into his arms with such force, it almost knocked the wind out of him. Tyler wrapped her tightly in his embrace, burying his face in Del's neck. God, she smelled good as she clung to him in return for a long, sweet moment. Then she backed away.

"I—I spent the last week dealing with the downfall of Carlson's scheme and writing my story. Preston loved it and asked me to stay on as a featured reporter."

"It's what you've always wanted." Tyler stiffened, fidgeted. He wanted to be happy for her, but inside he felt himself dying, becoming hollow and numb. She hadn't mentioned him coming back to California with her.

"It is what I've always wanted." She nodded. "Which made turning it down bittersweet, but still an easy decision. I know you love your family of friends, and clearly they care about Seth. I'm ready for a fresh start, so—"

"You turned it down?" Tyler snapped, his mind racing. She was ready for a fresh start. What did that mean? He winced. He hadn't let her finish her sentence so he could really listen to her. Jack had given him good advice; he just hadn't said how difficult it would be to follow.

"Yeah. Too many memories in Los Angeles. Seth needs a good place to grow up. Chasing the journalistic fast track isn't what I want anymore. You are." Her face dissolved, and tears welled in her so-blue eyes. "I love you."

That was all Tyler needed to hear. The last week of worry and anguish melted, and he dragged Del against him, fitting every inch of his body against hers. "I love you. I thought this would be like last time, that you wanted to leave me and . . . I was going insane."

She pressed a hard, quick kiss to his lips. "No. I needed time to wrap up with all the authorities. They took my phone into evidence, so it was harder to call you. Either way, I knew we needed to settle this in person. I didn't want to do it from across the country, over the phone. So I took that time to quit my job, put my condo up for sale, pack up my stuff, and ship it here. Then I bought a plane ticket and called Jack." She grimaced. "Actually, he tracked me down. Less than a minute after I bought my plane ticket, he called my house to ask me what the hell I was doing. I filled him in, and he offered to pick me up so I could surprise you and . . . here we are."

With every word out of her mouth, Tyler's joy increased. His heart pounded, and euphoria filled every corner of his body. "So you're definitely moving here?"

She nodded and fresh tears fell. "I . . . got a job with the paper here and I've come to be with you. If you'll have us."

Tyler kissed away her tears, feeling a few himself. She trusted him and believed in their future enough to give up everything, including her dream job. She was choosing to spend her tomorrows with him here in Lafayette. He wanted nothing more.

"Angel, I want you and Seth with me here for the rest of our lives. Come with me. I've got something for you."

He took her hand and dragged her into the house, his long steps making it difficult for her to keep up. He knew he should slow down, but he couldn't yet.

Once he reached his bedroom, he pulled Del inside and picked her up, tossing her onto the bed. He grabbed what he needed from the nightstand, then covered her body with his, pinning her down. She was going to hear every word of this; he would make sure of it.

"You're the only woman I want, Del. My mother was dead wrong about me. My father didn't love her, so leaving was easy for him. But I could barely bring myself to walk away from you the first time. It would kill me to do it again—for any reason. It's different—*I'm* different—because I love you. We belong together. I want to be a good father to Seth and a good husband to you. Please don't leave me, angel. Stay." He settled the precious metal and stone into her hand. "Marry me."

She opened her palm and saw the diamond engagement ring he'd picked out for her the day he'd returned from L.A. Her eyes grew saucer wide, and she blinked up at him with more tears. But if the smile on her face was any indication, these were tears of joy.

"Yes!" she squealed, then lifted up to cover his lips with her own.

Tyler put the ring on her finger, his heart bursting with relief and joy as he drowned in her familiar flavor and sweet kiss.

Within seconds, she began tugging at his shirt and yanking on his shorts. Rising up just enough to pull his shirt over his head, he shoved her T-shirt off, ripped into her capri pants, and jerked them down before opening his fly with trembling fingers. Fuck, he had to get inside her, claim her again, this time once and for all.

She kicked away her panties, then spread her legs for him. Tyler didn't hesitate, just slipped inside her, letting her warmth and need envelop him. *Home.* He closed his eyes to savor the feeling. Then reality intruded.

"Damn it," he cursed. "Should I get a condom?"

She sent him a sheepish smile. "If the pregnancy test I took this morning is right, I think it's too late."

His heart soared, and his cock grew even harder. "You're pregnant?"

"I'm pretty sure." She nodded. "Is that . . . okay? Are you going to be ready to be a dad again so soon? I know we didn't plan it this way, but—"

He cut her off with a kiss. "It's perfect."

Easing out of her body, he slid back in slowly, thrilled when she cried out and arched and threw her arms around his neck, looking utterly lost to passion. She was wonderful, and she was finally his. Fuck, he couldn't be happier.

"Guess that means we need to get married soon," he drawled, tormenting her with another slow glide of his dick inside her silky-wet sex.

"You sound pretty happy about that," she managed to eke out in between gasps of pleasure.

"Absolutely. You make me happy."

She smiled up at him, something so beautiful, his heart nearly stopped. "I fell hard for you the first time you touched me. I think I always knew, deep down, we were meant to be together, but over the last two weeks the feelings only got stronger. This is my dream coming true."

He'd suspected the same thing. "Mine, too. I love you, angel. Always."

About the Author

Shayla Black (aka Shelley Bradley) is the *New York Times* bestselling author of more than thirty sizzling contemporary, erotic, paranormal, and historical romances for multiple print and electronic publishers. She lives in Texas with her husband, munchkin, and one very spoiled cat. In her "free" time she enjoys watching reality TV, reading, and listening to an eclectic blend of music.

Shayla has won or placed in more than a dozen writing contests, including Passionate Ink's Passionate Plume, Colorado Romance Writers Award of Excellence, and the National Reader's Choice Awards. Romantic Times has awarded her Top Picks, a K.I.S.S. Hero Award, and a nomination for Best Erotic Romance.

A writing risk-taker, Shayla enjoys tackling writing challenges with every book.

Find Shayla at www.ShaylaBlack.com or visit her on her Shayla Black Author Facebook page.